TWO ACTION-PACKED
WILL COOK WESTERNS
FOR ONE LOW PRICE!

BULLET RANGE

"Entertaining!" —*Kansas City Star*

Reilly stood facing the man who'd come to kill him.

"It's just the two of us now," the man said. "That's the way you wanted it and that's the way you'll...."

Reilly wondered about all the talk. This was a gun duel, not a conversation.

And then he suddenly understood. Somewhere behind him was a man whose job was to make sure Reilly never had a chance to draw....

IRON MAN, IRON HORSE

"An enlivening mixture of redskins and railroading...*Iron Man, Iron Horse* is an exciting account...[wedding] romance to fact!"

—*New York Times*

Ben Holliday leaned back in his chair and surveyed Murray Singer in a frankly unfriendly manner. "You want the line; I know that. You want it for a song, but it'll be the dearest one you ever sang in your life. And as for the fight, Mr. Texas-Cattle-Baron, you're going to find out when this is finished that, up to now, you never knew what a real fight was."

BULLET RANGE/
IRON MAN, IRON HORSE
Will Cook

LEISURE BOOKS ⌐ NEW YORK CITY

A LEISURE BOOK®

November 1993

Published by special arrangement with Golden West Literary Agency.

Dorchester Publishing Co., Inc.
276 Fifth Avenue
New York, NY 10001

Printed in the United States of America.

BULLET RANGE

CHAPTER 1

Rising with the first light of dawn, Reilly Meyers boiled a pot of coffee to thaw the chill from his bones. In the valley below it was still early fall and trees were beginning to drop leaves, but in the mountains the air carried the first promise of winter. The valley he had crossed yesterday lay like an oblong bowl and the ridge on which he had made his camp was part of a backbone extending into Oregon far to the north.

This was a small clearing in the cedar breaks near the summit and water fell out of the rocks in a silver rope. A thicket of stunted cedars and pine hid him from the crest of the slope. This was Reilly Meyers' fifth day in an eastward direction and he had been moving leisurely, following the natural breaks in this rocky range. Around him lay the sharp wild odor of the forests and the never ceasing upcast rocks. The evergreens and manzanita layered the sharp slopes and from the dry face, sage flourished in dark clumps.

On the eastern side of the mountain the land tapered rapidly to dun colored flats, and farther on, lesser hills sat like small brown waves on a tossed sea. At the edge of this sea sat a ranch house, nestling against the base of a series of low hills. Smoke curled sluggishly from the cook shack chimney, breaking off in a wisp at the top as the morning breeze caught it.

Smiling slightly, Reilly Meyers gathered his gear, then began to work his way off the mountainside.

He was not a tall man, but the weight in his shoulders and chest gave him a bulkiness that made him appear big.

His face was blunt and his chin was like the base of a setting maul, square and heavy on the bottom. Hair lay in dark chunks around his ears and his eyes were drill straight with splinters of light in their dark depths. He wore an old suit and a gray flannel shirt. His hat was black and sat squarely on his head. In his right hand he carried a brass-receivered Winchester, almost twenty years old, and in his waistband he had thrust a single action Remington.

The early morning chill disappeared quickly under the sun's blast and he removed his coat. Making his way down the tilting face of the slope, Reilly kept his eyes on the ranch house below as though he couldn't bear to lose sight of it even for an instant.

Sweat began to make runnels along his cheeks and his shirt turned dark along the back and under the arms. Heat bounced from the barren rocks and began to soak through the thin soles of his boots. He moved with familiarity down this slope, taking obscure game trails that clung at times to a sheer drop-off of several hundred feet. This was his land and he had traveled it before many times.

By noon he had worked down to the flats and passed beneath the pole arch with the chain-hung sign proclaiming this to be Broken Bit range. The ranch house was square with a wide porch running around all four sides. Flat-roofed with no attic, the house seemed wide and squat compared to the large barn and other outbuildings.

Back of the barn lay an inclosed area and three men worked horses there, raising a column of tan dust. Their yelling was faint and slightly distorted by distance. Far out on the flats a rider approached and Reilly Meyers gave this a study before turning to the well. Throwing off his bedroll and leaning his .44 Winchester against the stone curbing, Reilly worked the windlass and listened to the dry shaft squeak. As he lifted the dipper a second time, the screen door opened and a tall man came out, slightly bent with age. He put a shielding hand to his eyes and stood still in the drenching sunlight.

For a moment he stared against the distance with a grave face, and then he spoke. "Reilly?" He came off the

6

porch and closed the distance between them with long strides and then shook Reilly Meyers' hand.

Tension ran out of Reilly. He said, "How are you, Paul? It's been a damn long time."

"A little over four years," Paul Childress said, and studied Reilly carefully. Childress was lean and age had left wrinkles around his eyes. He had a tolerant face, even slightly humorous if one discounted the stubborn set of the jaw.

"You walk over them hills?" Childress favored t.. Sierra Nevada mountains with a glance. "You could have let me know, Reilly. Did you think I'd turned on you?"

"I wasn't too sure," Reilly said. "Somehow I never got much of a chance to explain what happened. You never answered my letters, Paul."

"I know," Childress said, and studied the dusty ground. "I'm ashamed, boy, but there's things a man can't help. There was others to think of besides me." He took Reilly by the arm. "Come on in. There's coffee on."

Going into the house, Reilly turned down the long hall with easy familiarity and went into the large kitchen. He laid his hat on the floor and sat down at the table. Looking around the room at the pine cupboards, the wooden sink, he recalled things nearly forgotten. At another time he had come here, but there had been a difference. He'd had a gun in his hand and a fear pushing him and outside men had called to each other and talked of a rope. Paul Childress had made no move to stop them when they took him away and for a long time Reilly held a deep resentment. Now he wasn't sure whether he still had it or if he had left it in a California prison.

Childress took two cups from the kitchen cabinet and placed them on the table, then poured from a gallon coffee pot. He said, "I didn't think you was coming back, Reilly. And if you did, I figured you'd shoot me."

"Do I have anything to shoot you for, Paul?"

"I left you when you needed me," Childress said, and sat down. "I was thinkin' of Emily, Reilly. I'm thinkin' of her now. You got a record, boy, and some people don't take kindly to that."

"I'm clean," Reilly said, and added sugar to the coffee. He listened to the quiet in the house, catching the sounds

7

of activity around the corral. When he raised his eyes he found Paul Childress studying him.

Reilly said, "I'm back to stay, Paul. Am I going to have to take it up where I left off?"

Childress moved his shoulders slightly. "There's better places than here. You got a bad deal. Staying won't make it better."

"I'm not the only man around here who's shot a man."

The old man scrubbed a hand across his face, lifting the ends of his mustache with his fingertip. "That's so, but the wild ones are after you and that makes it different. I wanted to help you that night, but I got enough sense to know I can't buck that crowd. Burk Seever wanted to see you dead, and from the talk he passes around, he ain't changed his mind none about it."

A horse drummed across the yard and stopped. The back door opened, slamming shut behind a young girl who halted suddenly when she saw Reilly Meyers. She stood like a rabbit in a field who is suddenly confronted by a strange force, poised, uncertain, and then she ran to him, bowling over a chair in her haste to throw her arms around Reilly's neck.

She was laughing and crying and kissing him. When he put her away to speak, his voice sounded choked and deeper than it had been before. "Little sister's grown up, it seems."

Emily Meyers laced her arms around Reilly's waist and buried her face against the folds of his shirt. Her voice was muffled. "I waited a long time, Reilly. A very long time."

"The waiting's over now," Reilly said. He stepped away from her, then sat down again. She remained standing and he raised his eyes to her. Emily Meyers was nearly nineteen, tall for a girl, with frank eyes and a skin that was tanned golden. She wore a heavy riding skirt and a white shirtwaist, open at the throat. When she removed her hat, hair fell loosely across her shoulders in a dark wave.

Taking a place at the table across from her brother, she crossed her arms, frankly admiring him. "You should have written to me, Reilly. I'd have gone to Carson City and met the stage."

"I came over the hills this morning," he said, and took

his cup to the stove for a refill. His movements were easy and gave people the impression that he had trained all surplus motion out of him, leaving him lithe and efficient. He turned with the cup half-raised and said, "Better this way, Emily. Four years have gone by and folks might be on the edge of forgettin' I've been to prison." He glanced at Childress. "Where's Ma?"

"In town with Al Murdock," Emily said quickly. "Reilly, you are going to stay here with us, aren't you?"

"No," he said. "My coming back will be bad enough. Bad names rub off, Emily. I'm sure sorry if mine's bothered you."

"That's silly talk," she said shortly. "I'm going to get married, Reilly. Al's asked me."

"Is that what you want?"

"That's what I want," she said. "Believe me, Reilly, I'll be happy."

"Then that's all that counts," he said, and drank deeply.

"Why did you have to come back, Reilly?" Childress voice was flat and unemotional.

"This is my home," Reilly said. Then he frowned. "Or is it?

Emily glanced from Reilly to Paul Childress, then back to Reilly. The old man pursed his lips and packed his pipe. "I don't mean to hurt your feelings, boy, but I ain't lyin' when I say you ain't got many friends. The Slaughter boys went with Buttelow when you got sent up, but the crowd you fooled around with is still ridin' the big white horse."

Hunching his shoulders, Reilly came back to the table and sat down, his hands laced around the cup. "I'm not asking you for anything," he said. "I guess you made your position clear enough the night the sheriff and his posse came here. Maybe I don't have any friends, just like you say, but I've thought about this for a long time —how it was going to be, meeting people and lookin' 'em in the eye. Right now, I don't give much of a damn. I'll get started again. Goin' someplace else is the easy way." He smiled slightly. "A man can leave a lot behind him, no matter what happens. All the time I was in prison I've been thinkin' about Sally. Maybe I'll get married now and settle down. You think that's impossible?"

9

A vaguely worried expression appeared on Childress' face. Emily opened her mouth to speak, but the old man gave her a quick glance with a definite warning in it. She looked at her hands and said nothing.

"Better get your feet on the ground before you make any plans," Childress said. "There ain't much left of your old place, I hear tell."

"It was all right when I left it."

"Run down some now," Childress said, and knocked the dottle from his pipe. "Nothin' remains the same, son. The crowd that turned on you is still the big augur. Burk Seever's telling the sheriff where to head in all the time, and Horgan and Winehaven still ride where they please and no one dares open their mouth about it."

Finishing his coffee, Reilly shied the grounds into the coal scuttle and rinsed his cup. "I've got a bone to pick with Seever and Max Horgan," Reilly said. "Winehaven too, but this time I'm going to do it careful. That's your trouble, Paul. You stand still and let these people walk all over you. I never would do that."

"No," Childress said softly, "you never would. Shooting one wasn't so smart either. You didn't get your cattle back." He thrust his hands deep into his pockets and leaned against the wall. "I suppose I could have taken a rifle and stood 'em off the night they was after you, but what would it have got me? My herd raided. My buildings fired while I was in town." He shook his head. "They'd have got you anyway, regardless of what I could have done."

"That's your story," Reilly said flatly. "You just stick with it."

"I'm not goin' to squabble with you about it," Childress said. "Reilly, you was twelve years old when you came staggerin' out of the desert with a baby girl in your arms. Your pants was in rags and the baby near dead. Even then you was a stubborn little devil, full of pride and fight. I clearly remember when I told you to do something you told me to mind my own damned business, that you'd get along. You were the kind that always had to find out for themselves, the hard way. I guess you'll still have to be that way, Reilly."

Leaning against the sink, Reilly shook out his tobacco

and rolled a cigaret. "Do you think I came back to buck the wild bunch, Paul?"

The old man's shoulders rose and fell. "I've give up guessin' about what you'll do next," Childress said. "You was pretty thick with Horgan and Winehaven." He held up his hand as Reilly opened his mouth to speak. "Now let me finish. You always said that they left you alone and you was returnin' the favor, but when your toes got stepped on it was a different story. Once I was neither for you or against you, and I ain't changed a damned bit, Reilly. It was your idea to play it the lone wolf and I'll give you all the rope you want."

"You hate me, Paul?"

The old man shook his head. "Reckon I care for you like you was my own son, but you got a way of holdin' folks away, not takin' help. You done it to me all your life and a man can get tired of it. Times have changed, Reilly. The country's divided now between those who like Winehaven's money and those who're tired of havin' their beef rustled. While you was in the pen, Max Horgan used your place and he made damn sure everyone understood that you told him it was all right."

"Used it?" Reilly's eyes narrowed. "I never told him no such a thing!"

"He had a paper, son. I asked the sheriff about it and we both went to Burk Seever. He said it was legal, and crooked or not, he's a lawyer and ought to know."

Reilly struck the sink with his fist. "I never signed a thing. As for what people think, I don't give a damn. I just came back for Sally and then I'm getting out."

"Gettin' sore won't help you, Reilly." Childress glanced at Emily, but she had turned away and was staring out the kitchen door. "A woman is the most unpredictable thing of all, Reilly. You ever think of that?"

"For four years I've thought of her," Reilly said. "Sally believed in me when you and the others turned away. That's what I remember, Paul." Moving away from the sink he walked to the window, and stood there staring out on the blandness of the bleached desert. "For three days you sat there during the trial, listening to Burk Seever try to hang me, but never a change in your expression." He turned and faced Paul Childress. "Did you think I drew first, like Seever said?"

11

"I never thought that," Childress murmured as he refilled his pipe. "I'm not a brave man, son. I'm old and don't want to lose what I've worked a lifetime for. The wild bunch is big business, Reilly. A man who wants to go on livin' has to keep his mouth shut."

"Thanks for nothin' then," Reilly said bitterly.

Emily raised her hand and she was near crying. "Please, Reilly—don't. Try to understand."

"Understand what?" He shook out his tobacco and rolled a smoke, kicking his unruly temper in place.

"I've wondered why Seever and Winehaven lied you into the pen, Reilly." Childress' voice was softly puzzled. "They had a rope waiting and it's bothered me. What did you see there that day that scared 'em that much?"

"See? I didn't see anything," Reilly said. "I trailed my steers for a week until the trail petered out near Winehaven's slaughter house across the California line. They were there, but he had a bill of sale that I never signed." Reilly slapped the window sill with his palm. "It was my signature and yet it wasn't. I don't know what got into me. There was my steers and here was this bastard sayin' I couldn't have 'em. When he reached for his gun I shot him." He paused and looked at his sister and foster father. "The mistake I made was to come here, thinkin' you'd stick up for me. I should have stayed in the hills and toughed it out."

"What does it matter now?" Childress said. "You're a free man now and everything's paid up. Remember that, Reilly, and you'll be all right."

"Sure. I paid for something that I didn't do." He sighed and added, "You got a horse I can borrow?"

"I've got a horse I'll give you," Childress said. He went outside, Reilly and his sister following him. By the well, Reilly retrieved his blanket roll and crossed to the barn. A gangly rider with legs like parentheses left the shade of the bunkhouse and came over.

"Turn the buckskin stud out," Childress said, and the rider shook out a rope, entered the corral and made a deft cast. The horse was loose-legged with a deep chest and the round barrel of a runner.

"There's a saddle in the barn you can have," Childress said, and the rider went in after it. Saddling up, Reilly lashed his blankets behind the cantle and slid the .44 Winchester into the boot.

Pausing with a foot in the stirrup, he said, "I'm happy to be back, Paul. I want you to know that."

Childress nodded and his eyes were mere slits as he looked at the flat desert vastness. Something solidified in his mind and he said, "Stay away from Buckeye, Reilly. The town's no good for you."

"Sally's there," Reilly said. He mounted. "I'd like to pay you for the horse and hull, Paul. I'm not broke. There was a poker game in Marysville—" He let the rest trail off.

"Consider it a gift," Childress said. He offered his hand. "I hope everything turns out well for you, Reilly."

"Hope? You don't believe it, do you?"

Childress shook his head. "Trouble's always found you mighty easy. You never listened to advice very good."

"I've had my trouble," he said gravely. "All I want is my own place and people to leave me alone." He glanced at Emily and gave her a smile. "Sure is amazin' what four years will do for a leggy female." He bent from the saddle and lifted her. She put her arm around him and kissed his cheek before he set her down.

"Come back here and stay, Reilly," she said, and in her eyes there was a troubled pleading.

"A man has to make his own way," he told her gently. "I'm quotin' Paul when I say it." He rapped the stud with his heels and rode from the yard, not looking back.

Once on the flats, the land changed. Water being scarce here, the ground was sandy, dotted with cacti, soapweed and lupin. Reilly rode slack in the saddle, letting the monotonous miles drift by. Toward midafternoon he saw a rising column of dust and cut toward it.

Drawing closer, Reilly felt mild disappointment when he recognized a buggy, but with only one man in it. Halting, he waited for the rig to clatter nearer, and when identification came to him, his attention sharpened.

When the buggy drew abreast, Reilly Meyers hooked a leg over the saddlehorn. He watched the man holding the reins and caught the sudden shock that was quickly smothered.

Reilly said, "Max, friend. The last time I saw you

13

was at Winehaven's slaughter house when I shot a man. As I remember it, you didn't show up at the trial and tell the good folks how it really happened."

"I like to stay out of courtrooms," Max Horgan said. His face was blocky, with high cheekbones and deepset eyes. Reilly studied Horgan, searching for some small sign around the lips and eyes. He saw no change there.

In Horgan, humanity had been pushed aside, leaving him coldly methodical and without friendship for anyone. "You were a damn fool to come back," Horgan said. "Be careful what you get into now. The next time you'll get your hands slapped a lot harder."

"A little lecture, Max?"

"Personally, I don't give a damn one way or another," Horgan said. "Just leave the bunch alone and you'll live to be an old man."

Shifting his Winchester, Reilly pointed it casually toward the buggy. "Once I thought some of the men in this country were gutless because they didn't step on you a long time ago, but now I've learned to mind my own business. Paul was tellin' me that you've been using my place. If there's any of your boys there now, you better get 'em off, because I don't like squatters."

"Maybe they'll move you instead," Horgan suggested quietly. "There's no one there now, Reilly, but it wouldn't worry me if there was. You're a restless man and you like to move around. It could be that you won't be staying here long."

"I'll be staying, Max. I'm goin' to get married and settle down so don't do anything now to make my plans go cockeyed."

"Married? To Sally Isham?" Horgan grinned.

"Does that strike you as funny?"

Max Horgan began to laugh. It started with a chuckle and blossomed into a wild gale of mirth. Reilly sat his horse, his puzzlement turning to sharp anger. Finally Max Horgan wiped tears from his eyes and said, "Reilly, I wouldn't dream of changin' your plans." He lifted the reins to slap the horses into motion.

"Wait a minute!" Reilly snapped and wheeled the buckskin. "Let me in on the joke, Max." His voice was low but brittle.

14

"You wouldn't think it's funny," Max said softly, all humor fading from his dark eyes.

"That's all right," Reilly said. "I'll watch you and laugh when you laugh. I mean it, Max—better tell me."

Raising his hand, Horgan pawed his face out of shape. "Remember that you asked me, Reilly." His smile widened behind his flowing mustache. "You can't marry Sally Isham because she up and got married to someone else."

For a moment, Reilly stared at him. "If you're making a joke of this, I'll kill you, Max."

"Go ask her yourself," Horgan said, and lifted the reins.

"Hold on! Who did she marry, Max?"

"Uh, uh," Horgan said. "You go find out from her. If your foster pa and sister wouldn't tell you, I don't guess I will either."

"I could make you tell," Reilly said softly.

Horgan's smile faded slightly and he brushed his coat away from the short barreled Colt in a cross-draw holster. "Easy now, Reilly. I'm a lot better than that fella you shot at Winehaven's."

For a moment a strong feeling moved back and forth between them and then Reilly relaxed. "If this is a joke, Max—"

"I told you you wouldn't think it was funny," Horgan said, and clucked to his team. Turning in the saddle, Reilly followed the retreating buggy until Horgan had gone a half mile down the road. Seeing Horgan again brought back a flood of half-forgotten memories. Reilly could still smell Winehaven's slaughter house as he rode toward it that spring day. The smell of blood and manure was strong and in spite of the fact that he had been there a dozen times before, he still disliked the place. Horgan had stood to one side during the argument, not speaking, and after the quick crash of gunfire he had stepped up to the dead man, rolled him over with his boot, and said, "You ought to have let him draw first, son." Horgan's eyes were cold and without feeling and Reilly mounted his horse and rode away.

Horgan had been with Sheriff Henderson and the posse that came to Paul Childress' ranch the same night and it had been Horgan who coldly, implacably insisted that he be given a trial and then hanged. Reilly remembered the sound of Horgan's voice, soft, demanding. No one had argued, either. Horgan had much power over men.

Moving on toward town, Reilly felt no inclination to hurry. Within an hour he saw another spiral of dust approaching and in a few minutes he recognized Al Murdock with Mrs. Childress. Jabbing the horse into a run, Reilly was in the buggy and embracing the plump woman before the rig stopped. Mrs. Childress cried a little and patted his cheek, saying, "I'm being silly."

Murdock leaned across Mrs. Childress to shake hands with Reilly. He was tall, with shoulders like a spreading oak. His face was flat and somewhat square, but he smiled easily and the smile made people forget his homeliness. Hair lay in dark chunks across his forehead and his eyes were bold and stabbing, the eyes of a man who gives orders with the complete knowledge that they will be obeyed.

Mrs. Childress dabbed at her eyes with the corner of a handkerchief. "I was afraid you wouldn't come back, Reilly."

"I almost didn't," Reilly admitted. He sighed and looked around at the land. "I met Max Horgan a few miles down the road. He mentioned Sally Isham's gettin' married."

Between Al Murdock and Mrs. Childress there passed an embarrassed glance and the awkward silence when there is nothing to say.

"Yes," Murdock said flatly, "she did." He studied Reilly with a certain reserve for he was in the delicate position of becoming a brother-in-law to a man he couldn't be sure of. Reilly understood Murdock well and knew that the man would hew to a line of moral exactitude, offering only as much friendliness as his position dictated, nothing more. Murdock spoke again. "You're takin' it good, Reilly. I figured you'd be killin' mad."

"Jail cools a man off. All I want to do is to be left alone."

"That's nice to hear," Murdock said, obviously relieved. "You know, there's been some speculation goin' around that you'd come back just to blow Burk Seever's head off."

16

Reilly said slowly, "Sally married Burk?"

"Lands sake, I thought you knew!" Mrs. Childress raised a hand and pushed a strand of gray hair from her face. "You just said Max told you."

"He just said she was married," Reilly murmured, and recalled Paul Childress' deft handling of the subject. *He thought I'd kill Burk,* Reilly reflected, and sat quiet for a moment.

"Don't blame her too much," Mrs. Childress said quickly. "Reilly, you was in bad trouble and she had to make the best of things, with her pa dead and her sister to take care of."

"Sure," Reilly said. "Sure."

Murdock stirred on the buggy seat and rolled a smoke. "Burk's come up in the world, Reilly. He's moved his law office from the feed store to above the bank and he wears fancy suits and smokes ten cent cigars. Times have changed. The government's built a big Piute reservation about fifty miles east of here. Now there's big beef contracts and Burk's got himself appointed to handle all of it. You do business with him or none at all."

"I'll have to go look him up," Reilly said with deceptive softness.

The dancing light in his eyes provoked Mrs. Childress to worry. That was the way it went with a woman who had raised a son. The knowledge was too complete, the signs all too familiar. "Don't be a hothead now, Reilly. Turn around and come home where you belong."

"Can't," he said. "Ma, Paul and I don't agree on a lot of things. You know it wouldn't work out."

"You're the son we never had, Reilly. Can't you see that?"

"I'd have never let a posse take him," Reilly said.

Murdock grunted something unintelligible, then said, "Go on then. Get yourself in another jam. For some reason the wild bunch is really after you. Seever would like to whip a horse out from under you and he just may do it if you get too big for your pants."

"Seever and I have something to talk over—and I don't mean his wife. Four years is a long time to spend for something I didn't do. That wasn't manslaughter, Al. That was self-defense."

17

"Reilly," Mrs. Childress said, "give it time. Sometimes that's the best."

"Time is something that I don't have much of," Reilly said.

He lifted his hat and goaded the buckskin into a trot. A hundred yards down the road he looked back and found them still sitting there. Finally Al Murdock slapped the team with the reins and Reilly continued across the flatlands toward the town barely outlined five miles away.

He rode at a faster pace now. He was seeing a big man, a handsome man with a booming voice and a driving ambition that crushed other men without afterthought. Burk Seever stood out bold and clear in Reilly's mind. Seever was an easy man to hate, and Reilly wondered if he could hate Seever enough to kill him.

CHAPTER 2

Buckeye sprawled along the southern tip of Duck Lake, and although bracketed on three sides by mountains, the town itself reared up from the desert flatness, unpainted, a monument to hurry and unconcern. Other than being the focal point for trade in a fifty mile radius, it had little excuse for existence. The town had been born full-grown during the Civil War, eleven years ago, and now gave no indication of ever growing further.

Riding down a main street that was little more than a strip of dust flanked by boardwalks and building overhangs, Reilly Meyers found little that had changed during his absence. Selecting a shaded spot by the hardware store, he dismounted and tied his horse. A few mounts stood three-footed along the street, switching flies. A rig was parked before the feed store and a half dozen men cruised along the walks. In the distance a blacksmith hammer tolled like a church bell.

With his hat brim shielding his eyes, Reilly sauntered down the street, drawing no more than a casual glance from anyone. At the far corner he turned, walking on until he came to the alley. Traveling the length of it, he stopped when he came to the rear of a small bakery. The sweet smell of bread and pastries was thick and inviting when he opened the back door and stepped inside.

In the front of the building a young woman waited on a customer, but she was shielded from his view by a wall separating the rooms. The bell on the cash drawer tinkled musically and a moment later the front door opened and closed. Reilly leaned his Winchester against a baker's bench and waited for the girl to come into the back room.

"Just put the flour on the floor, Herbie," she called, and when she received no answer she came to the separating archway. She halted suddenly when she saw Reilly, her mouth dropping open in surprise. Then she dashed across the distance between them and threw her arms around his neck, kissing him soundly.

"Hey," Reilly said. "Where did you learn to do that?"

She laughed, a happy, musical sound, and cocked her head to one side, studying him. "You look older," she said. "I think I like you better this way, a little more serious and not so full of hell."

Tess Isham was a foot shorter than Reilly, but she had an hourglass figure with the sand settled in the right places. Her hair was a pale brown with definite reddish tints in it. She had green eyes and a peppering of freckles across the bridge of her nose.

"Where's your loving sister, Tess? The one who was going to wait for me?"

The ends of her eyebrows drew down and she placed a hand flat against his chest. "Reilly—damn it." The small bell over the front door rang and she said, "Customer. Wait here for me."

"Sure," he said, and watched the switch of her hips as she went into the other room. A moment later the low run of voices filtered into the back but he paid no attention to it. Leaning against a bench, he looked at the long baking ovens, the hanging pots and utensils. The bare floor had been scrubbed so often that the grain of the wood was upraised ridges. He had scrubbed this floor when Sally worked here because he wanted to be with her, even on his hands and knees with a scrub brush in his hands. He remembered Tess, skinny and flat-chested, but then he saw only Sally. Memory was like a silver thread that kept going back and farther back. He couldn't recall when he had not been in love with Sally Isham or when Burk Seever had not been around.

The voices in the other room grew sharper and Tess' became firm, almost overriding the man's deeper tones. Reilly, listening with half an ear, felt memory and reality blend; and then he stiffened, for he knew that voice. The man was saying, "Tess, I don't know what's got into you.

20

It seems that you're always trying to make a case against me."

"Just get out of here and leave me alone," Tess said flatly, and Reilly Meyers stepped toward the arch.

"You're being very childish about this," the man said. Then he stopped, his head coming around quickly as Reilly filled the archway. A heartbeat passed before the man regained his poise.

"Well, Reilly, I see that you find the back doors still the handiest."

"You seem to like 'em yourself, Burk," Reilly said. "What are you trying to sell this time?" He gave the big man a going over with his eyes, detecting no bulge that would indicate a gun. Burk Seever was very tall and carried the weight to go with it. He was a year younger than Reilly, near thirty, but his eyes were a lot older. They were quick eyes, moving like the rapid play of sunlight through the spokes of a wagon wheel. Seever had a thick mane of blond hair and a mustache to match. His face was unscarred and handsomely cast.

Catching a glimpse of the Remington in Reilly's waistband, Seever placed his hands flat on the glass showcase and stood motionless. He was like a runner waiting for the starting gun.

"I'm not carrying a gun," he said.

"You never did," Reilly said softly, sagging against the door frame. "I hear you got married since I've been in the pen. I'll have to drop around and kiss the bride." He smiled without humor. "Anyone I know, Burk?"

"Stop playing cat and mouse with me," Seever said tightly. "You got shut out and you might as well get used to the idea. You cause me any trouble and I'll bend you out of shape." The big man showed his vexation through the slight movements of his lips, but his close cropped mustache hid most of it. "You've come back asking for trouble. All right, Reilly. We'll give you all you can handle and then some."

"Some other time," Reilly said. "All I'm looking for is a little peace and quiet and for people to leave me alone. You tell that around to the bunch, Burk. *Just leave me alone!*"

"We'll see how that works out," Seever said, and he

21

whirled, slamming the door behind him before stalking down the street.

"That's a nice thing to have for a brother-in-law," Reilly muttered.

"Don't remind me," Tess said, and led him into the back room again. She took a fresh pie from the rack and cut a generous slice. Coffee was on the large range and she poured a cup, placing this on the long rolling bench. When he scraped a chair around and sat down, she took a seat across from him, leaning her elbows on the edge.

"Why did you have to come back, Reilly? Sally?"

"That's one of the reasons," he said between bites. "The others are hard to explain. When the judge handed me four years, all I could think about was gettin' out and puttin' a bullet in Burk Seever. But then I began to cool off. Gunnin' him would only put a rope around my neck because the wild bunch is in too solid for one man to break up with a sixshooter. No, I've thought it out. I'm goin' back to ranchin' and mindin' my own business. However, if someone starts to shove me around, there'll be trouble."

"All right," she said. "We'll let that pass, but why does Burk hate you so?"

"Does there have to be a reason? We just don't like each other. Hell, you can remember how we fought when we was ten years old."

She shook her head in disagreement. "That was kid stuff, Reilly. At the trial he wanted to put a rope around your neck and whip the horse out from under you. Why, Reilly?"

"I don't know," Reilly admitted.

"Do you have something on Burk or Winehaven?"

"Nothing. Do you think I'd have served four years if I had?" He lowered his voice. "Tess, what's the matter with everybody? I said I'd come back and yet everyone seems so damned surprised when I do show up."

"Because no one believed it except me," she said. "People are going to remember how you were friendly with the bunch, Reilly. I'm sorry I had to tell you that, but you always put a great store in the truth even when it pinched."

"Winehaven's man stood up in court and lied me into

22

the pen," Reilly said. "Don't that prove that I wasn't in on their dirty work?"

She shook her head. "I've heard some say that you had a falling out with them—that's why they tried to get you the hard way." She pressed her hands together and moved the palms against each other. "You can't stop people from talking, Reilly, and it's like you used to say: 'When you're catching hell, they're leaving some other poor devil alone.' Everything's changed some since you went away, even me. Since Sally and Burk got married, I've had to get along the best I can. Burk wants me to sell out the bakery and move in with them, but it wouldn't work. I'm not sure I'd like it if it did."

"Where are you living now?"

"Here," Tess said, and gave him a tight-lipped smile. "Don't look so shocked, Reilly. I'm a grown woman and I have a gun. There's a good lock on the door and I put the key under my pillow every night." She saw that he had finished the pie and patted his arm. "Wait here," she said and went out the back door. A moment later she came back and opened the door of a small side room. "This is my home now. Make yourself comfortable while I lock the front door. Business was slow anyway."

The room contained several chairs, a bed and two dressers. There was a familiarity here: the pictures on the walls and the curtains covering the three windows. Then he remembered them being in her room in the old house on Wells Street. Sometimes when he was waiting for Sally to dress, he would talk to her, sitting on the edge of her bed while she cut clothes patterns on the floor. Now that he thought about it, he remembered spending a great deal of time waiting for Sally. And while he waited, he had talked to Tess.

He heard her footsteps and then she came back, toeing the door closed. "I ordered you a meal from the restaurant next door." She motioned toward the bed. "Sit down, Reilly."

He smiled, for she always said this. Indicating the furniture, he said, "Did she throw you out of the house, Tess?"

A pained expression crossed her face but she covered her feelings with a laugh and sat in a deep chair. "Reilly,

23

there never was enough room in one house for two women, especially when they both figure they own it."

"There was plenty of room before Burk married her."

"That was before," Tess agreed. "I knew it wouldn't work, Reilly, so I took my things and moved in here."

"After she asked you to?"

She gnawed her lower lip for a moment, jumping up when a knock rattled the back door. She seemed relieved with the interruption and went out of the room to admit a man bearing a large tray. The wall hid them from Reilly's view, but he heard her soft voice say, "Just set it on the table, Mose," and a moment later the man went out.

Carrying it into her room, she placed it on a low table between them, whisking off the white towel. "Steak," she said, and reached across the table to touch him on the arm. "Reilly, things really do change and it does no good to worry about them. Just forget about what has happened and think about tomorrow."

"A nice trick if you can do it," he said, and began to eat.

After the meal, Tess rose to fix a pot of coffee on the small stove in the corner. She kindled a fire and placed the pot on the back by the pipe. Tipping his chair back, Reilly watched her while rolling a cigaret to top off his dinner.

"You sure are trying hard to keep me from seeing her, aren't you?"

"I'm trying to keep you out of trouble," Tess said. She gave him a sharp glance. "You have a temper like heat lightning and if you didn't shoot Burk, you'd try to fight him with your fists and you've done that before, but always lost. Beating Burk in a fight is something no one has done, Reilly. He's built up a nice reputation around here, believe me."

"You're wrong if you think I'm looking for trouble," Reilly told her. "I said that I'd learned a lesson. From now on I'm leaving people alone. I meant it when I said I didn't want trouble from anyone."

"It sometimes comes looking for you."

"This time I'll step aside," he promised. He leaned forward then, his manner changing. "What made her do it, Tess?"

The girl shrugged. "She never liked to wait, you know that. It pleased her to have people wait for her, but never the other way around."

"She knew I'd come back," Reilly said. "I promised her, Tess. You were there. You heard me promise her."

"You promised a lot of things and some of them didn't come out," she said. The coffee pot began to gurgle. She lifted the lid, then stood with her arms crossed under her breasts. "You've changed, Reilly. I think you'd fulfill a promise now." She gave him a wide smile. "See how canny I've gotten since I've grown up? I'm not the little girl you can tell tall stories to any more."

He smiled at her in spite of the seriousness of his thoughts. She was like mercury, never still. Her mind raced ahead, touching things, liking some, rejecting others. She had a natural exuberance that no amount of unpleasantness could dim for long.

"I've been noticing," Reilly said, "that you've filled out some. It seems that Burk Seever's been noticing it too."

"Then you can see why I couldn't live under the same roof with Sally and him." She switched the subject deftly. "What was it like, Reilly? Bad?"

"Prison? Pretty bad. Once a man's in jail he becomes just another animal." He stared at the ash on his cigarette, then rose to throw it in the stove. "Tell me, is Harry Peters still the U.S. marshal?"

"Yes," she said. "I think he was genuinely sorry about the deal you got, but you did the shooting in California and there was nothing he could do about it."

"Sure," Reilly said. He stared at the fire through the damper opening. "I get four years breaking rocks for trying to get back what was stolen from me in the first place, and Winehaven, who has a stockyard full of stolen beef is still in business. That doesn't make sense."

"Harry Peters has made three raids on Winehaven's place and never found a thing that wasn't covered with a bill of sale. You figure it out, Reilly. No one else can."

"It's not my problem any more," he said flatly. "I had four years to think this thing over and I made up my mind that I wasn't going to try to get even with anybody." He turned his head and looked at her. She remained half-turned toward him as though inviting his appraisal. Finally he pulled his eyes away and filled two coffee cups. "You used to sit like that, watching me," he said. "I often wondered what you were thinking, Tess."

"Did you?" She stood up, a half-smile lifting the ends of her lips. When she came near him she set his cup aside and he took her arm, pulling her against him. She did not fight him, but answered the pressure of his lips and the pull of his hands around the curved hips.

After they parted she studied him gravely. "Were you thinking of Sally?"

"I was thinking of you," he said.

"Then it's all right," she said. The sun was down now and gray shadows began to invade the corners of the room. She moved about, lighting the lamps. Finishing his coffee, Reilly stood up and walked back and forth as though a deep restlessness pushed him.

Tess Isham watched this for several minutes, then said, "You don't have to stay."

His pacing stopped. "Tess, it isn't that at all." From her expression he was sure that he hadn't convinced her.

"I understand, Reilly. Give me credit for it." She began to stack the dishes on the tray. Gathering a shawl from the closet, she moved to the door, pausing with her hand on the knob. "Wait here."

"Where are you going?"

She regarded him levelly. "Out. Just wait here."

He listened to her heels on the hardwood floor and then the back door slammed and quiet came into the building. The sounds of the street filtered through the walls, muffled and seemingly from a great distance. He crossed to the side window to look out but the night was thick and he could see nothing.

Rolling a cigarette he smoked it short and built another. There was some coffee left and he finished it by the time the back door opened and closed. Reilly put the cup down, feeling uncertain. He was like a man visiting in a strange house when the doorbell begins to ring. He knew that moment of uncertainty; should he answer it or not?

He stepped away from the table and moved across the room. Flinging the separating door open, he stepped through and to one side so that the shaft of lamplight would cut the darkness of the back room. A breath of perfume touched him and a familiar voice said, "Aren't you going to kiss me, Reilly?"

"Sally!" He was more shocked than surprised. "What are you doing here?"

She moved past him, into her sister's room. With the lamplight on her she turned slowly toward him as though conscious of her beauty and wanting to give it to him in small doses. Her hair was golden and piled high in a bun on the back of her head. She had full lips and dark eyes with lashes that touched her cheeks when she offered him half-veiled glances.

"Do I pass inspection?"

"You haven't changed," he said softly, his eyes traveling over the soft curves revealed by a flowing dress, tight at waist and bodice.

"But *you* have," she said. "I can see it, Reilly. More serious, I think, and not quite so impulsive." She studied his face as though attempting to read his thoughts. "You're angry because I married Burk, aren't you?"

"You want a silly answer to that one?"

"Sorry. Both to the question and not believing you when you said you'd come back to me. What was a girl to do? Sit and wait?"

"I had to sit and wait. They put bars around to make sure I didn't run off."

"I don't want to quarrel with you," she said. "All right, so I made a mistake. What do I have to do to prove that I'm sorry—draw blood?"

"Forget it," Reilly said, and studied the pattern of the rug. "You're sorry. I'm sorry. Let's forget it."

"Don't be that way," Sally said. She clasped her hands together. "I know you think it was foolish of me to come here like this, but when Tess came to the house and said you were here, I just had to see you again. Don't ask me why."

"I don't have to," Reilly told her. "You always had a tough time making up your mind who you liked. You had to come here because you're remembering how it used to be with us and you're wondering if it will be that way again. I'm not going to sneak off behind Burk's back, Sally. Don't think you can make me. You're trouble to me now, so you go your way and I'll go mine."

She tipped her head back and laughed at him. "I can see right through you, Reilly. You're jealous. Every time the sun goes down you'll begin to sweat, and whatever

27

you're doing, you'll stop, wondering about me and Burk. Go ahead and think, Reilly. Make up a lot of pictures, but remember that they'll only be pictures." Her smile widened and something sly moved into her eyes. "I've always wanted a child. I think I'll take the subject up with my husband."

"You can hate like a Piute," he said softly.

"You're the Indian," she said, her temper exposed now, "and the sign's on *you*. Winehaven is still in business, and with the agency buying beef, you'll be back with the wild bunch where the easy money is. You'll go back because without *me* that dirt pile you call a ranch will be unbearable."

"Are you finished?"

"No. Not until I have you back. You're going to take me back, aren't you, Reilly?" She came close to him and slipped her arms around his neck, pressing herself against him. She could use her body and her lips, and her fervor reached a fever pitch before she released him. In the beginning he resisted her, and when his emotion became too strong he tried to break away. But he ended with her crushed against him and all resolution gone.

When she pushed herself away she raised her hands to straighten her hair, the cloth of her dress pulling tight over her breasts. She wore a slightly superior smile and she said, "It isn't over between us, Reilly. It isn't even beginning."

Her casualness shocked him. He said, "Sally, I think you're trying to get me killed."

Her hand pressed against the butt of his Remington. "Perhaps I'm trying to get my husband killed."

"Get the hell out of here," he said. "What did you come here for? To pull me apart?"

"Don't make this any harder for me than it is," she said. "Reilly, we used to make a lot of plans. What happened to them?"

"They're dead," he told her. "Sally, keep away from me. You're married and no matter what I wanted, I couldn't have it now."

She turned again quickly, facing him, her mouth full and warm with pleasure. "Ah, it *is* that way. You do want me and Burk won't stand between us. Not up to you, he wouldn't. Reilly, you haven't changed, I can see that now.

28

You always took what you wanted. Take me. Do you think I really love him?"

"You married him. Sally, I don't want trouble with Burk or anybody."

"Why? Are you afraid of him?"

He shook his head. "That won't work any more, Sally. Once there was a time when that would have made me fight him, but not now. I have changed. The pen did that to me. You made a deal with Burk and you'd better go back to the house and sleep with it."

"I'll go back," she agreed, "but the other I won't do."

He reached out and touched her on the arm. "What do you want, Sally? Do you really know?"

Smiling, she turned her back to him. Her voice was silky. "I'm a selfish person. Maybe I don't want Tess to have you." She seemed to sense his coming protest and raised her hand. "Let's not pretend, Reilly. We both know she's been making calf-eyes at you since she's been thirteen." She laughed uneasily. "Once I was quite jealous because she rode double with you and always wanted to tussle. At times I wondered if you were taking her into the hayloft."

"Did that worry you?"

Her shoulders rose and fell slightly. "At the time it might have, but I've learned a few things since then. Now the competition doesn't bother me." She shot him a quick glance. "She's a little fool, coming to the house after me. Burk's up town with Jane Alford and he won't be home until morning. What he does doesn't concern me one way or another, Reilly."

"That's a coincidence," he said. "I don't give a damn either."

"I told you he wouldn't be home until morning," Sally said and gave him a bolder look. "We have lots of time, Reilly." Moving closer to him, she touched him lightly on the arm. "Tess is probably standing out in the alley. Turn the key and blow out the lamp and she'll go away. You really don't want me to leave, do you?"

"The sooner the better," he said.

She offered him a short, brittle laugh. "And here I had it all figured out." She dropped her hand and stepped away from him. "I believe I *am* sorry that I came here, but I'm not giving up."

"Don't come back," Reilly said, and took her arm, steering her to the door.

She offered no protest, but stopped in the doorway. "I've heard of people being thrown out, but I've never had it happen to me before." Reaching out, she put her arm around his neck, pulling him close. "Look at me, Reilly, and tell me that you don't love me."

"You'd better go."

Her laughter teased him and she came against him suddenly, her lips searching for his. Her arms held him with a new power and at last she pulled away, laughing and pleased and composed.

"I'll be back," she promised. "You won't stop me, Reilly. No matter what you say, you won't, because you want me with you."

She moved through the darkened back room. He listened to the back door open and close, and then he was alone. His coffee was cold but he lifted the cup anyway. When he glanced down at his hand he saw that it was trembling.

Tess came in a moment later and closed the door, leaning her back against it. She searched him with her eyes. She said, "Nothing's changed, has it?"

"You're talking like a fool," Reilly said, but he didn't look at her.

"Am I?" She pushed herself away from the door and took the cup from his hands, taking a long drink while watching him over the rim. Handing it back, she said, "From now on you'll do everything wrong because she won't let you do otherwise. She never lets go of a thing until it's ruined or destroyed. You think I'm horrible for talking about my sister that way? Maybe I am."

"She did all the talking, Tess."

"I know," Tess Isham said. "I know how it goes because I've heard it all before. She's heading you straight for trouble, Reilly."

"Not me," he maintained. "I'm not going to bother her."

"No," she said, "I don't suppose you will, but she'll bother you and then you'll forget which is which and nothing will matter but you and her being together again. I can remember, Reilly. She taught all the tricks to me

30

and I saw her work 'em on you." She turned her back to him suddenly. "You'd better go now, Reilly."

"Will I see you again, Tess?"

"Maybe. I don't know. I shouldn't have let you kiss me."

For a moment he stood there as though hoping she would turn around. When he saw that she was not going to, he picked up his hat. He paused at the door and looked at her. He said, "I wasn't lying, Tess. It was you I was thinking of."

"It doesn't matter. You're thinking of Sally now and that washes everything out."

"Does it?"

"Please go, Reilly."

"All right," he said and went into the darkened back room. Retrieving his rifle from the bench, he let himself out the front way, testing the door to see that it had locked behind him.

His horse was still tied in front of the hardware store and he led it to the stable at the end of the street. He off-saddled and eased the stud into a stall just as Ben Cannoyer came in.

"Better take that stud out back," Cannoyer said testily. "I got a mare that's horsin' and I don't want my stable kicked to pieces."

Without arguing about it, Reilly led the horse through the stable and bedded him down in a small out-building that once had served as a carriage shed. When he returned he found the old man waiting in the stable arch, puffing contentedly on his pipe.

Only one lantern hung on a stanchion. Reilly raised the lantern off the hook, setting it on a cross board to cast light onto the ground where his blanket roll lay. Cannoyer said, "Careful with that. I don't want no fires in here."

Reilly unrolled his double blanket, took a clean shirt from it, then peeled out of his coat. A watering trough sat a few feet from the stable archway and he walked to it, taking off his shirt to wash.

Cannoyer said, "The hotel's up the street, and if you want a bath go to the barbershop. They got a tub there."

Putting on the clean shirt, Reilly slipped back into his coat and went back into the stable to roll his blankets.

Cannoyer had left his place in the doorway and was leaning against the stanchion. He sucked on his pipe and watched Reilly carefully. Dropping his eyes to the gun in Reilly's waistband, he said, "Couldn't help notice that. Been a little work done on it, ain't there?"

"Some," Reilly said and tossed his rolled blankets in an empty feed bin.

"Knew a fella in Ellsworth who had his guns worked on," Cannoyer said. "Short barrels and no front sights. Trouble was, he tried to pull it one night and he found out a short barrel didn't make a damn bit of difference against a good man."

Reilly flipped his head around and stared at Cannoyer. "You got any good men around here?"

The old man shrugged and hooked one suspender strap farther up on his shoulder. "Noticed that was a Broken Bit stud. You and the old man make up?"

"Did we ever have a fallin' out?"

"He never went to see you," Cannoyer said. "A man do that to me and I'd be plumb aggravated."

He turned away from Reilly and went back to the stable door, closing one side and dropping the locking pin into the sill. Taking his chair, he elevated it against the door frame and cocked his feet up against the side that was closed.

Reilly watched this, and then Cannoyer smiled. Clearly, Ben Cannoyer was barring the exit. Reilly had no doubt of it when Cannoyer said softly, "You wasn't in no hurry now, was you, Reilly?"

CHAPTER 3

Past the stable door the street was bright with streaked lamplight and people moved up and down. In the stable archway an overhanging lantern puddled a yellow glow on the hoof-chopped yard. Reilly walked to where Ben Cannoyer waited and glanced down at the old man's outstretched feet.

"Let me through, Ben," he said mildly.

"Let's talk a spell," Cannoyer said. He knocked the dottle from his corncob pipe. "The news got around that you was comin' back, Reilly. There was some talk on what you'd do."

"You mean go after Winehaven?"

Cannoyer nodded. "Sheriff Henderson got word from the California law that you'd been released. He's been waitin' for you."

"Let him wait," Reilly said. He nodded at the old man's legs. "Better pick 'em up, Ben," he said, and finally Cannoyer lifted them. The old man wore a faded pair of denim pants and run-down boots. He had his shirt sleeves rolled to the elbow and the red flannel underwear sagged away from his skinny arms.

"Something on your mind, Ben?"

"Not much. Goin' to be a lively little town tonight," Cannoyer opined, "seein' how you had to show your muscles to Burk in the bakery." He bent forward in his chair, lowering his voice like a man passing on a smutty joke. "Sally was seen comin' out of th' alley behind th' restaurant about th' same time you was there. Now a

33

man'd have to be pretty dumb not to be able to figure that one out, wouldn't he?"

"I don't know. How dumb are you, Ben?"

In the light of the stable arch, Cannoyer conducted a study of Reilly. Deep shadows boxed Reilly's face, making him seem older. The gun tucked into the waistband gave him a touch of danger.

"I guess it's none of my business," Cannoyer admitted.

"That's right, Ben. It isn't."

"But I wouldn't hang around Buckeye if I was you. When Burk gets wind of this he's liable to come looking for you."

"I won't be hard to find," Reilly said, then broke off his talk as a fringed-top buggy wheeled into the yard. A small man dismounted, peering through the darkness at Reilly and Cannoyer. When he stepped closer, Reilly raised his head so the lantern light bathed his face.

"Well, Reilly," the man said, "I thought this country had seen the last of you."

"Don't bother to pull your badge, Peters," Reilly said. "I'm clean and you know it."

Harry Peters smiled and the ends of his heavy mustache lifted slightly. He was a moon-faced man with a derby and a shaggy buffalo coat. A cigar was fragrantly ignited between his teeth and the brown ends of a dozen more protruded past an inner coat pocket. Removing the cigar from his mouth, he rotated it between thumb and forefinger. He said, "A good cigar is like a loose woman, Reilly—a comfort a man may live to regret."

"Never use 'em," Reilly said.

"I like to see virtue in a man," Peters said. He shrugged his shoulders beneath his heavy coat. "Turning off chilly, Ben. Won't be long until winter."

Cannoyer grunted and refilled his charred pipe. "How's th' marshalin' business, Harry?"

"Tolerable when you think of it only as a steady job," Peters said. "Is Paul Childress and Jim Buttelow in town yet?"

"At the hotel," Cannoyer said. "Some of the others too."

"Thanks," Peters said, and licked a loose shard of tobacco dangling from his cigar. Glancing at Reilly, he

34

added: "Keep out of trouble. I don't want to spend the winter chasing you through the hills."

"Don't lose any sleep over it," Reilly told him. "I'm going to back the winter out at my place—all by myself."

"That," Peters said, "sounds monotonous." He walked down the street.

"That's some fella," Ben Cannoyer said. "He sure don't look like a U.S. marshal, does he?"

"How does a marshal look?"

"Hard to say. He seems kind of runty to be packin' so much authority around." Cannoyer slanted Reilly a shrewd glance. "Still, he ain't done much about stoppin' the rustlin', has he?"

"You're telling me the story," Reilly said. "I've been away."

Cannoyer grunted. Reilly walked up the main drag toward the saloon.

Thirty years ago, Paul Childress had learned how futile it was to worry, and being a strongly disciplined man, resolved to rule it out of his system. But like other planned controls, it slipped now and then and he was forced to acknowledge a vague rat-gnaw of uneasiness.

Sitting on the wide arcade of the new hotel, Childress watched the traffic flow past. He saw Al Murdock come out with Emily Meyers.

"I'm going to see if that linen came in from Fort Reno," Emily said, and left the porch, walking rapidly down the street to the mercantile.

Murdock spotted the empty chair and sat down. Studying Murdock, Childress decided that the foreman was fine-honed in his habits and thinking. It showed plainly on the man's blunt face.

Murdock said, "We're overstocked again for winter range, Paul. You want me to move some of 'em down from the north pasture and let them winter out by the creek?"

"Whatever you think is best," Childress murmured.

"We need another forty ton of hay," Murdock pointed out. "The cash is getting low so I'd better see Hammerslip at the bank in the mornin'." He removed his battered hat and ran fingers through unruly hair. Plainly, he was acting idle and feeling the opposite.

Childress observed him closely for these small clues.

"What's eating on you, Al?" The old man struck a match and laid it across the bowl of his pipe, waggling it back and forth until the fire glowed evenly. He gave Murdock a darting glance. "Worried about Reilly?"

"Some," Murdock admitted. "That hothead's going to get himself into it again if he ain't careful."

"He's a grown man," Childress said. "Reilly can take care of himself."

"Too damn well," Murdock said. He fell silent for a moment. "Paul, I've never stuck my nose in much that never concerned me, but what's between you and Reilly?"

"You think there's something?"

"Reilly could use a friend, and some understandin'. You ain't give him much of either."

"I guess not," Childress said. He sighed. "A man's got to take his own hard knocks, Al. Reilly wants it that way."

"I guess you know what you're doin'," Murdock said, and lapsed into silence.

Sitting quietly with his pipe, Childress decided that Murdock worried too much about trouble. In fact, most men worried too much about it. Yet man was born into trouble, waded through it most of his life, and then succumbed to it or surmounted it. The stronger a man was, the more he fought it, while the weak died easily. He wondered who was better off, the man who died bending to it or the one who died fighting it.

He said, "You and Reilly were never close, Al. Why all the concern?"

Tipping back his chair, Murdock elevated his feet to the railing and sat there, loose-muscled and easy in his manner. When his gaze moved along the street, it swung like the needle of a compass, quickly, restless in its searching, pausing only with reluctance.

"I'm goin' to be shirt-tail kin to Reilly come spring," Murdock said. "A man's got his obligations, that's all."

"Better leave Reilly alone," Childress counseled. "He's headstrong." He touched Murdock on the arm and drew his attention to the two riders dismounting across the street. "There's Reilly's two wild friends from Buttelow's. Go on over there before they come here. I'd hate to have 'em raise hell while I'm relaxin'."

36

Dropping his feet to the floor, Murdock went down the steps and across the street. Walt and Ernie Slaughter tied up, and as Murdock ducked under the hitchrail, they focused their attention along the boardwalk.

Reilly Meyers came toward them through the darkness.

Night lay in thick patches, broken only by the bars of outflung shop lights. Reilly flickered from patch to patch as he moved along the building edge. The Slaughters waited until he came abreast of them, then with wild shouting, leaped on him and smothered him in a flurry of arms. The force of the attack carried Reilly against the building with a jarring crash and he went down beneath their combined weight.

Murdock ran to them and fisted a handful of Ernie's hair, pulling him free. "Let him up," Murdock yelled. "You damn fool, don't you do anything but play?"

For a moment Reilly had fought with a wild stubbornness, but the sound of Murdock's voice cooled him and he struggled to his feet. Grabbing the Slaughters roughly, he pulled them into the light. Then his face wrinkled into a wide smile.

"Damn fool pranksters," he said. "When the hell you two goin' to grow up?"

"That's for old folks," Ernie said, and pounded Reilly on the back. "Now let's catch up on some livin'."

From the open door of Burkhauser's Saloon the sound of a tinkling piano floated out and a voice sang:

> *Fond of fun as fond can be,*
> *When it's on the strict q.t.*

They listened for a minute, then Walt Slaughter rubbed his stomach. He was a slat lean man, near thirty, and on his face a latent danger lay. Pleasure glowed in his pale eyes. "Damned if I don't feel like havin' a smile on this," he said. "When did you get back, Reilly?"

"Today. Things have changed some."

Ernie glanced at his brother and murmured, "Some have." He craned his head around restlessly, as though searching for someone. "Let's go have a look at the elephant."

"You think there's one in there?" Reilly asked and

37

shouldered the batwings aside. They filed in, Murdock trailing behind, and all bellied against the cherrywood. A girl was prancing across the stage, kicking her black stockinged legs high.

> *Ta-ra-ra-boom-de-ay*
> *Ta-ra-ra-boom-de-ay*

Reilly seemed fascinated with her, an odd stirring of remembrance on his face. Taking Ernie Slaughter by the arm, he pulled his attention around. "That widow that lived by Alder Creek—ain't that her daughter?"

"Yeah," Ernie said, and his eyes grew unpleasant. "Burk threw her over when he married Sally Isham."

Turning back to the bar, Reilly stared at the triangle formed by his forearms. "Is that all she can do for a living?"

"Singin's just a sideline," Murdock said, and Ernie showed a quick resentment. Walt saw this and braced a hand against his brother, giving him a gentle shove backward.

"Cinch up on it. Forget it now."

"Sure," Ernie murmured, and glanced at Al Murdock. The Broken Bit foreman looked ill at ease. "Sorry, Ernie. My damn mouth's too big." He studied the bar's polished surface.

The bartender came up cautiously. When Reilly raised his head, he stiffened slightly, his hands sliding to the carved edge of the bar. For a moment neither man spoke. Then the bartender said, "Don't try anything with me, Reilly. I got a double-barreled shotgun under here and I'll blow a hole in your guts if you so much as lay a hand on me."

"Now what would I have against you, Elmer?" Reilly kept his voice deceptively soft. He laughed. "When did you leave Winehaven's? Is this better than being his flunky?"

The bartender made a nervous movement with his feet. "You act like a man with a guilty conscience," Reilly said, and the good nature in his manner vanished like a puff of smoke. "There'll be no trouble *tonight*, Elmer. Just leave the bottle and get the hell out of my sight."

"Sure," Elmer said, and went to the far end of the bar.

38

The Slaughter brothers looked at each other and Murdock made a negative movement with his head. "Well," Ernie said, "someone drink to my health. I feel faint."

Murdock fisted the bottle and came to his rescue. Making a larve V with his index and little finger, Ernie said, "Whoop, whoop, whoop—just two fingers in a washtub now."

"Pour until it burns my hand," Walt told him, shoving his glass down the bar. To Reilly, he said, "It seems like Elmer is still on th' list, don't it?"

"Shouldn't he be? I did four years on the rock pile, remember?"

"So you did," Walt said dryly.

Reilly watched Elmer. The bartender grew increasingly nervous. Finally he could stand it no longer. He came back to where the four men stood.

Speaking to Reilly, Elmer said, "You want to start somethin' with me?" Elmer Loving was a round faced man with pop-eyes. He wore his hair slicked down in spit-bangs over the forehead.

"I'd like to unscrew your damned head," Reilly said pleasantly, "but I suppose that's a pleasure that will have to wait." He leaned forward on his elbows, his face only a foot from Loving's. "Who paid you to lie, Elmer?"

"You're barkin' up the wrong tree." Elmer made aimless motions with the bar rag. "Don't make trouble for me, Reilly. I've got friends—friends who'll eat you whole."

"No trouble," Reilly said. "I'm going to be around for a long time, Elmer. One of these days we're going to get together, just you and me, and have a nice, long talk."

"You're not scarin' me." Elmer waited a moment before moving away. It was as though he lingered only to create an illusion of fearlessness.

The girl finished her song and dance and Reilly turned his head to watch her. Leaving the stage, she walked among the tables, and a moment later she started for the bar. She was small and shapely and her dress was cheap. Beneath the rouge and lip paint she had a natural beauty, but she seemed to wear makeup to disguise, rather than accent it.

When she saw Ernie Slaughter at the bar she halted. Then her shoulders moved slightly as though shrugging

39

something aside. She came toward them, a wide, dead smile stretching her lips.

Ernie said, "How are you, Jane?" His voice was gravely serious.

Jane Alford laughed, a brittle, forced sound, and the smile remained on her lips although it did not creep into her eyes. They were deep blue and very remote, for she deliberately held herself back, never revealing what she really thought or what she felt. "I'm sober," she said. "But drunk or sober, I'm happy."

Reilly Meyers was half hidden by Al Murdock's shoulder. When Jane saw him, her smile died and her lips turned stiff. Reilly said, "Don't you remember me, Jane?"

"I—Reilly, get out of here! If these two knotheads had an ounce of brains between them they would have never brought you in here." She turned to Ernie Slaughter, openly angry. "Haven't you any better sense than to flaunt him under Burk's nose?"

When she glanced past Ernie Slaughter, she found Burk Seever's eyes boring into her from across the room. Seever sat at a table along the far wall and when Reilly looked, he found the big man's stare a thing so solid that it almost rang like a struck saber blade.

Placing his cards face down on the table, Burk excused himself and crossed to the bar, carefully threading his bulk between the filled tables. When he reached the bar, he raised a finger to Elmer and said, "Out of the private bottle, Loving." Then he looked at Ernie Slaughter. "If you'd move down," he said, "I'd have a little room."

"You move," Ernie said, and kept his body braced, preventing Seever from coming against the bar.

A dancing light began to shine in Burk's eyes. He laughed. He let his eyes wander over Jane Alford's stockinged legs and low-cut dress. "Run along, honey. Sell that charm to the customers."

"She likes it here," Ernie said.

Seever ran a hand over his mouth, pawing it out of shape. His eyes were bold and demanding, for he had physical power and used it ruthlessly.

Tension swirled around them, and then Reilly Meyers edged his voice in. "Before you get lathered up, Burk, I want to tell you that your wife called on me when I was at the bakery. I just thought you'd like to know."

"Damn you," Seever said. In his mind he had a good fight started with Ernie Slaughter and now Reilly had pulled his teeth. This rankled Burk Seever and he hid it poorly.

Reilly began to press him then from another angle. "We were having a friendly drink until you butted in. Why don't you pull your picket now?"

"Don't talk big to me, Meyers. You're not built for it." Burk didn't bother to look at Jane Alford when he added, "I said, peddle your charms."

She took a step away from them. Ernie reached out, fastening a hand on her bare arm.

Reilly saw anger vault into Seever's face. He said, "You've got yourself all primed for trouble tonight, Burk, but I'll tell you now—don't start it. There's enough of us here to stomp a mud hole in your head, so you'd better move on."

The taunt seemed to drive Seever's temper deeper. He said, "I'm not going to fool you, Reilly. I'll give it to you straight out—you're headed for trouble. I tied a can to your tail once and I'll do a better job of it the next time. Get out of the country. That's good advice."

"I wouldn't take advice from you on a bedbug race," Reilly said. "Go on back to your card game before your busted flush gets cold."

"You're getting nervy," Seever said. "You got nervy once before at Winehaven's place." He moved his heavy shoulders restlessly. "Keep away from my wife. If I hear of you bothering her, I'll break up your face so no woman will have you."

He struck the bar with his fist and wheeled away, striding rapidly back to the waiting card game.

Walt Slaughter grinned. "Mr. Seever is mad as hell, Reilly. He don't like you."

"I don't like him," Reilly said. He took another drink and felt it slide warmly down, settling into a pool of fire in his stomach.

"You're dumber than when you left," Jane Alford said. "Can't you see that he's out to get you, that it's always been that way?"

Reilly's interest sharpened. "Tell me why, Jane. What did I see at Winehaven's that he's afraid I'll remember?"

Her face turned smooth and her eyes became remote

41

and unfriendly. "I work here. I don't know anything." Ernie still held her arm and she said to him, "I have to go now, Ernie."

"You don't have to go any place," he told her, but he dropped his hand.

"I *have* to go," she repeated, and moved away. The four men watched her walk among the tables, smiling with her lips alone.

On Ernie Slaughter's face there was a quiet thoughtfulness that pushed the laughter out of his eyes as he turned to nurse his drink. Plainly he wished to be left alone and Murdock swung their attention away from him when he said, "Considering that Buckeye is a small town and the ranches are few and far between, Burk has really come up in the world. He handles all the beef contracts for the Piute Agency besides his law practice." He leaned against the bar and sagged until his weight was on his forearms. "Somehow money just seems to stick to his fingers, and the way he spends it, his addition must be somethin' new and different."

"You tryin' to say something?" Ernie asked.

"Maybe." Murdock swung around, hooking his elbows on the edge of the bar. "Let's say a man makes a hundred a week bein' a lawyer. If so, how can he spend a hundred and fifty?" He shook his head sadly. "You two clowns break horses for a livin' but I manage a ranch. When I lose ten head, I worry. A hundred turn up missing and I'm out a lot of sleep."

"Not that bad, is it?" Reilly said soberly.

Murdock snorted. "You know, I don't have enough money on the books to show a decent profit this last year? As a safe guess I'd say that at least a thousand head has been rustled in the past ten months." He tallied it up on his fingers. "Bob Ackroyd, at Hat, has lost some. Lovelock's Lazy U has been hit. Your Hangnoose brand is gone, Reilly. Max Horgan's Chain claims to have lost steers." Murdock smiled wryly. "Where do they go? The Piute Agency? Harry Peters says not, but when the beef contracts are posted in Seever's office, they don't buy enough to feed half the Piutes. Yet the Injuns never cry 'cause they're starving."

"This bores me," Walt said. "I'm a horse wrangler."

"Everything puts you to sleep," Murdock opined. He

hooked his drink off the bar and finished it, pushing the shot glass away from him. "I'd sure like to get on the reservation some day when they was issuin' beef."

"You mean you can't get in?" Reilly asked.

"Seever buys," Murdock repeated. "Everything goes through him and then the agent at Carson City. We fill out a contract and the check is mailed to him. After his cut, we get ours."

"That sounds like a tight little setup," Reilly murmured. He pushed his glass in aimless circles. "A deal between Seever and the agent?"

"What else?" Murdock said. "But what does that prove? Harry Peters has been rappin' his head against the wall tryin' to find the break, but there isn't any. Seever don't rustle cattle. Winehaven's been clean every time Peters crossed over the border with a warrant. Horgan's brand is clean—at least it has been when Sheriff Henderson and Peters looked it over." Murdock sighed and changed the subject. "You goin' back to your place, Reilly?"

"Nowhere else to go. The brand's registered and the land's mine."

"You could move on," Murdock suggested softly. "Reilly, sometimes a man gets to a point where there's nothin' else for him to do but move on. Why don't you think it over."

"I've thought it over."

"The deck's stacked, Reilly. Seever is out to get you because you and Sally—well, you know what I mean. Henderson and Horgan would like to see you dead and gone. You tell me why, because I can't figure it out. You make Winehaven very nervous. How can you buck a hand like that?"

"I'm going to try," Reilly said, patting the money belt beneath his shirt. "There's a little over six hundred there, enough to keep me going for a year. In that time I'll either make it back or be flat broke."

"All right," Murdock said with some resignation. Rolling a smoke, he kept his attention on the paper and tobacco. The sense of fairness that ruled Murdock was now satisfied. He owed Reilly Meyers nothing more. Raising his eyes, he looked at his future brother-in-law and added, "Another for the road?"

Reilly shook his head. "I'm going to get me a box of rifle cartridges and then head for the hills."

"Luck," Murdock said, and raised his glass. Ernie and Walt said nothing, but Ernie winked at Reilly before he went out.

Pausing on the porch for a moment, he surveyed the traffic, then cut across and went into the hardware store. Childress was still sitting on the hotel porch but Reilly did not speak. Two other men were with Childress, men who held no particular friendliness for Reilly Meyers.

Bolder's store was one large room, lamplit now and filled with the mingled smells of leather, bolted cloth and stored paint. At the counter, Reilly waited until Bolder finished waiting on Mrs. Ketchum.

Bolder was shriveled, fifty some, with the pinched face of a man who counts money in his sleep. He shuffled along behind the counter and Reilly laid a gold piece down. "Two boxes of forty-four-forty, Gabe."

The man took two from beneath the counter and made change in a slow, cautious way. Sounds of movement from the street came into the building and a man's boots hit the boardwalk with a hollow thump.

"You figure on stayin'?" Bolder asked.

"I might," Reilly said.

Bolder was leaning against the counter, his hands spread along the edge as a brace.

The heavy footsteps stopped. From the doorway, Burk Seever said, "He's not staying."

Reilly swung around slowly. Lamplight struck Burk's face, making an oily shine on his forehead. Seever took another step into the room. "You're leaving, Reilly."

"Are you looking for a little trouble, Burk?" Reilly raised his hand and touched the butt of his sawed off Remington. "I can give you trouble, Burk."

"You won't use that gun on me, Reilly." Seever turned his head slightly as footsteps approached from his rear. A young man paused in the doorway, his eyes round and innocent. He looked first at Reilly Meyers and then at Burk Seever.

He said, "If this is private I can go some place else."

"It's open to the public," Reilly said, and the young man smiled, taking another step into the room. He drew Reilly's attention like a magnet, for in him Reilly sensed

44

something daring and reckless, something that reminded him of times gone past, when he believed the world was fun and hills were made to be ridden over.

Burk Seever said, "Get out of here or get in front of me where I can see you."

"Something bothering you?" the young man asked.

"I won't ask you again," Seever said heavily.

"I'll bet you won't," the young man said, and leaned against the door frame, his legs crossed.

No more sounds came from the street. Even the piano in Burkhauser's Saloon was still. Burk Seever stood just inside the room, the problem seesawing back and forth in his mind, the urge to push this thing further prodding him hard.

Finally he stepped deeper into the room, putting the young man out of jumping distance. His feet made the plank floor protest, and in the coffee mill, a few beans that had clung to the rolled rim came loose and clattered loudly in the hopper.

Carefully, Seever removed his coat and unbuttoned his vest, tossing them on a stack of crates. Reilly shifted his weight and braced both hands against the counter. The young man stepped away from Seever and around him, placing himself on the big man's left and directly across from Reilly.

"Move away from there," Seever said.

Reilly left the counter, moving down to where a bunch of ax handles sat stacked in an empty barrel.

"I like to lean," he said, and shook out his sack of tobacco. Rolling a smoke, he struck a match against one of the handles. His eyes laughed at Seever over the flame.

Seever jumped slightly when Reilly tossed the makings to the young stranger. The only sound in the room was Seever's angry breathing.

Seever said, "This is between you and me, Reilly. You don't want this kid to get hurt, do you?"

"He can make up his own mind," Reilly said. He plucked one of the handles from the barrel, running his hand along the smooth wood. Out on the street a horse went by, the hoofs making dull sounds in the dust.

Reilly said, "If you don't want your skull caved in, put your coat and vest on and walk out of here."

Seever swung his head from the stranger to Reilly.

45

"You sure got guts," he said. "Are you afraid to use your fists?"

"Better get out now," Reilly murmured. "You're wearin' it pretty thin."

"Sure." Seever managed a forced smile. "Some other time, Reilly." His eyes went around and fastened on the young man. "I'll be seeing you too."

"Don't strain your eyes," the kid said, and then Seever picked up his coat and vest and went out with plunging strides. Bolder let out a long sigh and went to the back room for the bottle he kept hidden behind the cider press.

Reilly studied the stranger. He said, "You like your fun rough, don't you?"

"Any way that's fun," the young man said. He gave Reilly a lopsided grin and stepped through the doorway. He paused on the walk for a moment before crossing to Burkhauser's saloon.

The piano was going full blast again. Its tinkle filled the town.

CHAPTER 4

Bob Ackroyd of Hat, Swan Lovelock of the Lazy U and Paul Childress were still huddled on the hotel porch when Burk Seever came out of the hardware store and stalked across the street. On the boardwalk he rammed his shoulder against a man who partially blocked his path, and entered the saloon.

A moment later, Reilly Meyers came out and walked to Cannoyer's stable at the end of the street. He led his horse out, mounted and rode out of town. The young stranger who had left the hardware store a moment before Reilly, came sauntering up the walk and Bob Ackroyd leaned over the porch rail. "Hey, what happened?"

"You seen who come out first, didn't you?" The stranger took a final drag on his cigarette and shied it into the street. He gave Ackroyd a frank glance, neither bold nor wise. Just an appraisal. "That's what happened," he added and walked on down the street.

"That might have been worth seein'," Lovelock muttered. "Burk don't back up too easy."

Paul Childress slapped the arms of his chair. "I think it's time we paid Harry Peters a call."

"Buttelow's over to Burkhauser's. You want him in on this?"

"Tell him to come along," Childress said, and Ackroyd left the porch, cutting across the street. On Burkhauser's porch he fronted the swinging doors, then recoiled as two men charged through, locked in each others arms and fighting with drunken intensity.

For a moment Ackroyd watched them sway to the

porch edge and topple into the street. Farther down, the young stranger who had paused at the porch crossed over and elbowed his way to the inside of the ring of spectators.

The two men fought on, paying no attention to the crowd gathered around them. Ackroyd lost interest and went into the saloon.

Spilled lamplight fell on the two men as they struggled to their feet. One man swung at the other and missed, falling back against the cheering crowd. Suddenly the man whirled and lashed out and the young stranger who stood there watching caught the blow on the mouth.

Almost instantly he was in the fight, bearing the other man down with caroming blows. The crowd's cheering increased, for now it was two against one with the young stranger making a good showing for himself. Surprisingly, the two fighters seemed less drunk than they had been. They concentrated on a quick finish.

The stranger went down and was jumped before he had a chance to regain his feet. Childress and the others, sitting across the street, could hear the sodden impact of fists against flesh, and then Sheriff Henderson battled his way through the spectators and collared the young man, jerking him roughly to his feet.

Without warning, Henderson whipped his long barreled Smith & Wesson out of the holster and cracked the young man across the head with it. A murmured protest rose from the crowd and Murdock, Buttelow and Ackroyd came out of Burkhauser's in time to see this. Pushing his way through to Henderson, Ackroyd spoke tersely and the sheriff's head came around quick and sullen and ready for trouble.

Then Ackroyd and the other two men came across the street. Childress and Lovelock stepped off the porch and joined them. In a group they watched Henderson drag the unconscious man to jail.

"That seemed damn sudden to me," Lovelock said. "It's hell when a man can't have a little fun without gettin' his head cracked."

"The other two beat it quick enough," Buttelow said. He was a man in the shadow of sixty, rifle-straight, with a mane of white hair. He wore his mustaches long and a waterfall haircut touched his coat collar.

At the corner, the young stranger began to come around. He tried to stand, but Henderson cuffed him and they moved on.

"Somebody ought to go get him," Murdock said.

"Stay out of it," Childress warned. "We've got enough problems of our own." He addressed Jim Buttelow. "Did you see Reilly? He's goin' back to his old place. There could be trouble over that."

Buttelow grunted. "Trouble and Reilly always went hand in hand." He nodded toward the street where the sheriff and the young man had disappeared. "Like him, he's havin' fun, but tomorrow he'll be in jail."

"Not any more," Murdock said, raising his eyes from the cigarette he had been rolling. "Reilly's cooled off. He's different now."

"Harry Peters is at the New Congress Hotel," Childress said. "I thought we might walk over and have a talk with him."

They nodded and went down the street.

The New Congress was a two-story frame building on the back corner, the older of Buckeye's two hotels. Passing through the lobby, they mounted the protesting stairs and Childress rapped on a door halfway down the hall.

"Come in," the marshal's voice invited. Buttelow opened the door, then stepped aside for the others to pass in ahead of him.

Without his shaggy coat, Harry Peters seemed even smaller, a slightly dapper man. He shook hands all around and waved them to take seats. "I was getting ready to come to you," he said. He patted his pockets for a cigar, found one and touched a match to it. "If you're expecting good news from the Carson City office, though, I'll have to disappoint you. After three years of work we still have no evidence that will stand up in court."

"That song's gettin' on my nerves," Childress said. "We're still losing beef right and left."

"The country is against you," Peters said and puffed on his cigar. "It's against all of us. The land is too dry and the vegetation too poor. With a cow for every ten acres a man's holdings is spread over hell's back yard. You've got three men on your payroll, Paul, not counting Al. How many acres? Twenty thousand at least.

49

That's spreading the men out too thin and you know it."

"Dammit, I can't afford any more," Childress snapped. "With all the damn rustlin' goin' on, I'm not making enough to support a full crew."

"I know," Peters said. He paused to shy ashes into the wood box. "The rustlers know it too and they're taking advantage of it. We're up against a big thing here and we won't whip it easy. It seems they know where the cattle are bunched and by the time Henderson gets on the trail, they're in the rocks and the tracks peter out."

"One time the tracks didn't peter out," Murdock said softly. "But Reilly got four years for his trouble."

Harry Peters shot the Broken Bit foreman an irritated glance.

Lovelock said, "Can't we get Henderson out of office? He's no damned good."

"Vote him out," Peters suggested. "That's what the polls are for."

"Another two years until election," Bob Ackroyd said. "And who the hell are we goin' to get to run against him?" He took out the makings and shaped a cigarette. "I, for one, never voted for him."

"I don't think any of us did," Childress said. "Harry, did you know that Reilly's back?"

Peters nodded and studied the tip of his cigar. "Blame me if you want to, Paul, but I stood back and let Reilly get four years." Childress' head came up at this and the marshal smiled. "I'm sure he shot that man in self-defense. Elmer Loving was lying." Grimacing at his sour cigar stub, he went to the window and threw it into the street. Lighting a fresh one, he turned the air acrid with strong smoke.

"Reconstructing what happened that day, we all know that Reilly discovered the raid on his herd a few hours after it happened. He began to trail. That unexpected snowfall helped and at Winehaven's he found the steers bunched in a holding pen. There was an argument and Reilly pulled his gun. Max Horgan was there as well as Elmer Loving. Horgan didn't show for the trial, but Loving lied in his testimony. Personally, I believe that there was more to it than came out or Burk Seever would never have pressed such a strong case for a hanging. I tell you, gentlemen, Reilly saw something there at Winehaven's that scared the pants off of somebody. I'm not at all sure that Reilly understands how important this is or even what it was, but they knew he saw it and wanted to get rid of him."

"Seems funny to me you'd let Reilly go to the pen," Murdock said.

"Getting Reilly off the hook wouldn't make him remember what he saw. It's not a big thing or it would have been outstanding." Peters frowned. "I'd say it was a small piece of the puzzle, but once a man got his hands on it and thought about it, a lot would fall into place."

Al Murdock became very attentive. "You got something in mind, Harry?"

"Yes. We need a man to get in there and slug it out with Winehaven's bunch."

"Reilly?"

"Yes," Peters said after a pause. "He's got a record now and it might be that he won't make a go of it on his own place. He has as much to lose now as any of you have."

"I don't like it," Murdock said flatly. "I'm not takin' Reilly's side but the man's goin' to be my brother-in-law one of these days and I draw a line on what's fair and what ain't. You leave him alone, Peters."

Raising both hands palms out, Peters said, "Now don't jump down my throat. I just made a suggestion. Look at it this way for once. When Burk married Sally Isham, she opened up a lot of trouble for Reilly because Reilly never liked to take a licking from anyone and Burk's give him a couple already." Peters jabbed his cigar at Murdock. "I'm in sympathy with you, Emily and all, but I didn't mean that I'd throw Reilly to the wolves. Gentlemen, law enforcement is a coldly methodical profession, following just rules and mutual protection, innocent and guilty alike."

"A rope and a Winchester in the right places," Ackroyd said, "would do a lot of good."

"Yes," Peters said. "It would make us as lawless as the ones we shot or hung." He shook his head. "This matter will be brought to a court of law and aired there. Nothing less will satisfy me."

"You ought to quit marshalin' and run for sheriff," Childress said. "We need a man like you, Harry."

"Very complimentary," Peters said, "but I'm satisfied."

"What about Reilly?" Murdock asked.

Peters removed his cigar from his mouth and pulled at his bottom lip. "We'll play it straight. Let Burk Seever and his crowd make the first move against Reilly. Burk won't give up. He wants Reilly dead."

The meeting broke up and Harry Peters shook hands all around before they filed out. Murdock and Childress were the last to leave and Al paused to ask, "What kind of a man are you, Harry? I've known you since the war and I still haven't figured you out."

Peters placed the cigar in the corner of his mouth and smiled. "Right now, a sleepy man." He stood in the doorway and watched them walk down the stairs.

Closing the door then, he laid his cigar on the dresser. He removed his coat and rolled up his sleeves to wash his hands and face. His gun harness hung under the left armpit in a spring holster. It popped when he removed the gun, a .38 Smith & Wesson Sheriff's model with a shortened barrel. Laying this on a chair by his bed, he placed his hunting case watch beside it before snuffing out the lamp.

Springs squeaked as he settled himself for the night. Through the walls, the sound of the town came faintly.

Because it was her job, Jane Alford circulated among the tables, but several times she looked toward the bar where Ernie Slaughter stood. She saw Reilly Meyers leave, and soon after that, Burk Seever. She paid particular attention to Burk's face when he returned. Then Bob Ackroyd came in a moment later, only to go out again with Jim Buttelow and Al Murdock. The fight was going strong outside, but she paid no attention to it. She watched the batwings winnow after Ackroyd, and then she left the main floor. She went toward a door leading through the back room to the alley.

The night was cool and the muffled sounds coming from the saloon somehow seemed very far away. She leaned against the rough wall and breathed deeply as though her lungs were sick with the odors of spilled whiskey and cigar smoke.

From the gap between the saloon and the hardware

52

store, a slight rattle came to her. Then a man emerged, swinging his head left and right before he picked up the reflected light from her dress. She started to move away from the wall, but sagged back when Ernie Slaughter said, "Jane! Wait."

He moved past some stacked beer barrels, a tall shape with a voice as cool as the night wind. Jane said, "Get out of here, Ernie, before you get hurt."

"Don't play tough with me, Jane. I know what's beneath the paint."

"Do you?" She laughed softly. "You're a boy, Ernie. You don't know anything."

He stepped close to her. She raised a hand and placed it against his chest, but his fingers closed on her bare arms and pulled her and his lips held hers for a long moment. Finally she broke away from him. When she spoke, her voice was ragged and her breathing disturbed. "You kiss like a boy too."

"You're lying," Ernie said. "Why do you keep lying? What happened to us?"

"There was never anything there," she said. "You filled me with a lot of foolish notions, that's all." She put the smile back on her lips. "I wanted a little fun—some money. Don't feel sad for me, Ernie. I'm not complaining."

"You changed your mind too suddenly," Ernie said. "Right after Reilly went up, you changed your mind." He reached for her but she shifted and he dropped his hand. "What's the connection, Jane? I want to know."

She became angry then and pushed against him with stiffened arms. "Get away from me! You always want to know everything! Can't a girl have anything to herself? You come around like a sick calf. You want your fun with me and you'll have to pay for it like everybody else."

"You don't mean that," Ernie said.

She laughed at him, her voice lifting against the silence in the alley. "Grow up, Ernie. You want a girl to raise fat kids. I never wanted the raising part, just the fun."

"I see," he said. He touched her arm again. She brought her hand up and slapped him resoundingly.

"Get away from me, Ernie. I mean it!"

"All right," he said, and he went down the alley, making his way slowly past the litter of boxes and junk. She stood there watching him and the pale night light fell on her face, glistening in the streaks of moisture that ran down her cheeks.

The back door of the saloon opened and Burk Seever stepped out, his bulk magnified in the darkness. Jane Alford wiped her face.

"You sure can handle 'em, honey," Burk said.

Her shoulders stiffened, but her voice was smooth. "Did you see them leave? Ackroyd and the others?"

"Yeah. They'll talk and beat their brains out, but they won't get anywhere." He put his hand on her bare shoulder. She stood still, waiting for his hand to move away, but it slid past her breast and clasped her waist. "Better get inside," he told her.

"You go first," Jane said, still presenting her back to him. "What about Reilly, Burk? What if he remembers? Surely he will."

"Don't worry about it," Burk murmured, and touched his lips to her neck. "You just keep your mouth shut around Ernie Slaughter. You want that kid, don't you?"

"Do you have to keep asking me?"

"Just don't want you to forget," Seever said, and bit her ear.

She shrugged her shoulder, pushing his face away. "Not now," she said flatly. "You've got a wife of your own."

"I like variety," Burk said. He slapped her rounded hip, then moved away. A moment later the rear door closed and she was alone in the alley. She pressed her hands flat against her open mouth while tears broke past the dam of her eyelids.

Her lips moved and her voice was barely a whisper. "Ernie—help me, Ernie."

The hour was late when Reilly Meyers arrived at his place southeast of Buckeye. He put his horse in the barn, and trudged across the littered yard, kicking empty tin cans and cursing his unwelcome tenants for leaving such a mess behind.

He entered the darkened house. The door came off the hinges when he tried to close it, and this added to his aggravation. Disgusted with the filthy floors, he went outside again and spread his blankets on the porch. The night wind carried a thin chill and he inched closer to the wall to break the flow of air around him.

A sleeping man cannot always say what brings him awake. There may be no sound at all, but the instinct for survival is strong, preceeding sound. Almost a metaphysical force, it brings a man upright in his blankets, instantly alert.

The dawn was not far away and a faint light had begun rinsing away the blackness when Reilly came awake. He stopped all movement when he found the man sitting across from him, a .56 caliber Spencer balanced across his knees.

Sheriff Henderson was near fifty, wrinkle-faced, with a mustache sagging past the corners of his mouth. A star peeked from between the folds of his coat.

Reilly threw his blankets aside, his hand falling near the butt of his Remington.

"Be careful there," Henderson said. "I'd hate to shoot you just because you got careless."

Kicking free of his blankets, Reilly sat up and tugged on his boots. Henderson had leaned his rifle against the porch steps, safely out of reach. He took the sawed-off Remington from Reilly and stuck it into his waistband.

When the sheriff studied Reilly, he had a flat, lusterless expression in his eyes. "I like the dawn," he said. "Never a better time to take a man. He's lazy then and his mind's full of sleep."

"What the hell do you want with me?" Reilly asked.

"Comes under the heading of unfinished business," Henderson said. "You're a man with a record, Reilly, and as sheriff of this county I got to ask you a few questions."

"Go ahead and ask 'em."

"We'll go in town to my office," Henderson suggested. "These things take time. You know how the law is." He stood up, flourishing his rifle. "Let's not waste any of it now, shall we?"

With the sheriff's rifle covering him, Reilly saddled the buckskin and made up his blanket roll. Once Reilly's guns were secured to the saddlehorn, the sheriff mounted and told Reilly to move out ahead of him.

The sheriff kept his horse at a walk five paces behind Reilly. After a short silence, he said, "If you had been smart, you would never have come back here. There's some people around here who think you want to make trouble."

"Why don't you get off my back?" Reilly asked.

"Me?" Henderson laughed. "I'm a public servant, Reilly. When a man wants another brought in, then I have to do it. Nothin' personal, you understand."

"Like hell," Reilly said.

Henderson laughed louder this time and they finished the trip in silence. Riding down the main street, Henderson stayed behind Reilly, his rifle nonchalantly held across the saddle. They went down a short side street and Reilly dismounted. The sheriff unlocked the door and stepped aside for Reilly to enter ahead of him.

The outer office was a dingy room with a barred window, an oak desk and several straight backed chairs. Henderson racked Reilly's rifle and put the revolver in the desk drawer, then herded him toward a cell facing an open lot.

Reilly paused as Henderson swung the cell door open. He said, "You don't have a damn thing on me and you know it, Jack. What's this all about?"

"Spittin' on the sidewalk," Henderson said. "What difference does it make? We'll make something stick."

"You got it all figured out, haven't you?"

"Somebody has," Henderson admitted, and locked the door.

Through the barred window, Reilly could observe a large section of the main drag beyond the vacant lot. The morning sun climbed higher, and by noon the air was thick with heat.

There were two bunks in the cell, the bottom one occupied by a young man who snored on, his head thrown back, half in, half out of the bed. After listening to this for an hour, Reilly raised a foot and gave the young man a shove.

The snoring sputtered to a halt and he sat up, scrubbing a hand over his face. There was a long split in the young man's scalp and blood had dried and matted the blond hair.

"What a night," he said. He stood up then, staggered to the barred door and rattled it until Henderson came back. "How about some water in here?"

The sheriff nodded and went away, returning a few minutes later with a gallon bucket. He unlocked the door, set it inside, then snapped the key again before returning down the hall to the outer office.

The young man poured half the water over his head and stood dripping. Then he said, "I'm Milo Bucks, friend. Don't I know you from somewhere?" He didn't wait for an answer; just poured more water over his head. He set the bucket aside and added, "Sure, the hardware store. You wasn't in here when I got tossed in, was you?"

"No," Reilly said. He examined the split scalp. "Door knob?"

"Gun barrel." Bucks grinned. "There was a beautiful fight, but the sheriff broke it up." He sat down on the bunk and reached for the bucket, drinking until it was empty. "That was selfish of me. You thirsty?"

"It can wait," Reilly said. "You new around here?"

"Just passin' through," Milo Bucks said. "It's too bad I didn't. After I saw the elephant, it wasn't as pretty as I thought it was goin' to be." He sighed. "Like a woman's kiss, a mystery until you've had it, then quickly forgotten." His young face turned serious. "You didn't say what your name was," he said.

Reilly told him, then looked out the window. This being Saturday, traffic was brisk. All the outlying families had come into town for supplies and talk.

Henderson ambled back with two plates of stew, shoving them beneath the door. The two men ate in silence and pushed the plates back. Reilly rolled a smoke and passed the sack of tobacco to Milo Bucks.

The front door opened and Reilly looked around in time to see Tess Isham come in. She spoke briefly to Henderson. The sheriff came down the hall with Tess following him.

"Talk through the bars," Henderson said. "Five minutes."

After he went back to the front office, Tess said, "I'm sorry, Reilly, but I was afraid something like this would happen."

"I haven't done anything," he said. "They can't hold me. But get out of here, Tess. This is no place for you."

She gripped the bars until her knuckles turned white. "Reilly, this isn't anything to joke about. Don't you un-

57

derstand that Burk, through the sheriff, can reach out and take what he wants?"

"So that's what happened?"

"I'm not sure," she said in a heavy whisper. "Peters was having lunch with Childress and Murdock as I came over. They know Henderson has you, but Childress wants to stay out of it."

"I figured it would be that way," Reilly said.

"Harry Peters could get you out of here," Tess said, "but he refused to interfere. Reilly, isn't there anything you can do?"

"Not for a while." Reilly folded his hands over hers as they gripped the bars. "Thanks for coming, Tess."

She gave him a brief smile. "Somebody had to, Reilly."

He released her hands. Thrusting his arms through the bars, he took her face gently between his palms. She read his intent and said, "No, Reilly."

But he pulled her face close and kissed her, the cold bars pressed against their cheeks. "Damn you, Reilly," she said, and hurried down the corridor. Henderson let her out and went back to his desk, hidden from Reilly's view by the angle of the wall.

"Wow," Milo said. "For a girl like that I could stand this flea trap for six months." He nudged Reilly. "Here comes the law again."

Pausing at the cell door, Henderson produced a ring of keys and swung the door open. "All right, sonny. Get the hell out of here and next time don't stick your nose in where it don't belong."

Picking up his hat, Milo moved past Reilly. "Luck," he said, and went out.

After Bucks left the building, Henderson said, "Let's go, Reilly." He followed Reilly into the outer office. Waving him into a chair, Henderson took a position behind his desk and waited. A few minutes later, Burk Seever came in. He wore a new suit, a stiffly starched collar, and a flowing ascot tie tucked into a double-breasted vest.

"I see you let that meddling kid out," he said to the sheriff. Then he fixed his attention on Reilly. "I'm willing to be reasonable with you but I want you to get out of the country."

A grin broke across Reilly's face. "Go to hell, Burk. You may run the sheriff's office now but you sure as hell don't run me."

"You're going to make this tough on yourself," Seever began, and then the front door opened. Milo Bucks stepped inside. He closed the door gently behind him and leaned against it, his young face smooth and vaguely interested.

"Am I interrupting something?"

Henderson frowned at Burk Seever, who glared at Milo Bucks. "What the hell do you want?"

"I got a sixshooter in the drawer there," Bucks said. He pointed to Henderson's desk. "The sheriff there forgot to give it back."

"I got no gun that's yours," Henderson said flatly.

Milo Bucks smiled. "I was sure out cold when I got drug in here last night and I been locked up ever since, which is my way of sayin' that I wouldn't know what was in that desk. Howsomever, if you'd run your hand around in there, I guess you'd find my gun."

"Get the hell out of here," Henderson said, half rising from his chair. "What do you think you're pulling?"

"This, I guess," Bucks said and reached into his pocket. In his hand was a small nickel-plated Derringer, the over and under barrels staring at the sheriff. "Keep it in my saddlebag as a little friend," Milo said. "Now, Sheriff, if you'll open that drawer real careful, you'll find a short barreled forty-four Colt there with pretty pearl handles. Just lay it on the floor and slide it to where I'm standin'." He smiled pleasantly and Henderson reached into the drawer.

The gun was there and he slid it toward Milo Bucks. Milo stooped and picked it up. He put the Derringer away and held the forty-four loosely.

"Won this at Klamath Falls last year. Seems like every sheriff who sees it wants it for his own." He nodded to Seever and opened the door. "I'll be thankin' you gentlemen," he added, and closed the door between them.

"That wise sonofabitch," Henderson said.

"Forget about him," Seever snapped, paying all his attention to Reilly Meyers. "Now listen to me, Reilly. I'm not suggesting that you do a damn thing. I'm telling you. I won't fool with you."

"Were you ever fooling, Burk?"

"Get smart with me and I'll smash your face," Seever said. "You don't have any ax handle now." He rolled his heavy shoulders. "Hating you is easy, Reilly. The nice part of it is, you've given me a damn good excuse, one that any man can understand. A woman! Everytime I look at my wife I can think of you and how you used to eat out of the dish I wanted. I can blame all of it on your laughing ways and how a man can sweat his brains out wanting something and you come along and smile and she'd fall into your arms. In your case, I can get the job done and never explain anything because any man can add two and two and get the answer about you and Sally."

"Well," Reilly murmured. "You've turned into a first class sharpie, haven't you, Burk?"

Seever moved with surprising agility for a man his size, knocking Reilly out of the chair and splintering it under him. Reilly struck the floor, rolling, an odd roaring in his ears and a deadness in the left side of his face.

He heard Seever's soft-soled shoes whisper on the floor as the big man closed in.

CHAPTER 5

When Burk Seever knocked Reilly to the floor, Sheriff Henderson half-rose from his chair as though debating whether to interfere or not. Then he relaxed back into the chair.

Rolling to his hands and knees, Reilly settled there for a moment, blood dripping from his nose onto the worn wood floor. "Better lay off him, Burk," Henderson said, but there was no push behind his words, no desire to step in and stop Seever.

"Keep your nose out of it if you're scared," Seever said, and Reilly began to edge away as the big man's shoes shuffled on the floor. Reilly regained his feet in time to be knocked against the wall. A rifle shook loose from the rack and tumbled down with a loud rattle.

Shaking his head, Reilly tried to clear the fog that taxed his strength. He raised a hand to touch his bruised cheek. There was no feeling in his face, just a sickness gripping his stomach and making breathing a chore.

As yet, Seever had not hit him with all his strength, but the power in the man's arms was bone crushing.

Grabbing Reilly by the shirt front, Seever pulled the smaller man forward, but Reilly uncoiled a fist and smashed Burk flush in the mouth. Blood spurted and Seever roared. He was hurt, but not enough to relax his grip. He blocked Reilly's next punch and hit him twice, snapping his head back with each blow.

Kicking out, Reilly's boot connected with the big man's shin and for a relaxed second he had a chance to get free.

He twisted away, spearing Seever again with a knotted fist, at the same time ducking the man's windmilling arms.

With this new confidence, Reilly stepped in close and tried to put the big man down. Seever had a bull strength and absorbed punishment without effect. He drove Reilly backward across the sheriff's desk and onto the floor beyond. Reilly had the will to rise, but his legs refused to obey the mental command. Sickness began to plow through him and he knew that he did not have long before he would lose this fight.

Understanding this, Seever began to move forward and Reilly put out his hand to push himself erect. He felt the barrel and magazine tube of a rifle and folded his fingers around it. The cold feel of the metal gave his flagging strength a boost. He stood up, reversing the rifle until it pointed at Burk Seever.

"You—want one of these in—the gut, Burk?"

Reilly leaned back against the wall and looked at Seever. Henderson remained at his desk, his hands flat on the top. There was no sound in the room except heavy breathing.

Henderson made some vague motion and the rifle shifted to him. Whatever the sheriff had in his mind vanished and he remained perfectly still, his breath whistling through his nose.

Seever said, "You yellow bastard."

Reilly was recovering somewhat from the pounding. He said, "I'll fight you, Burk, but let's get this thing even."

Putting a hand behind him, Reilly fumbled along the wall until he found the rifle rack. He grabbed one of Henderson's guns from the wall and tossed it to Seever, who caught it and held it stupidly before him.

"You'll have to take a chance on it bein' loaded," Reilly said and lowered the muzzle of his rifle to the floor. "Now you do as you damn please, Burk."

"My fists have always been good enough," Seever said. "I don't like a gun."

"Fight or run," Reilly said. "I won't wait long for you to decide."

"Let's fight," Seever said.

He swung the rifle like an ax. The move caught Reilly unprepared and he barely raised the barrel before Seever's gun caught it with enough force to jar his arms.

The thin metal of the magazine tube split open, spewing blunt-nosed cartridges on the floor as the two men came against each other, fighting for an opening. The sound of barrel upon barrel was a loud clashing and then Reilly swung the buttstock in a sideward sweep that caught Burk on the shoulder, knocking him halfway across the room.

Without hesitation, Reilly followed him, the rifle reversed now and gripped by the barrel. Seever tried to get up, raising his own gun to block Reilly's down-sweeping weapon. The stock broke and the piece struck Seever on the head, bringing bright blood.

The big man rolled, striking out at Reilly. The blow was not true, but it did catch Reilly on the hip and spin him half around, giving Seever time to get to his feet. Then they swung together, the barrels meeting with enough force to bend them.

There was a cartridge under the lowered hammer of Burk's rifle and the sudden impact touched it off. The room bloomed with sound. Henderson gave a frightened yelp as a foot-long gouge appeared across his desk top. Glass shattered as the lead escaped through the front window.

The blast stunned Seever. Reilly caught him in the stomach with a backhanded swing, bringing the man double. He raised the battered gun to hit Seever across the head, but the big man dropped his weapon and locked his arms around Reilly's middle, lifting him completely clear of the floor.

Seever carried him like a belly-hugged sack of meal and slammed Reilly into the wall with enough force to rattle the door. Pawing for Seever's face, Reilly tried to break free. His breathing was all but cut off and hot flashes charged back and forth in his head.

Backing up, Seever pounded him into the wall again, this time lowering his head and ramming Reilly in the mouth. For a moment, Reilly relaxed completely, drained of strength. Then Seever dropped him and brought up his knee, catching him flush in the chest.

Seever's knee lifted Reilly clear of the floor and flung him backward. He struck heavily and when he tried to work his elbow under him to rise, he found that he could not move. Seever swayed before him, then began a slow advance while Reilly tried to rally muscles that were too tired to obey.

A wide grin started on Seever's face. He said, "I've always wanted to stomp your guts out, Reilly."

He moved another step forward then stopped dead still.

On the floor, Reilly heard the faint squeak as the door opened. He felt the draft. He turned his head slowly and saw Al Murdock standing there, a long barreled Rogers and Spencer in his hand.

Seever said, "What the hell is this, Al? You owe him something?"

"Some," Murdock said. "I'm marryin' into the family." To Reilly he said, "Pick up your gun and get. This is the last favor."

Reilly pulled himself erect slowly. He stood there swaying. He went to Henderson's desk and pushed the sheriff aside. He took his Remington and looked for his rifle, then realized that he had just battered it to pieces. For a moment he considered taking one of Henderson's, but put the thought aside and shuffled toward the door.

"You can get your butt in the fire for this, Al," Henderson said. "This is jailbreak."

A smile creased Murdock's lips. "I doubt it, Jack." He cast a quick glance at Reilly who stood by the door, weaving. "Can you make it? I brought your horse around front."

"I'll make it," Reilly said in a loose mumble, and went outside. Seever and the sheriff remained rooted under Al Murdock's .44.

Reilly's horse was tied to the hitchrack and Harry Peters stood nearby, smoking one of his cigars. He looked at Reilly's face and said, "Better get out of town, Reilly. I'll see that you don't have to go through this again."

"Why didn't you come in and stop it then?" Reilly asked, and untied the reins.

"Politics," Peters said. He shifted the cigar. He had a habit of rolling it from one corner of his mouth to the other. "Sometimes a citizen like Al can do more than a lawman." He nodded to the horse. "Can you get on him?"

"I'll get on him," Reilly said, but when he tried to mount he found that there was no strength in his arms.

"Lean against the hitchrail," Peters said. He walked to

the watering trough in front of the next building, soaked a handkerchief and handed it to Reilly. Reilly washed his face and laid the wet cloth against the back of his neck.

Murdock called through the open door, "Still there, Reilly?"

"Give him time," Peters said, and Reilly swung up after the second try. Reining away from the hitchrail, he moved slowly down the side street and then cut over to take the main road to his own place.

The afternoon sun was hot on his back as he followed the creek for three miles. He dismounted to sit in the cold water. After some of the aches diminished, he climbed out, dripping. Picking up his revolver, he mounted again and cut across the flats toward the rougher land on whose fringe his ranch lay.

Sheriff Henderson and Burk Seever stayed against the wall, both eyeing the revolver in Al Murdock's hand. After hearing Reilly's horse leave, Harry Peters stepped to the open doorway and stood there, a slight smile on his face.

"I'd say it was all right now, Al." Peter's voice was bland.

"Just how long do you think we'll stand like this?" Henderson asked.

"Until I say, 'scat,' " Murdock said.

"I'll have your butt for this, Al," Seever threatened.

"Come and get it," Murdock invited.

Using a different approach, Henderson said, "Damn it all, Al, I can't figure what got into you—pullin' a stunt like this. What the hell's marryin' his sister got to do with it?"

"A man owes something, he pays it," Murdock said. "Now I'm paid up." He stepped backward into the doorway.

Seever said, "I'll remember you for this, Al."

"Who gives a damn?" Murdock said. He backed to the boardwalk. He reached in and slammed the door, then walked rapidly down the street with Harry Peters.

"I hope you don't have the idea that Henderson or Seever will let this go," Peters said, kindling a fresh fire to his cigar.

"He might get hurt monkeyin' around," Al said quietly. "Seever engineered that, Harry."

"Of course he did," Peters said as they turned the corner. "Now we know who's the law around here. It makes a man pause and think."

Pausing before the hotel porch, Murdock went to his horse and put the Rogers and Spencer in the saddlebag. On the porch, Tess Isham and Emily Meyers waited, grave and worried. Murdock took Emily's arm. Drawing her aside, he spoke a few soft words, erasing the strain around her lips.

Harry Peters sat on the railing of the porch by Childress' chair. No one said anything until Tess Isham murmured, "Burk got to him, didn't he?"

"Yes," Murdock said. He paused. "One of these days Reilly is going to even that up. I'd like to see it and at the same time I'm sorry. That man can cut some mighty big chores out for himself."

"It was bound to come one way or another," Childress said, refilling his pipe. "Reilly's different. There's somethin' in him that won't let go when he gets his jaws locked. I'm thinkin' he still figures Winehaven owes him for a herd of cattle, and if that's so, he'll get 'em back or cut the price out of someone's hide."

"I believe it," Harry Peters said. He rotated the cigar between his lips. He seemed pleased.

At the next corner, Seever paused to say a few final words to Sheriff Henderson, then went across while Henderson came toward the hotel. Childress slapped his thighs and stood up. "Time to be gettin' home," he said, and stepped down to the buggy tied by the hitchrail. Emily and Tess Isham promised to see each other and then Murdock handed Emily into the rig.

He turned as Henderson clumped up, his boots rattling the boardwalk. "By rights," he said, "I could lock you up for interferin', but I'm goin' to forget it, see. If Reilly wasn't so damned smart, he wouldn't be in trouble all the time."

Childress said, "Let's go, Al."

Murdock walked around Henderson and untied his horse. The sheriff followed him and when Al tried to mount, Henderson took him by the coat sleeve. Murdock looked at the hand and the sheriff let go.

"I'm entitled to a little respect around here," Henderson said.

"Better start earnin' it," Al said, and mounted.

"Now just a minute—"

"Jack, you've been coastin' along free and easy for a long time," Murdock said, "but the free part is over. I think you started somethin' with Reilly that you might wish you hadn't. At Winehaven's that time—you'd have been money ahead by just givin' him back his cattle."

"Are you accusin' me—"

"Take it any way you like," Murdock said. He swung the horse, almost knocking Henderson over. Childress pulled out in the buggy and Murdock brought up the rear, not looking back.

Reilly found that riding bent over in the saddle eased the pounding at the base of his skull, but his face still remained stiff from the drum of Burk Seever's fists. In the lonely distance his own ranch loomed on the flatlands bordering country that rose high and rough half a mile behind the house.

Ten minutes later he paused to study the sluggish spiral of smoke easing from the kitchen chimney. The sun was dropping now. It cast long shadows on the ground as he dismounted by the watering trough.

Easing onto the porch, Reilly opened the front door and tip-toed through the dim hall. The kitchen door was open and he saw the man at the table, his shoulders hunched, both hands wrapped lovingly around a coffee cup. The lamp hadn't been lighted and darkness increased in the room. A holstered revolver sat on the back of the man's hip, the pearl handle shiny in the last remaining daylight coming through the window.

Drawing his short-barreled Remington, Reilly said, "Sit still if you want to keep livin'."

The man's shoulders stiffened and his ears moved slightly as his scalp tightened, but that was all. Reilly stepped into the room and moved around the table. He put his gun back into his belt and said, "What are you doing here?"

"Hungry," Milo Bucks said. "I thought the place was deserted."

"You thought wrong," Reilly said. "I'll see what we

can find to eat." In the cupboard he rummaged around until he found a can of beans. Kicking open the door of the stove, he fed wood to the blaze until it roared, then placed a frying pan on the top.

"How long you been here?" he asked. He dumped in the can of beans and stirred them with an old spoon.

"About an hour," Bucks said. He squinted at Reilly's puffed face. "The big fella get to you?" Bucks moved his shoulders restlessly. "No man would do that to me."

Reilly's head came around quickly. He studied the young man for a moment. "I used to talk like that. Hit first and think afterward. That's no good, Milo."

"Good for me," Bucks said. "The big man's got it in for you, hasn't he?"

"Everybody's got it in for somebody," Reilly murmured. He could only find one tin plate so he dished half the beans onto it. He sat down across from Milo Bucks and ate from the skillet. "Where are you headin'?"

Bucks' shoulders rose and fell. He had a round face, without guile, and eyes that were a deep brown, almost black now that night had invaded the room. Reilly touched a match to the lamp and settled back in his chair again.

"I'm just ridin'," Bucks said. "Seems like a waste, don't it?"

"Depends on who's doin' the wastin'," Reilly said. "You lookin' for a winter roost? Not much pay, but three meals a day and a wall to break the wind."

"I could use that," Bucks said, and as he smiled his face changed, revealing a certain gaiety that time and trouble couldn't hide completely.

Downing the last beans, Reilly shook out his tobacco sack and rolled a smoke, afterward offering the makings to Milo Bucks. The young man fashioned a stubby cigarette, raced a match and drew deeply. "The weed's a comfort sometimes," he said. "Like a cool drink of water or a fire on a chilly night." He raised his eyes and looked at Reilly. "That was a hell of a jail, wasn't it?"

"The sheriff makes it that way," Reilly opined. He flicked ashes onto the floor and added, "You could have got your tail in a crack, buttin' in on Burk like you did."

"A man's a damn fool in lots of ways," Bucks admitted. "He'll get boozed up, shoot off his mouth and get in a fight, or hunt himself some woman for a gallop on the two-headed beast, but he don't mean none of it."

"I used to think like that," Reilly said. "But there's more to life than that."

"Sure, sure, but who the devil thinks about it when they're twenty?" Bucks rose and shied his smoke into the fire. "A man's got so much runnin' in him, like a colt. Bayin' at the moon ain't confined to dogs, you know."

"I guess not," Reilly said. He checked the coffee can, found a cup left and dumped it in the pot. The well was on the back porch and he went out, banging around in the darkness. The windlass squeaked and he came back in, setting the pot on the stove to boil.

While the coffee cooked, Reilly went to the barn and put up his horse. In the tack shed he found a piece of leather and took it to the kitchen, along with a head knife, an awl and ten feet of rawhide lacing. His head pounded fiercely but working took his mind off it so he laid his gun on the table and cut a pattern around it. He buck-laced the holster together, then spent an hour making a cartridge belt.

Milo Bucks sat across from him, watching and smoking. He picked up Reilly's gun and examined it. "I've seen guns like this," he said. "Short barrel, lightened main spring for fanning." He put the gun back on the table. "Not a bad job."

"You know about those things?" Reilly asked. He completed the bullet loops and filled them from the two boxes of shells he had bought in the hardware store. His rifle was broken and these black powder loads might rear back a little in a short-barreled pistol, but such technicalities did not concern him much.

He threaded the belt through the holster, buckled the rig on and felt pleased with the mild sag. He whipped the gun out of the leather, cocking it on the upswing in one smooth motion. This test satisfied him so he replaced the gun in the scabbard and ignored it thereafter.

The coffee had boiled over and was now cool enough to drink. They filled their cups and took them to the front porch, squatting on the steps to listen to the night sounds and study the enveloping blackness.

In the yard a broken bottle lay, catching the faint rays

of the moon and flinging them away like a distant star. Across the outline of the land, a coyote paused to cry out, then moved on, a shifting shape.

Far out on the road a party of horsemen made a steady drumming. When they drew nearer, Milo Bucks drew his pearl handled .44, half-cocked it and spun the cylinder. He sat holding it in his lap while the riders approached.

They slowed before coming into the yard and one man said, "He's here. I see a light." They stopped by the watering trough and Reilly stood up, taking care to keep away from the light streaming through the open door.

Ten feet from them he recognized Max Horgan, Indian Jim and Herb Winehaven. Reilly gave Milo Bucks a short nod and Milo said to no one in particular, "I think I hear the horses gettin' restless."

He walked rapidly toward the barn.

Reilly said, "What do you want, Max?"

"Talk," Horgan said. "Can we get down?"

"Come in if you want," Reilly said.

"We'll just get down," Horgan said, and saddle leather protested as they dismounted. Indian Jim held the horses. He was a big man with a face the color of old leather and a pair of shoe button eyes.

"What's on your minds?" Reilly asked.

"I don't see why we should be on the peck at each other," Herb Winehaven said. He was a runt and he wore an old suit of clothes with gaping holes at the elbows. His face was pointed at the chin and his mustache dropped past the ends of his lips.

"You've got guts, Herb," Reilly said. "I've always said that."

"Now don't go gettin' hot under the collar," Horgan said. "We want you in with us, Reilly."

"What are you into?"

Horgan laughed at this, but Winehaven didn't smile. The horses shifted and Indian Jim grunted to quiet them.

"That reminds me," Reilly said, and moved Horgan and Winehaven aside to walk up to Indian Jim. The big man shifted nervously and Reilly said, "You remember what you said to me the last time we met?"

"Been long time," Jim said. "Forget easy."

"I haven't," Reilly said, and knocked the man beneath the horses. One snorted in surprise and they began to

70

mill, but Indian Jim had rolled out of the way and came to his feet again.

"You want to take it up from there?" Reilly asked.

"No," Indian Jim said.

Horgan moved his feet and said, "Now that you got it off your chest can we talk a little sense?"

"You talk," Reilly said. "I'll listen."

After a glance at Winehaven, Horgan said, "You got Burk mad as hell at you, Reilly, but that can be patched up. Get wise to yourself. You're on the outside looking in around here. We can use you."

"How?"

"This place you got here. It's got some pockets back in the rocks. A little water and enough grass, I'd say." Horgan shoved his hands deep in his coat pockets. "Make you a good proposition, Reilly. It would be hard to turn down."

"Make it then," Reilly said.

"I buy a lot of stock now and then—"

"Buy it or steal it?"

"Here, here," Horgan said gently. "We came friendly like, Reilly. You tryin' to make me mad or somethin'?"

"I don't give a damn." He turned to Herb Winehaven. "You get a good price for my cattle?"

There was an ugliness in Winehaven which he couldn't control. His unruly disposition made him say, "Maybe I did. What's it to you?"

"Not much to me," Reilly said. "Except that I'm going to cut the price of that beef off of your butt before I'm through."

"Pretty big talk," Winehaven said.

"Let's not get in a ruckus," Horgan said, pushing himself into the argument. "Who's that kid you got with you? Never mind. Get rid of him."

"I like him," Reilly said. "Don't ever tell me what to do, Max. I don't like it at all."

"All right, all right," Horgan said in a running voice. "About a deal now—a cut of everything that we hold here."

"How big a cut?"

Horgan hesitated. "What do you say to a tenth?"

"Go to hell," Reilly said.

Some of the softness went out of Horgan's voice. "Seems

71

to me you're gettin' damn proud, Reilly. Remember who you are. Burk's mad at you. You just upset Henderson. Maybe you better think it over a little while and we can come back in a day or two."

"Save yourself the trip," Reilly told him. "Your horses are gettin' spooky. They'll feel better with weight in the saddles."

"All right," Horgan said. He turned to his mount. Winehaven and Indian Jim swung up and waited.

"I meant what I said, Herb," Reilly murmured.

"I heard you," Winehaven said. "I'll be expecting you and it'll be different than the last time."

"We'll see," Reilly said, then looked sharply at Horgan's mare. He stepped close, took the bridle and swung the mare so that some lamplight fell on her face.

"Get the hell away from there!" Horgan said. "What do you think you're doing there?"

Reilly released the bridle and stepped back. "That's a dandy sorrel you got there, Max. Seems that I remember seein' that blaze face some place before."

"If you did, I was on him," Horgan said. "I raised this mare from a foal." He glanced at Winehaven and then back to Reilly. "You don't believe me? I can prove it."

"Nobody's arguing with you, Max. I just said that I saw this sorrel some place before, but I sure to hell can't recollect where."

"I wouldn't worry about it if I was you," Horgan advised. "We'll be back, Reilly."

"That wouldn't be smart, Max," Reilly said, and watched them carefully. Horgan seemed debating something in his mind, and then put it off. He rapped the sorrel with his heels and led the way out of the yard.

Reilly stood there, his legs spread, watching and listening until the night swallowed them and there was no sound at all coming back on the gentle breeze.

Milo Bucks' boots popped in the loose dust as he came across the yard. He rolled a smoke and a match flared, but Reilly saw nothing in his eyes except a strict neutrality.

"Nice people," Milo said. "That Indian didn't like to take that poke in the jaw."

"You're smart," Reilly said. "Be smarter and saddle

that horse of yours and ride over into Utah and join the church. It'll be safe there."

"Do I want to go where it's safe?" Bucks laughed and flipped his cigarette away, watching it hit in a shower of sparks. "This is the kind of hand I like—fast and with high stakes. A man makes it or breaks it in a hurry that way."

"That what you want to do?"

"It's less agony than losing it slow," Bucks opined.

Reilly nodded, for in spite of himself, that was his way, to stake it all on one card, win or lose. A part of him reached out to Milo Bucks, for in the young man he saw many failings, most of them he had had himself at that age.

"Let's get some sleep," Reilly said and went toward the house.

CHAPTER 6

As soon as the sky lightened next morning, Reilly Meyers gave Milo Bucks fifty dollars and sent him to Buckeye for supplies and a wagon. After Bucks rode out, Reilly saddled his horse and cut into the hills back of his place.

Through the morning he rode, finally breaking out on the flats that led to Paul Childress' place. Lifting the stud into a lope, he covered the remaining miles and tied up in front of Childress' porch.

Al Murdock had been working near the barn. He came across the yard when he saw Reilly. Reilly waited by the steps and Murdock said, "Your face don't look too bad. A little lopsided maybe."

Reilly waved it aside. "Paul at home?"

"Inside," Murdock said. He went up the steps, held the door open and motioned Reilly into the house. Childress came to the door of his study, his gold rimmed glasses perched halfway down his nose.

"Come in," he said, and turned away. Reilly and Murdock took chairs and Childress shoved his tally book in a cubbyhole. He took off his glasses, tossing them on the paper littered desk and rested his forearms flat. "Something on your mind, Reilly?"

"Cattle," Reilly said. He rolled a cigarette and blew a cloud of smoke to the ceiling. "You're overstocked, Paul. I'm understocked. Let's make a deal."

"Make it," Childress said.

Reilly cuffed his hat to the back of his head. "I'll go broke quick without a herd. I've got graze and a water-

74

shed. Suppose I was to bed down three hundred and fifty head for you. There's still time to drive them over and let them find a winter hole. I don't get the snow that you do. The hills break most of it. They'll get fat, Paul."

"What will it cost me?" Childress asked.

"One out of ten," Reilly said, "and I'll take it in calves."

Childress drummed his fingers on the desk, then shot Murdock a glance. "Al?"

The foreman's shoulders rose and fell. "Sounds about right. Figurin' the wages of a man up in the hills all winter—I'd say, do it."

"When do you want 'em?" Childress asked.

"Give me thirty days," Reilly said, and stood up. He stepped to the hall door and paused. "Emily and Ma in the kitchen?" Childress nodded and Reilly went to the rear of the house, pushing open the swinging door.

The thick odor of apple pie filled the room and the stove laid an oven heat in the kitchen. Mrs. Childress smiled at Reilly, and when she noticed his bruised face she scolded him with her eyes. Emily stood on her toes to kiss him in passing, then pulled a chair out for him to sit at the table.

She took a pie from the window sill and cut a wide wedge. Reilly said, "Hate to strain Paul's hospitality."

"He's a fool sometimes," Mrs. Childress said. She touched Reilly on the shoulder. "You'd make me happy if you and him would make up." She dropped her hand and went back to the stove. "He hates to be stood off, Reilly. He's a givin' man. That's his nature."

"And I never needed his help—is that it?" He waited but she didn't answer him. "I'm sorry, Ma."

Emily said. "Eat your pie, Reilly."

Reilly ate his pie and put on his hat. He crossed to the stove and gave Mrs. Childress a quick hug, slapped Emily as she bent over the table rolling dough and went to his horse.

Murdock was at the corrals with two men breaking horses, but he did not look at Reilly when he rode out. With the afternoon sun on his back, Reilly made for the end of a low range, passing Buckeye near sundown.

Darkness found him mounting a series of low hills where Jim Buttelow's horse ranch lay in a short valley rimmed by sage-stubbled rises. Away from the ranch house, breaking and holding corrals fanned out like spokes in a wheel.

Reilly rode into the darkened yard and dismounted. Lamplight made bright patches on the porch as Jim Buttelow came to the door, peering out into the night. He grunted when he recognized Reilly and held the door open.

Buttelow was a friendly man with big bones and a rough manner, a hard man in a hard land, tough when forced to be, but by nature, easygoing and soft spoken. He took Reilly into the parlor and waved him into a chair.

"Got a proposition for you," Reilly said.

"If it makes me some money, then I'm interested."

"I'm after a small remuda," Reilly said. "I made a deal with Paul to winter a herd, but I've got to have horses."

Buttelow paused to pack and light his pipe. "Maybe we can make a deal. I got myself into a little jackpot on an army contract and you might just be able to get me out of it." He puffed for a moment, then went on. "Got a telegram yesterday sayin' that Otis Fielding and his bunch over in Utah have a herd of three hundred that they're going to have to move out before winter comes. I *had* room for 'em, but the contract officer at Fort Bliss wired me that they were building a new stable and put a hold on the herd I was ready to ship. When Fielding gets here I'm goin' to be pinched for room."

"I don't know," Reilly said. "Holdin' a herd is somethin' I hadn't thought about."

"Build a corral," Buttelow said.

"No time," Reilly said. "Sounds good, but I don't have the time or men. I'd like to buy a few head from you though."

"You want Ernie and Walt Slaughter?"

Reilly looked at Buttelow. "You gettin' tired of 'em? I couldn't pay much, Jim."

"I just want 'em off the place," Buttelow said, and smiled at Reilly's expression. "They're good men, Reilly —too good. A man's a fool to stick with stompin' horses. That may sound strange comin' from a man who hires nothin' but bronc riders, but it's a fact. Walt and Ernie ought to get off by themselves. They'd be better off eatin' backfat and greens on a quarter section than they are here. Look in the saloons and see the cripples cadgin' drinks. Usually they're old stompers. It rips a man here, Reilly," He hit himself in the stomach. "Pretty soon you get a little crazy in the head, and then it's too late."

"Walt and Ernie know this."

"Sure," Buttelow said, "they know it. And like most men they figure it won't get them that way. I'm an old man, Reilly, and like all old men, I've begun to dream. One of these days you'll find me in front of some store, passin' out advice to people if they'd only stop and listen to it. That's sort of sad in a way, because most of that advice would be good. Take Ernie and Walt with you, Reilly. They'll work for you."

"I can't carry a payroll, Jim. I just can't do it."

"They won't worry about money," Buttelow said. "A man never does when he's young. Only old men want money, after all the other good things are gone." He stood up and offered his hand. "A deal?"

"A deal," Reilly said. "I'll build a stout holding corral."

Buttelow walked with him to his horse. "I'll send Walt and Ernie over in the morning."

"All right," Reilly said, and swung up.

"You comin' in with us against the rustlin'?" Buttelow asked.

"You think I ought to?"

"Keepin' the law's every man's job," Buttelow said. "We got to help one another to get along."

"No one broke their neck four years ago to help me," Reilly said. "You can tell Harry Peters that the next time he asks why I didn't come in this thing."

"I will," Buttelow said as Reilly turned the stud away. "But remember, boy—no man can mind his own business all the time, unless he lives completely alone."

"I'll get along," Reilly said, and rode out of Buttelow's yard.

It was after nine when he saw the lights of his own place and dismounted by the barn, off-saddled and walked to the house. He felt stiff and tired and he had eaten nothing since that piece of pie. Hunger gnawed an aching hole in his stomach.

He paused by the porch, peering around the side of the house at a heavy shape parked in the deep shadows. He took three steps toward it, then realized it was a buggy.

He whirled toward the porch when Sally said, "I was getting tired of waiting, Reilly."

From the kitchen came muffled noises made by Milo Bucks. A heavy wagon had been drawn up to the back porch and the back door opened and slammed as Milo carried provisions into the house and stored them.

"What are you doing here?" Reilly asked, and came onto the porch. He sat on the railing, his feet braced wide on the floor. The light streaming from the door touched him, but Sally sat partially concealed in the shadows against the house wall.

She laughed softly. "Don't you know, Reilly? Or is it that you like to have me keep telling you that I just can't stay away from you?"

"Cut it out," he said, and rolled a cigarette. "Was Burk to find out you're here, he'd shoot me."

"Or you'd shoot him," Sally said. "Would you do that for me, Reilly?"

"No," he said flatly. He scratched a match against the upright. Firelight made a halo of his face for an instant and then he whipped it out. The end of his cigarette glowed and died.

"You're a restrained man, Reilly. Somehow I always liked that. You never panted and I didn't have to fight off your hot, sticky hands." Cloth rustled as she stood up and came close to him. She leaned slightly until her thighs touched his and stood that way, daring him, trying to draw him out of his shell.

"If I hadn't married Burk, you'd be in my parlor now."

"That's *if*," Reilly said. "You did marry Burk and I'm not in your parlor."

She raised a hand and laid it against his chest. "But I'm here, Reilly. Why do you think I've come?"

"I know why you've come," he said, "and I told you before that I want no part of it." Her hand moved up his shirt front and caressed his cheek. He stood immobile for a moment, only a muscle in his jaw moving, and then his restraint gave way and he pulled her to him savagely. "Damn you," he said, and kissed her, his tight arms shutting off her breath.

It was a long kiss, the kind he remembered, and afterward she clung to him. "You're fire," he said. "You think I've ever got over it?"

"Neither of us has," Sally said in a fierce whisper. "Reilly, it need never end for us, you know that."

Her words were like a dash of water. Dropping his arms, he moved slightly away from her, once more composed and on guard. "It's ended," he said. "It ended when you married Burk. Neither of us can change that now."

"There's a way, Reilly. You know there's a way."

"Shut up about it!" He gave her a little push. "You better get back to town. He'll find out. Someone will tell him."

"I don't care."

"*I* care," Reilly said, and raised his voice. "Bucks!" He heard the movement in the kitchen stop, and then Milo Bucks came out and stood in the doorway. "Get Mrs. Seever's buggy around here."

Milo stepped off the porch, started to walk around the house, and halted, his head cocked to one side like a dog. From out on the flats, a horse beat a steady tattoo. "Someone comin', Reilly."

"I got ears," Reilly snapped. "Get that buggy put away in the barn."

He tried to steer Sally into the house but she shook free of his grip and stood in the deep shadows. "I like it here. If it's Burk, I want to see it."

Bucks led the team across the yard at a run. He had just closed the barn door when a horse entered the yard. Passing through the light, the rider showed himself for an instant. Reilly let out a relieved breath and stepped down from the porch.

He raised his arms and lifted Tess Isham from her side-saddle. She paused with her hands on his shoulders for a moment, then said, "I came as fast as I could, Reilly. I think Burk's on his way here and he's hopping mad." She peered past him, trying to cut the darkness along the wall. "Sally's here, isn't she?"

"Yes," Reilly said. "She was just leaving when we heard your horse."

"It's too late. I can't be more than ten minutes ahead of him." She slid past Reilly and stepped to the porch. Without ceremony she grabbed Sally's arm and hustled her into Reilly's house.

Once inside, she said, "You damn fool, Sally. Haven't you any better sense?"

79

"Don't preach to me," Sally snapped.

"Oh!" Tess said and bit her lip. Tears of rage filled her eyes but she shook her head stubbornly. "Have you a place we can hide, Reilly?"

"I don't like hiding," Reilly said. "Better to face a thing out."

"You're a damn fool too," she said, and started down the hall. Over her shoulder, she asked, "Which is your room?"

"The one on the end," Reilly said. He watched until the door closed. Milo came across the porch and paused in the doorway, his face grave and faintly worried.

"I put the other horse away too," he said, leaning against the frame. "Looks like a big night ahead, don't it?"

"Quit bein' funny," Reilly said. He stepped past Milo. Another rider had left the road and was coming across the flats.

"You want me to stick around?" Bucks asked.

"If you want," Reilly said. "No trouble now, regardless of how this turns out."

"All right," Bucks said, and went into the parlor, sweeping some discarded junk off a chair so he could sit down.

Reilly walked back to his porch and waited. Burk Seever pulled up a few minutes later. He dismounted, coming to the foot of the stairs.

"Reilly," he said, "I've come for my wife."

"She's not here, Burk."

"She's here," Burk said. "After I get her, I'm going to kill you."

"I said she wasn't here!"

"You're a liar, Reilly. She was seen leaving the house all rigged for a night ride." He stepped up one step. "I'm going to have a look around. Don't try to stop me."

"I'm not going to stop you," Reilly said. "Make a fool out of yourself if you want to."

He moved aside and Seever came across the porch. Reilly followed him inside. The big man glanced into the parlor and saw Milo Bucks sitting in a chair.

"Well," Seever said, his face wrinkling into a grin. "If it isn't the rooster. I've still got to pull some of your tail feathers, don't I?"

"Not tonight," Bucks said, and he stared at Seever.

The big man stood there for a while. Then he laughed

and turned to the kitchen. He gave it a thorough going over and came back to Reilly. "Where's the bedroom, lover?"

"You low minded bastard," Reilly said.

"Where is it, Reilly?"

"At the end of the hall," Reilly said.

Seever took three steps toward the door and stopped. The bedroom door came open. Tess Isham stepped out, said, "Oh!" in a startled voice and ducked part way behind the door. She had removed her heavy riding dress and wore only a thin shift that revealed her bare shoulders and most of her legs.

Seever stood there perfectly motionless, then wheeled and stomped out of the house. His boots rattled off the porch and saddle leather protested as he swung up. Reilly listened to the receding drum of hoofbeats.

There was no sound at all in the house for a moment. Then Reilly went outside, shaking, with a film of sweat on his face. In his mind he knew that he would always remember her as she had appeared for that brief time. When his thoughts became unbearable he wheeled and walked rapidly to his room, flinging the door open without bothering to knock.

Sally stood by the end of the four-poster bed, her face composed. Tess sat on his bed, her slim legs crossed and her hands folded placidly in her lap. She stared at some invisible spot on the floor and did not seem aware that Reilly was there.

Reilly said, "Wait for me outside, Sally."

"But—"

"Do as I tell you!"

"All right, Reilly." She moved past him with a rustle of skirts and smiled faintly at Tess as she closed the door. Reilly waited until her footsteps died out, then dropped to one knee and took Tess Isham's hands in his.

"Tess." She raised her head and her eyes brimmed with unshed tears. "You fool, Tess."

He folded her against him and she cried in earnest. For several minutes he comforted her, and then she pushed herself away from him and rose to slip into her dress. He watched her hook the buttons and said, "She wasn't worth that, Tess. Why didn't you let him look? He came here after a fight."

81

"I wasn't thinking of her," Tess said softly. She moved to the door and opened it, pausing in the aperture without turning around. "You would have shot him, wouldn't you?"

"Yes," he said. "I would have."

He stood dumbly as the full implication of her act registered on him. She had not ruined her reputation for her sister. She had done it for him. Nothing would ever be the same for her now. The talk would get around and men would come to the bakery who wouldn't be thinking of bread when they called.

Tess said, "You would have never found happiness with her if you had killed him, Reilly."

"Tess, wait." He moved toward her, but she stiffened.

"Don't touch me, Reilly! I have to go now."

She went down the hall. He followed her. Sally was waiting in the yard. Milo Bucks came from the barn leading the team and buggy, with Tess' horse tied to the baggage rack. Tess walked to her horse, accepted a hand-up from Milo Bucks and waited for her sister to settle herself in the rig.

Reilly took Sally's elbow to help her, but she turned and put her arms around his neck, holding him even as he pushed against her. Her lips came up to his, demanding and bold, and then she released him with a small laugh.

As she climbed in the buggy, she gave Tess a superior smile that spoke of more triumph than one. "I'll see you again, Reilly," she said, and whipped the team with the reins.

Reilly stood still until they left the yard and then he went back to the house, dimly aware that Milo Bucks was following him.

The next morning Walt and Ernie Slaughter came over. They showed a marked inclination to sit around and talk after breakfast, but Reilly put them to work digging post holes for the new corral.

The house was so littered that Reilly didn't have to ask himself where to start: one part was as filthy as another. Building a large fire in the kitchen range, he and Milo filled four fire buckets and placed them on the stove to heat.

Emptying the cupboards, they sorted the dishes, throwing away the cracked ones. By the time they finished this

82

job and cleared the sink, the water had come to a boil and they began on the floor. By noon the stove was clean and a large pile of rubbish by the back porch grew hourly.

The living room came next. They worked for an hour moving everything out to the porch, then beat the frayed rug until their arms ached. Reilly did not mention last night's affair and Milo was too discreet to bring it up. Reilly knew, though, that he hid nothing from Milo and the fact that he took his temper out in hard work caused the young man to smile now and then.

At four in the afternoon they paused to cook a hasty meal and then tackled the bedrooms. When darkness came the house smelled strongly of laundry soap but the walls and floors were clean and the place had begun to look like a home.

Reilly got up at four the next morning and started work before the others ate breakfast. Walt and Ernie went back to digging post holes while Reilly and Milo took lumber from the barn loft and began repairing ripped siding. The windows from the tack shed replaced the broken panes in the house and the sills from the tack shed repaired the rotting well curbing. After supper that night, Reilly hung a lantern by the door, carried paint from the toolshed, and painted the front porch.

It took Reilly and Milo a day and a half to remove the accumulated manure from the barn and an hour to scrub themselves so they could stand each other. Ernie and Walt continued to dig holes and complained about it over the supper table, but Reilly showed no sign of letting up.

By the week's end, Ernie and Walt had finished the post holes, while Reilly and Milo Bucks had completely painted the house. Reilly started to red-lead the barn. When he finished the job three days later, he took a team into the hills, and with Milo driving, began to fall pines for his corral.

Ernie and Walt set poles and within a week they erected the cross members. Now Reilly was ready to forge the hardware for the loading gate.

Reilly found an old forge buried under cast-off harness, repaired it, erected it and built a fire. Using scrap iron collected from a burned out buggy, he fashioned three heavy hinges and a clasp. With a heated running iron, one of the wild bunch's few useful remains, he burned the

83

holes for the lag screws. Finished at last, he tried the gate a few times, then casually suggested that they all go to town.

Ernie Slaughter seemed stunned. He spread his calloused and bleeding palms and said, "Damned if I think I can hold a whiskey glass now. My hands just naturally fit a post hole digger."

"I'll saddle up," Walt said, and walked to the barn with rapid strides.

Washing at the pump, Milo said to Reilly, "Feel that chill in the air? Snow's comin'. A man can smell it. It'll be a long hard winter and a man sort of looks forward to the last whoop-up before he tucks his head in."

"Still bayin' at the moon?" Reilly asked.

"Man has th' voice for it," Bucks said, and dried his dripping face on a flour sack towel.

Walt came from the barn leading four horses. Reilly went into the house. He came out a moment later buckling on his gun. "That reminds me," Milo said, and went in after his.

They mounted and rode from the yard, and before they were off the flats around the hills, Reilly paused to look back. His corral sat like a spindly legged animal in back of the barn. A large corral, he told himself, and was proud of the job.

In the perverse nature of Westerners, they took their time because they were in a hurry to get there and the sky had darkened when they came to the end of the main street and stopped. Milo leaned forward in the saddle and crossed his arms over the horn. "Now that sure is a pretty thing, ain't it? Does it come apart easy?"

"Let's leave it together," Reilly said, and moved out. He dismounted at the restaurant and they filed in, taking a table in the far corner. The waitress set four cups of coffee on the table. After three minutes of fooling around, she managed to extract their order from them. She went into the kitchen muttering about 'cowboys.'

Reilly sat hunched over in the chair, the lines of hard work not yet eased around his eyes and mouth. He toyed with the coffee cup, then took a sip from it.

Ernie said, "What the hell we want to eat now for. Burkhauser's got a bottle over there waitin' for me."

"Later," Reilly said. "I'm sick of my own cookin'."

84

Four steaks arrived. They ate in silence, for they had learned early that a meal is not a social function. Reilly paid the girl and they filed out onto the boardwalk, teetering with indecision on the street edge.

Milo said, "You goin' to see her?"

"Think I'm that crazy?" Reilly said. A part of his mind told him he should resent the question and put Milo in his place, but the young man's face was guileless.

"I didn't mean her," Milo said. "I meant the younger one."

"I've caused her enough trouble," Reilly said, and swung his head to look up and down the street. The traffic was growing heavier as more families came into town for the weekend shopping. He recognized Paul Childress' buggy tied up before the hotel.

Down the street, Burkhauser's saloon doors winnowed as men came and went and the throbbing strains of a small band issued forth. Walt Slaughter nudged Reilly.

"What do you say? Now?"

Reilly looked at him and smiled. "You thirsty?"

"Damned right I'm thirsty," Walt said, and they crossed the street. They mounted Burkhauser's porch, went inside and headed immediately for the bar.

Reilly bought a bottle and four glasses from Elmer Loving, who still eyed him nervously, and then they took a table on the floor. Walt poured, drank and sat back, a sudden ease running through him.

"There's nothin' like good whiskey," he said. He poured another. He cuffed his hat to the back of his head and said, "You know, I swore off once, but it was no good. I told myself I was a fool over women and whiskey, but then I found out that a fool was all I'd ever be."

"Sure," Reilly said, and nursed his drink. "There was a fella in the pen with me, from Kalispell. We got to talkin' about the back street ladies one time and he said that when you had cowboys, you'd always have them around. For a while I didn't understand him, but I guess I do now. Workin' cows is about the loneliest job a man can have. He don't get to town often and a good woman don't want to live in a soddy on thirty and found. So he gets roarin' drunk, lays up with some back street gal, and then goes back in the hills like a hermit for a couple more months."

"What the hell wound you up?" Ernie asked.

"Nothin'," Reilly said. "I just want you to know that we're in a hell of a business."

"Name me a better one," Walt challenged.

"I'm not tryin' to," Reilly said, and noticed Ernie Slaughter staring over his right shoulder. "What's so interestin'?"

"Burk Seever and Indian Jim," Ernie said. "Sittin' there like toads."

Reilly turned in his chair to see for himself. Seever and Indian Jim were in the corner, a bottle between them and in earnest conversation. "Burk's gettin' bold," Reilly said softly. "Everyone knows Indian Jim's in the wild bunch."

"Bold or big," Walt said.

The crowd in Burkhauser's kept growing. Jim Buttelow came in with Otis Fielding, his advance man from Utah. He saw Reilly, sent his brief nod across the room, then sat down at a table.

The musicians were trying to get together on a number and the curtain went up. Jane Alford came out to sing. She wore a red dress that ended just below her hips and her tapered legs glistened in the yellow glow of the footlights.

Noises began to die as she went into her song, a sad tale about a wandering father and an unpaid mortgage. The applause was scattered and indifferent and the men began to pick up their dropped conversation before she walked off the stage.

Reilly glanced at Ernie Slaughter and found him sitting with his hat tipped forward over his eyes, his face boxed in shadows. Reilly understood that there had been something between Ernie and Jane, but Ernie made no mention of it and Reilly knew of no way to bring it up without prying.

"Are we holdin' a wake or somethin'?" Walt asked. He looked around the table but no one brightened.

Reilly turned in his chair again and looked at Burk Seever. Somehow he kept remembering the man's face when Tess Isham had stepped out into the hall, half dressed. The fact that Seever also had that picture of her in his mind drove a deep rage through him.

Turning back to his friends, Reilly said, "I think I can lick that sonofabitch."

86

Their heads came up. "Seever?" Walt's voice held amazement.

"Yes," Reilly said.

"Man," Walt said, trying to grin the idea away, "you drunk already?"

"Cold sober," Reilly told him, and looked at Seever again. "I mean it. I got my reasons for tryin', too."

"Hell, this is your wake we're celebratin'," Ernie stated. His smile faded and he bent forward. "You're serious!"

Reilly slid his chair back and touched Milo on the shoulder. "Keep 'em off my back, will you?"

"Just worry about the big one," Milo said, and Reilly stepped away from their table, threading his way through the crowd.

Indian Jim stopped talking when Reilly dropped a hand on his shoulder. "Take a walk for yourself," Reilly said.

"Well," Seever said. "I'm surprised you can leave that poor girl alone long enough to come to town."

"I want to talk to you about that," Reilly said. He jabbed his thumb at Indian Jim who still remained seated. "I won't tell you again, Jim."

"He's bluffing," Seever said. "Sit still, Jim."

"Am I?" Reilly smiled and then backhanded Indian Jim out of the chair. Jim hit the floor, grunted and pawed for his gun. Reilly kicked out and sent the gun spinning and Milo's cool voice said, "Forget him. He'll behave himself."

Facing the table where Seever sat, Reilly leaned on the edge and said, "Burk, I think you and me have a waltz comin' up."

"Not with a gun," Seever said. "Insult me all you want with that gun on, but take it off and I'll tear you in two."

"I think you've made a deal," Reilly said, and unbuckled the gunbelt. A ring of men had formed quickly and there was little talk in the room. On the stage, Jane Alford peered around the curtain, her face pale and strained.

Reilly saw Walt raise his hand. He threw the holstered gun. He did not hear it hit the floor so he knew Walt had caught it.

"There's no gun now," Reilly said, and he waited, his hands once again on the edge of Seever's table.

The only sound was the ticking of the large wall clock.

CHAPTER 7

Because Reilly Meyers had fought Burk Seever off and on all his life, he knew the man's style and was able to anticipate Seever's move as he made it. The big man's hands dropped to the kidney-shaped table's edge and he threw his weight against it, shoving. This was calculated to push Reilly back and bring the table over on top of him, but Reilly pulled a scant second before Seever shoved and the big man lost his balance. Propelled by his own impetus, Seever sprawled face down, knocking cards and chips to the floor and sending bottle and shot glasses flying.

The sprawl carried him a good ten feet and Reilly found his shoulder point pressed against Walt Slaughter's chest. Walt pressed the cold neck of their whiskey bottle into Reilly's hand and said, "Take it. We can get another one."

Catching Seever as he rose, Reilly swung his arm in an arc and brought the bottle down across the crown of Seever's head. Whiskey and fragmented glass sprayed into the sawdust.

Behind Reilly, Walt Slaughter swung on a man, driving him back. When the man came in again, Walt hefted another bottle and fractured it. Reilly heard the body hit loosely and did not bother to glance back.

Seever was getting up.

The big man rolled over before propping himself up on all fours like a bear. Reilly threw the jagged neck of the bottle away and seized a chair. He splintered it over Seever's head and shoulders.

A mild commotion built up behind him and Reilly shot a quick glance that way. Walt was standing over the man he had downed, Ernie beside him. They faced four men who had an idea about fighting, but were making no move to start it.

Burk Seever had been flattened by the last blast but he gathered himself and rolled, his knees drawn up to protect his belly, the result of dim remembrance of brawls past. When he came erect, Reilly moved in on him with an oak chair leg.

Seever was dizzy and weaving. Reilly hit him with his fist, a blow that merely bounced off although he had put all his power into it. An animal lived in Seever, beneath that veneer of handsomeness. A big-boned, indestructible animal. Reilly used the chair leg like a setting maul, opening up ugly cuts on Seever's face and head. This was different from hitting a man with a fist and bringing quick blood. A fist distributes power over a wider area and has some give to it, but the oak chair leg left gashes that reached to the bone. The wounds showed white and stark, not bleeding at all for the moment.

With a mind numb from the sledging, Seever pawed out blindly and Reilly went over backward in a flailing somersault. The blow had lacked full power; actually it was a gigantic shove that punished severely. Reilly rolled his head aside in an effort to determine whether or not his neck had been broken. He had seen it coming in time to swerve and take the brunt of it on his neck muscles, but now his whole side was numb from the shock of it.

Moving forward, Seever planted his feet solidly. Reilly came erect in time to duck a wild swing that would have torn his head off and then jabbed viciously with the chair leg. This wrung a grunt from Seever, nothing more, and the big man tried to grapple.

Understanding what would happen if Seever ever managed to get his arms around him, Reilly struck out with the oak leg, cracking it across Seever's heavy forearm. Seever's eyes grew round with shock. He stood there flat-footed, looking at the sliver of bone sticking through the bloody coat sleeve.

Seever's fancy vest had been torn open and blood made ink splashes on his white shirt front. Reilly charged. He split open a four inch gash over Seever's eyebrows, then

89

threw the chair leg away. He speared Seever in the mouth with his fist.

Somebody behind Reilly yelped in sudden fright and he shot a rapid glance that way. Milo Bucks had his pearl handled gun out and three men stood against the bar. One was Indian Jim, scowling darkly.

Bleeding freely across the face now, Seever moaned and moved toward Reilly like a mechanical man. His muscles were battered, his mind blank. He acted purely from some deep primeval instinct.

"This is the kiss-off, bully boy," Reilly said, and hit Seever in the stomach. Behind his fist went all his strength, fed by many galling defeats in the past, beatings taken from this man with no hope of repayment. He had worn Seever numb and now he wanted to cut him down with his bare hands.

Reilly closed with a vengeance.

This was a near fatal mistake for Reilly misjudged the man's brute staying power. Seever reached out with his good hand and grabbed Reilly by the back of the neck, bringing him to his knees with the power of the grip.

The great difference in weight told. Reilly weighed no more than a hundred and seventy pounds, while Seever stood a head taller and topped that by fifty pounds.

As Reilly gasped, Seever lashed forward with his bloody head, smashing his brow against Reilly's cheekbone. Dimly Reilly recalled a man in prison, a Negro, who had played 'pop-skull,' breaking the bones of another man's face with his own smashing head.

The blow left him sick and half conscious and Seever used Reilly's head like an extension of his fist, battering it against his own massive brow until blood ran from Reilly's mouth and nose.

With a head that felt beaten out of shape, Reilly felt the sudden pain revive him. He gathered his strength for one last try. He understood that one was all he would get, for he was near gone now. Using his feet like flails, he raked Seever's shins then cracked the hard heel of his boot down across the man's instep.

A howl of pain rewarded him and a slackening of the grip followed. Breaking free, Reilly raised one knee and caught the big man squarely in the crotch. Seever doubled over, his eyes suddenly glazed. Whirling, Reilly lifted a chair, then threw it aside in disgust.

He'd finish this with his hands.

Bringing one up from the floor, he connected solidly. Seever arched backward and struck with enough force to bring bottles down behind the bar.

The man was more dead than alive and still he struggled to his feet, swaying blindly as blood flowed into his eyes. He walked in a short choppy circle, bent over like a chicken searching for bugs. His movement had no direction, no purpose. It was just movement.

Reilly began to stalk him.

He forced Seever back against a supporting post and tacked him against it with a whistling fist. He beat him with the steady cadence of a drum major leading a parade, literally supporting the man with the killing power of his fists.

Seever did not lift his hands.

Finally Reilly stepped back and Seever fell like a heavy tree. A nude on horseback broke free of the wall hanger, showering glass on the floor as it struck the baseboard.

Reilly stood there, legs spread wide to keep from falling, the wind tearing in and out of lungs that were afire. A muttering began to grow in the crowded saloon and Ernie Slaughter gave a shrill whoop. But Milo Bucks said something in a quietly dangerous voice to the group of men he faced and Reilly felt the power drain from his legs.

He sat down in an awkwardly cramped position, trying to decipher the loud talk that filled the saloon. He heard Milo Bucks shout something to Indian Jim, heard a fist strike meatily, heard a chair break into splinters.

Walt and Ernie were lifting him and Ernie was saying, "Damn it to hell, I sure never seen the beat of it. Damned if I have."

Milo Bucks was still standing before the three men. Indian Jim lay on the floor, stirring now and daubing at a bloody nose. Milo's voice came easy and unstrained: "Whoa there now. You fellas want more than you can handle, then come right ahead."

Walt and his brother got Reilly outside and Ernie plunged Reilly's head into the horse trough. He brought Reilly up twice, then ducked him a third time.

91

Walt said, "Stop it, Ernie. You tryin' to drown him?"

Reaching the point where he could finally control his legs, Reilly pushed Ernie's arm away. He weaved back and forth and Walt held him so that he would not fall. Water dripped down Reilly's ripped shirt front in a steady stream.

Milo Bucks came out on the saloon porch, his pearl handled .44 still relaxed and ready. Seever had friends who resented this. They began to crowd Bucks, but would not close completely with him.

Walt said, "Better get a doctor over here," and trotted across the street to the office above the barber shop. Reilly was able to manage by himself now and Ernie handed him his gun. He buckled it on, feeling his head expand and contract with every heartbeat.

Henderson hurried down the street and mounted the porch. Milo Bucks turned to him, the Colt still in his hand, and said, "Your boy just got his guts stomped out."

"I'm going in there," Henderson said, and put his hand on Bucks' shoulder to spin him out of the way.

Milo spun, but the short barrel of his Frontier arced up and down and Henderson cascaded limply off the porch. His rolling body hit one of the hitchrail posts and the dry wood split, dumping him into the street.

Putting the gun away, Milo said softly, "That was for nothin'. The same reason you pistol whipped me for, tin star." He was a cold man now, a driving man with a powerful force surging within him. He faced Seever's friends on the porch and said, "Move on, now. Move out."

He waited, cold, implacable, and one by one they bent to his will. In a minute the porch was bare, the men having gone back inside or drifted down the street.

Walt and the doctor came across on the run. The doctor stopped by the watering trough where Reilly stood, but Milo said, "In there. Seever's the one who needs you."

"Seever?" The man seemed amazed. He was short and peppery with a pair of gold-rimmed spectacles and an enormous watch fob that slid back and forth with his breathing. "Did Reilly lick Seever?"

"Better get on," Ernie murmured. "He's in a bad way."

"Of course," the doctor said, and hurried into the saloon.

"I'm goin' to get a new shirt," Reilly said. He walked

across the street to the mercantile. The large room was bright with lamplight and the clerk stepped away from the door with a good deal of respect.

Reilly looked the hickory shirts over, chose one his size and went into the back room to change. A mirror hung on one wall and he stared when he saw the face reflected there. One eye was nearly closed. Skin was missing from his cheekbones and forehead. He saw a gash high on his head that he did not remember getting.

He shrugged and slipped into the new shirt, tucking it into his waistband. A stiffness was beginning to creep into his shoulder and back muscles and just walking set up protests.

The clerk waited behind the counter and Reilly asked, "How much for the shirt, Roscoe?"

"One and a quarter, Mr. Meyers." He made change quickly and Reilly stepped to the doorway. The doctor came out of Burkhauser's, followed by four of Burk Seever's friends. Burk lay flat on a door that had been removed and they walked clumsily across to the office above the barbershop. Reilly could hear them cursing as they wrestled the weight upstairs.

Milo Bucks had disappeared and Reilly wondered where he was. Milo had proved to be somewhat of a big man in the saloon and Reilly wanted to talk to him. Ernie Slaughter pushed Burkhauser's swing-doors open and stepped outside. He saw Reilly and came across, peering anxiously at Reilly's face.

"How you feelin'?"

"Like somebody took an ax to me."

Ernie blew out his breath and rolled a smoke. "The doc ain't brought Burk around yet," he said, and scratched a match. "Henderson's got a split in his scalp where Milo banged him with the gun. Hell, that little rooster's got a craw full of sand, ain't he?"

"Where's he now?"

Ernie shrugged. "Walked off down the street with Walt ten minutes ago." He turned to look up and down the street, halting the motion of his head when Jane Alford came to the saloon doorway. She looked over the top at Ernie for a scant moment, then went back inside.

"I'll see you later," Ernie said. He crossed the street and moved along darkened store fronts until he came to the express office. Then after one final look up and down, he fitted himself into the narrow gap and traversed it with side steps.

He paused in the inkiness of the alley, carefully skirting the stacked litter. Three buildings down, the saloon's back door opened flush with a loading platform. Ernie moved toward this. He slid past the back of the feed store and jumped when Jane Alford reached out of the darkness and touched him.

"Hey," he said. "You gave me a scare."

"Talking's better here," Jane said. "Burkhauser's walls are too damn thin." She shivered slightly for her shoulders were bare and the night held a sharp chill. "Get Reilly out of town, Ernie. Do it now while he's still alive."

Ernie's relaxed manner changed to caution. "What's goin' on, Jane?" He touched her round shoulder and when she didn't draw away, he pulled her a little closer to him. "Jane—"

"No, Ernie." Her voice was like a hand, pushing against him, but he closed his mind to it. His eyes had adjusted to the darkness and he saw the pale oval of her face, the gentle bow of her lips. He pulled her to him, all the way.

His was the kiss of hunger and loneliness and of a man in love when he knew there was no reason for it and no certain happy ending to it. For a heartbeat her arms remained at her sides and then she moaned and clung to him, returning his love in a way that left him shaken.

That moment passed and she strained against him until she was free. He looked at her with solemnity and wonder, unable to believe what she had said without words.

"That was a fool thing to do," she said. "I ought to slap your face."

"You've been lyin' to me, Jane," Ernie began, the words tumbling together in his haste to say it all at once. "You love me—you've never stopped." He took her shoulders and shook her. "I know somethin's after you, somethin' you won't tell me about, but come with me. Nothin' will ever bother you."

"You're talking like a moon-struck schoolboy," she said. "Now do as I tell you and get Reilly out of town."

"I want to marry you," Ernie said. "Once you wanted to marry me too, Jane. You don't belong in a saloon, or with Burk Seever."

"So you know about that." Her shoulders moved in a small shrug. "I suppose you'd go noble on me and say that it didn't matter."

"It don't," Ernie said. "Whatever reasons you had would suit me. I wouldn't even ask what they were."

"You're not fooling me," Jane said. "I know how it would be. You'd work on me and pester me until you found out, and then we'd be through." She shook her head and her ringlets stirred. "And even if that didn't happen, I don't want to work my life away on some quarter section. I told you that before."

"You're lying. You love me and you can't hide that."

"Get out of here now," Jane told him. "Go on, take your fighting friend and beat it."

"All right," Ernie said, and touched her cheek. She slapped his hand away.

"You got away with it once," she snapped. "Don't press your luck."

"You're not fooling me," Ernie said. "I'll wait, Jane. Whatever's hangin' over you is goin' to show its hand one of these days, and when I find it out, I'd say you'll get out from under it mighty quick."

She said, "Be careful with that kind of talk. Get Reilly out of town now."

"I'll see what I can do," Ernie said. "I'll see you again, Jane. I'll see you lots of times."

"Don't count on it," she said, and watched him walk down the alley.

Ernie did not use the gap between the buildings. He walked to the end, came out the side street and crossed over on the other side. Reilly Meyers was sitting on a bench in front of the mercantile, smoking a cigarette, when Ernie came up and hunkered down to one side.

"Have a good visit?" Reilly asked.

"I guess," Ernie said. "Jane says to get you out of town, Reilly. She seemed real worried about your health."

Reilly took the cigarette from his lips and spun it into the street. "That's interesting. Tell me more."

"Nothin' to tell. She wouldn't say what or anything. Just to get you out."

"Somethin' in the wind?"

Ernie snorted. "You put a crimp in Seever's tail. Bucks lays Indian Jim low, then Henderson, and you want to know what's in the wind." He stood up. "I'll get Walt and Bucks and we'll get the hell out. What do you say?"

"All right," Reilly said, and flipped his head around sharply as a tin can clattered across the street. There was little movement along the other walk. Two men sat before the shoemaker's talking. Another man walked along a half a block up.

"That's peculiar," Reilly said. He shifted until shadows masked him. "Where'd that come from? That tin can?" He scanned the street, pausing at each gap between buildings. Then full awareness hit him and he gave Ernie a shove that sent him sprawling.

The dark slot on the near side of the saloon bloomed like a sunflower and a rifle bullet puckered the plank walk near Reilly's feet. Echoes pounded along the street and somewhere a man yelled.

Reilly pulled his gun and fired hurriedly at the muzzle flash. He started for the street but caution checked him. Ernie rolled to a sitting position in the dust and stood up, beating rank clouds from his levis.

"Damn it to hell," he said.

Kneeling, Reilly felt of the splintered walk. The clerk came out of the store, asking questions in a high, excited voice. "Get me a lantern," Reilly said, and the man hurried back inside.

By the time the clerk came back a good sized crowd had gathered. Reilly held the light low to examine the chewed spot. He whistled softly and said, "A forty-eighty-two. That bastard wasn't after quail."

Milo Bucks and Walt came up then, pushing their way through the crowd. Reilly spoke to the crowd. "Let's break it up. The fun's over."

"Didn't look like fun to me," one man said as he turned away. They broke off in chattering groups, leaving Reilly and his crew standing before the mercantile.

"There was the try I was tellin' you about," Ernie said.

"What was you tellin' him?" Walt wanted to know.

"Never mind," Reilly said. "Get the horses, Milo. We're goin' home."

"It's time," Bucks agreed. "We've had ourselves a real play party." He walked down the street, whistling softly between his teeth.

Reilly and the others waited until Bucks came back with the horses, and then they mounted. Childress stepped down from the hotel porch and walked toward them. "Wait a minute," Reilly said.

After looking Reilly over carefully, Childress said, "Well, Reilly, you always wanted to lick Burk."

"Is that what you came here to tell me?"

"No," Childress said. "We're moving stock tomorrow. You ready for it?"

"We'll take care of it," Reilly assured him. "Anything else on your mind, Paul?"

"There might be," Childress admitted. "I'd like to talk to you a little later, if you're not in a hurry. I have a room at the hotel."

"All right," Reilly said. He nodded to the others. "I'll meet you at the place."

"I think I'll stay," Ernie said in a blunt way that invited argument.

"Take this then," Milo said, and unbuckled his gun. "Seems that this here's a real live town and a man ain't sure what the hell he'll run into." He grinned, wheeled his horse and followed Walt out of town.

Childress patted his pockets absently for his pipe. He said, "I'll see you at the hotel," and walked away.

They dismounted and retied the horses in front of the store. Ernie fidgeted with the reins, then said, "You're a damn fool for sure. Somebody wants you to stay in town and you're playin' right along with 'em."

"Paul?"

"I didn't say that."

They went down the street toward the restaurant. The activity of the town had died down a little. Many families were already heading home. Bloom was closing his barbershop when Reilly and Ernie paused.

Bloom peered at the cuts on Reilly's face. "I got just the thing for them," he said.

"What? Cuttin' the head off?"

"I'm serious," Bloom said. He was a little man who took a great deal of pride in his profession. "I've patched up worse than that."

Footsteps rattled on the steps, and Bloom turned the key in the lock and walked off. The doctor stepped down to the street level and rubbed his stomach. He smelled strongly of shag tobacco and chemicals. Behind him, Sheriff Henderson paused, a large white bandage around his head.

He saw Reilly and Ernie standing there and pushed the doctor to one side. "What are you hangin' around for?" he asked.

Reilly grinned. It hurt his face, but he couldn't resist rubbing salt in Henderson's wounds. Now that the war had opened, he decided to declare it properly. "You don't like it?" he said.

Henderson scowled, and when the doctor moved to speak to Reilly, the sheriff gave him a shove that sent him off the boardwalk.

"I want to tell you somethin' now," Henderson said. "I'm declarin' open season on that punk friend of yours."

"Better be careful," Reilly said. "My punk friend has a hell of a big stinger." He turned as though to leave, and then swung back. "How's Burk? Dying, I hope."

"He's in bad shape," Henderson said. "You hit him with a lot of furniture." The sheriff tapped Reilly's chest with his finger. "Burk just may die, bucko boy, and if he does I'll be coming after you with a warrant."

"Somebody took a shot at me tonight," Reilly said. "Where were you?"

"With Burk," Henderson said. "Reilly, you're heading for a great big fall. First thing off you've got to start foolin' around with a man's wife. Burk was only doin' what any man would have done. When you fool around with a woman, you can figure on havin' to square the bill with her husband."

Reilly hit him with a suddenness that shocked even Ernie Slaughter. Henderson went back against the wall of the barbershop, both arms flailing to keep his balance, and Reilly was on him before he could set himself.

He hit the sheriff again, a spearing blow that brought him to his knees. Then he cracked Henderson on the base of the neck with a downsledging fist. Ernie jumped on Reilly's back, pinning his arms. He spread his legs wide and pulled Reilly away from Henderson, who braced himself on stiffened arms and tried to get up.

"Leave him alone!" Ernie snapped, and released Reilly.

"To hell with that noise," Reilly said. He moved toward Henderson again. "Get up, you mouthy bastard. You want a fight, then you can have it."

"No." Henderson raised a hand. "No."

"Then get out of my sight," Reilly told him.

The sheriff tried to stand. Reilly kicked out, driving his feet from under him. Henderson fell flat, rapping his head on the boardwalk. He cried out in sharp pain and Reilly said, "Crawl away. Don't walk."

Henderson began to inch toward the street on his hands and knees. He went into the dust and halfway across before he stood erect and weaved into the saloon. The crowd of men standing on the porch parted to let him pass, but they said nothing.

Ernie Slaughter said, "You were wrong, Reilly. Dead wrong."

"He had no right to say what he did."

"Man calls the shots as he sees 'em," Ernie said. "She came to you twice. The whole town knows it. You make a mistake with Jack. No need to give a man a reason to kill you."

"I play it the way I see it," Reilly said, but he felt ashamed for letting his temper get the best of him. "If you don't like it—"

"I didn't like it," Ernie said, "and I'm telling you so to your face. A man don't stand by and see his friends go wrong, not if he's anythin' himself."

"The damage is done now," Reilly said, and regret began to dig deep. He stirred restlessly. "Let's get something to eat."

The restaurant was nearly empty when they entered and took a back table. A cowboy, with too much to drink, slept across one table. The proprietor, a large man with hairy knuckles, woke him and moved him on his way.

"Coffee," Reilly said when the waitress came over. She had flushed cheeks and drooping skin under her eyes. She even walked tired.

The coffee came, hot and strong enough to float a .45 pistol cartridge. Reilly raised the cup and jumped when it burned his cut lips. He diluted it with water and then drank it.

In cowboy fashion, they ordered pie next, eating their meal backwards with the steak and potatoes following the pie. There were no niceties like soup or salad; they would not have known what to do with them anyway.

Reilly passed his tobacco to Ernie Slaughter after the steak had been reduced to a clean T bone, and they smoked. Reilly asked, "Kick me if I'm nosy, but how're you and Jane coming along?"

"No change," Ernie said, and took a last puff before letting it sizzle in the coffee cup. "What happened there, Reilly? You tell me."

"How can I tell you?" Reilly murmured. "Hell, when I left for the pen, you and her was fixin' to get married."

"Yeah," Ernie said. He rubbed the back of his neck. "Then her ma died and something went to hell. Jane got a job over at the Indian Agency and wouldn't let me come see her any more."

"How come she's singin' in Burkhauser's?"

Ernie's shoulders rose and fell. "She quit the Agency two years ago and the next time I saw her was in the saloon, dancin' with them bastards lookin' at her legs."

"Take her out of there if you want her that bad," Reilly said.

"That's your way, not mine." Ernie shook his head. "I know Jane, Reilly, and she's not doin' this 'cause she wants to. Somethin's makin' her do it."

"What? Any guesses?"

"Burk Seever, maybe. She's got a cabin at the edge of town. I followed him there one night. He didn't leave until dawn."

"And you still want her?"

Ernie's eyes were bleak. "I've done my hellin', Reilly. I'd be a poor one to preach to any woman."

"Better get yourself another girl," Reilly advised.

"Can't," Ernie said. "I didn't do the pickin'. Somethin' inside a man sort of takes care of that."

"Now who's the damn fool?"

"We all are, I suppose. It's funny, Reilly, but to me she ain't never done nothin' wrong. Inside, where it counts, she's clean."

Reilly stood up and dropped some money on the table. "Let's get out of here," he said.

They stepped to the boardwalk as a horseman rode down the street and dismounted by the saloon. Ernie murmured, "Max is a little late, ain't he? Or did he·plan it that way."

"I don't see a rifle," Reilly said. "But then, he could have borrowed one." Horgan turned, once he mounted Burkhauser's porch, and surveyed the street carefully. His eyes tarried a moment on Reilly Meyers, then he went in. The batwings flapped idly behind him.

His sorrel horse stood in the full light coming through Burkhauser's door and Reilly cast his attention on it. "I've seen that horse before," he said. "It's the damnedest feelin', seein' something and not bein' able to place it. Somehow I get the idea all the time that someone else owned that sorrel horse."

"What the hell difference does it make? You goin' to see Paul?"

"Later," Reilly said. "I thought I'd wander around a spell."

"Sure." Ernie smiled faintly. "I know how it is."

"Do you?"

"I reckon," Ernie said, and sauntered toward the hotel.

Reilly glanced toward the bakery. Finding it dark, he moved down the street to come in through the alley.

CHAPTER 8

Reilly tried the back door of the bakery. It wasn't locked. He stepped into the thick darkness and moved slowly, his hand outstretched before him. He came against the table edge and pots hanging from the center rack rattled.

A streak of light came from beneath Tess Isham's door and then it opened suddenly. She said, "Who's there?" and her voice was high pitched.

"Me," Reilly said, and stepped into the light. The lamp behind her laid shadows over her face as she stepped aside. He entered her room and she closed the door.

"Your face looks terrible," she said. "You ought to see the doctor."

"He's busy takin' care of the other fellow," Reilly said. He tossed his hat onto a small table and settled gingerly into a chair. His muscles felt tight now. Tight and aching.

The small potbellied stove in the corner sighed. Tess removed the top lid, laying it in the coal scuttle. She set the coffee pot over the open hole and then crossed her arms, leaning against the wall to watch him.

"Why did you do it, Reilly?"

He shrugged. "Been long overdue."

"You know how the talk will be now, don't you?"

He didn't answer for a moment. "I don't give a damn. I was thinking of what they'll be saying about you."

"Forget about me," Tess said. "I told you once, Reilly —I'm a big girl now and I can take care of myself." The coffee pot began to rumble and she took it off the stove. Two cups clinked against each other, chuckling in the saucers as she set them on the table. Over the rim of her cup, she said, "I thought you'd changed, but you haven't. You're still a mucklehead with more fight than sense."

"You trying to draw blood?"

"I would if I thought it would do any good." But abruptly the stiffness left her face and moisture gathered in her eyes. "Oh, Reilly, look at your face."

She came around the table and touched his face gently. "Go lie down, Reilly."

He settled himself on her bed, the springs protesting beneath his unaccustomed weight. She poured a pan full of water and ripped an old sheet into rags. Then she sat on the edge of the bed and bathed his cuts.

"I heard the fight going on," she said. "It sounded like you two were tearing the saloon down."

"Practically. Seever stomps his feet when he walks."

"That's not funny," Tess said sternly. "How do you think I felt, listening? And then Ernie carried you out. I thought Burk had won again."

"And then they carried Burk out," Reilly said. "For years I've wanted to see him horizontal."

She set the pan of pink water on the floor and folded her hands in her lap. "Maybe you liked it, but someone else didn't. At least enough to take a shot at you."

"Some drunk," he said.

"Was it?"

He sighed and swung his feet to the floor. "No," he admitted. "It's got me worried some, Tess. Is Burk in so solid with the wild bunch that they'd shoot me because I whipped him?"

"He could be Mister Big."

Reilly shook his head. "I can't believe it. Even if I was faced with the fact, I'd still not believe it."

"Why not? He's in a position to be, isn't he?"

"There's someone else, Tess. I know Burk. Even as a kid he was mean. Just plain ornery. He's never been any good and that kind of a man couldn't boss anyone. A man can be tough as hell, and ruthless, and still head other men—but as a general rule they don't like a mean man. They just won't work for him."

"Then who?"

"Horgan, maybe," Reilly said. "Or Winehaven. They've both got a crew of toughs working for them." He braced

103

his elbows on his knees and set his chin in his palms, the fingers splayed along the cheeks. "Don't know what's got into me, Tess, but all of a sudden I'm worried. Worried and scared."

She gripped his shirt. "Reilly, why don't you get out!"

"Give me a reason."

"The shot that missed you tonight," Tess said. "That would be all the reason I'd need."

He grunted in disagreement. "I need more than that, Tess." He studied her and the lamplight fell softly across her cheeks. He touched her bare arm and she didn't pull away. "Would you come with me, Tess?"

She turned her face away, presenting her profile. The silence in the room was like a shout. Finally she asked, "Why did you say that, Reilly? Because you're lonely?"

"Everybody's lonely," he said. "You're lonely living here. It isn't what you want."

Suddenly she seemed angry again. "I wouldn't marry a man because I was cold and needed blankets!" She made a move as if to get up, but he gripped her tighter and pulled her toward him.

"Can't you see what I'm trying to say to you?"

She looked into his good eye, as though trying to see past and into his mind. "How can I say what I see? Do you think I dare to read into your actions and words what I want there? Reilly, you never knew I was alive for a long time and now you're hinting—" She stopped. "I don't know what you're hinting."

Again she tried to twist free. He pulled her across his lap and held her against his chest. "Tess," he said. "Tess, you're different."

She slid her hands along his back and tried to kiss his bruised lips gently, but after they touched, she lost control and hurt him. He felt pain but he ignored it, and for a long moment they stayed locked in each other's arms.

After their lips parted, Reilly held her and she seemed content to lie quietly, her fingers moving slightly along his neck. They sat that way, not speaking, and then Tess glanced up as the lamp flickered. She pushed herself away from Reilly, staring at the open door.

Sally leaned her shoulder against the upright and a faint, mocking smile curved her lips. "Well," she said, closing the door and stepping into the room. "I always come at the most inopportune times, don't I?"

"What do you want?" Tess asked. Spots of color tinted her cheeks and her eyes had sharp, dancing lights in them.

"That's a good question," Sally said. "Maybe I want the same thing you do. You've been after him for six years. Don't you ever give up?"

"Get out of here," Tess said. "I mean it, Sally. I've had enough."

"You get out," Sally said. "Let me tell you something, honey. You'll never do Reilly Meyers any good. He's not your type. Get yourself some shoe clerk and scrub his floor. That's your speed."

Reilly stood up, hard and angular in the light. He said, "Shut your mouth, Sally."

"What for?" Sally said. "So you can blow out the lamp?"

"That's enough of that talk!" Reilly said.

"Is it now?" Sally's smile grew. "I saw the way you were when I came in." She faced her sister. "Get out, please."

"Don't order me around, Sally. This is my home and you're the one who's going to leave." Tess took a step toward Sally and Reilly put his hands on her shoulders, stopping her.

"You've always been a little fool," Sally said. "Your home? You've been fooling yourself. Do you think the place is paid for?" She laughed softly. "Tess, Burk bought this place a year ago. He gave me the deed, all signed and delivered." Her smile faded. "Now you get out. Close this up tomorrow and find yourself another place to bring your men."

Tess Isham stood stock still, the color drained from her face. "You're lying, Sally. This place is mine. Dad owned it outright."

"He didn't own the shirt on his own back," Sally told her. "Burk Seever paid off everything, even the house we lived in."

"I think this has gone far enough," Reilly said, and stepped around Tess. "Whatever you want, Sally, you've come to the wrong place at the wrong time. Now we don't want a squabble, so just leave."

"She's going to leave," Sally said flatly. "Damn you,

Reilly, why didn't you finish the job when you had the chance?"

"Burk?"

"Who else?" Sally reached up and removed her hat, laying it on the table. She stripped off her gloves, then shrugged out of her cape. Crossing to Tess Isham's bed, Sally tested it with an outstretched hand, then looked at her sister.

"Are you going to leave, or will I have to make you?"

"Make me."

"All right," Sally said. She reached behind her, unbuttoning the row of buttons up the back. The pale blue dress fell away from her arms and she kicked her legs free. She wore a thin white petticoat under it and unfastened the band at her waist. When she bent over to free her legs, lamplight threw deep shadows between her breasts.

She stood there, clad in only a brief shift that ended high on her thighs. She looked at Tess and smiled faintly. "Why don't you pull up a chair if you want to watch."

For a moment, only shock appeared on Tess' face. Then tears broke through and she ran blindly for the door, slamming it behind her. After the outside door closed, Sally sat down on the bed and said, "You're very angry, aren't you, Reilly?"

"I didn't know you could hit that low, Sally."

"Why not?" she said. "You're tough, Reilly and you fight your way. Why can't I be tough too? Or isn't that fair?" She raised her arms, drawing her shift tight across her breasts. "Do you want a soft woman, Reilly? I can be soft."

"Tess pulled you out of a tight one the other night," Reilly said. "You forget those things damn easy, don't you?"

"She didn't save me from anything," Sally snapped. "That was for you, Reilly. She's so crazy about you, she'd have walked out in the altogether if she'd thought it would help." She stood up, moving toward him. "Don't use an old saw on me. I know you too well for that."

She stood with the lamp behind her, letting the light come through the fabric. She watched the tightening of his jaw muscles. "You're not rid of me," she said. "Deny it, do anything you want, but we're for each other. Shall I prove it to you?"

"You don't have to prove anything," Reilly said. "I can admit somethin' and still stay away from it. You're under my skin, Sally. I never made no bones about that. You got somethin' I like and with all your meanness, that's what I want. But not the way you like to have it. I'm not goin' to kill Burk to get you."

"I ran Tess out of here," Sally said. "I can bring you into my arms the same way."

"Don't try it," Reilly said.

"A dare, Reilly?" She unlaced the drawstring that held up her shift and let it drop. Her hands were at her sides and she waited with the lamplight falling against her. There was no shyness in this woman. She knew what she was doing and did it boldly, aggressively.

Reilly walked to the table and bent down to pick up her dress from where she had kicked it. He came back to her and threw it at her. "Put it on," he said without emotion. "You remind me of a two-bit whore I knew in Stockton."

He heard her gasp, but his back was turned. He went out, closing the door behind him, and once in the alley with the cool night wind blowing against him, he realized that he was sweating. Farther down, he saw a shifting movement. He reached for his gun, but let his hand slide away when he saw Tess Isham.

He walked toward her, wondering what he could say. When he stopped before her, she did not offer to speak. Finally he said, "I'm sorry, kid. She's willful."

"Mean too," Tess said. "But you've always overlooked that. I'm sorry I pushed myself on you, Reilly. I ought to have known better."

"You're sore," Reilly said. "Sore at me. Did you think I—" He jerked his thumb toward the bakery, then shook his head. "You're wrong, Tess. Dead wrong."

"I'm not going back there now," Tess said. "She's been on the bed and I'd never be able to get it out of my mind."

"Now wait a minute—"

"You don't have to apologize, Reilly." A poor imitation of a smile passed over her face. "She's right. I was after something I couldn't have."

107

"Tess," he said, "why don't you shut up and listen?"

"Listen to what?" She drew a shaky breath. "I was just fourteen, Reilly, but I knew about the buggy rides. I used to lie awake at night and wish I was there instead of her. But even then I knew it wouldn't work. I'm just not enough woman for you, that's all."

"You goin' to talk all night?" He wanted to laugh at her, but he knew he would not. He thought how different she was from her sister, and wondered what kind of a wife she would make. He knew she would work beside her man and share his troubles, but he thought of another thing. That part of her he didn't know.

"I'll get me a place at the edge of town," she said. "There's some abandoned shanties left behind by the railroad survey crew. I'll get along." The façade ruptured and she buried her face in her hands and cried.

He stood there for a moment, then touched her shoulder and walked down the alley, emerging on a side street. At the corner he crossed over and turned left, walking slow and easy toward the saloon. There was not much light now for the business houses had closed for the night. Doorways stood dark and sunken and as he passed a crack between buildings, a voice said softly, "Reilly!"

He wheeled and drew his Remington in one motion, the click of the hammer loud in the stillness. Then he saw a pale face and put the gun away. He stepped into the gap, pushed Jane Alford back a pace and held her arm.

"What are you hiding here for?" Reilly asked.

"I had to see you," Jane said. "Keep your voice down if you don't want to get killed." She took his sleeve and pulled him close so she could whisper. "Elmer Loving was the one who fired that shot."

"How do you know?"

"Don't look a gift horse in the mouth, Reilly. I'm telling you. That's enough."

He sighed. "I guess that figures all right."

"That's not it," Jane said. "You guess he's getting even, figuring you'll do him in some day, but that's not it. Seever had orders to pick a fight with you. You remember what happened to Hank Walling eight years ago. He never came to after Burk hit him enough times."

"So-o," Reilly said.

"Burk didn't make it this time," Jane whispered, "so Loving was supposed to finish the job."

"Who paid him?"

"I've said enough." She tried to sidle away but he held her fast. Across the street, boots echoed hollowly on the boardwalk. Ernie Slaughter came into view and Milo Bucks turned up a minute later. They stood together over there.

"You've said too much," Reilly murmured. "I'm going after Elmer and when I do, the man who paid him will know you talked. Who was it, Jane."

She said slowly, "Max Horgan. It was Ben Cannoyer's rifle."

"Max the big boy?"

"You know better than that," Jane said. "Max is tough, but not smart enough."

"How do you know these things?"

"I just know them," she said. "Let me go, Reilly. I've been gone too long now."

"Goin' back to the saloon's no good now," Reilly said. "Seems to me not too many'd know of this. Once I go after Elmer, your neck won't be worth a nickel. You're gettin' out of the saloon business now, Jane."

"You're insane!" She began to struggle, but he wrapped an arm around her and held her almost motionless against him. Ernie and Milo Bucks still teetered on the boardwalk across the street so Reilly took a match from his pocket, wiping it against the building.

The cell of light flared for a moment, attracting their attention. Reilly said, "Ernie!" and both men came across, loose-legged and easy.

"What the hell?" Ernie said when he saw Jane Alford.

"Elmer tried to tag me," Reilly said. He nodded toward Jane. "Get her out of town, Ernie, and do it quick."

"Where?"

"She'll be safe at Jim Buttelow's," Reilly said.

"This is crazy," Jane said. "I won't go."

"Put her on a horse," Reilly said, as if he hadn't heard her. "Be careful of Ben Cannoyer. He's in this somehow. Just get her out and don't let anything happen to her."

"Nothin' will happen to her."

"Ernie," Jane said, "please. You're getting yourself in

109

trouble and I don't want that. Can't you see I've never wanted you to get mixed up in it?"

"Is that why you keep slappin' my face an' tellin' me to stay the hell away from you?"

"Yes," she said in an intense whisper. "Oh, Ernie, don't be a fool now. Forget about me."

"Maybe you've been lyin'," Ernie said. "Maybe you never did stop bein' in love with me. Is that how it is, Jane?"

"Yes. Yes, I love you, you blind saddlebum. Now will you leave me alone?"

Ernie spat on the ground. "You sure as hell are goin' with me now—nice and easy, or across my shoulder."

Her shoulders sagged. She said, "All right, but I'll have to get some clothes."

"You're dressed fine," Ernie said, and took her arm.

As he pulled her to the boardwalk, Jane turned her head to Reilly. "What do you do with a man like that?"

"Marry him," Reilly said.

He stood there while Ernie and Jane Alford hurried down the dark street. After the night swallowed them he said, "Feel up to some rough stuff, Milo?"

"Hell, you bet," Milo said, and followed Reilly toward the shanties east of town.

The shanties were not much: tarpaper shacks mostly, left behind by a railroad crew that came through but did not build a railroad. Reilly saw no light anywhere as he led the way down a narrow lane. The shacks were small one-room affairs and in the night they resembled squat rocks. A Mexican swamper at the saloon lived down here, and so did two saddlebums in town for the winter. Reilly made up his mind that he'd burn this section out before he'd let Tess move here.

Reilly stopped near the last shack. Milo crossed over behind him and stood on the other side of the door. He drew his Frontier and cocked it, holding it ready as Reilly raised his foot.

The door splintered and fell flat. He got inside with one bound. He collided with a table and upset it. The lamp on the table shattered. He stopped, but heard no sound.

After a moment he wiped a match alight, holding it far away from his body in case he drew fire.

110

The shack was empty.

Milo backed through the door and Reilly flipped the match. The spilled coal oil caught with a *whoof*. The dry boards of the shack burned quickly.

Half a block away they looked back at the red glow. They heard some yelling from that quarter as the Mexican and the two saddlebums rushed around trying to keep the other buildings from catching.

Burkhauser was locking his saloon when Reilly and Bucks came down the street. He said, "Don't you two have a home?"

"Where's Elmer Loving?" Reilly asked.

Burkhauser looked surprised. "Loving? He went home an hour ago."

"That's a batch of—" Milo began, and Reilly cut him off.

They walked on down the street. Once out of earshot, Milo said, "I got a loose mouth."

"Forget it," Reilly said, and stepped into the harness maker's doorway. His shoulder collided with something soft and a woman let out a frightened bleat. The man tried to push Reilly out of the way, but Reilly brought up a forearm and cracked him across the mouth. Then he wiped a match alive and looked into four startled eyes. Jim Reagan, who clerked in the Bon Marche, swallowed heavily and felt of his bruised mouth.

"Get out of here," Reilly said. The woman tried to cover her face with her arm, but Reilly pulled it down. "What's the matter with your husband, Mrs. Cox? He getting old?"

"Now see here," Reagan said, but Reilly whipped the match out, took him by the coat collar and pitched him sprawling onto the sidewalk. The woman cried out and tried to go to him, but Reilly held her.

"Get a little sense," he said. "Jules find this out and Reagan's a dead man."

"It's never happened before," Mrs. Cox began in a run-together voice. "I swear it's—"

"I've got troubles of my own," Reilly said. He stepped through the doorway. Bucks waited nearby, his face inscrutable. Reilly started to walk away, then said as an afterthought, "Let Reagan go first. Wait a couple minutes."

"You're a real gentleman," Mrs. Cox said, relieved and yet still worried because she had been caught.

Reilly walked down the street. He turned at the corner and looked back, but Reagan was gone. Milo said, "You're sure a virtuous cuss."

"A man ought to have better sense than to get caught." Reilly scanned the darkened street. Ben Cannoyer's stable made a huge dark shadow on the left side and he gave this a long study.

"That was Ben's rifle," he said. "I'm just wonderin—" He let the rest trail off and began to walk toward the stable.

The lantern over the archway had long been extinguished, and a deeper night outlined the open doors. Cannoyer's quarters were off to one side: a bare room with stove and cot, the stark necessities for a man who lived alone.

Entering the stable, Reilly moved along cautiously until he touched the wall, then shifted left until he found the door. "Go light the lantern hanging over the door," he said, and Milo drifted away.

Reilly hammered on Cannoyer's door until he heard the old man's grumble and the slide of the bolt. Milo arced a match and Reilly thrust against the door, pushing Cannoyer back and stepping inside.

Milo came over with the light. Reilly closed the door. Cannoyer looked from one to the other and said, "What the devil is this, fellas? A little devilment with an old man?"

"I'm lookin' for one of your friends," Reilly said. "Loving."

Cannoyer spread his age-wrinkled hands. His long underwear sagged at the knees and behind. "Friend?" He smiled, showing gaps in his teeth. "You got it all wrong, Reilly. He's no friend of mine. Why, I hardly know the fella. I'm not a drinkin' man, you know."

"You a loanin' man?" Reilly asked.

Cannoyer laughed as if this were a joke that he would get later. "What have I got to loan, Reilly? I'm a poor man. Everybody knows old Ben ain't got nothin'."

"You got a forty-eighty-two Winchester," Reilly said. "Elmer Loving took a shot at me with it tonight."

"Why—why," Cannoyer said. "You're teasin' me,

Reilly. Why would I do such a thing if I had such a thing?"

Reilly spoke to Milo without turning his head. "Find the gun."

Milo began a systematic search of the room while Cannoyer stood there in his underwear, the lantern making a splashy, thin light in the room. "Reilly," he said, "you know I ain't got nothin'. What you doin' this to old Ben for?"

"Shut your mouth, old Ben," Reilly said. "Look in the tick, Milo. Tear it apart."

"That's my bed!" Cannoyer said in a high voice and made a lunge toward Milo. Reilly tripped him with an outthrust foot and the old man sprawled on the floor.

Milo threw the straw mattress on the floor and pulled it apart. He began to scatter straw. Then Reilly raised the lantern and said, "Hold it, kid." He walked around Cannoyer, who still huddled on the floor, and picked up the Winchester that was used for a bed slat.

Reilly worked the lever and spun an empty onto the floor. Cannoyer watched the slightly bottlenecked cartridge roll in ever increasing circles. He reminded Reilly of a small boy watching his first top spin.

"Suppose you tell me about it now," Reilly said.

Cannoyer sat there shaking his head slowly. Fear showed in his eyes and around the pinched ends of his lips.

"I'll tell you then," Reilly said. "Burk was supposed to do the job, but he didn't make it. Horgan told Elmer to do it with a gun, so he used your rifle. Ain't that right, Ben?"

Cannoyer said, "What you goin' to do, Reilly?"

"Shoot you!" Reilly snorted. "Go get our horses, kid."

Milo went out immediately. Cannoyer began to hunch himself along the floor until he came to the wall. He stayed there, his eyes never leaving Reilly's face. The scrawny arms that braced his body began to tremble slightly.

"What's inside you, old man? Hate? Who do you hate and why? What does it get you, Ben—money? What's money to a dead man?" Reilly's voice was barely stronger than a whisper, but Cannoyer read grave things in it.

"Elmer asked me for the loan of it," Cannoyer said at last. "He said he'd take good care of it. I guess he brought it back when I was outside some place. Hell, Reilly, I wouldn't have let him have it if I'd known he was going to shoot at a man."

"I'll bet you wouldn't," Reilly said, and listened. Milo was leading the horses into the yard. "Where's Elmer now?"

"How would I know?"

"I heard you loaned him a horse too," Reilly said, and was surprised at how good his guess had been. Cannoyer's face fell. He nodded, his head sagging forward.

"An hour ago. He rode out. Didn't say when he was coming back."

"All right," Reilly told him. "I'm going after him, but I'm comin' back, Ben. Be gone when I get here."

Cannoyer said, "Now wait a minute—" but Reilly was walking toward the door.

He turned there and speared Ben Cannoyer with a glance. "Remember what I said, Ben. Be gone."

Reilly swung into the saddle. Milo mounted with him and they walked their horses to the edge of town. Reilly stopped there. At the east end, the glow had widened somewhat and the faint sound of voices rose and faded on the night wind. The other shanties had caught and somehow he was both saddened and pleased. He did not like the thought of putting the Mexican and the two drifters out in the night, but there would be no shacks there in case Tess Isham made good her threat.

He didn't think she would, but he couldn't be sure. She was a stubborn woman when she set her mind to it and she had been hurt. Reilly wished he knew of some way to ease that for her, but times had changed, along with values, and he could do no more now.

He tried to remember Sally as she had looked in the lamplight, the last of her clothes around her ankles, but somehow the picture wouldn't focus. He could see Tess Isham's face clearly, and this puzzled him, for she had always been in his mind much the same as a pesky younger sister.

Milo's voice pulled his mind away from his thoughts. "We goin' to sit here all night?"

"No," Reilly said. "Let's go find ourselves a man."

"Where?"

"Just guessin' now, mind you, but Horgan was in on this and Horgan's in with Winehaven. Elmer used to work for Winehaven." He nodded. "Let's go see what California looks like, kid."

He lifted his horse into a trot. It wasn't an easy pace, but a horse could cover miles that way and be fresh the next day.

Reilly meant to take care of the horse. He had a long way to go and he wanted to be damned sure he got there.

CHAPTER 9

Milo Bucks was a tough young man, saddle-pounded since his sixth birthday, but he felt a strong inclination to lag behind, for Reilly Meyers did not bend to fatigue, nor slacken his pace. For three hours they rode northward through climbing land, pushing through brush and dried creek beds. Finally Reilly came to a stream and paused, allowing his horse to drink. He did not dismount and when Bucks moved to swing off, Reilly said, "No time for that," and rode out again.

They were high and in timbered land when the dawn bloomed beyond the stony summits. A dark stubble tinted Reilly's cheeks and his good eye was bloodshot, but still he pushed on.

The top edge of the sun showed itself and they passed between lanes of pines. A rabbit left the roadside thicket in a bound, sky-hopping, and Reilly's horse shied violently, wheeling around. But he controlled the horse and started off again.

Reilly angled off a sharp rise and pointed to a town below. Bucks didn't see much there—one street and half a dozen buildings.

"We'll get a meal there," Reilly said. They rolled their coats and tied them behind their saddles. They approached the end of the street. A saloon stood on the corner, a rooming house across from it. They dismounted and went into the rooming house.

A fat woman waddled down the hall, drying her hands on her apron. "Can we get a meal here?"

The woman let her eyes travel over Reilly's battered face and the dust that clung like a mantle on his shoulders. Milo Bucks shifted his feet self-consciously when she looked at him.

"Fifty cents apiece," the woman said. "Pay now."

Reilly gave her a dollar and followed her into the warm kitchen. She placed a steaming pot of coffee on the table and they sat down, letting warmth soak into them. Surprisingly, the riding had loosened Reilly's muscles to the point where he no longer ached every time he moved.

The woman fried beef steak and hotcakes, along with a dozen eggs. She put the food on the table and went out the back door. Reilly and Bucks ate in silence. A few minutes later, they were rolling cigarettes and having their third cup of coffee.

The back door opened and the woman came in, followed by a slat-lean man with drooping mustaches. He came up to the table and said, "I don't recollect seein' you around here before."

"You never have," Reilly said.

"Where you fellas from?"

Reilly gave him a level stare. "That's not your business, mister."

"I reckon I got a right to ask," he said. "I'm a deputy sheriff in these parts. You fellas don't look right to me."

"We're all right," Reilly said. "Now just leave us alone."

"Your horses look rode out," the deputy said. "Been travelin' all night?" Bucks glanced at Reilly and this exchange cemented something in the man's mind.

He pulled a gun from beneath his coat.

"Reckon I'll just hold you two boys here a couple days until I get a line on you."

"Put that away," Reilly said softly. "You're buying into somethin', mister."

"I know my way around," the deputy said. "Can tell a hardcase when I see one. Now you two just raise your hands. Myrtle, you sashay around the other side and lift their pistols."

"I'd guess we'd better give up," Reilly said resignedly, and glanced at Milo. He lifted his coffee cup halfway to his lips and then threw it into the deputy's face. The man

117

yelped and stepped back and Reilly hit him, a chopping blow that drove him halfway across the room.

The long barreled gun hit the floor and Reilly scooped it up. Milo left his chair and stood facing the fat woman. Her face was pale and her jaws jiggled slightly.

"Now nobody's goin' to get hurt," Reilly said, and watched the deputy as he struggled to his feet, massaging a sore jaw. He dipped two fingers into his pocket and laid three silver dollars on the table. "Gather a fryin' pan and a little grub," he told Milo.

Milo put bacon and pan, flour, salt and three cans of beans in a flour sack. Crossing to the doorway, he halted until Reilly joined him. "Now behave yourselves," Reilly said, and went out.

He threw the deputy's gun on the roof, heard it skid along until it caught in the eave, then mounted.

They rode slowly from the one street town, lifting their horses into a trot as soon as the last buildings passed behind them.

Late that afternoon Reilly turned east, rode on a few miles and then camped high in the rocks where water rippled over round stones and the odor of the forest was ancient and musky. He took the flour sack of grub, cooked a hasty meal, and then lay down in the squaw carpet, his head on his saddle.

The horses were hobbled and grazing a few yards away.

They slept for nearly four hours. Reilly woke first, nudging Milo awake. Night was not far away. Already a grayness was thickening.

"Let's go," Reilly said. They saddled up, and after a last drink at the mountain stream they rode away, pushing toward a high pass to the west.

Night slowed them, and all around, great forests loomed darkly and animals made snapping noises as they broke brush getting out of the way. Twice deer scudded down the trail ahead of them and from a bramble thicket a black bear snorted at the horse scent, then ambled off on stiff hind legs.

Milo said, "Hell, we must have got ahead of him by this time."

"No," Reilly said. "Elmer's pushing his horse."

At dawn they reached the summit of the Sierra

118

Nevada range. California lay beyond. Reilly sat his horse, his shoulders rounded with fatigue. His face felt better and the puffiness had receded somewhat. He turned the horse and skirted the ridge for two hours. Then he pointed.

In an elongated valley below lay a cluster of buildings and wide expanses of corrals, all interlocking with blocking gates and chutes leading into the huge tin barn near one corner. Smoke rolled from a tall stack and the rank mixed odor of cooking meat and manure and dust hung in the air.

"Winehaven's," Reilly said. "We'll have a look around."

They rode slowly off the mountainside. They had to go two miles over rough terrain. Crossing a small edge of the valley, Reilly studied the buildings carefully.

The slaughtering chute was near the north side of the siding and stripping plant. A man stood on an overhead platform, a big man with a ten pound sledge in his hands. Two helpers hazed steers into the long chute and as they passed beneath the man on the platform, his sledge crushed their frontal lobes, dropping them in their tracks.

Another slaughterer, armed with a long knife, stuck the steers and fastened a rope around their forefeet. From within the building, a steam engine huffed, turning a conveyor belt that resembled a seamless chain. Someone fastened a hook between rope and belt and the steer was dragged away, slowly, inexorably, toward the gutting shack where more men waited.

In the still mountain air the thunk of the slaughterer's sledge, the muffled laboring of the steam engine, and the rattle of conveyor chains made foreign sounds. And in the air there was that stench.

Reilly moved to the left side of the big building where cattle were bunched together. "Stay here," he told Milo, and dismounted. He ducked between the bars and began to work his way afoot through the herd. A man could do that with Herefords, and live to tell about it.

A man came out of the side door and saw Milo sitting there. Reilly caught this and worked his way back to the outside. He was stepping through the bars when Indian Jim came up, a seven-shot Spencer in his hands.

"What the hell are you doin' around here?" he asked. A mouse showed under his left eye where Milo's fist had

119

struck. He hefted the Spencer, but had too much sense to point it at anyone.

"Winehaven around?"

"No," Jim said sullenly. "Get the hell out of here now."

"We'll see Loving then," Reilly said. "It don't make much difference to me."

"Loving ain't here either," Indian Jim said. He shifted the big fifty caliber a little and Reilly nodded at it.

"Be careful with it now."

Indian Jim stopped moving the rifle around.

Without taking his eyes from Indian Jim, Reilly said, "Look around for Loving's horse, Milo. He's stable branded, Flying C."

"I said, get out of here." Indian Jim's face darkened beneath his flop-brimmed hat. He wore faded jeans and a dark corduroy jacket. A belt of silver disks held it together.

Milo took an experimental step away. Reilly's stare held the half-breed motionless. Reilly said, "You're actin suspicious as hell, Jim. What would we want to hur Elmer for?"

"Damned if I know," Jim said. "We had trouble with you once and Winehaven don't want you snoopin' around."

"When we find Elmer and have a talk with him, we'll leave." Reilly smiled. "You sure made damn good time leavin' town the other night. Was you in a hurry to tell Winehaven that Burk didn't make it and that Loving was goin' to do the job?"

"I don't know what you're talking about."

"Ben Cannoyer loaned Loving the rifle," Reilly said smoothly. "A forty-eighty-two Winchester. We went to Ben's stable and had a look at it."

Indian Jim licked his lips and turned his head as Milo Bucks came back.

Milo said, "There's a horse with that brand in the barn. He here?"

"He's here," Reilly said. "Hand him over, Jim!"

Jim said, "Damned if I will!" and whipped the Spencer up to his shoulder.

Reilly sensed the man's move and ducked under the barrel as the carbine coughed. Echoes woke in the hills. He rammed Jim in the pit of the stomach with his elbow,

120

driving wind from the man, then wrested the rifle away and stunned him with his fist.

Jim staggered, hurt, and Reilly sledged him again, dropping him. Picking up the Spencer, Reilly tossed it in the grass by the holding corral. He motioned toward the far corner of the slaughtering shed.

"Take the horses and wait there. I'm going inside."

"Two can do that better," Bucks said.

"Do as I tell you," Reilly snapped, and trotted toward the side door Indian Jim had come out of.

Inside, the building was damp and dark and stinking. He passed through the packing section where men turned from their steam tubs to stare at him. Along one wall, a canning line tinned beef, the cooked meat passing along on a slow moving belt.

Reilly went through the building and into a warehouse section. On his right, heavy insulated doors indicated a cold storage section. He opened a door. Steers hung in double rows and the blocks of ice were piled high with sawdust covering them. There was no one in there and Reilly closed the door.

On the other side, the skinning and stripping section added to the ripe odor. The pile of guts lay man-high at the base of a long chute and flies droned thick and busy.

Reilly passed this to the outside where the slaughtering went on. He climbed upon the top rail of a chute to look around, and on the far side of the corral he saw a man duck under the bars.

He cursed and leaped into the pens while Elmer Loving dodged among the restless steers. The ground here had been cut to dust by thousands of hooves and churned with the manure until the stench was almost overpowering.

From across the backs of the steers, a gun popped. Loving wheeled and Reilly came on, his own gun out now. The noise started the steers to milling but Reilly battled his way through, trying to close with Loving. Sixty yards separated them when Loving climbed to the top rail, trying to break clear.

Sighting quickly, Reilly fired. Loving paused, straddling the fence. His back arched and then he fell forward, his foot hooking the between rails. His leg snapped as he fell.

Using his gun as a club, Reilly battered his way through the herd and vaulted the corral. Loving lay moaning on the ground, a wide stain spreading around his hip. His right leg lay bent at an awkward angle below the knee.

The man clawed for his gun, but Reilly kicked it away and kneeled. "You played a poor hand," he said. "Who's behind it, Elmer?"

"My leg," Loving said faintly. His eyes rolled wildly and color left his face as shock began to work him over. "My leg's broke."

"You got a bullet in you too," Reilly said. "Let me have it, Elmer. What are you getting that should be worth all this?"

From the other side, the Spencer boomed again. Reilly stood up quickly. A sixgun answered in a quick snapping voice and Reilly cursed. He left Loving where he had fallen and skirted the perimeter of the holding corral. At the corner he saw Milo Bucks behind the shelter of a hide shed, firing at Indian Jim who had taken cover behind baled hay.

Reilly whistled sharply and Milo's head came around. Bucks mounted and, keeping himself screened by the hide shed, rode over to join Reilly. Reilly mounted on the run and they bent low in the saddles as Indian Jim shot at them. The heavy bullet plowed dirt a few yards to Milo's left, and then they extended the range beyond the limits of Indian Jim's gun and were in the clear.

Reilly broke the horse's run when the trees began to screen them. Milo kept looking back, but Reilly said, "They won't follow us. Loving's hit bad."

"For a while there," Milo admitted, "I was a little worried." He pulled his gun, rocked open the loading gate and jacked the empties onto the ground. "Loving dead?"

"No," Reilly said. "He'll live." He stirred restlessly. "Let's get back to Buckeye, kid. I saw somethin' Peters ought to know about."

"I could use a meal and some sleep," Milo said.

"Tonight," Reilly told him. "Let's make miles now."

Four days from the time they had left, Reilly and Milo paused at the end of Buckeye's main street. The swelling had diminished in Reilly's face and he could see out of both eyes, although one still puffed slightly and remained a yellow black. Whiskered now, and dirty, he looked like an out-of-the-pants saddle bum.

Milo Bucks matched his appearance easily, for he had eaten Reilly's dust all the way back. Both men dismounted by Ben Cannoyer's stable, swinging off stiffly, testing muscles long unused. They watered their horses at the trough and led them to the open maw, and then Sheriff Henderson, Max Horgan and Winehaven came out of what once had been Cannoyer's home.

Reilly said, "Winehaven, you'd better get back. I just shot Elmer Loving at your place."

Winehaven cleared his throat. "He dead?"

"He's still alive," Reilly said, and speared Max Horgan with a blank stare. "You wasted your money the other night, Max. I just paid Elmer off in coin he understands."

"You're going to step in a big hole one of these days," Horgan said softly. He still wore a tan suit with a heavy vest. His bone handled gun sat high on his left hip in a cross-draw holster.

"You had no right to run Ben Cannoyer out," Henderson said heavily.

"He knew better than to stay," Reilly said. "I made it clear when I came back, I wanted to be left alone. I told you on the road, Max. Now you just keep gettin' in my way and I'll whittle you down to a nub."

Henderson shifted his feet and looked at Milo Bucks. "I've got a bone to pick with you, kid. A big bone."

"Pick it then," Milo invited.

Henderson's eyes widened. Then he rubbed his hand against his leg and laughed without humor. "You two're a pair all right. There ain't a damn bit of difference between you. You're as bad as Reilly ever was, Bucks."

"To me that's good," Milo said, and waited. Horgan nudged Winehaven and the two men walked away. Henderson hesitated for an instant, then followed them down the street.

When they entered Burkhauser's saloon, Reilly led the horses into the stable and off-saddled. He guided them into a stall, rubbed them down with an old blanket and rationed out half a bucket of oats.

Reilly saw Harry Peters' buggy parked by the rear door, the shafts empty and lying on the ground. He went out and walked to the New Congress Hotel.

Milo waited in the lobby while Reilly went up the squeaking stairs and rapped on Harry Peters' door. Peters opened it, grunting in surprise. "Come in," he said, and took his cigar out of his mouth to smile.

He closed the door and waved Reilly into a chair. "You look like you've covered miles."

"I have," Reilly admitted, and related the events leading up to the shooting of Elmer Loving.

Peters listened carefully, then sat back, his hands laced together. "Reilly," he said, "I'm an officer of the law and I deal only in facts. Jane Alford told you it was Loving. On her word you ran an old man out of town and shot Elmer. Now you want me to arrest Max Horgan and Winehaven." He shook his head. "I can't do it. Seever or another lawyer would have them out in twenty-four hours. Even if it came to trial, there would be no conviction. I'm sorry, Reilly, but I have to have facts."

"I'll give you some facts," Reilly said. "You got a pencil and paper?"

Peters rummaged through his coat pocket and produced an old envelope. He handed this to Reilly, along with a pencil, and Reilly drew the five major brands:

Childress' Broken Bit   ⊙-⊙
Bob Ackroyd's Hat   ⌂
Swan Lovelock's Lazy U   ⊂
Reilly's Hangnoose   ♭
Max Horgan's Chain   ∞∞

Then Reilly drew them in a row:

⊙-⊙   ⌂   ⊂   ♭   ∞∞

and after that he added the lines that made them into the Chain, Max Horgan's Brand:

∞⊙   ⊂⊐   ♂⬦   ♭   ∞∞

"There," Reilly said. "That's how they're altered, with a running iron. When I moved through the herd at

124

Winehaven's, I saw Chain cattle with brands runnin' every which way. Some brands were a little bigger than others, with the chain links different size." He waggled the pencil at Harry Peters. "There's your proof. Now go make the arrest."

Peters stood up and went to the window. He lit a fresh cigar and puffed it for several minutes, looking outside. He turned at last and said, "Will you come with me?"

"What for?" Reilly asked. "You get paid for upholdin' the law. Go ahead and uphold it."

"It's not as easy as all that," Peters said slowly. "Reilly, I've looked over Horgan's herd several times and I've never found anything like this. Winehaven's been clean when I went there." He paused to flick ashes off his cigar. "I'd like to work on what information you've given me, but I'd feel pretty foolish if I swore out a warrant and then had to come away empty handed, wouldn't I?"

"What the hell do you want for proof?" Reilly flared. He was tired and saddle sore and he didn't give a damn.

Peters stroked his mustache. "Reilly, you could get me proof."

"How?"

"It seems to me you ought to act like an asset to the wild bunch. It could be they'd rather have you on their side than fighting you. I'd like to see you make a deal with Horgan. Get on the inside and get me real information."

"No thanks," Reilly said, and stood up. "I've got enough troubles of my own without buying yours. I told you what I found out. Now you can do as you please about it."

He went out without glancing back. He picked up Milo Bucks in the lobby and they walked toward the barbershop.

The public bath was in the back room. They stayed an hour, then settled in the chair for their shave. With the dust off his clothes and his face shiny in the sun, Reilly felt better although the riding had set up a stiffness in his shoulders.

Next, Reilly went into the hotel on a hunch and palmed the bell to call the clerk. Milo sat down on the porch and elevated his feet on the railing.

The clerk came out of the back room. Reilly said, "Did Tess Isham take a room here?"

"Number seven at the end of the hall, street side."

Reilly nodded his thanks. He climbed the stairs and jingled his spurs along the hall to the last door. He rapped lightly.

"Who is it?"

"Me, Reilly." From the quickness that the bolt slid back, he knew that she had heard the steps and waited at the door. He stepped inside and smiled at her.

She closed and locked the door and he looked around the room. The place was not new and the furniture second rate. He said, "This is a poor place for you, Tess."

"Better than what I left," she said, and went over to the window. She pulled her chair around and faced away from him. The sunlight streamed into the room, staining the faded green rug.

"I'm going back to my place," Reilly said. "I wanted to see you before I did."

"Why?"

"To set things straight between us."

"There's nothing to set straight," she said. "Sally wants you and she'll end up having you."

"Takes two to make a pair," Reilly said. "You're forgetting that."

"I'm not forgetting anything," Tess said. "I know her, Reilly. Somehow she'll have you, just like she's always had you."

He sighed and shook out his Durham, sifting it into a paper. After he had licked it and struck a match, he asked, "Childress been through yet?"

"Two days ago," she said. "He and Murdock came through early this morning with the crew." She got up abruptly and came to stand before him. "What are you getting into, Reilly? Did you have to run Cannoyer out?"

"I thought I did," Reilly said. "I want to be left alone, Tess. The bunch don't seem to understand that."

"They're after you. They've been after you since you came back." She raised her hand and massaged her cheek. "And I don't know why. What have you done, Reilly?"

"Nothing. Absolutely nothing."

He turned to crush out his cigarette in a dish by her bedside.

"Emily left a message for you," Tess said. "She's marrying Al next month."

"They'll be happy," he said and lifted his hat. "I wish we could be happy, Tess."

"We?"

"You and me." He tossed the hat on her bed and became intense. "I mean it. Why couldn't we? We need each other and isn't that what it takes, a need?"

"Not our kind of need," she said. "Reilly, if you married me, then you'd have one more defense to use against Sally. I don't want to be used. When a man thinks he needs someone like that, he's telling me he hasn't made up his mind yet."

"Tess," he said softly, "you know how it's always been with us. We'd get along."

"I need more than that, Reilly. If there had never been Sally I might have settled for that, but she is there and I can't forget what she's been to you."

"I see."

"I wonder if you do," Tess said, and handed him his hat. "You'd better go, Reilly."

He could do no more now, so he obeyed her. The door closed behind him and he paused in the hall, listening to the bolt click shut again. Somehow this seemed to close something out in his mind and he felt a fleeting regret.

He walked down into the lobby. Through the front window he saw Harry Peters on the porch with Milo Bucks. The marshal was talking and waving his cigar.

Peters straightened when Reilly stepped out the door. "Ah," he said, "I've been talking about you."

"You're wearing the handle of that pump out," Reilly said.

"Perhaps I am," Peters admitted. "However, I got damned little information." He stood up and poked through his pockets for a match. "I was just going down to the doctor's office to see Burk Seever. He's mending nicely."

"Too bad," Reilly said.

"Yes, isn't it?" Peters pushed his finger against the

127

dead end of his cigar, then lit it. "I keep after him though. He may tell me something voluntarily."

"Voluntarily?" Reilly laughed. "I'd sit on that broken arm until he talked."

"We can't all be Apaches, now can we?" Peters smiled pleasantly and stepped off the porch.

"Just a second," Reilly said, remembering something. "Max Horgan's horse has my curiosity stirred. You know the one, the blaze-face sorrel? I've seen that horse somewhere, but I can't connect Max with it."

Peters' face was bland behind a gray film of cigar smoke. He took the cigar from his mouth and said, "You're worrying about nothing. Forget the damned horse."

He walked down the street.

Milo Bucks unkinked his legs and came off the porch. "He's a funny little man, ain't he?"

"I guess he knows his business," Reilly murmured, and led the way to the stable.

CHAPTER 10

Reilly and Milo rode into the yard near sundown. Milo took the jaded horses to the barn while Reilly walked stiffly to the house. Childress' cattle milled in a loose bunch half a mile away and he paused on the porch to look at them.

A new building had been added to the right of the bunkhouse, the planed boards tawny in the last remaining sunlight. Inside the house, Reilly heard quick footsteps in the kitchen. He frowned when a woman's faint humming came to him.

Opening the door, he went down the hall, stopping in the archway to the kitchen. Jane Alford turned from the stove and perspiration lent a shine to her face. She wore a cotton dress with the sleeves rolled above the elbow.

"What are you doing here?" Reilly asked.

"I live here," Jane said, "with Ernie Slaughter. Is that wrong?"

"I'd be the last man in the world to tell you anything was wrong, Jane."

"I've shocked you," Jane said, "but it isn't like that. Ernie built me a small place out by the bunkhouse."

"I saw it," Reilly said. He came up to the stove, lifting the lids on the pots. "Where are they now?"

"Walt went out to relieve Ernie," Jane said. "They've been riding herd since Childress drove them over. It's new ground and they're pretty restless." She smiled. "Ernie'll be back soon."

He turned his back to the range and felt the heat drill

through him. With the sun going down, the day's heat faded rapidly and a coming winter chill blew across the land. Reilly said, "You're happy now, aren't you?"

"Yes," she said. "Yes, I'm very happy."

"Why wait so long, Jane? It don't make sense."

"It did to me," she said. "Reilly, I made a mistake once, a bad mistake. I'm still paying for it."

"Ernie know about it?"

"No. No one knows about it. No one's going to know." She grabbed a pot holder and pulled a boiling kettle to the back of the stove. "Now get out of here and wash up. You're ruining my cooking."

Reilly met Milo and Ernie at the pump. After slicking their hair back they came into the kitchen and sat down at the table. Jane heaped the platters full and took her place at the far end. Silverware clattered briskly. They ate until they were full, and then they began to talk.

"That beef will winter out fine here," Ernie said. "I'm thinkin' the snow will stay off the flats for another month. They'll have found a place to bed down by then."

The sun died completely. Jane got up to light the lamps. Somehow the talk drifted around to the affair at Winehaven's and Reilly covered it briefly. They were on the second cup of coffee when Milo put his hand on Reilly's arm, closing off his voice with that one movement.

A buckboard wheeled into the yard and stopped by the front porch. Reilly slid back his chair to go out and then a man's boots thumped across the porch. The front door opened. The front of the house was dark and the lamps in the kitchen threw light only part way down the hall.

The man came ahead. He stopped in the doorway. Reilly pulled his breath in sharply and said, "Burk, do you want to get killed?"

"Not tonight I won't," Seever said. His right arm hung in a sling and he put his left hand up as if to adjust it. The fingers went inside the cloth and came out with a nickel-plated .32. "I brought a friend along tonight," he said.

Light fell fully on Seever and Reilly winced with shock. One side of Seever's face seemed to sag as though tired muscles no longer chose to support the flesh. A ragged

130

scar traced itself around his eyebrow, the stitches showing plainly. He had a dozen scabs.

"You fixed me up good," Seever said. "This one side is dead." He touched his cheek with the barrel of his gun.

Ernie and Milo sat motionless, their hands on the table edge. Seever looked at Jane Alford and said, "If you're through passing it around to the boys, then come on back with me. I need somebody to warm the sheets."

Ernie tried to rise, but Reilly jerked him back down.

"You're not so dumb," Seever said. "The next time he pops up I'll put a bullet in his head."

"I'm not going anywhere with you," Jane Alford said.

"Yes you are," Seever said. "You're going with me and you know why."

"Don't push it too far with me," Jane said. "There'll come a time, Burk—"

"You'll never see that time," he interrupted. "Tell me why you'll come with me."

"I won't!" Jane said. "I've lied enough!"

"Think," Seever said, almost whispering. "Think, Jane. Who's going to get it in the neck if you don't behave?"

"All right," she said numbly. "All right, Burk." She got up slowly from the table.

"Jane!" Ernie said, and there was pain in his voice.

She tried to meet his eyes and couldn't. Burk Seever laughed. Reilly put both hands on Ernie Slaughter's shoulders to keep him in his chair.

"She's in love with me," Seever said. "Aren't you, Jane?" When she failed to answer, he repeated it. "Tell this punk, Jane!"

"I'm in love with him," Jane Alford said dully with her back turned. "I'm sorry, Ernie."

"Sorry?" He sounded as if he had lost the power to understand even a simple word.

"Then take her and get out of here!" Reilly snapped.

Jane shot Reilly a frightened glance and then complete defeat glazed her eyes. Her shoulders slumped. She came near Seever and he took her arm. He backed up until he stood just in the hall. "Now be smart," he said, "or I'll have to sacrifice this little honey. You know what I mean."

"We know," Reilly said, and watched them retreat down the hall. The sound of them moving off the porch and into the rig was loud in the quiet. Then the horses wheeled and raced from the yard.

Ernie Slaughter dashed his chair aside and slammed out the back door. He walked rapidly across the yard and Reilly tracked him, afraid that he would catch up a horse to follow Seever.

Reilly saw Ernie come against the corral and bend his head down, and then he turned away. He said, "I'm goin' back to town."

"That makes two of us," Milo said.

Reilly studied him as he had done a dozen times, trying to fathom what motives drove the boy along such reckless paths. He didn't know any more than he knew about his own yearnings when he was that age. Reilly decided that he liked Milo because the kid was more like him than he cared to admit.

Ernie still leaned against the corral, head down, when Reilly and Milo saddled their horses and rode back over the Buckeye road. The night wind had a bite to it and they unrolled their coats.

Finally Milo said, "She went with him because she was afraid. Besides, she ain't the kind a man can push over."

"No," Reilly admitted. "She's not that kind."

The ride was a silent one after that, for neither felt the inclination to talk. When they arrived and dropped their horses off at Cannoyer's abandoned stable, Reilly was in a vicious frame of mind. The streets were bare and there were few customers in the stores. The hardware was closed and darkened. Only the hotel, saloon and mercantile showed lights.

They walked down the street and met Harry Peters coming out of the restaurant. He paused with his back to the wind to light up a fresh cigar. When he saw Reilly and Milo he looked mildly surprised. "I thought you'd be home now," he said, and pulled his collar up. "Feel that? Be snow in the pass in a few days. I can always tell."

"To hell with the snow," Reilly said. "You see Burk Seever come in town a while ago?"

"No," Peters said. "Can't say as I have. Indian Jim came in this afternoon with a mad on about something. He's over in Burkhauser's now drinking it off."

132

"It's Seever I'm looking for," Reilly said, and walked on. He traveled the length of the side street to the two-story house sitting on the corner. At the front gate he said, "Wait here," and walked on alone.

He saw a light burning in one of the upstairs windows. He knocked heavily, then watched a bobbing light descend the winding stairs. A voice close against the door said, "Who is it?"

"Reilly."

The lock turned and Sally stepped aside. She wore a white robe over her flannel nightgown and her hair was braided down her back.

"Where's Burk?" Reilly asked.

"I don't know and don't care," she said. "I keep the house locked to him."

"There's something I want to see him about," Reilly said, then cocked his head around as a quick rattle of gunfire broke out on the main street. He jerked the door open and bolted halfway down the path while Sally called, "Reilly! Damn you, Reilly, come back here!"

Reilly was surprised to find Milo still at the gate, for somehow he had connected the shooting with Milo. Another shot splintered the night, and together they cut through the alley and came out near the harness maker's.

Burkhauser's saloon doors flapped, testifying to someone's hasty exit. A shot ripped through the building and light faded from one of the windows as a lamp came down with a tinkling crash.

"Indian Jim!" Reilly said. He started across the street just as a man filled Burkhauser's doorway.

Indian Jim saw Reilly crossing over and swung his Spencer repeater to his shoulder. Milo Bucks yelled and Indian Jim's attention wavered. With two targets and a belly full of whiskey he had a difficult time picking one. By the time he had swung the gun to Milo, then back to Reilly, Reilly had disappeared.

Cursing, Indian Jim took another shot, this time at Milo, but Milo Bucks eased himself into a dark doorway and let the night hide him.

Once in the alley, Reilly ran along the darkened pathway until he came to the rear door of Burkhauser's saloon. He let himself in through the crowded storeroom. A twist of the knob told him the back door leading into the main room was unlocked. He pushed it open a crack, drawing his gun with his other hand.

Indian Jim fired again at Milo Bucks and Reilly peered out. The man's back was toward him and from the corner of his vision, Reilly saw Burkhauser crouched behind the bar. Milo, still on the other side of the street, yelled something and Indian Jim ripped the tube from the buttstock, inserting seven more blunt cartridges. He levered one into the chamber, cocked the Spencer and fired one more shot.

Reilly opened the door, slipped out and ducked behind the bar to his left. The sawdust muffled his spurs, but he took them off anyway and eased along, his gun still ready.

He heard some muffled cursing from the doorway, and then Indian Jim came back into the room, his footsteps dragging along the foot rail.

"Burkhauser! You sonofabitch! Where are you, Burkhauser?"

Reilly canted his head and glanced into the back bar mirror. From his position he could see the top of Indian Jim's head and he gathered himself for a rush. The man hooked one arm against the bar for support and stood with his back to it. Holding the Spencer out at arms' length, he fired through the batwings and laughed when splinters flew.

Reilly raised himself then, and saw in an instant that he had read the mirror backward. Expecting Indian Jim to be to his right, he was shocked to see him to the left, and Jim whirled as Reilly stretched to connect with his arcing gun.

He missed Indian Jim's head and struck his shoulder with the barrel. The man cried out and dropped the Spencer and Reilly came over the bar, clubbing with the gun again. He caught Indian Jim squarely this time and the man wilted, his head rapping the brass spittoon as he fell.

Reilly called to Milo Bucks and Milo came over. Peters paused on the hotel porch, then followed Milo. Burkhauser darted frantically about, counting the damage in his mind.

Harry Peters stopped just inside the door and looked quite impersonally at Indian Jim.

Reilly said, "Where were you when the shooting started?"

"In bed, asleep," Peters said with no apology in his voice. "By the time I got my pants on, you'd already crossed the street and come in the back way. Rather than interfere with your play and get you killed, I waited."

Milo leaned against the bar and looked at Indian Jim's rifle. He said, "That's twice I damned near got killed with that thing." He picked it up, carried it outside and hammered it to pieces on the metal ring atop the hitching post by the watering trough. He threw the pieces in the gutter and came back in.

Milo Bucks threw a pail of water in Indian Jim's face and Jim tried to sit up.

"Now we'll get him to say a few words," Reilly stated.

"No rough stuff," Peters warned. "Testimony got that way won't hold up in court."

Reilly's temper slipped. "You played it nice and safe, Peters, and I got him. Now you just go back to bed and I'll finish the job."

"Gladly," Peters said. "I want no part of it." He turned away to the door and paused there. "In the event that you do learn anything of value, you'll let me know, won't you?" He smiled and tapped his inner pocket. "After all, I have the badge."

After he had gone, Milo said, "Now ain't he the fancy one?"

Indian Jim was standing against the bar now, bracing himself with both hands. "Better get him outside," Burkhauser said. "He looks like he's goin' to be sick and I got enough mess in here."

Reilly and Milo took Jim through the storeroom into the alley. Indian Jim was sick. When his spasms subsided, Reilly said, "Let's have a little talk, Jim."

"Nothing to say," Indian Jim said, and Reilly hit him. He cascaded backward into a stack of empty beer barrels, which fell over on him. When the last one stopped rolling down the alley, Reilly pulled him out of there and said, "I won't ask you again, Jim."

Jim bled from the nose and sniffed like a small boy with a cold. He said, "What you want to know?"

"Who's the top man?"

Indian Jim shook his head and Reilly hit him flush in the mouth. Reilly had a hold of his shirt front, which ripped but held. Indian Jim's head snapped back and blood spurted from a cut lip.

"What the hell," Jim said, "I'm finished anyway. Horgan's the man you want. Him and Winehaven and Henderson."

"Henderson?"

"Sure," Indian Jim said. "He can ride where he pleases so he spots the herds that ain't protected. Horgan's bunch does the actual movin'. Winehaven butchers what can't be doctored so the brands won't show. The rest Seever peddles to the reservation."

"You said you were finished," Reilly reminded him. "What's that mean?"

"Horgan shoved me out because I let you two get away the other day," Indian Jim said, then laughed. "You're real tough, Reilly, and half smart. You figured out how the brands got changed, but that ain't smart enough. You want to know somethin'? Horgan's bunch is raidin' your place right now. When you get back, Childress' cattle is goin' to be gone."

"Why you—" Reilly began, but Indian Jim held up his hands.

"I give it to you straight, Reilly, what you wanted to know. Don't I get some kind of a break?"

Reilly pondered this, then said, "Bring his horse around here, Milo." And after Milo ducked through the saloon he told Jim, "I'll give you a head start. You're gettin' off lucky."

"I know it," Jim said, and scrambled to his feet. They stood there in the darkness until Milo came back with Indian Jim's horse. Jim mounted and rode out of town.

Reilly and Milo walked across the street. They found Harry Peters in the lobby of the hotel. He studied Reilly and said, "Well, what did you learn?"

"Horgan's the boss," Reilly said. "So's Seever, Winehaven and Henderson." He explained their parts in the rustling. "You're a federal officer, Peters. You'd better see that Indian agent too."

"And the proof?" Peters inquired very gently.

Reilly stared at him then, trying to remember something else Indian Jim had said—something important

—but it wouldn't come to him. "To hell with you," Reilly said. "I told you the facts. Now do what you damn please about it."

"What about the herd?" Milo asked Reilly.

"What herd?" Peters took his cigar from his mouth and sat straighter in the chair.

"I got it from Jim that Horgan is runnin' off Childress' herd, the ones that are winterin' out on my place." Reilly bit his lower lip. "Someone is goin' to get hurt for this, Harry."

"You don't believe that, do you?"

"I'm sure as hell goin' to find out," Reilly said. "And while I'm at it, I'll give you some advice: Do somethin' about Henderson while I'm gone."

Peters sighed. "Taking to running the marshal's office now, Reilly?"

"You've set still long enough," Reilly said, and moved to the door with Milo. He turned there, that vague thing Indian Jim mentioned almost on the tip of his tongue. Then it receded.

They got their horses from the stable and rode out of town at a fast trot. A deep impatience began to churn in Reilly and he urged the horse to a faster pace. Milo increased his to match and they ran on into the night.

As soon as Reilly and Milo had cleared town, Harry Peters left the hotel and walked along the quiet back street to the jail. He paused by the door and withdrew the .38 from beneath his armpit. He broke it open, then replaced it in the spring holster, leaving his coat open.

He rapped on the jail door and heard Henderson's answering grumble. Then the lock snapped and he stepped inside. Henderson popped a match on his thumbnail, lifted the lamp chimney and stood squinting at the light.

"What the hell was all the shooting about?" Henderson asked, plainly not giving a damn.

Peters smiled. "That was your friend, Indian Jim, shooting up the bar. The shooting you didn't hear was done with his mouth in an alley. Reilly and Milo heard him spout off."

"About the bunch?" Henderson's eyes were wary now.

"I'm afraid so," Peters said. "This might make it awkward for you, Jack."

"I suppose it will," Henderson agreed. "You don't like this, do you, Harry?"

"I never like it when people get caught," Peters said. He leaned against the wall. "What are you going to do about it, Jack?"

"Pretty sudden," Henderson hedged. He picked up a pair of pants from the foot of his bed and stepped into them. Next he donned his shirt and stood with the suspenders around his hips, tucking in the tail.

"What do you think I ought to do, Harry?"

"I'm a federal officer," Peters said quietly. "You know what I have to do, Jack."

"Damn," Henderson said. "What the hell got into Indian Jim anyway?"

"Reilly," Peters said. "He got into you four years ago and he was bound to do the same now. The man don't let go, Jack. You ought to have known that."

"I guess," Henderson said, and put on his boots. He sat there on his bed, his big hands outstretched, bracing himself. "I know you too, Harry. You don't like to let go either."

"That's right," Peters said. He rotated the cigar from one side of his mouth to the other. "Hurry up and make up your mind, Jack."

"You going to give me any kind of a break?" Henderson's hand moved slightly, almost twitching.

"You think you got one coming?"

"Yeah," he said. "The thing's coming apart. Why pick on me?"

"Better come along now," Peters murmured, and he watched Henderson. He saw the refusal in the man's eyes before his hand darted under the pillow. When Henderson pulled the gun, Peters had him beat.

He shot three times, double action, three times fast, and then watched Henderson wilt and strike the floor on his back.

"You damn fool," Peters said to Henderson's corpse. "You knew it had to be done this way, didn't you?"

He reloaded the gun with loose cartridges from his pocket, put it away and let himself out. The night held a definite chill so he pulled his collar tighter. Then he retraced his steps to the hotel to make out his report.

Reilly saw the glow of the fire three miles away and nearly killed the stud running him. He tore into the yard, Milo right behind him, and flung off when he saw Walt Slaughter.

Ernie lay face down on the ground, and in the flickering firelight, the bullet hole in his side showed the white splintered ends of ribs. Walt stood there, saying nothing.

The outbuildings were just piles of glowing ashes, but the house and barn, being larger, still burned with hellish fury. Reilly did not look toward the holding pasture. He knew the herd was gone.

"All the horses were turned out before the barn caught," Walt said, and motioned limply toward Ernie. "He got it then. I was holed up by the well."

"You see 'em?"

"Horgan's bunch." Walt looked tired and there was no life in his voice. "I was supposed to get it too, but it didn't work out that way." He gulped audibly. "Why did it have to be him?"

"There's no answer to some things," Reilly said, and nudged Milo. "Go saddle me a fresh horse, kid."

"You goin' after Horgan?"

"That's right. Now do as I told you."

"I'll saddle two horses," Bucks said.

Reilly's voice followed him across the yard, hard and without room for argument. "I said *one* horse. You're needed here."

For a moment Reilly thought Milo would take it up, but he just shrugged and mounted his own horse. Shaking out his rope, he rode off to where the horses milled a quarter mile from the barn.

Walt spoke, almost to himself. "People's lives get all twisted up. Sally and you. Ernie and Jane. Why couldn't she have stayed with him, Reilly? What kind of a little tramp is she?"

"I think she loved him," Reilly said. "I only hope he never lost faith in her."

"He didn't talk at all last night," Walt said. "From then on he never said a word."

139

Of course not, Reilly thought, and raised his head as Milo came back leading a calico gelding. Reilly switched saddles and retied his blankets and coat. "Let me have your rifle," he said to Walt and Walt handed over a single shot Sharps carbine.

After mounting, Reilly dropped the rawhide thong over the saddle horn and let the carbine dangle by his leg. "I'll be back," he said.

"A two man job," Milo reminded him. "You'll never drive that herd back by yourself." He squinted at Reilly. "Or were you just aimin' to kill Horgan and let the cattle go to hell?"

Reilly's lips tightened because Milo's talk had pushed his reason back in place. He had intended to kill Max Horgan and let it go at that. "Catch up another horse," Reilly said.

"I'm in this," Walt said. "Can't we bury him now?"

Reilly stepped out of the saddle and left the horse ground tied. "Get a shovel, Milo."

"Where? The tool shed's burned up."

"There's an old plow in back of the barn. We'll make a Joe McGee hitch and scoop out a trench." Milo shrugged and crossed the yard again.

The rig couldn't be called fancy. The harness was rope and rolled blankets bound with leather strips. The horse didn't like it and it took fifteen minutes of fighting to convince her otherwise.

With a ground baked hard as caliche, Milo and Reilly had to combine their weight to make the dull plowshare bite deep. And then the harness gave way. Yet within an hour they had a shallow grave scooped out.

They wrapped Ernie Slaughter in a horse blanket, and gathering rocks, they heaped a cairn. When they finished they could find no words to speak over the grave. To Reilly Meyers, who had known Ernie well, a thousand memories were better than words, anyway.

He removed the crude harness from the horse, gave Walt back the Sharps, and then waited while Milo caught up another horse. They were still in the yard when a horse pounded across the flats, and each man drew his gun and waited.

The light from the burning house had faded to almost nothing. Occasionally an upright timber burned through and fell with a shower of sparks, but other than that it was all over.

The rider came plunging on. Finally he caught sight of them and pulled his horse up so short it reared. They recognized Jim Buttelow in the dim light. Buttelow stared at the dying fire.

He said, "I seen it five miles away from my front porch," and then he noticed the mound of rocks. He counted faces, nodding recognition one by one. "Ernie," he said. "Know who done it?"

"Horgan," Reilly said. "We're goin' after the herd, and him."

"I'll run home for some blankets and come along."

"No," Reilly said, and quickly told him all that had happened.

Buttelow listened with a respectful silence, then said, "I'll go get Childress and Al Murdock. Lovelock's up in the hills or I'd get him too." He shifted the cartridge belt on his hips. "Three'll be enough to take that bunch at Winehaven's."

"We'll get Winehaven," Reilly said. "You get Burk Seever, but I want that bastard alive. I want to stand by the scaffold and listen to the rope sing."

"We'll get him," Buttelow said and spurred his horse away.

Reilly Meyers did not hurry his men when they rode from his ranch yard. He knew how slowly cattle moved. There would be plenty of time, even with Horgan and his bunch pushing them.

The cold wind told him that he could expect weather within the next few days. Overhead, thin mare's tail clouds tried to blot out the starlight. Tomorrow morning the clouds would be thicker, wiping out the sun, and by evening there would be rain.

Ahead lay a tough trail. They were ill equipped for it, but that didn't bother Reilly at all. He considered the weather—rain here on the flats, but in the mountains, snow. Passes would fill up with wind drifts and the going would be tough. The tougher the better, he decided, and settled down for a long night.

By morning they had skirted the west shore of the lake and were approaching an isolated cabin. A small pole corral with two skinny milk cows stood behind the house.

A man came out and watched them come into the yard. They all rode round-shouldered, stiffened by a near freezing night. The sky gave no promise of sun, and when they swung off they stamped their feet to restore circulation.

"Coffee's on," the man said, and stood aside while they filed in. The room was low and warm and tingles ran through Reilly's fingers as he spread them over the sheet iron stove. Mud and grass chinking stuck from between the logs and a rickety pole bunk sat in one corner.

"You fellas must have come a ways," the man said, gently prying.

"Quite a ways," Reilly admitted, and accepted a steaming mug of coffee. The fire seemed to thaw them and by the time the man had fried more wheat cakes and another pound of bacon, they were talking.

"Any cattle go through here last night?" Reilly asked.

"By jingle!" the man said. "I thought I heard cattle lowin'." He nodded. "Yeah, I'd say some did. Bein' pushed too. They yours?"

"In a manner of speakin'," Reilly said. "I was winterin' 'em on the flats for a friend."

"Nigh on to four hours ago," the man said. He motioned for them to sit down, paused and examined each of their faces. Walt's was black with soot and burned holes showed in his clothes. The man said, "Reckon I'm glad I wasn't drivin' them steers. By jingle, I sure am."

Talk stopped while they ate. After a second cup of coffee, Reilly rose and the others got up with him. He thanked the man and went outside to the horses.

At the edge of a small rise he turned to look back, but the man had gone back inside and closed the door. They moved on.

CHAPTER 11

Because he knew now where the stolen herd was heading, Reilly swung farther north into solid timber country. For two days he led them on at a leisurely pace and the days grew colder. On the afternoon of the third day it began to rain, a cold drizzle that soaked them to the skin, later turning into fatly swollen drops.

Through the day's last remaining light they wound upward, always screened by the thick timber. When Reilly halted to build a fire, the rain had turned to a light snow. By the time they had warmed themselves, the ground was thinly covered and moisture dripped from the trees with a steady drumming.

Neither Walt nor Milo said anything when Reilly mounted again. They followed him in weary silence, on into the night. Around nine they began to let down off the slopes to a cluster of lighted windows below.

The raw odor of sawed pine and spruce grew stronger as the distance narrowed, and from the shadowy outlines of the buildings, as well as the gaunt skeleton of the 'A' frame loading jammer, Walt Slaughter recognized the logging camp.

By a bunkhouse bright with light, Reilly dismounted. The cook house sat nearby, the sharp clatter of pans coming from within. The three men walked toward the cook house and opened the back door.

The warm, moist air washed over them in a smothering wave. They cuddled the long stove while the cook took in their wet clothes, saw the guns, and drew his own conclusions.

"Coffee there," he said, and gave the dishwasher hell for hanging up a greasy pan.

They poured the bowls full of coffee and stood next to the stove, letting the heat make their clothes steam. The cook said something quiet to the dishwasher and the little man hurried out.

The smell of horses and hot woolens began to fill the room and then the back door opened and a man came in. He looked big enough to fight a grizzly with a switch. The dishwasher came in a moment later and went back to work.

The big man came over and said, "I'm Monaghan, the side-rod here."

"You've good coffee," Reilly said. "We appreciate the heat."

"A man'd have to be in a hurry to be out this night," Monaghan said. He wore a plaid shirt and tufts of dark hair fluffed up at the collar. His hands were hairy across the knuckles and full of strength. Monaghan's dark eyes moved from one man to the other and there was no fear in the man. They might have been desperate characters for all he knew, but the thought did not bother him.

"I'm Meyers of Hangnoose." Reilly waved his hand. "Southeast of here. These men are my crew, Walt and Milo. It seems that we had a whole herd stray all at one time. Since we're afraid they'll get lonesome, we thought we'd better go get 'em and bring 'em back."

Monaghan looked at Walt Slaughter. "Is that soot on your face, man?"

"We had a fire," Reilly murmured over the rim of his cup. "Add to that a dead man. A good man."

"Ah now," Monaghan said, his manner changing. "You're not fit to go on without gear." He flipped his head around. "Cookie! Give these men anything they want."

"That's kind of you," Reilly said. "We're willin' to pay."

"Faith now," Monaghan said, "trouble makes all men brothers. I'd do no less for my own. Ye'll need slickers for this weather. Snow's buildin' thick in the hills."

"There's a good pass twenty miles from here," Reilly said. "They'll drive through there. And that's where we'll be waitin'."

"You're free to bunk here," Monaghan said. "From the looks of you, you need it."

"The horses can use it," Reilly agreed, then nodded. "All right. We'll put up and get a few hours. In case we pull out early I'll thank you now for the help."

"It's nothin', man," Monaghan said. He went out into the night and the cook filled a large sack with supplies. Milo took it out to the horses, led them to a dry leanto, and forked down some hay.

Reilly and Walt came out. Reilly said, "This is good enough," and took his blankets off the saddle. He made a bed in the hay and rolled up, falling asleep almost immediately.

He slept soundlessly and in four hours he woke up. The snow was still falling, heavier now. He found a lantern hanging on a nail and lit it. Walt and Milo stirred, then sat up, still groggy with sleep.

They were rolling their blankets and saddling up when Monaghan came through the falling snow with three slickers and a heavy coat apiece.

Reilly put his on, as did the others. "We'll see that these get back here," he said.

"Be sure to be in 'em," Monaghan said. "We'll not be leaving dead men up there for the wolves." He motioned off to where the hills flattened. "That's longer, but there'll be less snow with the wind blowin' it. On the way back, you can bed your cattle down up there. There's a burn, mostly growed over now. I'm thinkin' you'll all be needin' the rest."

"We'll see you on the way back," Reilly said, and swung into the saddle.

After leaving the lumber camp, Reilly faced the blunt-topped ridge. After an hour's ride he crossed over it. The wind here was ripping and snow slanted at a sharp angle as it fell, but the logging boss had been right. The ridge was almost clean and traveling easy.

Through the rest of the night they worked their way west, dropping off now as the land let down into a high pass. The snow grew deeper and the wind whisked it into cone-shaped drifts and piled it into windrows.

The cold came through their clothes and feeling deserted their feet. By dawn—a dawn slow in coming and dirty gray—they were deep into this canyon.

Reilly pushed his horse ahead and studied the ground, although no track would last more than an hour in this sweeping wind. He came back and said, "I think we're ahead of 'em. Let's find ourselves a hole and crawl into it."

They rode on up canyon for a mile, and then Reilly pointed to some high rocks that formed an overhang. "Up there, Walt. You'll be on the point. Milo and I will let the herd pass through to you and then we'll seal off the back. When you hear the shooting, cut loose and close the stopper at the front. Can you shoot a man?"

"Thinkin' about Ernie, I can," Walt said.

He rode halfway up, then dismounted and led the rest of the way. Milo crossed over to the other side, for he did not want to leave tracks for Horgan and his crew to stumble onto.

He picked his way back carefully, and when he had gone four hundred yards downwind from Walt, he stopped and picketed his horse. Reilly took a place across from him and lay belly flat in the screening brush.

Waiting is always the hardest and the cold made it worse. At times a man just had to get up and flail his arms a little and move around, but they did not do this often. By noon Reilly began to think he had guessed wrong. At three in the afternoon he felt sure of it. He was about to signal Milo Bucks when he heard the first lowing of cattle below.

Milo and Walt heard it also, for the wind was right. Waiting stopped being a chore.

Through the deeper drifts the leaders plowed on, following two men at the point. Across the bobbing hairy backs, Reilly saw four more men, one of them Horgan, behind the herd, pushing them on. He cocked his .44 Remington and waited.

They came on slowly, for the snow was deep and they were tired from being pushed hard. Reilly let the leaders pass him. Then, when the drag began to close in, he thrust his gun forward. Holding his gun wrist with the other hand to steady it, he shot a man cleanly from the saddle.

Someone yelled and whipped his head around quickly, and from the other side Milo Bucks' .45 Colt bellowed. The rider jackknifed from his horse and lay still.

146

Reilly saw Max Horgan then and flipped a shot at him, but Horgan whirled away and the bullet passed clear of him. Up ahead, the deep bass of Walt's Sharps woke echoes in the hills, and a horse screamed as it went down.

The cattle stopped and tried to mill, but the snow formed a chute on each side of them. The other rider with Horgan was shooting at anything he thought could conceal a man. Reilly followed him in his sights, then squeezed off. The .44 recoiled and the man dropped his gun, falling forward in the saddle and clutching a shattered arm.

Horgan and Milo Bucks were exchanging shots so Reilly shifted his aim, trying to get a good bead on the man. Horgan spurred his horse in circles to make a difficult target and Reilly shot twice more without effect.

Suddenly, Horgan had had enough. He drove his spurs to the horse and ran down the back trail. Milo fired a tardy shot after him but it missed. There was no further shooting from the point, so Reilly rose from his position. Cupping his hands around his mouth, he yelled, "Come on out! It's all over!"

Milo had trouble mounting his horse and when he worked his way down to the drag Reilly saw the bloody bandage Milo had fashioned out of his neckerchief. The bullet had passed through his thigh, for blood showed on both sides.

"That bad?" Reilly yelled.

"I'll live!" Milo shouted. "How the hell do we turn 'em in here?"

"From the other end!" Reilly said, and moved up the side hill again. They fought their way through the snow to the point and found Walt sitting his horse. A dead man lay in the snow, half out of sight.

Turning a herd in this closed place wouldn't be easy. They removed their slickers, waving them and shouting to startle the leaders. For a few minutes there was only frantic milling. Then Reilly and Milo worked their way into the herd. Pressing incessantly, they began to turn the cattle, one by one. Within an hour the steers were moving back down the slash they had trampled in the snow.

Walt kept looking back until Reilly snapped, "Leave the bastards. They paid for what they got."

147

At noon the snowing stopped and Reilly felt easier. He ached all over and his eyes burned continually from lack of sleep. Milo rode hunched over in the saddle. His leg bothered him, but he said nothing about it.

They pushed on, covering ten more miles before nightfall, leaving the canyon trail, angling up the windblown side hills. The steepness made rough going, which was in turn canceled out by the lightness of the snow.

At nightfall the herd entered a wide burn area. Reilly began to bed them down, circling the herd until they milled at a slow walk, then stopped altogether.

Walt Slaughter slumped in the saddle, bone weary and troubled in mind. Milo tilted his chin to his chest when he stopped, and sat his horse without moving. Reilly came up and said, "Stay here, Walt. Build a fire. I'm going in to the logging camp with Milo. He's been hit."

"Hit?" Walt's head came up slowly. "Hell, I didn't know that."

"I'll be back in the morning," Reilly said.

He led Milo's horse from there on, letting the young man cling to the saddlehorn with both hands. Milo rode with his leg dangling and the cold had made the bleeding stop.

For three hours Reilly kept working his way deeper into the timber, guided by a natural sense of direction that never seemed to leave him. Near midnight he raised the first lights of the logging camp.

Reilly dipped off the last downcast slope, moving around bare stumps upthrust through the snow. He pulled his gun to fire it as a signal, but then remembered that he had never reloaded it. Putting it away, he moved across the flats, past the log stack and tailing pile, and dismounted wearily by the cook shack.

Milo could barely stand when Reilly lifted him off the horse and staggered with him into the cook shack. The spindly cook dropped a magazine and stared goggle-eyed when they came in. Reilly's face bristled with stiff whiskers and his eyes burned deep in their sockets.

"Get Monaghan," Reilly said, and hoisted Milo to a table close to the stove. He stripped off Milo's coat to get the heat to him and was heating water when Monaghan came storming in, his suspenders dangling.

Monaghan's caulked boots plucked up small tufts of

pine, leaving clear indented tracks on the floor behind him. He looked at Milo, pale and drawn on the table.

"You got your cattle, I see."

"I've got a hurt boy here," Reilly said, and leaned his hands on the table edge because he felt weak.

"Get some coffee in you, man." Monaghan ripped open Milo's pant leg. He made a hasty inspection, clucking his tongue against the roof of his mouth. "He's lost blood, but there's no broken bones. I hate 'em. A man has to suffer so."

Reilly turned from the stove, a steaming mug in his hand. He went to the table and lifted Milo. Milo drank weakly, then lay back again.

"Where's the cattle?" Monaghan asked. "And the other man?"

"He's with 'em," Reilly said. "I didn't want to leave him alone."

"Go on back, man," Monaghan said. "We'll take care of the lad and send him along when he's better." He saw Reilly waver and gave him a slight shove. "Get along with you now. No man can fight it all by himself." Monaghan grinned. "Faith, how could I turn down another fine Irishman named Reilly?"

Reilly nodded and put his hand on Monaghan's shoulder, then went outside to his horse. The tired gelding wanted to go to the leanto and eat hay, but Reilly pulled him around and rode back toward the burn.

He traveled faster this time, for he could rest when he got there. Within two hours he saw the feeble cell of light that was Walt Slaughter's fire. Walt was sitting up, a blanket over his shoulders, and he did not hear Reilly approach until firelight touched the legs and chest of Reilly's horse.

Walt raised the Sharps suddenly, then let it sag. Reilly dismounted and hobbled the gelding, then came near the fire, spreading his hands to warm them. He had knotted his neckerchief over his hat, folding it down around his ears like a bonnet. Now he took the neckerchief off and cupped his hands to his ears, inducing warmth.

"The storm's breaking," he said. "Everything all right here?"

"It's all right," Walt said.

149

"We'll stay here tomorrow," Reilly said. "Move out the day after." He blew out his breath and watched it plume white. "Better turn in, Walt. I'll stay up."

Walt spread his slicker to lie on. He rolled up in his blankets and did not stir. Reilly sat there, staring at the fire until it died out to faint coals. A chilly dawn came on, and with it, the crimson edge of the winter sun.

The sight of it made him feel a lot better.

Reilly did not hurry on the way back and ten days passed before he halted on the flats on Buckeye's outskirts. He left Walt Slaughter to hold the herd there, and rode into town. He had done a lot of thinking during those ten days, for a good deal had happened to change a man. With Ernie dead, things would not be the same again. He had been a part of Reilly's life, abiding in that warm spot which a man reserves for only the closest of friends.

He had the wild bunch on the run now but the fact gave him no satisfaction. He lacked the instincts of a man-hunter. He was tired enough now to look at himself with some objectivity, and he realized that the wild bunch never had been his problem. Even if he wiped them out the problem would still exist, for he carried it with him.

Nor could he convince himself that Sally had created his discontent. He had become too honest for that. Because he wanted flame and tumult in a woman, he had sold his own integrity and it still left him dissatisfied. She was not complete. A part of her was selfish and mean, too selfish ever to know the pleasure of giving.

Reilly stopped and dismounted and stood thinking. That was the trouble. Because Sally never gave, but only took, he had formed himself the same way, trying to match her, trying to establish some semblance of compatability where none could exist.

Reilly tied his horse and stepped to the boardwalk. He had wanted her and had pushed and twisted things to conform to his desires. He blamed her for letting him but then, she was the kind who took pleasure in watching a man destroy himself for her. This fed some starved sinkhole in her soul.

Reilly entered the hotel and went up the stairs. He walked down the long hall and paused by Tess Isham's door, hearing the ring of arguing voices from within.

150

He opened the door without knocking and the voices chopped off suddenly. Tess and Sally turned and looked at him, and then Sally hurried across the room and threw her arms around him.

She kissed him longingly, holding him tight, but he stood there stiffly, a man disinterested. His eyes went past Sally's face and locked with Tess Isham's.

Realizing that she was embracing stone, Sally released him and stepped back. Reilly said, "Somehow, it didn't work, did it?"

"Oh, Reilly," she said, and put her hands against him. "I've been frantic with worry."

"About me?" He smiled. "Sally, you don't lie worth a damn."

"I'm not lying," she said. "Reilly, I love you more than anything in the world."

"More than yourself? Where's your husband?"

"At home," she said. "He brought a woman with him. Jane Alford." She moved close again and pleaded, "Reilly, can you ever forget how we once were?"

"I've already forgotten it," he said, and looked past her to Tess. She stood with her hands at her sides, not taking her eyes from his face. There was a hope there, an expectancy that had always been missing before. She looked as though she had stopped breathing, so still did she stand.

"Reilly!" Sally said. "You can't mean that!"

"I do mean it," he said. "You'd be no good for any man, not for long anyway. There's more to being married than sleepin' with a woman. There should be room for other things in a man's mind besides worryin' whether his wife will behave herself when he leaves the house. I'd have to keep you locked up, Sally, and frankly, you ain't worth it."

"How—how dare you speak to me like that?"

"It's easy," Reilly said without malice. "I've suddenly found out that I wouldn't want you, not at any price."

She tried to slap him then but he caught her arm and pushed her aside. "Go on, Sally. Go on now."

She stared at him and saw nothing to give her hope. Then she hardened. She went to the door, and she paused to speak over her shoulder. "Reilly, this is going to cost you more than you can afford to pay."

151

"It isn't going to cost me anything," Reilly said, and watched her close the door. Her footsteps receded rapidly down the hall and he let out a long breath.

Tess Isham still remained motionless and he faced her, a great gentleness in his eyes. "Sometimes a man don't know what love is, girl. He thinks a lot of foolish things and makes believe that he's in love, but it isn't the feeling I have for you." He laughed softly. "The strange part is that I've always had that feelin' for you, Tess. It was always a restin' feelin' when I was with you. I guess that's why I always come to you when I'm troubled in the mind."

He made a fan-like motion with his hands.

"A man's mistakes can be pretty big. I've made 'em. You know what they are without me tellin' you. The times I've hurt you have been plenty and I guess the hurt's too deep to wipe out, but if I had it to do over again, we'd sure been married years ago."

When he turned to the door, she found her voice and spoke his name. He turned back to her and found that she was crying, the tears moving down her cheeks in tiny rivulets. "I'm not a fancy woman," she said. "Maybe I'm not enough woman, like she says, but I'd be good to you, Reilly, because I've loved you for such a very long time."

He did not touch her; there was no need now. They looked at each other and the bond was there. No power could ever break it. "I've got some work cut out for me," he said. "I'll be back."

"I don't mind waiting," she said, and he went out, closing the door quietly behind him. There was no hurry now and he stopped at the head of the stairs to thumb cartridges out of his gun and reload it.

He went down into the lobby. At the desk he said, "Have you seen Harry Peters?"

"At the New Congress," the clerk said; and Reilly went out. He reached the edge of the porch and saw Jane Alford running toward him. She stumbled in her haste to mount the steps.

Her hair hung loosely and her breath came in short gusts. "Reilly, I'm glad I found you!"

"Are you?" He was remembering Ernie Slaughter by the corral the night she went away with Burk Seever and he could not keep it out of his voice.

"I don't blame you for hating me," Jane said, "but you've got to listen to me."

"I don't hate you. I just don't understand you, Jane."

She pressed her hands against her cheeks and tears welled up in her eyes. "You think I'm not thinking of him? I loved him so much that it killed me inside when he died."

"Then why did you leave him, Jane?"

"I had no choice," Jane said. "I wish to God I'd told Ernie, but Winehaven and that squaw he lives with over by the slaughter house have my baby." She looked quickly up and down the street. "Burk's always held that over my head, threatening to take him away if I didn't do what he said."

"What baby?" Reilly asked. "I never heard about it."

"I made a mistake. Before we moved here. My mother—we left after he was born and came here. She met Winehaven and married him, but it didn't work out. Reilly, I thought I could get a new start with Ernie, but then ma died. Winehaven said I couldn't have the boy back." She smiled feebly. "He's seven now, Reilly, and I want him back. He's all I got left."

"We'll get him for you," Reilly said. "I'll tell Peters and he'll get him."

"No!" Jane snapped. "No, don't tell him." Her voice became thin and defeated. "I'll never see him again, I know that. What I'm telling you now will fix everything, but that's all right. Maybe it'll pay some back for the way I've hurt Ernie."

"You're not making sense," he said. A man came out of the hotel then and they stood awkwardly until he moved out of earshot.

"Winehaven used me, Reilly. I didn't want anything to happen to the baby, so I went to the Agency like he wanted me to. After—after I had something on the Indian agent, Winehaven told me to get out and got me a job in Burkhauser's. Burk and Henderson were in this for the money, Reilly. So was Winehaven and—" She took his arms and tried to shake him. "Reilly, do you remember what you saw at Winehaven's that day of the shooting? Remember it, Reilly, because I don't want to tell you."

For a reason he couldn't explain, he saw a sorrel horse

153

with a blaze. Suddenly he said, "I saw Harry Peters' sorrel there." He wondered where the statement came from, but he knew it was true. "Harry Peters!" he said.

"He killed Henderson. You didn't know that, did you?" Jane was frantic. "I got away from Burk. He's after you, Reilly, and he has a gun now. Max Horgan's with him and they mean to kill you."

Reilly acted as though he hadn't heard her. "Harry Peters," he repeated, and remembered a lot of small things: The way Peters acted, the way he talked, the things he didn't do and the pat excuses he had for doing the things he did. Somehow it all fell into place and he recalled clearly the thing that had teetered on the edge of his mind the last time he talked to Peters. Indian Jim had said he was half smart, figuring out how the brands had been changed—and he had mentioned that only to Harry Peters.

He said, "Is Horgan in town now?"

"He must be," Jane said. "Burk locked me in the upstairs room, but I climbed out the window and jumped down on the trellis."

"Go up to Tess Isham's hotel room," Reilly said gently, giving her a small push. "Everything's going to turn out all right, Jane."

"Nothing will ever be right with Ernie Slaughter dead," she said, and went inside.

Reilly remained on the porch a moment longer, listening to the whine of the wind as it husked down the street. He took off his heavy coat to give his arms more freedom and stepped to the boardwalk.

He walked carefully. He had no idea where Horgan or Seever would be waiting; he only knew they would wait. There was no traffic at all on the street and the town reminded him of deserted places he had seen in the lode country. Just buildings with the wind echoing against them.

Clinging to the buildings, Reilly searched every doorway, every gap that could hold a man with a gun. A door banged somewhere in the alley and he jumped, ready to draw his gun and start shooting.

He stopped and got a grip on himself.

Down the street and across from him, Ben Cannoyer's old stable reared up in the middle of a large lot, one door banging listlessly in the wind. From the far edge of town, the brown-and white Hereford herd grazed while Walt Slaughter walked his horse around them.

All this seemed very far away to Reilly.

He halted when a man started to come out of a small store next to the stable. The man paused in the doorway, then went back inside. This rang a warning bell in Reilly's mind. There was no reason for the man's hasty retreat.

He had been walking slowly, casually, with nothing in his manner to tip off impending trouble, yet the man knew it was coming. Reilly focused his attention on the doorway of the store, and then Max Horgan came out and stood on the boardwalk.

"Well, Reilly," he said. "One by one you've got all of us."

"But not you, Max," Reilly said, just loud enough to carry across the street. Twenty yards separated them and dust rose in swirls, pelting the raw board buildings.

"Man to man," Horgan said, his voice wind-whipped. "That's how it'll be between us, Reilly."

The man's talking too much, Reilly thought, and from the corner of his eye he picked up a slight movement in the door of the vacant stable. In that second he saw clearly what a sucker he had been, for the stable was seventy yards away and Burk Seever had a rifle.

He drew on Horgan then, and although he slapped leather first, Max Horgan matched him. Reilly cocked on the upswing and let the hammer slide from under his thumb as the gun came level. The sudden pop vanished in the wind and then Horgan's bullet chipped wood by Reilly's shoulder. Horgan's knees bent slowly, like melting wax. His gun went off again as he sprawled in the gutter.

A gun went off from a distance, but Reilly was moving and the rifle bullet tore through a window, bringing it down in a tinny sounding shower. On one knee, Reilly raised his gun and braced his arm against the tie rail. He fired as Burk Seever frantically worked the lever for another shot.

The shot took the big man high somewhere. He spun half around, but braced himself on his legs and tried to raise his rifle. Reilly cocked the Remington and waited, held by a force he couldn't resist. He saw Seever's gun come to the shoulder and still he held off.

Burk fired again, but he was falling. The bullet spanged in the dust and Burk Seever lay across the rifle, his legs working, trying to get back on his feet. He made it to his hands and knees once, but fell flat again.

Reilly stood up slowly and put his gun away. Seever had quit moving.

The wind must have carried the sound of shooting to Walt Slaughter, for he left the herd and rode toward town at a fast clip. Reilly stood at the boardwalk's edge, waiting for him. When Walt came off his horse, Reilly said, "There's one more. Harry Peters."

"Peters?" Walt couldn't believe it.

From the other end of town a party of horsemen came on at a trot. When they breached the far end of the street, Reilly recognized Jim Buttelow and Al Murdock in the lead. Paul Childress brought up the rear, a small boy riding the saddle with him. Winehaven rode a horse between them and Al Murdock held the lead rope which was looped around Winehaven's neck.

They saw Reilly and Walt and came on, pulling in at the hitch-rail to dismount. They made a tough looking bunch, all with a week's growth of whiskers and gaunt from much riding. Reilly stared at the boy, who regarded him with round eyes.

Buttelow saw the two men lying in the dust. "This is the last of 'em," he said, and the wind stirred their clothes and a gust whisked Horgan's fallen hat down the street, bouncing it along the boardwalk.

"What happened?" Reilly asked.

"Winehaven's up in smoke," Buttelow said. "Swan Lovelock and his crew are rounding up what beef's left. Everything's cleaned out."

"Not quite," Reilly said, and he moved through them, going toward the New Congress hotel on the side street.

The men frowned at each other, puzzled, but they turned as one man, still leading Winehaven, and followed him. Walt reached out and took the boy away from Childress. "I'll take care of him," Walt said.

The boy put his arms around Walt's neck, and over the tall man's face there passed an expression that was almost relief.

CHAPTER 12

The shooting had brought a crowd to the street. Reilly walked past them, paying no attention at all. At the corner he stopped to watch a man who was standing on the narrow hotel porch.

Puffing his cigar with seeming contentment, the man turned his head slowly. He looked at Reilly Meyers, and at the hard-faced group behind him, and went on puffing.

Reilly came on, halting on the boardwalk three steps below Harry Peters. The little man took the cigar from his mouth and glanced at the ash. "I heard shooting," he said.

"Max and Burk had to have a last try," Reilly said. "They didn't make it, Harry."

"I didn't think they would," Peters said, and put the cigar back in his mouth. He hunched his shoulders and swayed slightly as the wind hit him. "Winter's here. Likely to bring snow to the flats in another week."

Buttelow didn't understand this. Neither did Childress. He said, "We've got a man here for you," and shoved Winehaven forward a pace.

Harry Peters glanced at Winehaven and his face was inscrutable.

Reilly said, "He don't want him, Paul."

"What?" Childress said. "Hell, he's the—"

"Later," Reilly said, not taking his gaze off Peters.

The dapper little man took a couple of long pulls on his cigar, then spun it into the street. The wind caught it and rolled it along, sparks flying in a brief shower. He looked at Reilly. "You think you have something?"

"I've got enough," Reilly said. "She's all over, Harry. Let's not have any trouble now."

"What the hell—" Childress began, but Buttelow silenced him with a brief pressure of his hands.

"Your friends don't seem to agree with you," Peters said, and a smile appeared beneath his mustache.

"They don't know about it yet," Reilly said. "I remember what I saw that day at Winehaven's, Harry. You sold your sorrel to Horgan afterward, hoping that I would connect the fact that he was there with the horse being there. Were you inside hiding, Harry?"

"That's pretty thin," Peters said. "You'll have to do better, Reilly. Remember, it's evidence that convicts a man, not loose guessing."

"That's your song and I guess you can't sing any other," Reilly said. "All right, Harry. I've got the evidence." He grabbed Winehaven and pulled him forward. "He's going to talk, Harry."

"I see," Peters said. He pursed his lips. "What do you want me to do, Reilly?"

"You're under arrest," Reilly told him. "There's been enough killin' on this range to last a long time. I expect you'd better come along without any fuss."

"I suppose I'd better," Peters said mildly. He fished a match from his vest pocket, and then he reached again, with a completely natural movement, inside his coat toward the pocket which contained his ever-present cigars.

Reilly Meyers caught the blued surface of Harry Peters' .38 as it came free of the coat. He made a dive for the man's legs as the gun went off. The report almost deafened him and powder stung his neck. Winehaven cried out as the bullet struck his hip, and then Reilly hit Peters, tumbling him to the porch.

Reilly outweighed Peters by fifteen pounds, but the little man's wiry strength amazed him. Knocking the gun hand aside, Reilly tried to hit Peters along the shelf of the jaw, but Peters jerked his head aside and took the blow on the neck.

Reilly kept flailing out with his left hand, trying to get a grip on Peters' wrist. The gun went off again and the bullet ripped into the porch ceiling. Then Reilly kneed the marshal and felt him relax for an instant.

158

His hand closed over the cylinder and frame and he hung on. Peters tried to pull the trigger double action, but Reilly had the cylinder locked and Peters couldn't cock the gun. He beat at Reilly's face with his free hand and Reilly kicked out with his elbow, catching Peters in the mouth.

By twisting on the gun, Reilly bent it against Peters' finger, still curled in the trigger guard. The little man's face turned white and he cried out. Reilly got off him then and came erect, holding Harry Peters' gun in his hand.

He backed away a step and watched Peters nurse his tortured fingers. Winehaven squirmed on the ground, clutching his hip, and blood welled up from between his fingers. The crowd had come around the corner and all but blocked the street.

Reilly reached down and pulled Peters to his feet. He shoved Peters toward Jim Buttelow, who grabbed his arms and held him. "Better get a doctor for Winehaven," Reilly said, and Buttelow nodded. He released Peters, spoke roughly and pushed his way through the crowd, disappearing on the other side.

Peters stood without indication of further resistance and Paul Childress scrubbed a hand across his whiskered face. "Things has been happenin' pretty fast," he said vaguely.

"Yeah," Reilly admitted. "We got your steers back. Thought you'd like to know."

"It don't make a hell of a lot of difference," Childress said. "I was sick worried when Jim said you was trailin' Horgan."

Reilly looked sharply at the older man. "I never thought you gave a damn one way or another." He sighed and sat down on the porch steps, Peters' gun still reversed in his hand. "Seems like I've cleaned myself right in the hole. By spring my money'll be gone and I'll be wearin' through the seat of my pants, not able to buy a new pair." He tipped up his head and found Childress watching him.

"I've never asked you for a damn thing in my life, Paul, but I'm askin' you now. Could you see your way clear to loan me five hundred? There's lumber to buy and—"

"Boy," Childress said, and his voice had a frog in it. He sniffed and wiped the back of his hand across his nose. "Damn it, boy, you don't know how long I've been waitin' to be wanted. You always was so blamed independent. Never needin' a man's help." He dropped his head and stared at his feet a minute. "We'll get you set up again, son. Damn it, we'll set you up in fine style."

Buttelow came back through the crowd with the doctor and stayed behind to break the crowd up. His words were loud and braying and he got them moving. A few minutes later he came up to the hotel porch.

The doctor worked fast on Winehaven, securing a pack bandage to stop the bleeding. Buttelow stood behind Harry Peters like an angry dog just waiting for the opportunity to bite. He looked at Reilly and said, "There's a girl waitin' at the hotel, boy. You keep her in the dark much longer and she's liable to go crazy."

"All right," Reilly said. He started away. He turned back and said, "Take care of those—"

"Go on," Buttelow interrupted. "We know what to do."

Reilly nodded and walked on. When he turned the corner and saw Tess Isham on the porch down the street, his easy stride lengthened considerably.

She came off the porch to meet him, running into his arms. Two dozen people stood along both sides of the street, watching, but neither Reilly nor Tess noticed them.

"I'm flat," Reilly said. "Burned out. Busted. Can you take that, Tess?"

"I'd rather build my own future with you anyway," she said, and kissed him.

This came as a shock to Reilly, because it seemed like she'd been holding out on him when he kissed her before. Her mouth was fire and she hurt him with the intensity of her ardor. When they parted at last, Reilly said softly, "Well I'll be go to hell."

Tess Isham smiled. She understood what he meant. She liked the idea of being a woman of fire.

IRON MAN, IRON HORSE

CHAPTER ONE

Ben Holliday always started his day with a careful shave because he was a methodical man even in the smallest details of his day-to-day living. When the seven o'clock roundhouse whistle called the men to work, he was either wiping the blade of his razor or putting it in its case. Holliday was an angular man, nearly six feet tall, and a bit on the slender side, but a month of this dry summer air of North Texas had so improved his appetite that he expected this condition to change, and after each shave he examined his cheeks to see if there was any increase in fullness there. His face, at thirty-two, was beginning to show more of what he was; his manner of thinking was casting permanent lines on his forehead, pulling his rather thin lips into continually sterner lines until the general impression he gave upon first glance was that here was a man who did not laugh enough.

Holliday was a man seemingly overcome by his desire to do well.

Perhaps it was this honesty, this ambition, that made him a little bitter every time he walked a few steps from his quarters to his office and saw the name on the frosted glass of the door. It had a pomposity, a touch of sham, like a man who went around and bragged about his horse which was dying.

BENJAMIN C. HOLLIDAY
CHAIRMAN OF THE BOARD
MIDLAND-PACIFIC RAILROAD

He liked the office because it gave him an uninterrupted, second-story view of the empty cattle pens, and the idle switchyard, and the roundhouse, which was rap-

163

idly running out of work to do. He could also see the miles of track running south through the dry valley where the wind blew the weeds growing between the ties and rolled tumbleweeds and piled dust in windrows against the rails, now dull red with rust. Holliday felt that he should look at that every day, to remind him of what he had to do, to remind him that two men from before him had failed. One hundred and eighty miles of railroad going broke, and it was his job, his sole function, to get the rust off those rails.

It had been nearly six months since a train had gone south; his only knowledge of the country was what he could see from his window, the miles stretched out flat and lonely and baked under a constant sun. It was Indian country, and cattle country, with the only civilized mark upon it being the railroad tracks arcing out toward a blue haze-veiled rim of mountains nestled low against a far horizon.

In the other direction, northward, the roadbed swept past a yellow depot and freight shed, curved to miss the tawny adobe town, and pushed toward some low foothills ten miles away. Miles beyond, the rails joined at Dodge City, and every two days an engine pulled a mail car and one coach back and forth to fill the requirements of a mail contract.

This was, Holliday thought, a poor excuse for a railroad's being. In the beginning, Holliday's father had built the line on speculation, to have something to trade. From the beginning it fell in a puddle of red ink and stayed there. Morgansen had been sent out from Chicago to make it pay, and lasted six months. He was a genius, in his own way, but he couldn't beat the Indians, or the Texans, who figured it was better to have no railroad at all than to fight the Indians again.

The second man Holliday hadn't known at all; he'd heard that he had a background of politics, and he'd lasted four months, and the rails continued to gather rust.

All this drove home to Ben Holliday his own sense of

unimportance; he was neither a genius nor a politician, yet he was supposed to succeed where they had failed.

He opened his coat because he knew today would be as hot as yesterday; he hadn't known a genuinely cool day since he'd arrived. The tin roof didn't do anything to lessen the bake-oven heat either. On his desk were some letters that had come in on last night's train. He recognized his father's handwriting on one, and Ben Holliday knew without opening it what the gist of it would be. It would be full of advice, and questions, and more advice, and a reminder that there wouldn't be any salary until the line was paying its own way. His oldest brother, Lon, would probably enclose a note; he was always doing that, never writing a letter, just enclosing notes, as though any opinion he had was a fringe comment on what someone else had already said.

Adam, who was only a year older than Ben, had written, and this letter was quickly opened. A cashier's check for three hundred dollars fluttered to the desk, and Ben Holliday let it lie there.

He began to read.

Chicago, May 7, 1882

Dear Brother Ben:

A fantastic bit of luck here. That case I was working on was settled out of court, so I enclose a small check to tide you over until you get control of things. Before you get righteous and indignant, let me say that I now consider having paid you in full for that small book of addresses you left in my care. Your taste in femininity is exemplary; Alice is particularly delightful, and she misses you terribly. although I am doing my best to make her forget. I shall probably plunge beyond my financial capabilities in doing so, but I figure it will be worth it.

Brother Lon still puts in his ten hours a day; he's in charge of the Chicago office now and more like Father every day. I hope he succeeds; you know how badly he takes failure, and if he ever does, he's just the kind of silly ass who'd think it fitting to fall on his sword. The rooms in our family "museum" are as empty as ever; we need a woman here to liven it up, and I've been talking about it to Alice; I must either marry her or drop her before I go broke.

Conclude your business with the Texans as soon as possible and come home, Ben. Really, Friday night poker is not the same without you; I have yet to find another who so consistently loses to me. And stay away from the Indian squaws; I understand they are treacherous in matters of breach of promise.

Affectionately,
Adam

Ben Holliday chuckled and put this letter, and his father's, in his coat pocket, then stepped out of his office. The second floor contained the administrative staff of Midland-Pacific: the timekeeper and accountant shared one office, the freight superintendent and maintenance head another, with the chief telegrapher and the dispatcher together. Well, we'll all be out of a job soon, Holliday thought, and went down the back stairs, which opened into the equipment yard, with the cookshack on the other side. He made his way through mountains of railroad ties and stacked rails and rolls of telegraph wire.

By rule of thumb, he figured Midland-Pacific had about thirty or forty days of life left before the money ran out. After that, it was either pull up the rails or run a train over them and make it pay.

A triphammer banged away in the round house, and he could hear the steam donkey huffing away, and smell the hot metal from the foundry; the sounds were busy, prosperous sounds, full of industry, and he hated to think of it just stopping.

He went into the cookshack and sat at a table near the door, where he could smell the bacon frying and the pitch odor from the tie piles. He ate his breakfast and looked out the door at the rolling stock idle on the yard sidings.

Two good engines there, both coal burners, young, full of power, and nowhere to go.

This was the point of thinking he always came back to, that urge to get up steam, give the whistle cord one long pull, and roll out, heading south. That stretch of rusting track beckoned him like the invitation in a women's eyes, almost beyond resistance.

While he was having his coffee, Ollie Skinner came in, his battered hat respectfully held in his hands. Skinner was fifty some, dry humored, as sun-cooked as the land, and as shiftless as the wind that never quite seemed to stop blowing. "Mr. Holliday," he said, "I found you a couple of fellas who want to see a horse and buggy."

"How much?" Ben asked.

"Sixty dollars," Ollie Skinner said. He had a slow Texas drawl in his voice, and his skin was like a piece of old leather that had lain in the sun too long. This was his second year with the railroad, but he wasn't a company man and never would be, for he was a Texan and his thinking was pretty well defined, his opinions already established. Holliday felt a little irritated by Skinner's manner; the man seemed to work for the pay, with no loyalty or feeling, and Holliday always felt that behind Skinner's wrinkled face there was a joke somewhere, and not on himself.

"All right," Ben said, rising. "Where are they?"

'By the depot."

Holliday frowned. "Couldn't they come here?"

"A man learns to stay in his place," Skinner said, and went out.

The depot and freight shed sat alone, halfway between the town and the railroad yard, like some unwanted relative. Across the tracks, rows of identical yellow houses were crowded together, railroad owned, built for railroad employees. The houses weren't much, Holliday knew, just three rooms, slab siding, sheet-iron roofs, and cinders for a yard. They needed paint now; this climate was hard on any finish. But there was no money to spare for painting. Although he had never been there, he knew how poor their living standard was; he could see the people from his office window, and hear them on a still day, the children yelling, the women yelling in Polish and German and Italian.

By comparison, the town looked good, and it wasn't much, just a wide dirt street with manure piles attracting flies, and adobe buildings crammed close together, and a few trees carefully tended so that they grew to shady usefulness. It was a rough town in a rough land, quick to spring up and built to do, and that was all.

Do for Texans, Holliday thought, as he approached the depot. It would never do for me.

The two men sat in the shade, and they stood up when Skinner and Holliday approached. The horse and buggy were standing to one side. "Thet's a purty good rig," one of the Texans said. He had a hound-lean face and his jaws worked rhythmically on his chew of tobacco. He stood with his hands tucked into the waistband of his jeans, which rode very low on his hips; Holliday expected them to slip off any minute. Both Texans carried revolvers; Holliday felt this was more from custom than necessity, and he eyed them with a certain suspicion because of it.

"A good head," the other said. He glanced at his partner and jabbed him in the ribs with an elbow. "Ain't you got nothin' to say, Satchel? Brag him up a little."

"Heeheehee, well, mister, he's lively, I reckon."

Holliday looked the buggy over; it seemed sound, although well used. Then he walked around and looked at the horse, a lithe, walleyed brute that kept rearing his head and rolling his eyes.

Satchel said, "He's just nervous aroun' stranger, mister."

"He does seem to have spirit," Ben said.

Satchel's crackling laugh seemed almost uncontrollable. "You're a good judge of horseflesh there, mister. Heeheeheeheeheeheehee!"

168

Holliday looked at Ollie Skinner. "What do you think?" think?"

"I just brung you here." He took hold of the buggy wheel and gave it a shake. "Seems solid enough. Worth sixty dollars."

The horse was unusually active, stamping his feet, throwing his head, and either trying to back up or go forward a little. "We wouldn't be sellin' him," Satchel said, "except that we need the money. Sixty's our bottom price, friend. Take it or leave it."

"Well," Ben said, with some hesitation. "I've got a have a horse and buggy." He reached into his vest pocket and counted out six ten-dollar gold pieces. "Give the bill of sale to Skinner." He stepped into the rig and picked up the reins. "Whoa there! Whoa now!"

"He jest needs a bit of exercise," Satchel said smiling. Then he jabbed his friend in the ribs and winked at Ollie Skinner. He picked the revolver from his holster, pointed it straight up, and triggered it.

Ben Holliday, sitting there trying to quiet the horse, thought that the animal had gone from a dead standstill to a dead run in one jump. His feet flew straight out and up and he almost cascaded over the seat. By the time he regained some position of security, the horse was going over the tracks, the buggy flailing along behind like a string-held stick dragged behind a running boy. One of the rear wheels shed its spokes on the rails, and Ben saw the iron-shod rim roll crazily by, and this frightened the horse to renewed frenzy.

They tore wildly through the first row of shacks and the buggy slewed around, the tail end clipping an outhouse with enough force to topple it. Women and children were running out of the shacks and waving, and this didn't improve the horse's disposition.

Holliday was shouting and tugging at the reins and trying to slow the animal, but it was useless. Even the hub with splintered spokes gouging out a trail failed to slow him.

Ahead of him, between two buildings, a slender blond woman was busily washing clothes; she had them strung on a line and turned to see the rig bearing down on her.

"Get out of the way!" Ben yelled, then he was plowing through. The near front wheel struck the washtub and sent it spinning like a big wooden bowl, the water pinwheeling out of it. Then the horse caught the clothesline and the flapping sheets and shirts and underwear drove him completely mad.

Leaving the yard and a swatch of litter, Holliday only hoped that the woman had escaped being trampled; his memory was only of her sprawling, dress flying, then her rolling on the ground.

Ahead of him lay a wash, and the horse took the jump down, but he knew the buggy wasn't going to make it. He felt it hit, the axle fracture, both wheels collapse, and knew the buggy was not going to land right side up. So he left it, pushing with his legs to get clear and trusting to luck for the rest. He hit the dirt and felt the wind jar out of him, then he rolled five or six times and ended in a sitting position in eight inches of muddy water.

The horse kept on going and Ben Holliday didn't give a damn now. He got up slowly, expecting broken bones, but there didn't seem to be any. His only thought was for the woman, and he knew she must be dead or severely trampled.

Quickly he crawled out of the wash and ran back toward the gathering crowd of noisy women and children, picking up clothes and bed sheets that he had been whipped off the line by the horse's speed. They were torn and dirty, and he had quite an armful by the time he got there. The people were so tightly packed that he could not find a way through, then he started to pull at them, saying, "Pardon me. Please let me through. Let me through, will you?"

Not many understood his words, and they all began to shout at once, and without knowing a word of their respective languages, he was certain they were not compli-

170

menting him on his driving skill. Then he saw the blond woman, dirty from being thrown to the ground, and water-soaked from the wheeling tub. She began to push at the people gathered there, driving them away, back to their own homes. And Ben Holliday was relieved, because he hated a public row, and this one was going to be a good one.

He stood there, her ruined laundry in his arms. His coat was completely split up the back seam, and both knees protruded from gaping rents, and he couldn't have got any more mud on him if he'd shared a sow's wallow.

"Du bist ein Esel!" the girl shouted. Her anger was as intense as any he had ever seen. Her hair was in disarray and her white blouse was ripped, exposing a shoulder that was delightfully smooth and rounded. Still he expected her to see that this had been an accident; there was no call for her to be so angry, and he just knew that she'd sworn at him.

"What was that you said? What did you call me?"

"I called you an ass! A donkey!" Then she snatched the clothes from him, looked at them in horror, and threw them on the ground. Immediately she burst into tears "Oh, just look at what you've done! Just look at my clothes, my tub!"

"Well you don't have to bawl about it," he said. "I'll buy you a new tub. Look at my wrecked buggy!" He had his hands on his hips now, and his voice rose in volume. She was rather tall, he noticed, a slender, shapely girl with good bones and a real temper. He had never seen eyes so full of fire.

"I'll cry if I want!" Tears rolled down her cheeks, into the dirt streaks there, and she turned and kicked at the clothes and he knew that she pretended she was kicking him. Then she went loose and sat down on the clothes and let her head tip forward, her sobbing shaking her shoulders.

He felt a strong compassion for her and bent and put his hand on her arm. She bit him suddenly, bit him hard,

171

and he yelped and snatched his hand back and looked at the row of even teeth marks.

"Why, you damned wildcat!" He felt his temper flare like a sudden fire. "I ought to paddle you where it'll do the most good!" And to show her that he wasn't fooling, he took off his ruined coat and threw it to one side.

She sprang to her feet and faced him, her face inches from his. "You touch me and I'll make you sorry, you *dummkopf! Warum bist du so dumm?*" She pointed back toward the depot. "Get out!"

"Won't you let me explain? The horse ran away!"

She struck him with the heels of her hands, holding her arms stiff, and he retreated a step. "Go on, get out!" She rammed him again. "Do you hear what I say?" Then she dropped her arms loosely and looked at the clothes as though she couldn't yet believe it.

"I'm sorry," he said.

"Just leave me alone," she said, almost begging him.

He hated to leave, with her blaming him. But what did he really expect after turning order into a shambles? He looked around and saw the Texans standing across the tracks, taking it all in; they thought it was a big joke. Ben said, "Can't I come back later when you're feeling better? We can talk about it then."

"I don't want you to come back," she said. Then she looked at him and he was surprised to find her no longer angry. It seemed that she was more defeated now, and this state of mind alarmed him. "Each time I wash, I tell myself, now Anna, you be careful and not rub too hard and make the clothes last longer. They were the last of my mother's sheets that I brought here from Germany. The last thing of hers that I had left. Now they're gone." She studied him as though puzzled. "Why do you stand there and look at me? Do you like to see me cry?

"No," Ben said. "And it would please me if you never had to cry again." Then he quickly turned and walked across the tracks to where the crowd of Texans stood.

Ollie Skinner was there, his wrinkled face bland and unreadable.

"That hoss could sure run, couldn't it, Mr. Holliday?"

He looked intently at Skinner and resisted the impulse to hit him. "Where did Satchel and his friend go with my money?"

"A man shouldn't go back on a deal once he's made it," Skinner pointed out, but then saw that this advice fell on deaf ears. "In the saloon, I reckon. The story will be worth tellin'." He glanced at the good citizens from town, then at Holliday. "You got somethin' on your mind, Mr. Holliday?"

Skinner's amusement solidified Holliday's resolve. He said. "Come along and see, and afterward pick up your money from the timekeeper. You're fired!"

He left Skinner standing there with a slack jaw and walked toward the head of Comanche's single street. The sun bounced off the adobe walls and shade lay dark and inviting beneath the store overhangs. From the saloon halfway down the street, Holliday could hear the foot stamping and thigh slapping and a whinny of laughter that sounded familiar.

As Holliday passed the marshal's office, the door swung wide and Jim Bender stepped out. He was a tall, blunt-faced man, as tough as a horseshoe and about as flexible in his ways. He wore a white shirt and trousers tucked into his boots and a well-oiled, bone-handled pistol in a cross-draw holster.

He cuffed his hat to the back of his head and said, "Mr. Holliday, I can't recall ever seein' you look more determined." His glance traveled back down the street to the group of townspeople who had stopped. "They had their joke, so why don't you let it go at that?"

"Would you? Ben asked.

"No," Bender said. "But we're different."

"Tell me how different?" He looked at Bender and waited.

The marshal's young face grew serious. "Well then, if

173

you've got your hackles up, I'd better go along to keep it fair."

"Fair for them, or for me?"

A hard tone came into Bender's soft voice. "Friend, that word only has one meaning for me. Be well if you'd learn that."

"So far I haven't seen anything to show me," Ben Holliday said.

He walked on to the saloon, and Jim Bender watched him and waited for the crowd to come along. He held out his hand and it stopped, eyeing him curiously.

"I want Holliday to have all the room he wants," Bender said. "Don't make me repeat that."

One of the Texans scowled. "Say, are you a railroad man now, Jim?"

"I've spent my life being for nothing," Bender said. "Now don't anyone go and mix me up." He stepped to the street, taking Holliday's route to the saloon.

As Ben mounted the porch, he heard the crackling laugh, "Heeheeheeheeheehee you should have seen him thar, arms 'n' legs a-flyin', and yellin', 'Whoa!' as loud as he could. Heeheeheeheeheehee, that hoss hadn't heard whoa in his life."

A gale of laughter and bar slapping followed, and Ben Holliday got as far as the poker tables before anyone noticed him. Then a hush came over them and Holliday picked up a straight-backed chair, crashed it to kindling on a table, then sorted through the pieces for one that suited him. He selected a leg, a round, heavy piece of ash and stepped toward Satchel and his friend.

The others faded back to make room, and Satchel said, "Now you ain't got yourself all riled up, have you?"

"No," Ben Holliday said. "But it's my turn now. Suppose you put the sixty dollars on the bar."

Jim Bender stepped through the door and stood just inside, his arms crossed nonchalantly. Satchel looked like a man who didn't know whether to laugh or swear. Finally he said, "Aw now, you're sore. That's too bad. The next thing you'll be wantin' to fight."

"Put the money on the bar."

Satchel smiled, then shook his head, and Ben Holliday hit him across the jaw hinge with the chair leg, and it cracked like a snapped twig. Satchel whipped into the bar and sagged like a sun-wilted flower and he lay with his head against the brass footrail.

His friend looked at him and said, "That was sudden, warn't it?"

"Where's the money?" Holliday asked.

"I ain't—he's got it."

"Then take it out of his pocket," Ben said. He stood there while this was being done. then he threw the chair leg away. "How do you feel about this, horse trader? Do you want to make another joke?"

"Naw, I've had enough laughin' fer one day," he said. "Too hot to fight too. Could I buy you a drink?"

Ben Holliday looked at him and thought that here was a man with more brass than he knew what to do with, and he was on the verge of telling him to go to the devil when Jim Bender eased up quietly and put his hand on Ben's shoulder.

"Sure," Bender said. "Why not?" His fingers forced down hard, and Holliday knew enough not to object. Bender's dark eyes were smiling, yet there was a caution there, directed at Holliday. "You're not going to carry a grudge now, are you, Mr. Holliday?"

"No," Ben said. "Like he says, it's too hot."

The bartender filled the glasses and Ben tossed his off, and it was filled again. "Let's go sit down," Bender suggested and they went to a corner table. He took off his hat and ran his fingers through his dark hair. The bartender was upending a bucket of water on Satchel and two men pulled him to his feet while a third stuck the neck of a whisky bottle between his lips. Ben Holliday observed this, and Bender said, "Disappointed, Mr. Holliday?"

"What do you mean?"

"Well, there isn't much satisfaction in just whacking a man once. Anyway, it was Satchel's idea to sell you the horse, and he got the crack on the head. Too bad you can't solve all your problems that easy."

"Are you any good as a marshal?" Ben Holliday asked.

Bender pursed his lips. "It's a sideline with me, when you come right down to it. If the railroad can use a good man who knows Indians, can figure a Texan eighty per cent of the time, and duck the other twenty, I'm available."

"If you're serious, maybe something can be done," Ben said. "I'll know more in a day or so."

"You mean, when your accountant comes back?"

Holliday did not bother to hide his surprise. "You know about it? How?"

"Saw him pumpin' the handcar south," Jim Bender said. He came forward in his chair and put his arms flat on the table. "I'd say he went to make peace with the Texans. Right?"

"Not peace exactly," Ben said. "The railroad is asking favors."

"From the Texans?"

"We're giving something in return. Marshal, when Harry Lovell comes back, I'll invite you to the meeting. Until then, I'll be happy to know where I can get a dozen linen bed sheets."

"Sheets?" Bender frowned, as though this were a joke he hadn't heard. "Not in Comanche, Mr. Holliday. We're still sleeping on shucks around here. The railroad ain't quite brought civilization here yet." He grinned. "Ain't that your stock in trade? Your main-line stump speech? Call it 'land grab' if you want, but we bring churches and schools?" He chuckled. "Drink up, Mr. Holliday; it's a rough world and this puts a rosy tint to it."

CHAPTER TWO

Ben Holliday returned to his quarters and stripped to the waist to wash away the grime, then realized the hopelessness of it and fetched the tub and took a bath. He was dressing when Ollie Skinner timidly knocked on the door, then came in. Holliday was before the mirror, tying his tie. He said, "The timekeeper's office is three doors down, on the right."

"I just came to say that you left your money on the bar." He held it out as though he wasn't sure whether Holliday would take it or not, and when Ben went on knotting his tie, Skinner edged into the room and laid it on the dresser. Then he stood there, rocking back and forth on his run-over heels. "You wasn't serious about firin' me, was you, Mr. Holliday?"

"Did I act like I was fooling?"

"Well no, which is what bothers me," Skinner admitted.

"You're a fool, Skinner," Holliday said. "How long do you think I'll put up with your games?" He turned to his writing desk and sat down, drawing paper and pencil to him. He ignored Skinner when he wrote.

Chief Telegrapher - Midland - Pacific - Dodge City on night train one dozen linen bed sheets . . . Have wife pick out six dresses, light colors, to fit slender woman, about five-six tall . . . Include unmentionables with lace, etc. . . . If you mention this to my father you're fired.

Ben Holliday

He pushed back his chair, folded the message, and started to put it in his pocket. Ollie Skinner said, "I could drop that off for you before I check out, Mr. Holliday. Be no trouble at all."

Ben studied him for a moment, then asked, "Skinner, what the hell am I going to do with you?"

177

Ollie Skinner seemed genuinely puzzled. "Sure don't know, Mr. Holliday. To tell you the truth, I'd sure hate to get fired. I ain't done an honest day's work since I hired on two years ago, and now I don't know's I can." He scratched his thatch of gray hair. "It sure is a problem fer a man to have, ain't it?"

"I'm sick of you dragging your feet," Holliday said. Then he handed him the message. "See that it gets sent right away. Then find me another horse and buggy."

"Sure will."

"And Skinner, this time I want to see a *child* leading him, you understand?"

Color came into the old man's face; his expression was contrite. "Sure am sorry, Mr. Holliday. Then again, I ain't. That was the first stand any you railroad fellas made again' the Texans." He grinned and clapped his hat on his head solidly. "You just want anything, Mr. Holliday, just holler."

"I'm going to holler right now if you don't get the hell out of here."

After Skinner left, Holliday tidied up a bit, emptied the bath water, and hung up the damp towel. His quarters were on the spartan side, one wooden bedstead, three upholstered chairs, a skimpy rug, a battered writing desk, and a dresser, all handed down from former occupants and all showing signs of much use. Someday, he thought, when Midland-Pacific paid regular and generous dividends, he'd order everything new, the very best money could buy. But until then, he'd like what he had.

Returning to his office, he stood by the corner windows for a time and looked south along the unused roadbed. His concentration seemed to center on a point far down the tracks, then he got a pair of binoculars out of his desk and adjusted them. For a full minute he made his observations through the glasses, then put them away and stepped out to the smaller office across the hall.

Fred Casten, the timekeeper, was bringing his daily pay sheets up to date, and he looked around as Holliday stuck his head in the door. Casten was a quiet man of forty, and half of his life had been spent railroading; he didn't like a young man for a boss and tried hard to hide it, which to Holliday's way of thinking was worse than showing it.

"Harry Lovell is pumping the handcar up the track," Holliday said. "I want a meeting of all superintendents in my office in an hour."

Casten considered it as though he had some say about it, then nodded, and Ben Holiday went down the stairs and walked to the switchyard. The maintenance super came out of the roundhouse, and when he saw Holliday standing by the tracks he walked over. "Is that Lovell coming back? He lit a cigar, then held it tightly clamped between his teeth. "Well, good luck, Mr. Holliday. So far all we're having is bad."

"A man makes his own luck," Ben said.

Kisdeen grinned. "I said that myself, when I was thirty."

He turned and went back to his job and Ben Holliday waited while the handcar grew larger and finally came to a stop on one of the sidings.

Harry Lovell brushed the dust from his clothes and picked up his coat, and a small leather brief case. He was tucking a rifle in the crook of his arm when Ben Holliday came up. A grin came over Lovell's florid face and he patted the brief case. "Four signatures, Ben. Is that enough?"

"Yes," Holliday said, relieved. "I wanted more, but I can force the others into line now." He laughed. "Get cleaned up, then come to my office. And thanks for a good job, Harry."

"I was a little disappointed myself," Lovell said.

They walked back to the administration building together and Lovell went into his room on the lower floor while Ben climbed the stairs to his office. When he sat down behind his desk, he felt good for the first time since he'd arrived. Four signatures; he considered this a good start. A very good start.

Ollie Skinner came back and Ben Holliday sent him right out again, to Comanche to invite Marshal Jim Bender to the meeting. He wasn't sure whether Bender had just been talking through his hat or not, but he was going to find out. And if he wasn't, Ben Holliday was going to hire an important man.

Bender arrived early. He came in and wiped sweat from his face with a large bandana. "Hell can't be much hotter than this," he said. "This morning I promised God I'd quit cussin' if He'd cool it off. Guess He didn't believe me."

"They say we're judged on past performances," Holliday said. "Marshal, what does that job pay you a month?"

"Sixty."

"I'll pay seventy-five."

Bender raised his eyebrows. "Must be a big job."

"It could work into that," Holliday said. "The salary will go up in relation to your value to the railroad." He leaned back in his chair and studied Jim Bender. "You've been a puzzle to me. I've never been able to figure out who you're for or against. Have you been walking the fence long?"

"All my life," Bender said. "It's easier to be for everything and against nothing, as long as I get what I want." He shook out his tobacco into a paper and rolled it. "You think I want to be a small-town marshal all my life?" Jim Bender laughed. "A town's just a town, Mr. Holliday, just so big and not much chance of gettin' bigger. Now a railroad's different. This line is part of another line, which is part of another. A man could grow and never worry about bumpin' his head against the top. Are you still interested in hiring me?"

"Yes," Ben Holliday said. I'm of the opinion that you'll make a good company man, Jim."

"I guess there are worse things," Bender admitted. "Your man came back, huh?"

"Yes," Holliday said, "and with some luck." He leaned

forward and folded his hands tightly together. "I'm going to take a train south to the end of line. In thirty days I intend to have the rust worn off those rails."

"And Indian trouble," Bender said. "They don't like the railroad. Claim they scare the buffalo, and they ain't going to stand still for it. Sure, they won't bother you, because they can't shoot a train off the track, but they'll raid every ranch house in North Texas to get even. That's how come you're not running trains now; surely you know it. The Texans figure it's simpler to drive cattle than to ship them and fight Indians over it."

"Do they think this situation can last forever?" Holliday asked. "The railroad is here to stay, Jim. The Indians have to face that, and so do the Texans. I know they've been fighting Comanches and Apaches for fifty years and they're tired of it. But what if I could run the road without a fight?"

Bender laughed. "Mr. Holliday, you'd find it easier to walk on water. You don't see that trick very often."

Footsteps came down the hall, and Holliday's door opened. Harry Lovell came in first with his brief case, and he frowned slightly when he saw Jim Bender sitting there. The others filed in and sat down. and Holiday didn't bother to introduce Bender, since they all knew him by sight. He waved them into chairs, then glanced at Harry Lovell, who was taking papers from his brief case.

These were slid across Holliday's desk, and he studied them carefully for a few minutes. Finally he pushed them aside and swiveled his chair around so he could cock his feet up on an open drawer.

"Kisdeen, if I wanted to take a train south, how soon could a work train leave?"

"As soon as the engineer got steam up, Mr. Holliday."

They all straightened in their chairs and their attention sharpened as they looked at Emil Kisdeen. Ben Holliday said, "I want every telegraph pole we have loaded, every roll of wire, every glass insulator. A full work crew will be ready to leave tonight." His glance switched to Matt

Donovan, the chief telegrapher. "Get me four telegraphers, Matt. And have their gear with them because they won't be coming back for a while."

"Just what the divvil's going on?" Donovan asked.

"We're going to run a railroad," Ben Holliday said. "You all knew that Mr. Lovell went to the end of track, and now I'll tell you what for. The Texans have refused to ship on our railroad because they all believe we'll stir up the Indians, then stand back while they fight them for us. Until they change their minds, our rolling stock will stay on sidings. So my first concern has been to convince the ranchers that the railroad is ready to stand shoulder to shoulder with them in any fight that comes up. I sent Harry south with a proposition: the railroad will set poles and string wires to any ranch who uses our line on a contract basis. A telegrapher will stay at the ranch, and at the first sign of trouble he'll let us know and a train will be dispatched with horses and men and guns to help the Texans. We've got four outfits signed up, gentlemen. It's enough to start operation on, at a profit."

"It sounds good," Jim Bender said. "But tell me somethin'. What about the ones who didn't sign anything? Who the hell helps them out when the Indians start raidin'? The Comanches ain't going to care who's with you and who ain't."

"You've touched on the heart of the answer," Holliday said. "Gentlemen, those who have not signed a contract with us will have no choice but to join us. Without the telegraph, they're wide open to more trouble than they can handle. And to get a telegraph, they've got to ship on our railroad. They've got to join or get licked." He smiled. "Now before anyone howls about what a dirty trick this is, let me remind them that we're fighting for our lives, and for the good of the country. As soon as possible, I want to put down a siding about fifty miles south of here, with a full crew there all the time, to bring them closer to any trouble that develops. It'll cost money, but if we start shipping, it won't be long before we pull out of the red."

"We can't afford much expansion now," Lovell pointed out. "As it stands, we have finances for forty-three days."

"By then I'll be running steady trains," Ben Holliday said. "Gentlemen, we have to make the big effort now. We can't afford to wait. If we fail, then we'll do a good job of that too."

"Only one thing bothers me," Bender said. What's going to keep the Comanches from pulling that wire down as fast as you can string it?"

"I've given that some thought too," Holiday said. "According to Skinner, the Indians make medicine for everything. If it's good medicine, they make wars and go hunting and think that they've got all the luck on their side. But when the medicine is bad, they keep pretty much in line. So I think we ought to make some bad medicine for the Indians."

"It's going to have to be real bad," Bender said.

"I'll let you be the judge," Ben said. "Donovan, I want you to rig up something with the telegraph wires that'll shock the hell out of anyone who touches it. Bender, I want you to go south and ask all the Indians to come to a big talk and a demonstration of the wire. Then I want to invite them to touch the wire and get a jolt. Then we'll touch it after a switch has been opened, and get none at all."

"I can go you one better than that," Donovan said. "A switch would have to be hid and a man there to throw it off and on. We could all wear rubber boots and be insulated from the wire."

Holliday looked at all of them. "Any comments?"

Jim Bender began to laugh. "Ben, you're a sneaky bastard, but I'll go along with you."

"When can you leave?"

"Tonight."

"Fine," Holliday said. "Casten, put Bender on the payroll. Seventy-five a month. Kisdeen, you'd better check with me before you pull out with the work train. I'll have maps for both of you. For the meeting, I think the junction of the telegraph wires will do fine. It's open country there, and we can rig up all the wires so the Indians will understand that this isn't just something special."

"I don't know what else you'd call it," Lovell said. He closed his brief case. "Mr. Holliday, this is one hell of a way to run a railroad." Then he smiled and got up. "However, if it gets a train on the track, it's better than the other two did. I'll make up a cost sheet to send to your father."

"The only thing I want to send him," Ben said, "is an operating sheet. He knows the line is going broke, so anything else along that line is old information rehashed." He tapped his finger on the desk. "In twenty days, gentlemen, I want cattle cars coming into this siding loaded."

"That's pushing it pretty hard," Kisdeen said. "I don't think all the wire will be strung by then."

Holliday picked up the papers Lovell had given him. "Lazy T has sixteen hundred head ready for shipment. You run your wires there, and when the telegrapher tests the line I want those cattle loaded. Then you take your work train north about twelve miles and string a wire to Box X, and so on down the line. For Christ's sake, do I have to work out all the details?"

Ben got up and jammed his hands deep into his pockets, then stood by the window and observed the roundhouse activity. "Lovell expected this job, and he hasn't gotten over his disappointment yet. The others, well, they've already admitted to themselves that we're licked and are counting the days until we pull up the rails and go back East." Then he turned and looked at Bender. "I don't want to go back. My father, if he knew what was going on, would roar like a bull and tell me that never in his fifty-nine years had he heard of a railroad being run this way. And he'd be right. Lon, my oldest brother, is a corporation man, and he'd cuss me out for forgetting my obligation to the stockholders, and scold me in a high-finance sort of way because everything in his life is reduced to profit and loss. My other brother, Adam, is a lawyer, and he'd want to talk about all the possible litigation involved, but he'd admire me for getting into this mess without even half trying."

"I'd like to know him," Jim Bender said. "Tell me, how come your old man sent you here, Ben?"

"Because my father firmly believes that every man has to experience failure before he can appreciate success," Holliday said. "So he bought up twenty-eight per cent of the stock; it only cost him a few cents on the dollar, then gave it to me and told me to make it worth something, if I could."

"Mmmm, well it's one way of looking at the world," Bender admitted. "What's he going to say if you carry this off?

"He'll like it," Holliday said. "Above all else, he admires success." Then he sat down, a worried frown creasing his forehead. "Of course there's more to it than just appeasing the Texans and fooling the Indians. Midland-Pacific is in bad financial shape. It would have to operate well for at least six months before she could see the top of the hole she's in. And another four months before any kind of a dividend could be declared." He shook his head sadly. "She's a broke railroad, Jim, and there's damned little hope of any new blood being pumped into her." He pulled a ten-day-old New York paper from his desk and slapped it with his hand. "To get more money, you have to sell stock, and Midland-Pacific stock has about as much value as wallpaper. I could buy any of it for sixty cents a share. If I had the sixty cents."

Jim Bender's eyes were veiled and his voice was soft when he said, "Seems to me that someone around here, who could see that the railroad might make it, could buy up a hog's share, hold it a while, and amass himself quite a hunk of money." He got up and shifted his pistol to a more comfortable position. "I'll have to think on it."

"Stop by before you leave," Holliday suggested.

"I'll do that," Bender said, and went out.

During the next hour, Holliday cleaned up some paperwork that he had neglected. Skinner came around with a telegram from the Dodge City operator, stating that the shipment would be on the night train, and asking what the devil was going on there. Holliday wrinkled the telegram and threw it in the wastebasket.

He wasn't quite sure how he'd present the German girl with the sheets and things; she might even resent it and create another row. Perhaps, he thought, it would be better if he just sent them over with Lovell or someone. Still, taking them himself was going to be half the pleasure, and he was curious to see her with a clean face.

Most of the day was spent in the yard or roundhouse where the work train was being loaded. A steam donkey hoisted poles and wire rolls onto flatcars, and the crews were being made up, and a cook's car was stuffed with provisions before hooking it in front of the caboose.

Holliday skipped his noon day meal; he was too busy to eat, and he had a late supper, not bothering with it until Jim Bender came and went, heading south with a pack horse. The work train pulled out and it was a good sight to see the engine belching fire and smoke, and just listen to the rattle of the cars fade off into the night. This was what he had been working for, and he felt a little closer to some results; he felt impatient for the day when he could wire north a financial and operation report that wasn't all bad. And when he thought about it, he had to laugh, for in his mind he could visualize his father's reaction, a bellow of surprise, a moment of disbelief, then the half-grudging acknowledgment that "the boy's done it"——

It would be a good thing, Holliday thought, and walked to his quarters. There he found the door ajar and the lamps lighted, and he paused just outside the door, wondering who was there. He pushed open the door and the hinges squeaked, and with a startled leap the blond German girl got out of her chair.

"I—the man let me in," she said. "I don't know his name."

"Skinner," Ben Holliday said. "Sit down. I didn't mean to startle you." Her hair was braided now, and coiled into a bun on the back of her head, and she stood with her hands folded before her like a child who has been instructed to go cut a switch. She wore a white blouse and a dark skirt and no jewelry except a brooch at her throat. "I don't even know your name," he said.

"Anna. Anna Neubauer."

"Sit down, Anna. I'm Ben Holliday."

"I know," she said softly. Then she sat down and he walked to the door and looked up and down the hall. He saw Skinner leaning against the far end. "Come here." When Skinner came up, Holliday put his hand on the old man's shoulder. "Go on over to the cookshack and bring back some coffee."

"It was all right, me lettin' her in, wasn't it?"

"Yes. Go on now." Then he turned back into the room; she was watching him intently, and he wondered what to say. "Will you let me tell you how sorry I am about ruining your clothes?" He grinned. "And I didn't mean what I said about taking you over my knee."

Color came into her cheeks. "You make it hard to say what I came to say. When I called you an—an ass, I didn't know who you were."

"Well, I can be an ass at times. My brothers would tell you that."

"But it was wrong to call the boss such a name," she said. Then she picked up a wrapped bundle and put it on the table. "This is your coat. I took it away from some boys who were playing with it. There were some letters, but someone had already opened them. I'm sorry I didn't find it sooner."

He broke the string and took the letters from the inside pocket; there were enough finger smudges on them to convince him they had been well looked over. "Thanks for bringing them. I've sent Skinner for coffee. You'll stay and have some, won't you?"

"Is it all right?"

He frowned. "Is what all right?"

"To drink coffee with the boss?"

He laughed and reached for her hand, then remembered the last time he'd tried that and pulled his hand back. She caught the meaning of the gesture and quickly clapped a hand to her mouth; her expression was one of chagrin.

"I forgot about that!"

"Well, I haven't," Holliday said, meaning it as a joke.

But she didn't take it that way at all. "I told my father what I said. He will leave tomorrow."

"Leave? What the devil for?"

"Because he is too proud to be fired," Anna said.

"Now wait a minute," Ben said, sitting down across from her. "Anna, I'm not going to fire anyone. And surely not your father for something that was my fault."

She regarded him with wide eyes. "You're not? But I called you an ass, and bit your hand." She shook her head. "I thought—"

"You thought wrong," Ben Holliday said. Then he leaned back and laughed. "Anna, what other foolish notions do you have?"

"To me it isn't foolish," she said. "In Germany, we do not swear at the boss or bite his hand. But I've never seen a boss before."

Skinner came back with the coffee; he brought the tray in and placed it on the table, then acted as though he'd appreciate an invitation to sit. Ben said, "You can take it back tomorrow."

"Huh? Oh, sure." He went out and down the back steps, and Ben Holliday could hear him grumbling clear to the bottom of the landing. He poured the coffee, then said, "I made a wreck out of your washing, In the morning I'll send Skinner over with a new tub."

"You don't have to."

"What'll you do without a tub?"

"Borrow from Mrs. Bartocci, who lives next door."

"You're too proud to borrow," Ben said. "You'll get a new tub in the morning." He drank some of his coffee and looked at her. She was a very attractive girl, twenty some, with a face a bit squarish, and lips that were soft and long. She caught him staring, and he covered it up by saying, "I noticed that you speak English with hardly a trace of accent. Where did you learn that?"

"In night school in Chicago. My father worked for the railroad there." She made descriptive motions with her hands. "In the foundry he makes things of wood and sand, then parts for the trains are made from hot metal."

Holliday thought a moment. "Is he a big man with a stomach and a mustache drooping to his chin?"

Anna Neubauer laughed. "He drinks too much beer, but he works hard, so I say nothing about the beer." She sighed wistfully. "Someday I say that he won't have to work so hard, but I really don't believe it. It is like my sheets; I'm a fool to think they will last forever."

"You'll get other sheets, Anna."

"But they won't be the same."

"No, we can never have things the same. Every day there's a change, a little more wear somewhere. We've got to figure on the wear, Anna."

"I know." She finished her coffee and put the cup aside before standing up. "You're nice. But I knew that this morning when you gathered up my things and brought them to me. I'm sorry I was too angry to see it, and tell you."

"I'm glad you came here, Anna."

"And I am too, now," she said. He offered her his hand and she took it and he held hers a little longer than was proper, but didn't care and didn't think she cared either.

"Could I walk you home?"

She shook her head. "It would cause the neighbors to talk. And they are not always kind in what they say."

"Well, at least to the bottom of the stairs then," he said, taking her arm. At the bottom of the landing he held her

189

arm to keep her from just disappearing in the darkness. He thought of telling her that he was going to replace the things he had ruined, then decided not to; it would give him an excellent excuse to call on her.

"I have to go," she said softly.

He relaxed his grip and she slipped from his fingers and was gone. He stood there for a moment, then turned to go back up the stairs. From the shadows near the end of the building, Ellie Skinner said, "Some things just end too quick, don't they?"

Holliday was annoyed to find the man there, then he laughed. "Come on up and tell me a lot of lies about yourself and the state of Texas."

Skinner followed him, and once he got into the room he flopped in a chair and stretched out his legs. "If I told you about myself, it would be so plumb excitin' you wouldn't believe it. And I ain't got enough years left to tell you all about Texas." He raised his disgraceful hat in a mock salute. "However, I feel plumb privileged to be a part of this here vast enterprise of yours, Mr. Holliday."

Ben frowned good-naturedly. "Ollie, are you turning into a company man or something?"

"Well, let's put it this way. You're the first boss I've had on this job who didn't treat me like somethin' the cat dragged in. You got a style, Mr. Holliday. Don't know rightly what it is, but you got a style. A genuine wind cutter and a dog howler." He smacked his lips several times. "Say, you don't happen to keep any hard liquor about, do you?"

CHAPTER THREE

Just before noon, Ben Holliday walked from his office to the depot to meet the night train from Dodge City; it rattled into the station amid a flurry of swirling cinders and a hiss of brakes. A small crowd of passengers waited in the shade of the depot, and some local freight was stacked for loading. The single coach emptied quickly, just a few local businessmen and a young army officer in a uniform still bearing packing-box wrinkles. The others walked away, but he stood there looking around as though he didn't think much of any of it.

The door of the baggage car was opened and some freight was loaded on handcarts while a three-man cavalry detail from Fort Elliot waited for the mail. The young officer glanced at them briefly, then came over to Holliday.

"I'm Lieutenant Gary, and the conductor tells me this is as far as the train goes." He was a young man, crisp in manner, with the sharp hone of Academy training much in evidence. His face was long and rather thin, and a downy mustache was bravely trying to mature on his upper lip.

"This is the end of the line, Lieutenant. But nevertheless, welcome to Texas.

"A dubious pleasure, I can assure you," Gary said. "Is there a decent hotel in town?"

"If you consider a lumpy mattress and a few sand fleas decent," Holliday said. "Excuse me. I have some baggage to pick up." He smiled and walked over to the express car. "George, have you got a package for me?"

The express agent handed down a wrapped bundle. "I heard you're keeping a woman, Mr. Holliday."

Holliday grinned. "How would you like to be working for the Arkansas line?" He signed the express agent's book and turned back to the depot where shade lay cool and inviting along the wall. The young officer was still walking about, apparently undecided about what to do. After observing him for a moment, Ben Holliday left the shade, walked around the back of the train, and crossed over to railroad town, carrying the package.

The children were yelling and two boys were throwing cinders at each other, while around them an excited group urged them on. Holliday walked around them, but a small boy and his sister ran after him.

"Hey, meester!" He stopped and looked at the boy, eight or so, dark, with wavy black hair and the deepest brown eyes he had ever seen. The boy grinned. "Meester, you want see my seester t'row opp?" He took Holliday's sleeve and pulled it. "For nickel, she t'row opp for you."

Then a woman ran out of one of the shacks and came up and slapped the boy and yelled at him in Italian; Holliday walked on to Anna Neubauer's house, his step quicker now, as though he only wanted to do what he had to do and get out.

Skinner had already taken the tub over; it sat by her door, full of water to swell the cedar staves. He shifted the bundle and knocked, and Anna opened the door, a fleeting surprise on her face.

"May I come in?" Ben asked.

"Ja bitte herein." Then she laughed. "Yes, please." She stepped aside for him, then closed the door.

Without consciously thinking about it, Ben Holliday had schooled himself on showing no reaction to her poverty-level dwelling; from the outside it was a shack with paint peeling off the sides and the tar-paper roof curling along the edges. And from the outside he had pre-judged the inside, so what he found rattled him completely.

The furniture, every stick of it, had been carefully packed to endure the journey from Germany without damage, and all of it was black walnut, heavily carved, built to endure generations of use without showing a trace of deterioration. A glass-fronted cupboard held her dishes, fine bone china, and silver that could only have been hand-crafted by a master.

She watched him look around, then said, "My grand-mother was a rich woman, Mr. Holliday. These were things I could not leave behind, but I often wish that I had." She turned to the stove where a coffeepot warmed. "Nearly all of the women here are poor, and I no longer invite them into the house. It only makes them angry, and they won't understand that these things were given to me." Her shoulders rose and fell. "Thank you for the tub, but there'll be talk."

"As much as I hate to say it, there's going to be more talk." He laid the bundle on the table, and she looked questioningly at it. "God ahead, open it."

Before she touched it he knew she'd untie the string and save both that and the wrapping paper. She gasped when she saw the sheets and dresses and underclothes, and she ran her hands over the folded sheets for a moment.

"What can I say, they're so nice? There will be gossip about me when I hang them on the line, but it'll be worth it, I think."

"I hope you can explain it to your father," Ben said, smiling. "In Chicago, I gave a girl a pair of stockings." He rolled his eyes toward the ceiling. "It almost became a scandal. I'm sure this will make trouble for you."

"It's something I'm used to," she said. "Will you stay for coffee?"

He shook his head. "No doubt the ladies here are keep-ing track of the time from when I entered. Which makes it important for me to leave early." He opened the door and stood there a moment. "How do I cross from where I live to here, Anna?"

"Are you sure you want to?"

"I think so." He raised both hands and looked at them. "How does one break down walls he can't see, but knows are there?" Then he closed the door and walked back across the tracks and on to his office.

The sun was making an oven of it, and he took off his

coat and tie and rolled his sleeves. Ollie Skinner came in a few minutes later with Holliday's shredded coat rolled into a untidy ball.

"You want me to throw this out, Mr. Holliday?"

"Yes. Wait! There are a couple letters in the pocket." Skinner felt and patted the cloth until he heard paper rustle, then took them out and laid them on Holliday's desk.

After he went out, Ben picked up the letter from his father and gave it a tardy reading.

Chicago, May 6, 1882

Dear Ben:

At hand I have a communication from an attorney in Dodge City, who represents local interests. He has made a bona fide offer to purchase Midland-Pacific. I don't know why he got in touch with me, unless he was unaware that you are now chairman of the board. But I think this is unlikely. For some reason or another he does not want to do business with you.

Have you been alienating these people? God knows they're uncooperative enough.

I've studied this offer at length, and Adam has looked it over, and in spite of the fact that he disagrees with me, I believe it is an answer to a sticky problem. M-P has lost money at an alarming rate, and I believe will continue to do so in spite of any effort you might make. Sincerity does not count in this business, Ben. Only results, and I fear there will be precious little of those.

Naturally the sale will leave you nothing; the common stockholders will have to be paid off first, and their share will be pitifully small. But you'll be out from under it with a clean bill of health, and you can come back to Chicago; there is plenty to do here.

Since I've already approved of this offer, I will not enclose the papers. Of course, legally you are the chairman of the board and can do as you wish, but

194

don't fly in the face of providence and sound judgment, Ben. I urge you to write me your letter of acceptance at your earliest opportunity.

Midland-Pacific is broke, dead, finished. Bury her without tears and take the last train to Dodge and home.

Your father,
Julius

Holliday laid the letter on his desk and sat with his chin in his hands, considering this unexpected turn of events. The fact that there was a buyer for the line surprised him, but after thinking a moment, it made a lot of sense. His father had started that way, buying a defunct line for a few cents on the dollar and making it pay handsomely. That was evidently someone's idea here.

But who?

He didn't have a chance to think about it, for Skinner came back. "Some sojer wants to see you," he said. "Says he talked to you at the depot."

"All right, send him in," Holliday said. "And go over to the cookshack and bring back some sandwiches and some coffee."

Skinner went out and Lieutenant Gary stepped in, his manner hesitant. "I'm sorry to intrude, but they told me at the depot that you run the railroad."

"Have a chair. Run it?" Holliday smiled. "You're very generous, Lieutenant. However, you have problems of your own, I'm sure."

"Mainly, getting to Fort Elliot. It's my understanding that the roadbed runs within eight miles of the post."

"Yes, to the west, and terminates about twenty miles beyond, at a water tank, a telegraph shack, and a small bunkhouse. Is Fort Elliot your assignment?"

Gary nodded. "And I'm going to be late for it, damn it. A man's first duty and he has to botch it." He sighed. "I spent too much time with my sisters, I'm afraid, and did not take into consideration the abominable traveling conditions." He crossed one leg over the other and put his hands on his knee. "I was told that you sent a train south last night. May I ask how far?"

"To the end of track."

Gary swore softly, in a gentlemanly manner. "I've been missing connections since St. Louis!" He slapped his knee. "I don't suppose there's another train—no, I thought not. Damn, but there is an ominous tone to a man being tardy for his first assignment."

Ben Holliday was thinking about this when Skinner came back, a tray of sandwiches and a pot of coffee in hand. Gary said, "That looks good. I haven't had anything since supper last night."

"Help yourself," Holliday said. "Skinner, I think I'll take the handcar to the end of track. See that it's ready in about an hour."

"You aint goin' alone, are you?" Skinner asked.

"I thought I'd take Lieutenant Gary along." He smiled at Ollie Skinner. "Well, don't look like that. I can pump a handcar. And get me a rifle and some shells from the freight office. I'll take care of the rest."

"All right," Skinner said, his tone predicting dire things to come.

After he left, Lieutenant Gary said, "If you're doing this for me, I——"

"I can't run a railroad sitting down," Holiday told him. "We can pump ten miles an hour, spend the night on the prairie, and leave you with only an eight-mile walk to the post." He bit into one of the sandwiches. "I thought a military escort was supposed to meet you officers."

"Likely there was one, at Tascosa, a week ago," Gary said. "I'm really that far behind, I'm sorry to say." He shrugged and picked up his cup of coffee. "I tried to send a wire, but the telegraph only runs to here. Oh, what a dismal state of affairs."

"I thought the army had its own signal service."

"Of course, heliograph and dispatch riders." He snorted in disgust. "But not telegraph, except when near the main

196

ine. You say the post is eight miles from your telegraph lines? What a shame they're not tied into it."

"Take it up with your congressman the next time you're in Washington. Poles and wire and insulators cost money. Who's going to foot the bill? The railroad? We built this line out of our own pocket, for railroad business." He jerked open a desk drawer. "I've three letters there from Colonel Dawson asking if we'd string wire to Fort Elliot. We would, only he hasn't the authority or the money to pay the bill."

"You're certainly not much of a visionary," Gary said frankly.

"How so?" He got up and took his coffee to the windows and stood there, sipping it and looking out.

"Fort Elliot's function is to keep the Indians in line, Mr. Holliday. It seems to me that it would serve your function admirably if you put the line in at your expense. You railroaders are always stirring up the Indians. A telegraph wire would bring the army in a hurry."

Holliday turned and looked at him for a moment, then came back to his desk and sat down. "Mr. Gary, I assume that you are a genius."

"I was sixty-third in my class," Gary said. There were seventy-one, all told." He frowned pleasantly. "Did I say something bright? By golly, I'm due for a change, you know."

"Finish your sandwich and coffee," Holliday said, picking up his coat. He stepped out and went down the hall to Dan Rawlins's office. The freight superintendent was reading an old newspaper and he put it away quickly when Holliday came in, as though ashamed at getting caught. "Have you made up that string of empty cattle cars yet?" Rawlins handed him a sheet and Holliday looked at it, then gave it back. "When the first cattle train rolls out for Dodge, deadhead six flatcars. Tell Lovell to handle the paper work, but I want all the poles and wire Western Union can spare. Enough to string an additional eight miles."

"All right, but who's going to pay for it, Mr. Holliday? We can't afford those kind of expenditures." He scratched a day-old-beard stubble. "I hate to remind you, but everyone knows we're broke, or close to it. We don't have enough credit to buy a ton of coal."

"Do you play poker, Mr. Rawlins?"

"Well, I do now and then. But I'm not crazy about the game."

"You should play with my brother, Adam; he can bluff the money out of a cardshark's pocket." Holliday slapped Rawlins on the shoulder. "I'm not bad at bluffing myself."

He whistled on the way back to his office, then looked in Donovan's office. The telegrapher was cat napping, his feet on the desk, and Holliday shook him awake. "Curly, are you friendly with the Dodge City operator?"

"Why, sure. We used to work connecting shifts for Western Union."

"Then I got a bit of gossip for you to pass along to him. Be worth three drinks at least." He bent forward to speak softly, and glanced over his shoulder before he really came out with it. "We've got some fresh money, Curly. Over hundred thousand dollars from a Dodge City investor." He clapped the man on the back. "We're out of the hole. And I've been thinking about a raise to celebrate."

He went out while the man was still a little open mouthed over it, and before he stepped into his office Holliday puffed his cheeks and blew out a long breath. The telegrapher was asking for a clear signal, and Holliday stepped in and closed the door.

Gary was smoking a cigar and he said nothing, and Holliday was glad because he wanted a chance to think this out. He had no doubt that there was already some talk in Dodge about a buying interest in Midland-Pacific; you just couldn't keep those things absolutely quiet, especially among the bankers and money men. And this bit of nothing Curly was spreading would catch on, enough Holliday hoped, to convince the manager of Western Union that this shaky railroad was good for five carloads of poles and ten spools of wire. Holiday knew that there would be a lot of nosing around to find out just how true the rumor was, but he knew investors; they were all hunch players with big ears from keyhole listening. His own father had made his first million by taking advantage of rumors and getting there first with the right things.

"Are you working on a plan to assassinate the President?" Gary asked, drawing Holliday's attention back with a snap.

Ben laughed. "I'm playing big business with a busted flush. Do you have any luggage?"

"Sitting by the bottom landing."

"I'll meet you there after I change clothes," Holliday said. "Skinner ought to have the handcar ready."

In his quarters, he changed to some old hunting clothes he'd brought along, and laughed silently while he put them on. His notion, before he came here, was that he would have time to indulge in a few gentlemanly activities, like grouse hunting, and perhaps a buffalo hunt. As it turned out, he had twenty days of messed-up paper work to sort through before he even got a vivid picture of the railroad's ills. There was little time for thought of gentlemanly pursuits.

He found Gary waiting, and they walked together to the switchyard. Skinner was there, sitting in the sparse shade. He had some gear of his own stowed on the handcar, and Holliday looked at it.

"Where do you think you're going?"

"Along," Skinner said. He held up his hands. "Before you get to yellin' at me, let me just say that it ain't goin' to hurt you none, and it may do you a bit of good. I know this country. It would pay you to listen once in a while. That there chairman of the board thing don't make you that smart."

Lieutenant Gary frowned; he disapproved of this kind of talk from a hired man. But this was railroad business and he kept out of it. Finally Holliday said, "Let's go then.

Gary and I'll pump. We don't want you keeling over from overwork, Skinner."

They pushed the handcar past the switch, and while it was coasting the two men laid their weight on the handles and got up a little speed. Skinner sat on the bow, his Sharps rifle crossways on his knees.

It was a good feeling, the dripping sweat from Holliday's face soaking his shirt, and he liked the sound of the wheels clacking over the rail joints, eating the miles away, moving along briskly southward in a flat, dun-colored country with hardly a break in it. The string of telegraph poles marched by, and if a man wanted to count them and do a little mental arithmetic, he could calculate his rate of travel very accurately.

Skinner spelled them in turn, and they didn't stop at all until the sun was well down. They left the handcar on the track and camped near the roadbed. Skinner put together a fire, gathering the heavy stems of brush for fuel. The meal was mainly bacon and soggy pancakes, followed by coffee so strong you could etch copper with it. Gary brought out three cigars, and this pleased Skinner, who had a taste for them but was too tight with a nickel to buy his own.

"When you report to Colonel Dawson," Holliday said, "It might soften the effect of your tardiness if you mention that you'd talked me into building the telegraph line to the post."

Skinner raised his head and looked disgustedly at Ben Holliday. "That's a fool move. Ain't you got enough troubles without bringing in the army?"

"I never thought of it until Mr. Gary mentioned it, but it's the smartest advice I ever took. Skinner, our position's a lot stronger with the Texans if we string wire to Fort Elliot. It's like Mr. Gary says: the army is there to keep the Indians in line."

Ollie Skinner chuckled, but Lieutenant Gary didn't see the humor in it "The military," he said, "is not an instrument to be used by civilian enterprise, Mr. Holliday."

"It is if you want a telegraph," Ben pointed out.

"I see. If I'd known that——"

"You'd still need the telegraph," Holliday said. "Now before you accuse anybody of pulling a sneaky, try to see my position. If this railroad operates, army supplies will only be eight miles from the post, and instead of freighting them in on the stage road to Tascosa, they army will get them at much less rate. You're forgetting about the contract the government has with all railroads: men and material transported at a rock-bottom rate. Don't expect to get anything for nothing. It never works."

"I'm goin to inform Colonel Dawson of these ramifications," Gary said.

Ben Holliday laughed. "He already knows, and then some. The railroad is going to make his job easier."

"And tougher," Gary said. "I heard about all the Indian trouble you've stirred up."

"Then look at it this way," Holliday said. "If we didn't stir up the Indians, you wouldn't have a job to do."

Skinner stopped puffing on his cigar. "Sonny, don't argue with him; it don't do any good. His old man's one of them big moguls, and his brothers are swindlers from the word go. And most of it's rubbed off on him."

Gary said, "Are you going to let him talk to you like that?"

Holliday waved it aside. "All Texans are windbags, Mr. Gary. Now get some sleep." He turned to his blankets and stretched out, using his folded hands for a pillow. "Skinner, how are the rattlesnakes around here?"

"Friendly. Come right up and share your blankets. But don't roll on 'em. Makes 'em grouchy."

"Good advice," Holliday said blandly.

"Say, he's just joking, isn't he?" Gary asked.

"Don't go walkin' along the tracks at night," Skinner said. "You'll find out then whether I'm jokin' or not. They like to lay against the rails to keep warm."

"I think I'll sleep on the handcar," Gary said, and got his blankets. Skinner chuckled and lay there, his cigar end glowing redly for a time. Then he snuffed it out and went to sleep.

The dawn sunlight woke them, and Skinner booted first Holliday, then Garry. "Up! Up" he said. "Come on, up!"

Gary came to a sitting position and rubbed his backside. "By God, I'm not used to being woke like that," he said. "Don't you ever hear of shaking a man, Skinner?"

"Did that one time. Got my hand bit." He rubbed his hands together. "Let's get pumpin'. Who's going to take the other handle?"

"On an empty stomach?" Gary said. He stood there while Holliday and Skinner rolled the blankets and put them on handcar. Then Gary sighed and took a handle while Skinner pushed it into motion.

"If I had him in my outfit," Gary said, meaning Skinner, "I'd have him in the guardhouse."

"And I doubt if it'd hold him," Holliday said. He pointed to a spot far out on the prairie. "What's that?"

Skinner, who was riding backwards, turned his head for a look. He squinted his eyes for a moment, then said, "Oh, oh. Here, you pump." He picked up his rifle and sat on the prow. "Buffalo. Not many. Fifty-sixty maybe. Movin' this way too."

"Can't we outrun them?" Gary asked.

"No. you can't," Skinner said. "Maybe we don't have to, thought. Just keep up that steady pace, gents. Or a little faster, if you've a mind to. Speed at a time like this won't hurt nothin'." He took out the stale cigar stub he'd saved from last night, bit off the charred end, then chewed the rest. From his coat pocket he took out a box of .50-125 Sharps Express cartridges and held four of them in the palm of his left hand.

Holliday, who had a good view facing in the direction of their travel, could see that the buffalo herd was traveling a course converging on their own; they were likely to meet up ahead somewhere, and it wasn't good to think about.

He and Gary increased the cadence of their pumping and rattled along, only now he could no longer hear the clack of the wheels; the steady drum of hoofs closed it out. Yet he could feel the vibration at each rail joint, but only for a while as the approaching herd set up a vibration that made track and rail bed tremble. Gary's eyes were getting glassy and both men were breathing hard, yet they did not slacken their exertions.

Holliday could see clearly the humped backs and massive heads and the thick, filthy pelts, and the odor of the herd came to him strong and frightening. There was a time when only thirty yards separated them, then they passed on and the herd crossed the tracks at an angle and ran on to the other side and away from them.

They slowed somewhat but continued to pump for a mile or so, they sat down and let the handcar coast to the stop. The herd went on, to the west of them, the sounds of their passage dying until it was only a thunder rumble in the distance.

Skinner was sweating. He put his cartridges and rifle away and spat tobacco. "Close, that was. Can't take it much closer. Gives a man a bad heart, too much of that."

This joking admission of fright from Ollie Skinner was unnerving for Gary and Ben Holliday. They drank from their canteens, then Ben said, "Why the hell didn't you shoot? Or did you forget to load it?"

"No sense in it," Skinner said. "I didn't want to take a chance on turnin' 'em. They could have turned into us."

"How often does a man run into something like that?" Gary asked.

"Enough to make him old at thirty-five," Skinner said. He squinted and studied the farthest reaches of the prairie. "There's Indians about. They got that herd running."

"I thought I saw blood on a couple of cows," Holliday said.

Skinner grinned and slapped his leg. "By golly, you ain't as blind as I thought. Yep, you saw blood all right. Some brave put a .44 into her, or an arrer, then broke it off feelin' fer the life."

"What's he talking about?" Gary said.

"Feelin' fer the life?" Skinner smiled. "It's brave doin's, sonny. When they hunt with arrers, they sink a shaft, then side alongside, lean from the horses, and with their hand shove the arrer home, guidin' it into the heart or lung. Call it feelin' fer the life."

"It sounds like a damned good way to die," Gary said flatly, considering it foolish.

"Death ain't nothin' to an Indian," Skinner said. "Just an event, like bein' born. It's what's in-between that counts."

"Beer-barrel philosophy," Holliday. said. "You ready? I'll give us a push." He hopped down and set his shoulder against the car and got it going.

They stopped in midmorning on a spot of barren prairie, and Skinner pointed to the southeast. "Fort Elliot's out there, sonny. About three hours off, if you don't sit down too often."

"Hell, I can't even see it," Gary said.

"Take a look at your shadow. Keep it there as you walk. By the time the sun moves enough to put you off course, you'll be able to see the post," Skinner said. "You feel like shakin', or are you mad at me?"

Gary shook hands with him, then with Holliday, and walked off. When he passed out of earshot, Ben Holliday said, "You were a little rough on him, Skinner."

"Got to grow up fast out here, Mr. Holliday. In Texas, a boy's a boy, and a man's a man. One day he ain't ready to shave, and the next day he's got a beard." He sighed. "Sure wish I'd got a couple of them cigars off him." He threw his weight onto the handle, and the car started to move toward the end of track.

CHAPTER FOUR

End of track was turning into a tent town surrounded by piles of telegraph polies and boxed equipment, and after Holliday and Skinner wrestled the handcar off the rails, they walked down a ways to where Emil Kisdeen had set up headquarters.

When he saw them he made a surprised face, then took Holliday inside his tent and waved him into a folding chair. Already a line of poles was stretching southwest and the wagons were coming and going regularly; Kisdeen was working three shifts around the clock.

"What's this about you finding some new money?" Kisdeen asked. "My operator picked up Curly's transmission to Dodge. It caused a flurry of excitement around here."

Holliday dippered some water from a nearby bucket and slowly poured it over his head. Then he sighed and wiped his face with a handkerchief. "Let's hope it creates the some flurry in Dodge, enough to give me some credit for more poles and wire."

"There's nothing to the rumor?" Kisdeen asked.

"Not a damned thing," Holliday said. He liked Kisdeen, and he trusted him, still he did not mention that there were some buyers interested in the line. Not that he felt it was none of Kisdeen's business, but because he hadn't quite figured out the ramifications of the offer. Without a doubt, someone thought he could make money with the line, and to do that he'd have to operate it.

"It's a bad way to do business," Kisdeen said softly. "What makes you think anyone in Dodge will believe it?"

"A hunch," Holliday said. He got up and went to the flap door and ducked his head to step outside. A fringe-topped buggy was approaching, pulled by a pair of matched roans. The rig wheeled into the camp and stopped in a swelter of dust. A burly, heavy-shouldered man got down and started to walk around the rig to help the woman, but Ben Holliday stepped forward, put his hands on the soft roundness of her waist, and lowered her to the ground.

"Thank you," she said, smiling with her eyes. She was not tall, and her hair reminded him of polished burl walnut. Her face was round and deeply tanned, and a scatter of freckles tinted the bridge of her nose.

The man said, "Fella, we help our own women. You understand?"

Emil Kisdeen came out of his tent then and offered his hand to the man. "Mr. Singer, I'd like to have you meet Mr. Holliday."

Singer reared a little in surprise. Then he laughed. "If I'd know that, I wouldn't have spoken so quickly. This is my daughter, Betty." He plucked two cigars from his pocket and pressed one on Ben Holliday. "My son, Carl, is standing by on the other end. We can see the poles from our front porch. In another hour the hookup ought to be made and the first message sent. Here, let me give you a light." He chuckled softly. "That's the way to get the job done; work day and night until it's finished. And I can assure you, Mr. Holliday, that Lazy T is not ungrateful for this mark of progress."

Ben Holliday smiled. "Well that's fine, Mr. Singer. I may have to remind you of what you said in six months or so when we come to acquire a right of way, so you'll be friendly to the idea."

"Right of way?" Singer said.

"Of course. Did you think end of track would always remain here? Mr. Singer, a railroad has to terminate, yes, but not in the middle of the prairie." He rolled the cigar from one side of his mouth to the other. "The railroad takes your cattle north, but it can bring supplies in. And we pay for the right of way, if the price is right." Then he laughed. "Well, it's too hot to talk business today anyway."

"Yes," Singer said, glad the subject was being dropped. "We came here to invite Mr. Kisdeen to the ranch for the night. I'd like to extend the invitation to you, Mr. Holliday."

"I think I'd better stay here," Kisdeen said. "After I get a clear signal I want to start putting together some kind of a loading chute." His glance touched Singer. "I can expect the cattle to arrive day after tomorrow, can't I."

"Oh, I think so," Singer said. "Yes, yes, I suppose so. But you don't even have any cars here."

"Mr. Singer, we can get a train here in four hours," Holliday said. "Now we're pretty anxious to complete your shipping contract and get on with other business." He took a hunting case watch from his pocket and glanced at it. "Don't you think we ought to get started if we're going to reach your place by dark?"

A frown came to Singer's blunt face. "I thought you wanted to hear the signal when the wires were connected."

Holiday laughed. "We're not experimenting with a new invention. It'll work and that's all I care about." Betty laughed and he looked at her. "What did I say?"

"It's not what you say, Mr. Holliday, but the way you say it, as though there was one burning desire in you—to run a railroad."

"I suppose," Ben said. "that's about the size of it. Don't you have a burning desire?"

"That's almost an improper question," Betty Singer said. "I'll have to think about it."

"I suppose we'd better go," Singer said, turning to the buggy. "But damn it, I did want to hear the wire come alive. There ought to be a celebration or something." He was still grumbling when he climbed in and Holliday lifted Betty up, then got in back. Ollie Skinner came trotting along the track and when he stopped by the off-wheel he was out of breath. Singer looked at him and said, "I thought you left the country." He pointed to Skinner. "I threw this man off my place once." His heavy lips mir-

207

rored an unyielding opinion of Skinner. "The man's a thief."

"He works for me," Holliday said. "And I've found him loyal, hard-working, honest, and sober." He caught Skinner's astonished expression from the corner of his eye, but kept his face straight.

"This man?" Singer yelled, pointing.

"You heard him, didn't you?" Skinner asked. He unbuckled his shell belt, wrapped it around the holstered .44, and handed it to Ben Holliday. "You just sleep with that tonight; he'll accuse you of anything."

Anger stained Singer's face. "Damn you, Skinner, you stole eight dollars from me."

"Did eight months in the Tascosa jail fer it too!" He stepped back, his wrinkled face bland, the unfriendliness hidden behind drooped eyelids. "See you when you get back, Mr. Holliday."

As Murray Singer drove away, Betty said, "That dirty old man!" She glanced at Holliday as though she expected him to agree with her, and found that he didn't. "Don't you believe my father?"

"Sure, but like Skinner said, he's already been in jail."

Singer turned his attention away from his driving to speak. "I'll tell you plainly, Holliday, that it lowers my opinion of the railroad to see you're hiring men like that."

"Probably all your men sing in the choir," Holliday said casually. "It's wonderful to be pure."

Murray Singer said something unintelligible and Betty pouted. She said, "And I thought I was going to like you, Mr. Holliday."

The ride turned out to be dusty and silent and very long, and Ben Holliday rather enjoyed it, for he had prodded this stuffed-shirt cattleman on the peck, which wasn't especially hard to do with these Texans, except when it was done for a reason.

And Ben Holliday had a reason.

One long look at Singer, and five minutes of conversation, and Ben knew which way the wind blew. Singer was a big man, with a lot of land and a lot of cattle and two dozen men working for him, and the habit of running things was pretty well ingrained. The telegraph line gave him the notion that now he controlled a little bit of the railroad too. Well, to Ben's way of thinking, he didn't feel any too secure as the boss to begin with, so he had no wish for a dominant man like Singer to even touch the controls.

Some men just wouldn't let go once they got hold, and Holliday was certain that Singer was that kind.

Singer had built a sizable place, a large, rambling house with a small-town-size scatter of outbuildings and corrals. He was, Holliday could see, proud of the place, and when he stopped by the porch and got down, he said, "Out here there's only one thing that holds a man down. Water. Could hardly make a go of it until I got water. Dug four wells to get it, though."

"Dry holes?" Holliday asked.

"Just a lot of stinkin' wind," Singer said, turning to the porch.

Holliday handed Betty Singer to the ground; she flounced into the house, and Murray Singer scowled slightly. "A high-strung girl there. Come on in, Holliday. A whisky would settle some of this dust."

"Sounds good," Ben said, and started across the porch. Then he stopped and studied two men walking toward him from the barn. They would have passed on without noticing him if he hadn't said, "How's your jaw, Satchel?"

The stooped and Satchel looked at him, then did a right face and walked to the porch. His jaw was swollen and discolored clear up to the eye and down into the neck. "Well, if it ain't the railroad man," Satchel said. He raised a hand to his face and let it drop away, as though he hadn't meant to do that at all, but couldn't help it. "Maybe I'll see you before you leave."

"If you think you have to," Holliday said. He stood there while the other man pulled Satchel's arm, then Holliday went into the house with Murray Singer.

"Heard about the horse and buggy," Singer said. "Satchel doesn't like to be jumped."

"I had somewhat of a surprise myself," Holliday said. They went into the parlor, a wide, spacious room filled with Spanish furniture and olla jugs hanging from the beam ceiling. The chandelier was a wagon wheel hung on a chain, with the lamps dangling from hooks set into the rim. "A beautiful place," Holliday said. He sat down when Singer made a motion to his hand, then a Mexican servant came in.

"Bring up two whiskies. Ortiz. Then see if you can find my son." He turned to Holliday. "Carl is like my right arm, Holliday. Without him, Lazy T would only run half as smooth."

The servant came back with the whisky and Holliday took his glass, trying to think of an appropriate toast, something about cattle and railroads being wedded, but he had no opportunity to propose it. Singer tossed off his drink, then wiped his watering eyes.

"I suppose you'd like to see the telegraph installation," Singer said. "We've put the operator in an old tool shed." He opened a side door and they walked down a short hall to the side entrance. The tool shed was behind the barn, identified by the string of poles leading to it, and the wire disappearing inside.

While they were crossing the yard, two horsemen rode toward the house. Singer stopped and said, "Here's Hutchins and Vale. I thought it would be nice if we got together this evening, since we're all in business together."

Vale was a big man, heading a big outfit, the Cross A. He had a full, florid face and a roan mustache and a pearl-handled pistol at his hip. His handclasp was bone-bruising, and his voice a strong bass. "Glad to meet you, Holliday. I was beginning to take you for an office man." He touched Hutchins on the shoulder. "Bert Hutchins, of the Box X."

Holliday shook hands with him. Hutchins was like a

small rooster, proud standing, bold in the eye, and assertive as only a short man can be.

"We were going to have a look at the telegraph," Singer said. He laughed. "Lacking Holliday's confidence, I don't even know if the damned thing works yet."

They went on together to the tool shed, and Holliday stopped in the open door. The operator was lying on his bunk, and he got up quickly. "Hello, Mr. Holliday. I guess you caught me loafin'."

"I don't expect you to stand at attention all the time," Ben said. "When did you get through?"

"Some time ago," the operator said. The key started to chatter, and he listened a moment. "That's Curly, sir. Want me to take it down? He's calling end of track."

"Let's find out what's going on," Singer said. "That's what he's here for, ain't he?"

"Go ahead," Holliday said, and the operator wrote the message out. He handed it to Holliday, and Singer crowded in to see and Ben turned to him with a flat, irritated stare. "Do you mind? This is railroad business." He read the message and put it in his pocket, then looked at the anger staining Singer's face. "The cattle train is leaving the yard at sundown."

"You could have let me read that," Singer said.

"I could let you put your feet on my office desk, but I won't," Holliday said. Then he stepped outside and the others turned with him. A horseman cantered to the barn and flung off, and from the way one of the hands rushed out to take the horse, Holliday knew this was Carl Singer. He was dressed in denims and chaps and a wide-brimmed hat, yet as he walked across the yard, Holliday had the distinct feeling that he had seen the man before, but not dressed like that. He let his mind work on it and by the time Carl Singer came up to them, he had it.

"This is my son, Carl," Singer said.

Holliday observed him while they shook hands. Young, thirty or thirty-one, he was rather handsome, with a square jaw and fierce dark eyes. Holliday said, "Didn't I see you get off the train in Comanche yesterday morning?"

Carl Singer's eyes changed for the barest instant, becoming alert. Then he smiled. "Sorry, you must have me mixed up with someone else. I haven't left the ranch for ten days."

"My mistake," Holliday said.

"Well, let's go on into the house," Singer said, his manner jolly. "Where are you stringing wire to next, Holliday?"

"Who's ready to ship next?" He looked at Hutchins. "My maintenance foreman is working three shifts, stringing eight to ten miles of wire every day. We could be at your place by Thursday."

"That sounds good to me," Hutchins said.

Betty Singer was in the parlor when they stepped into the room. She had changed her dress to something light and white and she gave Ben Holliday her best smile. "The heat and dust always make me rude, Mr. Holliday. Will you forgive me?" She put her hand on his and let the fingers bite in a little, and in this way she squeezed an answering smile out of him. "May I call you Ben?"

"I'd like that."

"Then we'll go sit on the east veranda," she said. "It's always nice there close to sundown, and you can see the prairie change hues before growing dark."

Holliday hesitated an instant, then spoke to the men. "If you gentlemen will excuse me?"

They murmured their assent and he went out with her; she was telling him of some amusing happening and he was giving her a gentleman's polite attention.

After they passed from earshot, Carl Singer swore softly and said, "God damn it, I didn't think he'd recognize me."

"Let's go in the study," Murray Singer said, and led the way; after the door was closed and they'd taken chairs, he let his face draw into a pucker. "We've got to watch ourselves around him; he's not exactly stupid." He turned to a liquor cabinet and brought out a bottle and four glasses. "I'd like to know what kind of a scheme he's hatching with the Indians to keep them from pulling the wires down." He waved his finger like a baton. "Make up your mind to it, that here is a man who covers all his bets."

"Not all of them," Carl said. "When I got off the train, the town was still talking about the trouble he had with Satchel. I think you can make him go off half cocked without much trouble." He brought out his tobacco and papers and rolled a smoke. His glance went to Hutchins and Vale. "Like I was telling Dad, Holliday's in a bad spot. His old man has advised him to sell the line."

"You don't know this," Murray said quickly. "Let's stick to what we know."

"I think it's a sound assumption," Carl maintained. "I was in Holly Bristow's Dodge City office when he showed me a letter from Julius Holliday. The old man thinks the offer is sound and so much as said he would advise his son of the same."

"But that doesn't mean he'll take it," Jerry Vale said. "If he was going to sell, he wouldn't be running a train south and putting up wire."

"We'll have to make him sell," Murray Singer said. "But I want the lines up. It was our original agreement when we signed contracts to get as much out of the railroad as we could for the same offer." He spread his hands. "I'd rather have the poles set and the wire up than laying in the equipment yard and have to do it ourselves." He finished his drink and put the glass aside. "Holliday's got some idea of how he's going to handle the Indians. Oh, I know, the telegraph will put us in touch with the railroad if the Indians start raiding, but the scheme I'm talking about is the one he's cooked up to keep the Comanches away from the wires." He gnawed his lip a moment. "If that scheme didn't work, gentlemen, Ben Holliday would go bust in a hurry."

"I'd like to see the wires stay up," Bert Hutchins said. "One way or another, we'll have Indian trouble."

"You've fought Indians before," Vale reminded him.

"Can't you do it again?" He laughed without humor. "Bert, you always want everything for nothing. We've gone along with Murray this far. I'm for following it all the way through."

Hutchins shrugged and sat back in his chair, having no more to say. Carl refilled his glass and held it for a moment. "Holliday intends to string more wire than just to our places. We don't want that."

"He won't," Murray said flatly. "If ever a man was over our barrel, Ben Holliday is. He's broke and everyone knows it. And the only revenue he can get right away is the profit on our shipment. How much is that going to amount to?"

"Enough to keep him on his feet," Hutchins said. "He's an odds player, a man who will draw to a busted flush and fill it. Hell, it isn't that hard to figure him out. Any revenue he takes in he'll pour into more poles and wire until every rancher within a decent distance will be shipping." He shook his finger at Murray Singer. "And that is something we can't control. That's the profit that will make Midland-Pacific stock jump, and our offer worthless."

"Sure," Singer said. "But if the Indians tear down the wire and start raiding, how easy do you think it will be to talk anyone else into the idea?" He shook his head. "I've never known a man who couldn't be broken, and that sure as hell includes Ben Holliday. So we ship, so he pockets a profit. That's company money, and when we buy the company, we get all the assets, along with the rolling stock and equipment. Once it's ours, God help any Indian who gets in the way."

The study was filling with evening shadows, and Murray Singer got up, lit several lamps, then poured a little more whisky into his glass. "I found out today that Ollie Skinner is working for the railroad."

"Hell, I knew that," Carl said. "He's been working for them since he got out of jail."

"You never said anything to me," Murray said.

Carl shrugged. "Now how important did you think it was? Hell, after you had Skinner locked up, you said you never wanted to see him again. That's why I didn't say anything."

"Skinner's worked his way into Holliday's good graces," Murray said. "So I'll assume that Skinner knows some things we ought to know."

"Could be," Carl said. "So?"

"Since Skinner would never come here, better take Satchel with you and ride to end of line. Maybe you can get Skinner alone."

Carl Singer laughed. "What the hell do you think Skinner will tell me? Except to go to hell."

"Don't you know how to get what you want from a man?" Vale asked.

Carl Singer frowned. "You want it that way, Dad? Skinner is tough. He'll have to be hurt."

"We're talking about a hundred-thousand dollar investment," Bert Hutchins said flatly. "Who the devil cares who gets hurt?"

A soft run of talk came from the hall, then Betty Singer laughed at something Holliday said, and knocked on the study door. She opened it and pouted prettily. "You're like hermits. It's a beautiful sunset," she said, and sat down. "I've been trying to talk Ben into staying a few days, but he's very stubborn. I think he's dedicated to working himself to death before he's thirty-five."

"Never knock an ambitious man," Vale said, smiling. "Sit down, Holliday. Care for a drink?"

"Too close to supper," Ben said. "But I'll sit." He let a smile build slowly. "However, with such a beautiful daughter, Mr. Singer, I was sorely tempted to let the railroad go to pot for a few days."

"Things have a way of taking care of themselves." Hutchins opined. "When I was thirty and running four hundred head, I wouldn't leave the place if one of my cows was ready to drop a calf. Now I let it happen and count heads every spring and fall."

"Unfortunately," Holliday said, "when I need a new boxcar, I can't expect the caboose to give birth to it. I have to buy it with hard cash, and there is a shortage of that at the present which I hope to remedy," He turned his head as the servant quietly entered.

"A man to see Señor Holliday, *jefe*."

"Send him in," Murray Singer said. He looked at Ben Holliday. "Were you expecting anyone?"

"No," Holliday said, genuinely puzzled. He waited and then he heard hard boots coming down the hall. When Ollie Skinner stopped in the doorway, Ben said, "Don't you believe in the telegraph?"

"Got to talk to you," Skinner said.

"Excuse me," Holliday said, and stepped out of the room. But this didn't satisfy Skinner, who took him out of the house, out to where his horse was waiting. Ben said, "What the hell's the matter with you, Skinner?"

"Bender came back," Skinner said. "He's waitin' fer you at end of line."

"Why didn't you telegraph it and save the ride?"

Skinner wiped his face. "I don't want anyone to know but you, Mr. Holliday. Me, I don't trust nothin' here, or nobody. You know, I never took that eight dollars like Singer said. But I did a stretch in jail for it." He glanced past Holliday to the house. "A man does me mean once, and I got no use for him from then on. Maybe you'd better borrow a horse. I'll wait and ride back with you."

Holliday nodded and went back into the house, thinking how easy it would be to tell Skinner he was imagining things. But Holliday wasn't going to dismuss the man's opinion that casually, especially when Carl Singer said he hadn't left the ranch, while he'd gotten off the train in Comanche. A man had a reason to lie, maybe a personal one, but Holliday would be better off, he knew, if he didn't let any of the Singers get too friendly until he knew more about this.

He made his excuses, the best in the world; business, and Murray Singer made a fuss about being sorry this had come up, but he didn't argue about it. Holliday said good-by to Betty, and promised he'd see her again, then went out with Murray and Carl.

Skinner was still waiting by his horse, and Carl went to the barn to fetch one for Ben Holliday. Murray said, "It's a long ride on an empty stomach, Holliday. Are you sure you couldn't——"

"Skinner says it's important."

Singer shrugged. "You're the best judge of that. But it's still a shame you both have to ride hungry. Skinner, why don't you stay and eat before going back?"

"I guess not," the old man said sourly.

"Now you're not letting bitter feelings stand in the way of a full belly, are you?" Singer laughed softly. "Can't a man show that he was wrong and sorry about it?" Carl came back with a saddle horse, and Murray Singer said, "I've just asked Skinner to stay for supper, but he won't accept my apologies."

"You never were very good at it," Carl said. "Ollie, we found out that someone else took that eight dollars. None of us knew how to tell you, knowing how you felt about us and all." He scuffed dust with his feet. "Hell, man, you can hold it against us forever. Have supper, anyway."

"Nope," Skinner said bluntly, stubbornly.

Murray was beginning to lose patience, but Carl stayed amiable. "We said we were sorry. What more do you want?"

"Who took the money?" Skinner asked.

"The one they called Rio," Carl said. "You remember him. He told us he took it."

"That's right," Murray said, backing his son up. "Rio said he took the money."

Skinner squeezed tobacco juice between his lips and stepped into the saddle. He sat there and looked at the Singers. "I always said you was liars, and I'll still say it. Rio never took the money. I did. He owed it to me from poker and wouldn't pay up." He grinned. "You want to try another story?

Carl Singer swore and took a step toward the old man, but Murray flung out his arm, blocking him. "All right, get out of here, Skinner. The next time I see you on my place, you won't ride off."

"Suits me," Skinner said, and turned his horse, but Ben Holliday did not.

"When I first met you, Carl, I mentioned that I'd seen you get off the train in Comanche. And I did, in spite of what you said. Now you come up with this story. Playing games, gentlemen?"

"It's our business," Murray Singer said. "Leave it that way."

"We'll see," Holliday said, and joined Skinner; they trotted away together. When they were out of the yard, Ben said, "Now you tell the straight of it. Did you or didn't you take the money?"

"Told you once I didn't. Rio didn't either. He couldn't have, because he'd been loaned to Vale on roundup." He checkled softly. "That's why I confessed that I took it; they was ready to believe that. It sure threw 'em, didn't it?"

"But not hard," Holliday said. "This is a high-stake game, Ollie, and the pot is a railroad." He thought about it a moment. "And it makes me wonder if Hutchins and Vale are counting chips."

"Think you dare chance that they ain't?" Skinner asked He turned and looked back at the Singer ranch, bright with lights. "Was a man to come ridin' across the prairie at night and see that, he'd think it was the friendliest sight he'd ever seen. Shows how wrong a man can be without even tryin'."

CHAPTER FIVE

Jim Bender was in the cook tent when Holliday pushed the flap aside and stepped in. Bender sat with his hands enclosing a cup of coffee, and Holliday poured some for himself before sitting down. The cook was washing the last of the supper dishes and he set a pan of stew on the back of the stove to warm for Holliday and Skinner, who was putting up the horses.

"I thought you were hunting Indians," Holliday said.

"I was," Bender said. "That's why I went to Fort Elliot, who makes a business of keeping track of the Indians." He grinned and rubbed his beard stubble. "A man can save a lot of riding that way." He grinned at Ben Holliday. "I didn't expect to find you out here at end of track. I was going to telegraph you, but Skinner said you were with the Singers."

"You know them well?"

Bender shrugged. "Well enough. Murray likes to get what he wants, and the best way to stay clear of him is never to have what he wants." He leaned back and rolled a cigarette. "While I was at Fort Elliot, a new lieutenant wandered in off the prairie. Created somewhat of a stir; they usually don't arrive that way. As it happened, I was in Dawson's office when he reported. He said you were going to string wire to the post. Naturally I was some surprised."

"If I can get wire and poles," Holliday said. "What did Dawson say about the telegraph?"

"He'd like to believe it," Bender said. "Fact is, he'll be here in the mornin' to talk it over, among other things."

"What other things?"

"I don't know," Bender admitted. "He don't take me into his confidence." He got up to refill his coffee cup, then Skinner came in and headed for the stove and the pot of stew there. "Now there's a suspicious old man, Ben." There was more praise in Bender's voice than condemnation. "If you want to know about the Singers, ask Skinner. It'll be bad, because he never saw anything good in any of 'em, and it'll be the truth.

"Who do I see to get the other side?"

Bender thought a minute. "Holly Bristow. He used to have a law office in Comanche, but he moved to Dodge four years ago."

"Now that's real interesting," Holliday said, thinking of his father's letter and the offer from the Dodge City lawyer.

"What's real interestin'?" Skinner asked, bringing his plate to the table.

"Holly Bristow," Holliday said. "I just found out he was thick with Murray Singer."

"That crook," Skinner said, and began eating. Bender glanced at Holliday and shrugged, then got up.

"There's no sense in me hanging around, Ben. According to Dawson, the Indians are somewhere to the north huntin' buffalo. Maybe I'll see you in a week or ten days." He pushed Skinner's hat down over his eyes. "Didn't anyone ever tell you to take your hat off when you eat?"

After he walked out, Skinner said, "There was a time when Jim and Betty Singer was talkin' about settin' up housekeepin'. Thought I'd mention that for what it's worth."

"Just what is it worth?" Holliday asked.

"Wouldn't know," Skinner said. "Maybe you'd better ask him sometime."

Holliday went out and stood in the darkness for a time then walked over to the tent Emil Kisdeen had left behind. The maintenance superintendent had taken the work trail a ways north, where the night shift, working by lantern light, were setting poles for the line to Bert Hutchins place. As he took off his boots, Holliday wondered what kind of a reply Harry Lovell got from the Western Union stockyard in Dodge concerning the poles and wire. There was no particular good will between Midland-Pacific and Western Union, since the railroad had already cost the telegraph company considerable money. The wire and poles from Dodge to Comanche had been put in by Western Union, for the railroad, but when bad turned to worse, Western Union sold it to Midland-Pacific at a loss, expecting the railroad to go broke so they could buy it back and break even. But the railroad was stubborn and kept hanging on, and now they were asking for more credit.

He was thinking about his dismal prospects when he fell asleep.

Carl Singer dismounted a hundred yards from the tents and squatted for a time. Satchel remained on his horse, his hands crossed on the pommel. Finally Singer said, "You'd better go in alone; he'd spook if he saw me."

"He's no friend of mine," Satchel said. "What makes you think——"

"Just get him away from the camp. I'll foot in and wait for you."

"How'll I know where he's sleepin'?"

"It won't be in a tent," Carl Singer said. "Look on the ground around the edge of camp." He gave the man a shove. "Get going and don't wake everyone up." He watched Satchel disappear in the darkness, then moved in closer.

Every tent was dark, and there was no one about when Satchel soft-footed it around the camp. He found Skinner sleeping on a tie pile, and eased his revolver clear of the holster before moving in too close.

Carefully, Satchel advanced until he could hear Skinner breathe, then he pressed the cold muzzle of the pistol against Skinner's temple. "One sound," Satchel said, "and I'll blow you to kingdom come."

Without moving his head, Skinner opened his eyes with a snap, rolled them, and saw Satchel standing there.

"Up," Satchel said softly. "Come on, up!" Without taking the pistol away from Skinner's head, the man patted around, trying to find Skinner's gun.

"I gave it to Holliday," Skinner said. "You want to do the smart thing, Satchel? Take that pistol away from my head and vanish. If you don't, I swear, I'll even this with you."

"Let's go," Satchel said. "We'll go or I'll scatter your brains now."

"You got a good argument there," Skinner said, and jumped down off the tie pile. The pistol prodding him in the back directed him past the camp, then he saw Carl Singer standing there in the darkness. "I might have known it," he said gruffly. "Was you scared to come in fer me yourself?"

"Go catch up his horse, Satchel," Singer said. "I'll keep Ollie company."

"Some company," Skinner grumbled. He waited in silence for a time, then turned to Singer. "If this is your notion, it ain't a good one."

"I only want to talk to you," Singer said. "Ollie, you're a hard man to get along with."

"Haven't heard any complaints," Skinner said. Satchel came back with a horse, and Carl Singer motioned for him to mount up. When Skinner showed some reluctance Singer hit him with the gun barrel, not hard enough to knock him out, but hard enough to hurt him.

"I'm not going to fool with you," Singer said, and got on his own horse. They rode out with Ollie Skinner between them, and kept up a steady pace for over an hour.

Their destination was a dry wash, a ten-foot-deep gully splitting the face of the prairie in an irregular line. Satchel took care of the horses and Carl Singer crouched down, his gun still covering Skinner.

"We can talk here," Singer said. "I'll ask questions, and you'll answer 'em, Ollie."

"If I know the answers," Skinner said.

"Oh, you're a smart old bastard," Carl said. "You know a lot, say a lot." He turned his head as Satchel came back

"Fix a fire. I saw some brush along here earlier today."

Satchel stomped around, breaking up brush, and finally got a small fire going. Then he sat down and pointed his gun at Ollie Skinner. "I'll keep an eye on him, Mr. Singer."

"Be careful, he's sneaky as hell," Carl said. He took a cigar from his pocket and lit it. "I'll save you the butt, Ollie. You always used to pick up snipes for chewing tobacco." He laughed. "When I put my mind to it, there's a lot of things about you I don't like."

"Same here," Skinner said, "only I don't have to put my mind to it."

"Let's get on with this," Satchel said. "I want to get out of here by daylight."

"You're right," Carl said. "We want to talk over some railroad business, Ollie."

"I fetch meals, tend horses, and run errands," Skinner said. "What do I know?"

"You've got your ear to every keyhole, Ollie. I figure you know what's goin' on. Is Holliday going to take the offer made to him?"

"What offer?"

Satchel hit him with a heavy stick and Skinner fell over. But he sat up again, a red welt on the side of his head. Carl Singer spoke. "A lawyer in Dodge made an offer to buy the line. Is Holliday going to take it?"

"Ask Holliday. He's the boss."

Again Satchel struck him with the club, across the mouth, and Skinner bled from the lips. He sat up more slowly this time and spat out a broken tooth. Carl said, "What do you want to be like that for, Ollie? You cooperate, and I'll give you a horse and fifty dollars." He looked at Skinner to see how the offer was goin to be taken, but there was nothing in the old man's expression except disgust. "All right, we've got some time. How does Holliday expect to keep the Indians from tearing down the telegraph wires?"

"Are they goin' to tear down the wires? I didn't hear nobody say that."

Satchel would have hit him again, but Carl blocked his arm. "He's not afraid of that club, Satchel. Ollie, we don't want to hurt you, but we want to know about these things. The Indians will sure as hell tear the wires down once they find out what they're for. Now what's Holliday goin' to do about it?"

"Pray," Skinner said. "Write to his congressman. How the hell do I know?"

"You know," Carl said. He looked at Satchel. "We've been too easy on Ollie. Strip him to the waist."

The man got up and started for Skinner, but made the mistake of putting his pistol into the holster first. It was all the break Skinner needed; he kicked Satchel flush in the face and drove him backwards full into the fire. Satchel lit in a sitting position, his tight denims no protection at all. With a scream he vaulted up and started rolling away, and Skinner dived for Carl Singer.

For a moment they just rolled on the ground, their arms locked tightly about each other, legs thrashing for purchase; then Skinner battered Singer's face with his knuckles and tried to break away, to climb the gully wall.

He almost made the top when Singer pulled his gun, sighted quickly, and smashed Ollie Skinner's hip. The old man cried out and tumbled down, than Singer got up and went over and stood there, looking at him.

"I could have killed you easy," Carl said.

"You'd have—saved time if—you had," Skinner said, panting.

"Satchel, quit that moaning and strip him like I said!"

Skinner was shorn of shirt, and his underwear was ripped clean to the waist, then Satchel went to his saddlebags and brought back four picket pins and some short lengths of rope. In spite of his wound, Skinner fought, and it took both of them to spread-eagle him.

After Skinner's arms and legs were both tied tightly, Carl sat back and wiped sweat from his face. "Ollie, you're makîng me do this."

"I ain't makin' you do nothin'," Skinner snapped. "It's your own damned meanness."

"Put a little fire on his belly," Singer said.

Skinner drew taut like a violin string when Satchel laid a burning twig on him, and he moaned and bit his lips and sawed his head from side to side until Singer couldn't stand it any longer.

"Get it off him," Carl said, and Satchel flicked the burning wood away. "Ollie, I've got to know about Holliday's plans. What's he to you, anyway? It's just a job, ain't it?"

"You wouldn't understand," Skinner said softly. "He only cusses me when I got it comin', not when he feels like it. Burn me if you want. That's all I'm going to say."

Carl Singer didn't believe that, so they put some more fire on Skinner, and after a while, when he lost consciousness, Singer realized that it was the truth; Skinner just wasn't going to speak again.

"I should have known him better," Singer said softly. "He was never known to back down on anythin' in his life." He got up and brushed off the seat of his pants. "Let's go."

"He'll talk if we leave him," Satchel said.

"No. You get the horses." When Satchel turned, Carl Singer drew his gun and cocked it. "Damn you, Ollie, you're the world's worst fool." He fired and then cocked the gun and shot two more times, because he was a little frightened now and doubted his own ability to kill this old man. Then he turned and walked down the gully to where Satchel waited with the horses. "Leave Skinner's horse here." He stepped into the saddle, but Satchel remained dismounted. "Well, you want to stay here with him?"

"I can't ride," Satchel said. "My butt's one big blister."

"Then walk," Carl Singer said harshly. "You'll make it all right."

"I don't want to be found anywhere around here," Satchel said flatly.

"Who the hell's going to find you?" Singer asked. "If

225

he's missed, it won't be until daylight. And who the hell cares enough about him to go looking for him?"

"Holliday."

"He's a greenhorn who has a hell of a time finding his way from the house to the barn." He gigged his horse and ran up the steep walls of the gully, and once clear, he set a brisk pace back to his father's place. He wasn't sorry he had killed Ollie Skinner; he was bothered more by the possible consequences of what he had done; he'd hang for it if he was caught, and this seemed grossly unfair to Carl, hanging for killing a worthless old coot like Skinner.

Murray Singer was still up when Carl rode in. The house was dark, save for a lamp on in the parlor, and Murray came out to the porch as his son dismounted.

"Well?"

Carl shook his head and sat on the steps. "He wouldn't talk."

Murray Singer took the cigar from his mouth. "What the hell do you mean, he didn't talk? Can't you get information out of a man?"

"Not him," Carl said. "Satchel and I put fire to him, but he still wouldn't say. Maybe if he'd hated me less, he'd have been less stubborn."

"Where's Satchel?" Murray asked, peering around in the darkness.

"Walking. Skinner put up a fight. Knocked Satchel in the fire and he burned his hind end."

"Why, you damned bunglers," Murray said softly. "Where's Skinner now?"

"In a dry wash. Dead."

"Well, at least you had enough sense to do that," Murray said. "You didn't leave anything behind to point to you, did you? Like some empty shells or something?"

"No, I've still got the empties in my gun," Carl said.

"Well, go in and clean it and put it away. Start carrying another from now on. There's no telling when Jim Bender will come snooping around."

"If he does," Carl said, "Betty can handle him."

"Like the last time?" Murray shook his head. "He surprised the hell out of me, thinking more of that damned badge than he did Betty. You clean the gun and put it away someplace. I want everyone to be lily white when Bender shows up."

The cavalry arrived shortly after dawn, a ten-man escort for the colonel. Holliday was having his breakfast when they pulled into camp and he told the cook to set out some more plates in a hurry; it wouldn't hurt to feed the cavalry for the sake of public relations.

Colonel Cameron Dawson was a tall, gaunt man with a roan mustache and a constantly worried air. He shook hands briefly, then sat down and ignited a cigar. The fact that the cook was setting a place for his line troopers pleased Dawson, and he gave orders for the sergeant to see that every man was washed before he came in.

With some coffee before him, Dawson's manner thawed somewhat. "Mr. Holliday, since your response to my written appeals could hardly be classified as encouraging, it's come as considerable surprise to me that your attitude has been reversed."

"Blame it on a bright lieutenant," Holliday said.

Dawson's eyebrow arched. "Mr. Gary? He is now working off a bit of stable detail for arriving late. Now about the telegraph line to Fort Elliot. Fact or fiction?"

"Fact, if I can promote the poles and wire from Western Union."

"The eternal catch," Dawson said sadly. "I was afraid something like this was going to happen."

"There's about a seventy-thirty chance," Ben pointed out. "That's better than before, isn't it?"

"Good reasoning, but which is it? Seventy against getting the poles, or for?"

"Against," Holliday said frankly. "Our credit is none too good. However, I hope to convince others that it will improve."

"You're a gambler," Dawson said. "And they make me nervous. Always gambling with something not entirely

227

theirs." Then he shrugged. "But this telegraph is going to cost me. How much?"

"No more than you're used to paying," Ben said. "Colonel, I've got to move beef and freight over the line or go broke. And to do that, I have to assure the Texans that when there's Indian trouble, the railroad will do its fair share in putting it down. Naturally I'm going to pass as much of this off to the army as I can, and so they can do a good job of it I'll put in a telegraph." He smiled. "I think you're clever enough to see that when it comes to whether the Indians go or the railroad does, it'll be the Indians. So we end up making deals with each other. For taking care of the Indians, you'll get a supply line moved a lot nearer, and communication with Fort Dodge. Progress, Colonel, is a complicated thing."

Cameron Dawson thought about it, then nodded. "And I can see why you held out. No profit in it for you."

"Exactly. You'd have done the same." The troopers came in and sat down, and the cook brought out platters of hot cakes and bacon. "Cookie, when you're through there, go out and find Skinner. I've got a job for him."

"Sure, Mr. Holliday."

Holliday gave his attention then to the colonel. "Jim Bender, who's working for me now, is going to arrange a meeting with the Indians. We're going to demonstrate to them how dangerous it will be to tamper with the telegraph wires."

"How? Shoot the first one that touches it?"

Holliday laughed and shook his head. He then explained his plan to Colonel Dawson, and Dawson was pleased with it, although sparing in his praise. "It would be a good thing, Colonel, if you were present at the demonstration. It's my opinion that this ought to be carried out with considerable pomp and ceremony. I hope I can count on you, Colonel, for some original thoughts."

Dawson laughed. "Mr. Holliday, God help us if you run for the United States Senate. Yes, I think I can add some touches." He turned his head and spoke to a sergeant sitting at the third mess table. "DuJoise!"

He was a small peppery man with a waxed mustache and a manner of clicking his heels together that suggested foreign service, and a lot of it. Dawson introduced him. "Mr. Holliday, this is Sergeant Jean Jacques DuJoise, late of the French Artillery, the Prussian Royal Lancers, and the Confederate States Army. We call him John-Jack for short, and it's my eternal regret that he isn't a captain." He motioned for DuJoise to sit down, and he explained Holliday's plan. The Frenchman's eyes brightened and he smiled widely. "Since you've mastered the Comanche language, John-Jack, I suggest that you consider yourself attached to Mr. Holliday until recalled by me."

"As you wish," DuJoise said. "I'll be delighted to work with you, m'sieu. And we certainly can put on a show for the Comanches."

"John-Jack had a long and satisfying relationship with a Comanche girl," Dawson explained. "If anyone knows their customs better than he does, I've yet to meet him." He slapped Sergeant DuJoise on the shoulder and got up to have his coffee cup refilled and fetch back a plate of bacon and hot cakes. "The Indians are on a hunt; I told Bender that yesterday morning. But when the hunt is over, they're going to mix paint and dance some. When's your first load of cattle moving north?"

"I expect a train through today," Holliday said. "Probably two days before we're ready to pull out. Why?"

"I was just trying to get your schedule so I could activate a few more patrols," Dawson said. "The Indians are getting the idea finally that they can't lick the army, and they hesitate to cut up when patrols are roaming about."

The cook came back into the tent and approached the table. "Mr. Holliday, I can't find Skinner anyplace. His horse is here, but there's another one missing, the one you brought back from the Singer place."

"That's odd," Ben said. "Did you have a look around the tie pile? Skinner likes to roost there."

"Yes, sir, but he ain't there. But his blankets are, though."

Holliday got up from the table, a frown on his face. "I think I'll have a look for myself. If you'll excuse me?"

"We'll join you, if you don't mind," Dawson said. "John-Jack is pretty good at reading stories from tracks."

They walked together to the tie pile, but before they got to it, John-Jack stopped. "A question, m'sieu. Does anyone here wear the boots of the cowboy? With the little heels?"

"Hell no," Holliday said. "Mostly work boots around here. Flat heels." Then he amended that statement. "Except Skinner."

DuJoise pointed to the soft earth. "There to see is another man's boot marks." He puffed his cheek and thumped it. "Ah, we follow them to the tie pile, so!" He walked bent over, examining the ground. "Hah! Two pair of tracks walk away, in that direction." He pointed south to the flat stretch of prairie.

"Skinner had no reason to leave camp," Ben Holliday said. "I don't understand it.'

"Nor do I, m'sieu," DuJoise said. "But it would be worth a ride to find out." He shrugged. "There is the missing horse also."

"Skinner had his own horse," Holliday said. "He wouldn't take the one belonging to Murray Singer. He hated Singer." Then he fell silent a moment. "Could it be that someone got the horse for him?"

"A logical thought," Dawson said. "Well, I've got an army to run. If you and John-Jack want to follow this up, go ahead." He shook hands with Ben Holliday. "I enjoyed the bargaining, but I'm not sure what kind of cards I held." He smiled and walked back to the cook tent.

"I'm going to get my gun," Holliday said. "I'll meet you here in ten minutes."

He was going to take the rifle, then picked up Skinner's .44 instead and buckled the belt around his waist. He caught up Skinner's horse, saddled him, and joined the sergeant, who was already mounted.

With DuJoise slightly in the lead, they moved away from camp, taking wide arcs and finally finding the place where Carl Singer had waited.

DuJoise held up three fingers, then they cut to the southeast, moving at a walk, following a trail so faint that Holliday continually lost it, and relied on DuJoise to pick it up. The Frenchman had a profound knowledge of the land, and he read accurately the slightest sign, and watching him ork, Holliday could understand in part why so many of the early explorers were French; they seemed temperamentally suited to this exciting work.

Holliday could not imagine why the two men who took Skinner left such a trail. Then he tried to reason it from their point of view and decided that they figured no one in the railroad camp could find a washtub with both hands, so it didn't matter how much of a trail they left.

This made him smile, this mistaken impression, for many times in his own life he had been tripped up by the unexpected, the uncounted happening. Who could have known the army would show up, and that a good tracker would be available?

It was a sobering reminder to Ben Holliday that a man's plans were often thrown into a cocked hat by new elements he hadn't even considered. He promised himself he'd be careful with his own affairs.

They found the dry wash and Ollie Skinner. The flies were gathering and the sun wasn't helping much either. Holliday thought he was going to be sick, but he fought it down. DuJoise brought from his pack a small shovel and Holliday dug the grave while the Frenchman had his look around.

"Not Indians," DuJoise said softly. "No, m'sieu, the cowboys do this to your friend. An Indian does not put on fire that way. Just little pieces for the slow pain. And to shoot the victim three times; it is a waste of bullets, and the Indian has none to waste. He would have used a war club." He stood there, shaking his head. "And the pins, they are what the cowboys use to tie their horses." He pointed to the scars on the bank, where they had come down, and where one mounted man had gone up. "The other was not riding his horse, but leading him." He came over and spelled Holliday with the digging. "What is your wish, m'sieu? Return to the camp, or go on?"

"We'll go on," Holliday said grimly. "If we can catch the two who did this, I'm going to see they hang for it."

DuJoise glanced at him. "And if they choose to fight?"

"Then I'll save the state of Texas the price of a hanging."

CHAPTER SIX

As soon as Harry Lovell got off the train in Dodge City, he walked along Front Street to Holly Bristow's office, which was over a saddle maker's shop. He used the side stairs, not particularly worried about anyone seeing him, because he didn't come to Dodge often enough to be well known. And Lovell always conducted his business quietly, so as not to attract attention to himself.

A man had to do things that way when he held down three jobs at one time.

Bristow wasn't in his office, so Lovell made himself comfortable and waited, and in time Bristow came back, a fleeting look of surprise on his face when he saw Harry Lovell there.

"I wasn't expecting you," Bristow said, sitting down. He was a large, round man with a moon face and a dense black mustache. His suit was expensive, and a diamond stickpin in his tie reflected sunlight. "Have you sent your report to Julius Holliday yet?"

"No," Lovell said. "I may skip this one."

Holly Bristow laughed softly. "Lovell, you must be getting rich, drawing a salary from the railroad, and a bonus from the old man for checking up on the boy, and from me a generous fee for getting us in on the inside track. How's Holliday coming along?"

"He's trying desperately to save the line," Lovell said. "I came to Dodge to get some credit from Western Union. For poles and wire. He wants to string a telegraph to Fort Elliot."

"I don't like the sound of that," Bristow said softly. "There's been a strong rumor going around that Midland-Pacific got some financial help. Any truth to it?"

"None," Lovell said. "Holliday started that himself in order to bolster his credit with Western Union."

"The last time I talked to Carl Singer, he expressed an impatience at the way this is dragging out. Holliday's old man is for taking the offer. What makes Ben so stubborn?"

Lovell shrugged, then said, "Maybe he doesn't like to be licked, Holly. I can't blame him for that. What am I going to do about the poles and wire? I've got to try, and suppose I get them?"

"Don't do a thing until tomorrow morning," Bristow said. "That will give me time to spike your chances. Then you can report back to Ben Holliday with a straight face. Harry, how long is it going to be before his back breaks?"

"I'll be damned if I know," Lovell admitted. "He should be bleeding, but he isn't. The sooner this comes to a head, the better off we'll all be."

"Right," Bristow said. "That's what Carl Singer said. Some men have a habit of hanging on and hanging on. We don't want this to happen. Singer made it pretty plain that in a week or so he expects Holliday to throw up his hands and quit. Now if he's not going to do that, it's up to us to put the pressure on him hard."

"No rough stuff," Lovell cautioned.

Bristow laughed and waved his hand. "This is a business venture, Harry, not a war. Cut off his credit here and there, and he's done." He shuffled a few papers around on his desk. "We both know that more people have been stabbed to death with a bookkeeper's pencil than the sword. Now I want you to go over to the hotel, get a room, shave, clean up, have a good meal, and talk to anyone who wants to listen. Talk about railroading, Harry, and lay it on the line that Holliday is broke. You know what I mean. Loosen up with the inside information, like a man will when he can't see the sense of keeping quiet when the outfit is staggering its last steps. I'll take it from there, and when you ask for poles and wire, you can bet you won't get them."

"All right," Lovell said. Then he sighed. "God, I wish it would end, Holly. But I've said that before, haven't I? What takes a piddlin' little railroad so long to die?"

"The man at the throttle," Bristow said. "Holliday's got his hand on it and he doesn't want to turn loose of it." He straightened in his chair. "Be patient, Harry. Remember, we can afford to be."

"Of course," Lovell said.

Bristow got up when someone knocked at the door, and Harry Lovell straightened apprehensively, but Bristow motioned for him to sit back and relax. He opened the door and said, "Yes?" He glanced at the girl, and at the heavy man with the walrus mustache. "Could I help you?"

"I'm Anna Neubauer. This is my father. May we come in?"

Bristow stepped aside. "Of course. I was just finishing with a client." He turned to Harry Lovell. "I'm sure we'll find your wife, sir. You'll hear from me shortly." Then he shook hands with Lovell, who went right out. "Now, Miss Neubauer. Sit down, please. Right over there, sir, in the leather chair." Again he moved behind his desk and sat down. "Well, what can I do for you?"

"My father's English is not too good," Anna said. "But we want to know if it's true that in America, if you make a new thing, you can take out a paper to keep others from making it too."

"A patent," Bristow said, smiling. "Mr. Neubauer, have you an invention?"

Fritz Neubauer looked confused. *"Was sagt er?"*

Anna explained it in German, and he nodded. *"Ja,* I make this for the train." He got up. "I leave it in the hall." Then he hurried out and came back with a long, shallow box. He put this on Bristow's desk and took off the lid. A model of a railroad-car coupling handcrafted, with two complete sets of trunks, with air brakes, all operated by mechanical linkage made a polished steel and brass display on piano-finished mahogany. "My daughter, she vill

235

tell you about it. My English——" He shrugged and smiled as though embarrassed.

"This lever here represents the engineer's brake control," Anna said, demonstrating it. "The train is stopped when this valve is moved. But there have been many instances where the engineer and fireman were dead, or too badly hurt to operate the control, and the train ran on until an accident happened."

"Yes, I'm well aware of that," Bristow admitted. "Just last year there was a crash out of Sioux Falls—but go on."

"This is where the engineer stands," she said. "And this is a spring-loaded switch. The engineer puts his foot on it all the time he is running the train. If he so much as takes his foot off, the valve will automatically operate the brakes and stop the train."

"By golly," Bristow said, "that sounds very good." He drew pen and paper to him. "Now, we have some work to do. First, a complete description of the invention, its parts, and function." He smiled at Fritz Neubauer. "Smoke if you like. This is going to take some time."

After they registered at the hotel, Anna Neubauer understood how great was her father's thirst for a glass of beer, and urged him to go get one, but not to be late for supper; this was a strange town and she didn't want to eat alone.

She went upstairs and along the hall to her room, and as she unlocked the door, Harry Lovell stepped out of a room a few doors down. He glanced at her in passing and smiled fleetingly.

Anna said, "I hope you find your wife, sir."

Lovell stopped and frowned. "What was that?"

"I said that I hoped the lawyer finds your wife."

His recognition of her was complete then, and he nodded curtly and went on down the stairs. Just before he disappeared from view he turned his head and looked at her. Anna Neubauer shrugged and went into her room.

She knew her father would stay a while in the saloon, so

she washed her face, then went to do some shopping. Her purchases were carefully made—she was a born bargainer —then she walked back to the hotel just as her father crossed the street. He had, she knew, not limited himself to one beer, but three, but she expected this. Had she said three, he would have had five or six, for he was that way in some things, as though he sought to show in small harmless ways his independence from domesticity.

They ate in the dining room, and Fritz Neubauer seemed troubled, and finally he came out with it, speaking softly in German. "I've seen that man before, Anna."

"What man?"

"The one in the lawyer's office. I think he works for the railroad."

She shrugged. "So? We work for the railroad and we went there."

"I'm sure he works for the railroad. Not with the hands. For Mr. Holliday, in the office building." He shook his head and went on eating. "Maybe he invents something, yes?"

"He is trying to find his wife, Papa."

"How could a man lose his wife?" He seemed to think this was the most ridiculous thing he ever heard.

Through the heat of the day, Ben Holliday and John-Jack DuJoise followed the trail across the prairie, feeling it grow hotter with each mile. Finally DuJoise prodded some horse droppings. "No more than an hour, m'sieu. Perhaps even less. But no more." He pulled his hat low over his eyes and squinted at the shimmering reaches of land. "He still walks his horse, and at a slow pace. See how close are the marks of his feet." He paused to think a moment, then added, "I don't think he limps, m'sieu. Still it is not the stride of a well man. The feet are held too far apart." He turned to his horse. "Come. We move faster now."

Now and then they trotted their horses, and in the distance Ben Holliday could make out the buildings of the

Singer place, and as far as he was concerned, this pretty well settled the issue, for if it wasn't a Singer man who killed Skinner, then it was someone who felt pretty safe on Singer property.

As they drew close to the yard, they split, John-Jack going on toward the corral and bunkhouse, and Ben Holliday riding toward the front porch. Carl and Murray Singer came out to stand.

Holliday did not bother to dismount. He said, "Mr. Singer, Ollie Skinner is dead. The man that killed him is here, on your place. I want him."

For a moment, Murray Singer said nothing, then he smiled. "Son, I can't say that I know a Texas Ranger who'd have enough nerve to do what you just did. In Texas, we're a little more careful about what we say." He turned his head and looked at John-Jack DuJoise. "What the hell's that soldier doin' snoopin' around my corral and bunkhouse?"

"Smelling out rats," Holliday said. "Are you going to give him up, Mr. Singer?"

"Give who up?" He looked at his son. "Do you know what the hell he's talking about?"

"No, but I'll sure as hell get him if there's a killer on this place," Carl said, checking the loads in his gun. "Holliday, you and the soldier come around from behind. I'll break in the bunkhouse door and we'll surprise him, whoever it is."

After a brief hesitation, Holliday nodded and trotted his horse over to the corral where John-Jack waited. Murray observed this from the porch and said, "If they jump Satchel, he'll yell his head off. What he could say wouldn't be pretty."

"He ain't going to get a chance to say it," Carl assured him, and left the porch, trotting toward the bunkhouse. He waved his hands, first in one direction, then the other, and Holliday and the sergeant skirted the building to come in behind.

A group of hands came from the barn and watched

238

Carl kick the door open with his foot. Then he burst inside and there was a roll of gunfire and a man's long, surprised yell.

Holliday had to batter at the rear door with his shoulder before the latch tore away, and he staggered into the room, trying to catch his balance. Carl was standing over Satchel; he rolled him over with his toe and looked at the man's face.

"He went for his gun as soon as I came in," Carl said. "Who'd have thought it!" He looked at Holliday. "Where's the sergeant?"

It was a good question, and annoyed Ben, because he gave John-Jack credit for having a little guts. But instead the man had hung back. He came now to the doorway, looked in, then shrugged and leaned his shoulder against the frame.

"You have one, M'sieu Holliday. Now where is the other?"

"What other?" Carl Singer asked.

DuJoise held up two fingers. "The other who was with him." He pointed to Satchel. "I am always curious, m'sieus, why a man walks when he can ride. His horse is not lame. I looked." He left the doorway and rolled Satchel face down, then more closely examined the badly burned seat of Satchel's pants. "A man does not sit in a fire. Did he fall? Or was he knocked down?"

"Where's Satchel's gun?" Holliday asked. "You said that he went for it."

"Well, he stuck his hand under the mattress," Carl said. "I just guessed he was after a gun. What did you expect me to do? Wait and see? He turned as a shadow darkened the door, and Murray Singer stepped inside. "It was Satchel, Dad."

"Mmmm," Murray said. "It doesn't surprise me none." He looked at Ben Holliday. "What are you pawing under the mattress for?"

"His gun. Here." He lifted it to his nose and sniffed it, then handed it to John-Jack.

"Recently cleaned and oiled," the sergeant said. Then he turned impatiently. "There is nothing more here, m'sieu." He stepped outside.

"What's the army doing in this?" Murray asked impatiently. "I never liked the army around my place, and I never will."

"Take it up with Colonel Dawson," Holliday said. "He's my new aide." The whole notion seemed to insult Murray Singer, and Holliday went out. Sergeant DuJoise was at the watering trough, washing his hands and face, and Holliday crossed over to him. "Where the hell were you when I hit the door?"

"Looking in the window," DuJoise said, grinning. "It is surprising what a man sees through a window." He glanced past Ben Holliday to see if anyone was near enough to hear. "You know that Carl is lying? The dead man was on his stomach when the front door was opened. He rolled on his side and made no move at all when Carl shot him."

"You're sure of that?"

"I will swear it. And the gun under the mattress, it was too well oiled. A man does not dismantle his pistol and oil it while leading his horse, m'sieu."

"By God, that's so."

"And he was not far ahead of us," DuJoise pointed out. "I do not think he took the time to clean his gun, because he didn't have it."

"That's right. And a man with his tail burned isn't thinking about a clean Smith & Wesson." He pulled his face out of shape and gnawed his lip. "I'm going to assume that Satchel didn't kill Ollie, but knew who did. We got too close to him too quickly, Sergeant. That was my mistake."

"And mine," DuJoise said. Don't blame yourself." He tapped Holliday on the arm. "Ears coming, m'sieu."

Holliday washed up as Murray Singer and his son came over. Murray said, "I deeply regret this, Holliday."

"Do you?" Holliday raised his head and let the water stream off. "And you keep calling me Holliday, like I was

240

some damned flunky around here. I'm Mr. Holliday, and don't forget it."

A crimson rush of resentful anger stained Murray's face, and he took a cigar from his pocket and lit it as though he desperately needed something to do. Finally he said, "You're quick to take offense, *Mr.* Holliday." Then he chuckled. "Hell, let's not argue. This whole affair has made us jumpy. Why don't you come to the house and have a drink? Stay for supper; the offer's still good. The sergeant can eat in the cookshack."

"The cookshack?" Holliday stared at Murray Singer. "For your information, Sergeant DuJoise was a commissioned officer in three European armies. A colonel, no less. He eats at your table if I do."

"Of course," Singer said. "I'll tell the cook. Carl, you get a couple of men and get Satchel in the ground before he gets ripe." He walked off, trailing cigar smoke, and Carl turned to the barn.

Jean Jacques DuJoise smiled. *"Merci,* m'sieu. But I was only a lieutenant."

"The secret of getting along with Texans," Holliday said, "is to double everything, and triple it if you can. They liked to be impressed." Then he laughed. "What the hell, you'd have made a good colonel anyway." He glanced past DuJoise, and the sergeant looked around. Betty Singer had come out and was standing on the porch. "The last time I was here, she courted me, and I suspect for a good reason. If you've got any continental manner, John-Jack——"

"Ah, m'sieu, I am French!" He pulled his fingers together, placed them against puckered lips, and pulled them away with a loud smack. "You wish the table to be turned, eh?"

"It's worth a try," Holliday said. "Five will get you ten that Murray Singer wants to own my railroad, and pay nothing for it. Still I think the deal's too big for Singer to handle alone. That'll stand some looking into." He dried

241

his face with a handkerchief, then they walked on to the house.

Betty remained on the porch, and she smiled as Ben Holliday took her outstretched hand. "I want you to meet Colonel Jean Jacques DuJoise."

"Enchanted," DuJoise said, bringing his heels together with a wooden crash. He kissed her hand lingeringly, from a deep bow, and a burst of pleasure bloomed in Betty Singer's cheeks.

"But he's a sergeant."

"Only until his commission is reconfirmed," Holliday said smoothly.

"Well," she said, smiling, "you sure know how to kiss a hand, I must say."

"Perhaps you would show me this exciting house," DuJoise said. His glance touched Holliday. "I take it you've seen it, m'sieu, so there is no need for you to come along."

"Am I being excluded?" Holliday asked.

"Precisely," DuJoise said. "I will tell mademoiselle of Paris, which is a much more enchanting place than Chicago." He offered his arm and she took it, laughing at Ben Holliday.

"Daddy wanted me to bring you into the study, but I guess you know the way."

"If my tears of disappointment don't blind me," Holliday said, and went into the house.

As they walked slowly to the shady side of the house, Betty said, "Are you really a colonel?"

"But of course! I have fought many wars, but I would gladly fight another for you."

"Oh, that's silly. Men shouldn't talk like that."

"Why not? Don't your Texas men fight for their women?"

"Well, yes, but it's different."

He laughed. "True. I use the sword instead of a pistol. I believe it is a proper weapon for defending a lady. A pistol is much too crude for her sensitive nature, all that noise and smelly powder."

Betty Singer laughed. "I don't know whether to believe you or not."

"Test me."

"What? Why, I wouldn't want you to just kill a man to prove——"

"Then you do believe I would?"

"No, I don't believe it," she said. "Well, maybe I do. I wouldn't want to test you, though."

"Pick a man, and he is dead," DuJoise said. "M'sieu Holliday?"

This shocked her. "Your friend?"

"He is not my friend," he said. "Fah! I only met him this morning, and it is only with beautiful women like yourself that I form lasting fondnesses on such short acquaintance." He was a handsome man, smiling, charming, and behind him lay a trail of feminine conquests as long as his military record. He framed the picture with his hands as he talked. "I would pick a suitable time to challenge him, being of course most discreet so that no one ever suspected you were connected in any way. Perhaps I would find a flaw in the way he held his fork; I'm easily offended by vulgar manners. A slap across the face with a glove, lightly, of course, would bring him to his feet in a most insulting manner. He would challenge me, and as the challenged, 'I'd pick the weapons. A meeting at dawn, a quick thrust home, and an honor is saved."

"Why—why, you speak as though you'd already— planned it." She pulled slightly away from him as though suddenly chilled. "I—I don't want to hear any more about this."

"As you wish, but since your brother just killed a man, I thought—well, you're more sensitive than I imagined."

"What my brother does, I don't want to hear about," Betty said. "I don't understand Carl, or my father. My mother didn't either. Now I think we'd better go in." At the door, she paused. "The servant will show you to your room. He'll pour a bath for you if you wish it, and brush your uniform."

243

"Thank you," he said, bowing over her hand. She went down the length of the porch, and he observed her until she passed from his sight, then he walked down the hall. The study door was open and, as he passed, Murray Singer hailed him.

"Ah, come in. A drink?"

"Thank you, yes," DuJoise said. He took the glass Murray handed him and continued to stand.

"We were talking about this unfortunate trouble," Murray said. "I think Mr. Holliday will agree with me that it was an unforeseen development and will be best forgotten."

"Mr. Singer doesn't think we should call in the Texas Rangers to investigate."

"It's a local problem," Singer said. "Let's handle it as that." He spread his hands. "We'll never know what got into Satchel, and it's just as well. Here, Mr. Holliday, let me fill your glass."

"One's enough on an empty stomach," Ben Holliday said. "DuJoise, why don't you sit down? Frankly, I'm too busy with the railroad to go chasing around every time anyone gets shot. As Mr. Singer pointed out, the seeds of this thing probably were sown a long time ago, when Skinner worked here. Satchel's dead, and so is Skinner. We buried our man, and your buried yours. That's even enough."

"Now you're talking like a Texan," Singer said, smiling. "You know, Ben, we've had our differences, but I believe we think alike. You're a man who has to be going somewhere. Well, so do I. I'm never satisfied with what I have. When a man gets that way, he ought to dig a hole and crawl in it." He waved his hand. "When I married my wife I had thirteen hundred acres and a sod hut. When I wanted more land, I took it, and if a man got in my way I stepped on him so hard you could hear him yell in the next county."

"Then I take it you never met a man who stepped on you," Holliday said.

"A few have tried," Murray Singer admitted. He studied

Holliday, then laughed. "I can't help but measure you, because it's habit with me to measure a strong man. I don't think I'll ever get tired of testing my strength."

Carl came down the hall, then, and into the room. He poured himself a whisky and flopped in a leather chair. "Satchel's buried. One of his bunkhouse friends is carving a headboard. Beats me what the hell he'll put on it." His head swung around and he looked at Jean DuJoise. "Is the army working for the railroad now, or is it the other way around?"

"Trains fascinate me," DuJoise said, smiling.

"That's a hell of an answer to a serious question," Carl said.

"Mind your own business," Murray said. "Mr. Holliday, I hear that someone has made an offer to buy the line."

"Yes, that's so."

"You're considering it, I suppose."

"I have considered it," Ben said. "I don't think I'm interested."

"That hardly sounds sensible," Carl said flatly.

"Drink your whisky and keep out of this," Murray said. "Well, Ben, if the offer wasn't so small it was ridiculous, I think it would pay to give it some serious thought."

"Mr. Singer," Ben said, "if I think of a thing for five minutes, or for five years, it's been serious thinking. Now what would you do if your were in my place? Sell out and go home whipped? Maybe I can't win, but nobody, and I really mean nobody, is going to be able to say it wasn't because I didn't put up a good fight. I've got finances for another month, at the rate I'm going. And I'll spend every last nickel, use up every piece of equipment, trying to take in ten dollars in revenue from that line. If it goes bust, the receivers can have it, then whoever buys it won't be getting such a good bargain."

"I suppose you've considered what this is going to do to your career," Murray said. You'll never rise above an assistant manager's job with any railroad. Stockholders don't like men who run their investment to a tatter, then toss it in their lap."

"That's right," Ben Holliday admitted. "And I don't like to do it, but I'll tell you one thing here and now. It might be better for me if I got out of railroading, got out from under my father's thumb than to struggle on the way I've been going. If I make a railroad out of this financial wreck, how much good do you think it will do me? I work for no salary. Any profit for me will come as a dividend from the stock I hold. And, Mr. Singer, a lot of trains are going to have to travel up and down that track before I can declare a dividend." He leaned back in his chair and surveyed Murray Singer in a frankly unfriendly manner. "You want the line; I know that. You want it for a song, without a fight. Well, it may take a song, but it'll be the dearest one you ever sang in your life. And as for the fight, Mr. Texas-Cattle-Baron, you're going to find out when this is finished that, up to now, you never knew what a real fight was."

"That sounded like a declaration of war," Singer said.

"Well, what the hell did you expect, peace?"

CHAPTER SEVEN

As soon as the cattle train was loaded at end of track, Ben Holliday telegraphed Dodge City for the departure time of the southbound mail train; he wanted it into the siding at Comanche so he could take the northbound straight through. He felt that this was important, to highball through without a stop, sort of a symbol of the railroad's intentions, its way of doing business. Besides, it would be the first cattle train originating in Texas, and to Holliday's way of thinking it brought just a little nearer the end of the overland cattle drives.

He sat at the small desk in the rattling, swaying caboose, composing a carefully worded telegram to be sent to his father when he reached Dodge. Sergeant Jean DuJoise slept in one of the bunks, his hat covering his face. Holliday wanted his message to sound optimistic without being boastful, for the running of this train was in no way going to affect the fate of Midland-Pacific; it was simply something that hadn't been done before.

The freight train did not rocket along a twenty-five miles an hour. Closer to ten would have been right, and when it passed through the yard at Comanche, Ben Holliday was catching up on his sleep.

He woke to the brakie's hand on his shoulder. "We hooked this message as we passed through the yard, Mr. Holliday." The brakie turned up the lamp so Holliday could read, then went toward the front of the car to get some coffee.

The message was short. *No poles or wire . . . no credit . . . Harry.*

Holliday crumbled it into a ball and swore softly. Jean DuJoise stirred and then said, "Trouble, m'sieu?"

"The army is going to have to wait for their telegraph,"

Ben said. "And I hate like hell to think of telling Dawson that."

DuJoise shrugged eloquently. "It will not be the first time he's heard bad news." Then he settled back, his hands behind his head. "A pity, m'sieu. With a telegraph to the army post the job of watching the Indians would have been easier."

"Father used to tell me that I couldn't have everything, but I still like to try." He fell silent a moment. "Still, it's a smart man who admits he can't go any farther, and if they won't extend credit, then I'll have to try something else."

Just what that was, Holliday didn't know, and he was thinking about it when he went back to sleep.

The flavor of coffee and frying bacon woke him. Daylight streamed through the dirty windows, and Holliday got out of the bunk to stagger to the wash bucket. DuJoise was already up, sitting by a window, looking out on the prairie.

Suddenly he cried, "Ah! Well done, m'sieu!"

"What the hell are you looking at?" Holliday asked, peering over his shoulder. He had to scan a moment before he caught sight of the horseman, riding full tilt toward the train. And behind the lone man, a herd of Comanches whooped and charged along in pursuit. "He's trying to make the train!" Holliday said. Then he strained for a better look "That's Jim Bender! Slow the train."

"No, no!" DuJoise said. "He will make it. If you slow the train, the Indians will board her." He left his seat and got his carbine and Holliday's rifle. "But we can help him a little, eh?"

He jammed the muzzle through a window and began to fire at the Indians. This support spurred Bender on to a renewed effort, and the Indians seemed to drop back a little when Holliday's Winchester began to hammer. He wasn't hitting anything, but DuJoise scored, and Jim Bender altered his course, came alongside the train, and

248

left the saddle. Holliday put down his rifle and went to the rear platform.

There was a momentary flicker of surprise in Bender's eyes when he saw Holliday, then he said, "I found the Indians. You want to take a guess at what kind of luck I had?"

"No talks?"

"You are so right," Bender said, and went into the caboose.

DuJoise was cleaning his carbine, and he grinned at the ex-marshal. "A good ride, m'sieu."

"Got a little warm there for a spell, John-Jack." He looked at Ben and grinned. "That was a mighty pretty sight, that train huffin' along the track," He sniffed. "Is that horseshoe coffee?" He took a cup from the rack and went forward to fill it. When he came back, he scraped his whiskered face with his fingernails, and looked at DuJoise. "What are you doin' ridin' the railroad?"

"I am the new aide to M'sieu Holliday," DuJoise said. "The old one, Skinner, is dead."

Jim Bender frowned heavily. "Now that was kind of sudden, wasn't it?"

Holliday told him about it, and about the shooting at Singer's place. "Of course, Satchel didn't kill Ollie. But he knew who did, and that was enough to get him shot." He studied Jim Bender at length. "You were once pretty thick with the Singers. For my money they're a nest of rattlesnakes, and if they buzz at me I'm going to do what I have to do. Where would you stand, Jim?"

"With you," Bender said, "If you didn't include Betty."

"Jim, she's there with her father and brother. What can I do?"

Bender shook his head. "I keep my business to myself, Ben, but when we broke up, it wasn't because she was like her old man or Carl. It was because she wasn't."

"That I don't get."

"It's simple. She never liked the way either of them grabbed land, or whatever else they wanted."

249

"Then why didn't she leave?" Ben asked. "You wanted to marry her, didn't you, Jim?"

"Yep. But good or bad, they're her family, Ben, and she's loyal to 'em." He finished his coffee. "Ben, I'd ride with you against Murray and Carl, and take my chances that Betty would forgive me for it. You've made up your mind that Murray's after the line?"

"Yes, but I think he has partners," Holliday said. "I don't want a fight until they're all smoked out in to open." He sat there deep in thought for a minute. "No chance of getting the Indians to talk, huh?"

Bender shook his head. "They know a train went south, and as far as they're concerned, it was a breach of faith. Sorry, Ben, you'll just have to fight 'em. Better arm your train crews. They may try to stop the next one going south."

"You really think so?" Ben asked, his voice hopeful.

Bender's curiosity was aroused. "Ben, do you want that kind of a fight? It might drag out until winter."

"No, but it's good to know that I can get the Indians together whether they like it or not."

Bender glanced at Sergeant DuJoise. "Do you know what that means? I don't."

The Frenchman's shoulders rose and fell. "Who knows the thinking of a general?"

The last thing Ben Holliday expected when he arrived at Dodge was a celebration; the town seemed to go mad, and a brass band came marching onto the track, blocking them effectively. The crowd was immense, shouting, waving their hats, firing pistols into the air, and through it all came a delegation in buggies, the mayor and all the city officials, and a swarm of cattle buyers, all eager to sign checks and pay top prices.

Holliday, with Bender and DuJoise in tow, was whisked away by buggy and taken to a suite of rooms at the hotel. A bartender served and two waiters passed the drinks around to the jam of frock-coated men. Harry Lovell was there, but had no chance to talk to Holliday; the best Lovell could manage was a smile and a wave of the hand from across the room.

"A sterling achievement," the mayor said, raising his glass. The bankers with him nodded, and everyone took his whisky neat. "Perhaps, Mr. Holliday, you would consent to answer a few questions for us."

"Why not?"

The mayor clapped his hands for silence. "Gentlemen, Mr. Holliday has consented to answer our questions. Would you step right over there, sir, where everyone can see you. Thank you. As you are well aware, gentlemen, the success of Midland-Pacific has a direct bearing on our city. So does its failure, but today we are talking of success. Mr. Holliday, are you ready for the questions?"

"Yes," Ben said, and accepted a cigar and a light; he hoped it would cover his nervousness and make him appear as though he had done this many times.

One of the bankers had a question. "Mr. Holliday, you have done what two other men failed to do, bring a train from end of line to Dodge. Can we conclude from this that Midland-Pacific has resolved her difficulties?"

"No, you may not," Ben said. "However, we're working on them."

Another man asked, "Is there any truth to the rumor that you've accepted additional capital?"

"No additional capital has been offered. So we could hardly accept it." Another man was bidding for attention. "Yes?"

"Do you plan to run a freight on schedule?"

Holliday smiled. "I'd like to run one twice a day, but I hardly think business warrants it. In a few days, another train will come north with Box X steers, and return, I hope, with freight. Military supplies for Fort Elliot, and freight of any nature to ranchers along the line will be accepted."

"Do you have a solution for the Indian trouble this is bound to create, sir?"

251

"Yes," Ben said. "Fight."

There was some laughter, then Holly Bristow said, "Mr. Holliday, I don't believe I've ever met you, but since you've exhibited such frankness with us here, perhaps you'll answer my question: did you receive a legitimate offer for the line?"

"Yes."

Bristow smiled. "Are you going to accept it, sir?"

"I am not," Ben Holliday said. A murmur of surprise rippled among them, then died. Then Holliday asked, "Did you make the offer, sir?"

A cattle buyer laughed and said, "He's got you there, Bristow."

Bristow colored and hesitated. "I made the offer, yes, but as representative for a group of men."

"Would you care to name them?" Ben asked.

"No, sir, I would not."

"And why not? He smiled. "If the offer is as legitimate as you say, sir, then public knowledge of their names could harm no one."

"I'm not at liberty to do so," Bristow said. "You've answered my question; thank you."

"But you haven't answered mine," Holliday said flatly.

"No, and I'm not going to," Bristow said, sitting down.

"Perhaps I can answer it for you," Ben said. "Murray Singer, Bert Hutchins, and I think Jerry Vale." Singer he was sure of, and Hutchins was a good bet, but Vale had been a guess based on the close friendship of the three in Singer's study. And Bristow's dropped jaw told Holliday that he had scored in the X ring.

"You had no right to do that." Bristow said coolly. "No right at all."

"It's my railroad," Holliday said.

"But it may not be for long," Bristow said, and stalked out of the room.

There were a few more questions, and Holiday answered them honestly, then the gathering broke up, except for a portly, mustached man. He waited until the others had gone, then said, "I'm Swinner, Western Union. I refused you the poles and wire, Mr. Holliday."

Ben didn't want to argue about it. "You acted wisely for your company, Mr. Swinner. I was going to gamble with your equipment."

Swinner glanced at DuJoise and Jim Bender. "I'd like to talk to you alone, if I may."

"Consider us alone," Holliday said. "They're close associates."

Swinner shrugged and sat down, crossing his legs. "Have it your way, Mr. Holliday. I don't suppose, since I turned you down on the poles and wire, that you'd care to tell me what you were going to do."

"Why not? I was going to make a connection with Fort Elliot."

"Hardly profitable," Swinner said. "We've been asked to put in a line also. Too costly, running poles parallel to your right of way. Of course, if you'd give us an easement——"

Ben Holliday shook his head. "We use the telegraph for business and write off the expense of it. You're in business to make a profit off of what always is a loss to us. Sorry, no easement."

"Let me point out to you," Swinner said, "that if you do foot the bill for a line to Elliot, all you'll get out of it is some help with the Indians. That won't last forever. Then where's your investment?"

"Well at least I got something for it," Holliday said. "If Western Union wants to buy our existing poles and equipment——"

Swinner waved his hand and smiled. "No, I don't think so. However, we'd take this millstone from around your neck, and in return build the line to Fort Elliot for you. Naturally you'd use the line at the established railroad rate."

Ben Holliday laughed softly. "That's certainly decent of the company, Mr. Swinner, but it hardly meets the demands of Midland-Pacific."

"Oh? What do you suggest?"

"Midland-Pacific will pursue plans for expansion until the doors are locked by the receivers. Any agreement entered into would have to include areas of expansion."

Swinner shook his head. "We'll string wire to Fort Elliot and take the rest off your hands. That's our offer, Mr. Holliday. We're not going to buy easements until our till is pumped dry."

"We wouldn't want Western Union to go broke," Holliday said. "I think Midland-Pacific could provide easements along our right of way. However, we have operators who shouldn't be put out of a job just because the operation changes hands."

"We hire and train our own operators," Swinner said. "I'm sure the company wouldn't absorb your labor force."

Holliday ignored this. "And there would have to be a time clause in the contract, Mr. Swinner. That is to say, once the contracts are signed, construction of the Fort Elliot line would have to start immediately and be finished without interruption. This would prevent anyone from fulfilling the letter of the contract by starting, and getting off the hook by not finishing."

"That hardly sounds trustful," Swinner said.

"It's business. Naturally you'd be protected by an automatic easement on any right of way Midland-Pacific acquires. And I think poles ought to go up as the rails go down."

"You're not considering our other schedules."

"I'm considering the fact that if Midland-Pacific loses, so do you. Now about existing lines, and so forth. I think that under these terms, twenty thousand would be a fair price. That's a third of material and labor cost."

Swinner whisled, then said, "Now you've made me lose interest."

"Why don't you talk it over? I'll be in Dodge until tomorrow evening. Give me an answer then."

"All right, but I'm afraid you've pressed it too far. Look,

254

Holliday, I'm a reasonable man. Let me out from under on your labor force, and I'll present the offer."

"Done," Ben said, and shook hands.

After he stepped out, Jim Bender sighed and rubbed his stomach. "That wasn't much different from courthouse politics. You ought to run for Congress, Ben."

"Thanks, no."

"What's Western going to do about the wires strung to Singer's place?" Bender asked.

"Tear them down, probably," Holliday said.

"Ain't you got contracts with Singer and Hutchins and Vale?"

"Sure," Ben said. "Contracts with three men who want my railroad. What do you want me to do, Jim? Go on honoring the agreements?"

"I would," Bender said. "Even if it cost me."

"And that's why you're not running a railroad," Holliday said. "If it just cost me, personally, then maybe I'd stick it out. But with the railroad at stake, I'd cut a man's throat from ear to ear to save it."

"I guess," Bender said. "You save it and you save yourself, then you can report back to your pappy that you're a whoppin' success."

"Oh, hell, there's more to it than that!"

"Sure there is; I never doubted it." He turned to the door. "I'm going to get me a bath and a shave, then about six drinks in a row."

"Jim, you're not mad, are you?"

"Naw, but I've learned that one side of the fence is no cleaner than the other. You comin' along, John-Jack?"

"I stay with M'sieu Holliday." He shrugged. "I'm in the middle."

"No man's in the middle," Jim Bender said.

Holliday stared at him. "That's kind of a switch for you, isn't it Jim?"

"Well, I guess when a man wants to get off the fence, the best way is just to jump."

He went out and DuJoise said, "A good man but bound

255

by his own principles. To live, a man must be a little bit of the coward one day, a wise man the next, a hero another day, and a fool the day after. And all without a twinge of conscience. M'sieu is hot or cold, good or bad, never in between. It was his trouble with the woman; he wanted her to be all one way. It can't be done."

They went down to the lobby to get a room, and found that the one they had been in had been rented for them. Holliday ordered bath water brought up, and a meal, then went out to make arrangements for a tailor to fit him for a suit of clothes.

When he got back to the room, he found Harry Lovell waiting in the hallway. "I'm sorry," Lovell said. "I tried, Ben."

"That's all a man can do. Don't moon about it. Come on in."

He closed the door and heard DuJoise singing in the adjoining room. Then he came out, clad in the lower half of his underwear, toweling himself dry. Two vivid scars crossed his chest, old saber wounds, Holliday imagined, then tried to imagine himself facing cold steel—and couldn't. That called for a particularly acute sense of courage in a man, a kind he didn't have.

"Sit down, Harry. Sergeant, this is Mr. Lovell, my accountant. Sergeant John-Jack DuJoise."

The two shook hands, then Lovell sat down and lit a cigar. The tailor came, and DuJoise let him in. While the man took measurements and displayed his samples, Holliday and Harry Lovell talked.

"I never saw Dodge stirred up," Lovell said. "To look at it, you'd think something really important happened." He reached into his pocket for some papers. "The cattle buyer accepted our head count and made out the draft. It's good to have a little money for a change."

"Take a good look at it," Holliday said. "We won't have it tomorrow. You'd better take this down, Harry. I want an order of thirty-five ton of rail sent out before supper. And see what you can do about ties; we'll use all we have. I want to put this siding in; running one train at a time is foolish. And send a wire to my brother, Adam. Ask him if he can come out here for two weeks. I'm going to need some legal advice."

"What for?" Lovell asked.

"Well there's some contracts coming up and——" A knock on the door interrupted him and DuJoise opened it. "Well, for heaven's sake! Anna!"

"I'm sorry to intrude," she said, smiling. Then she saw Harry Lovell, and he turned quickly and went over to the window and stood looking out. "I heard you were here, and since—well, I thought I'd say hello."

"What are you doing in Dodge?"

"My father came to see a lawyer about a patent," she said. The tailor stood there, tape in hand, patience in his expression. "You're busy. I'll talk later to you, in Comanche."

"No, no!" He took her hand. Then he turned to the tailor. "You've got enough there. Something in a dark brown. And not a heavy material." He stepped into the hall and closed the door. "Will you have a cup of coffee with me?"

"My father's in a room downstairs," she said. "Would it be all right——"

"Of course," he said taking her arm.

As they walked down the stairs, Anna said, "Papa and I are going to take the night mail train back. Maybe I shouldn't have interruped you."

"If you hadn't and I found out about it, I wouldn't have forgiven you."

This pleased her; he could tell that from the sudden warmth in her eyes. "I do hope that man found his wife," she said. When he frowned, she went on to explain. "The man who was in your room talking to you. He was in the lawyer's office when Papa and I went there. The lawyer was trying to find his wife."

"Which man?"

"The short one with the suit."

"Harry Lovell? You must be mistaken, Anna."

She stopped at the base of the stairs. "I'm not. Papa thinks he works for you. Is that so?"

"Lovell's the accountant. Which lawyer did you go to?"

"Mr. Bristow."

Somehow he felt that he knew that even before she said it, and it gave him a sickness in the stomach to know that Lovell was working against him.

Anna said, "Is something wrong, Ben?"

"No, nothing now."

She opened the door for him, and Fritz Neubauer turned his head; he had been dozing in the chair. When he saw Ben Holliday he stood up and straightened his coat and unconsciously wiped the palm of his hand on his pant leg. "Papa, this is Mr. Holliday."

"So much a pleasure," Neubauer said, shaking hands. He was ill at ease, unsure of himself or what he should say or how he should act. "Anna spoke of you. My English is not good."

"It's fine," Ben said. His glance touched Anna Neubauer briefly. "Would you excuse me, for say ten or fifteen minutes?"

"I say something wrong?" Neubauer asked.

"No, no," Ben assured him. "I've got to talk to Lovell now, Anna. It's the way I am; I can't leave a thing go, or wait."

"I understand," she said.

When he turned to the door, Neubauer said, "You come, you go. I say something bad?"

"Explain it to him," Ben said, and went out.

As he made the top of the stairs, he saw Lovell walking toward him; Lovell stopped and said, "You didn't stay long."

"Do you feel nervous, Harry?"

"No."

"Guilty?"

"Why should I?"

"Did you ever find your wife, Harry?"

258

Lovell laughed. "Hell, you know I'm not married. So she said she saw me. What of it?"

"Tell me what you and Bristow had to talk about, Harry."

"A private matter, Ben. Believe me."

"Sorry, but I just can't do that now. Bristow represents interests that want me to go broke. You come to Dodge to see Swinner and you talk to Bristow first. What did you say to Swinner, Harry? Did you tell them I was broke, that I was going to stay broke? Or did you show them my balance sheets with red ink at the bottom?"

"You're accusing me without proof," Lovell said. "On the word of a foreigner." He shook his head and laughed I've worked for you father nearly eighteen years. You don't scare me, Ben, because I'll be working for him when you're through."

"Harry, you're through now."

"*You're* firing me?"

"As of now." He looked steadily at Lovell, as though sorry about this. "Would you tell me why, Harry?"

For a moment it seemed that Lovell was going to go on denying this, but then he shrugged and said, "For money. What the hell else?" He reached out and tapped Ben on the chest. "They've got you, son. Make it easy on yourself. That's why I went along with Bristow; I'm too old a man to lose."

"You were going to keep your job, is that it?"

"Yes, and a nice bonus." He sighed. "Why don't you just hit me, Ben? I'd feel better."

"Would it do any good? The damage is done. Singer knows all my business now."

"Your father too. I've been writing him letters. Not bad letters. He only wants to know how you're getting along."

"This is my railroad to run. It's about time he got his damned hand off the throttle. Go on back to Chicago, Harry. He'll give you a job and a gold watch for all those eighteen years of faithful service."

Lovell shook his head. "Eighteen years are a lot of years.

Too long to work for one man." He sighed and found a cigar in his pocket and lit it. "You know, I've been dreading the day when you found out; I like to think of myself as an honorable man. That must sound like a lie to you, after my selling you out. But I did it for the railroad."

"Get the hell away from me," Ben said flatly. "Get far away, Harry. And I'll tell you something else: don't say good-by to Holly Bristow. "I'll do that for you, right now."

"He only looks soft," Lovell warned.

"That'll make it all the more interesting," Holliday said, and went down the stairs, two at a time. As soon as he reached the street, he asked a man where Bristow's office was, then cut toward it, his stride long and determined.

CHAPTER EIGHT

Holly Bristow was studying some legal papers when Ben Holliday opened the office door with a crash and stood there. Bristow looked up, then motioned for him to come in. "You're going to bring me trouble, I suppose?"

"I just fired Harry Lovell," Ben said.

Bristow shrugged. "That was a fool thing to do."

"I don't want any spies in my outfit!" Holliday snapped.

Bristow threw down his pencil and leaned back in his chair. "Mr. Holliday, you don't have the situation in hand at all. You're on the ragged edge of being on the run, if you aren't there already. Now if you'd used your head, you'd have kept your mouth shut and never let on to Lovell that you knew about his arrangement. That way you'd have kept tabs on him, and used him more than he used you. What are you going to do for an accountant, Holliday? Who knows as much about your finances and business as Lovell?" He spread his hands and smiled. "Now you threw it all away because you stopped thinking. You know something, I think you're going to be easier to beat than Singer thinks, because you can be made to go off half cocked."

The fact that he was right angered Holliday, and even as he felt it rise in him, he knew that he was going to do something even more foolish than fire Harry Lovell. He stepped up to Bristow's desk and said, "I feel like knocking your head off."

"Aw, now you couldn't be that stupid," Bristow said. He looked at Holliday for a moment, then sighed and got up. As he came around his desk, he said, "I suppose you boxed in college?"

"I did."

Bristow started to take off his coat. "We don't use those rules out here." Then he whipped the coat back on and hit him, taking Holliday completely by surprise. He spun half around and fell across Bristow's desk, then shook his head and straightened up.

He started to raise his hands, to assume a posture of defense, but Bristow bent down, came in under Holliday's uplifted hands, and caught him with a belting hook in the stomach. Ben brought his fist down and struck Bristow on the back of the neck, not hard enough to hurt him, but enough to break the rhythm of Bristow's attack.

Holliday was forced to give ground, to back up when he wanted to carry the fight to Bristow, and it was going to be Bristow's fight; he could tell that much, and it was a sickness in his mind, to know that he was going to get licked.

He had the courage to stand up to Bristow and take it, and he went down three times, but he always managed to come back. And he even managed to hurt Bristow a little, opening a cut on his eyebrow and lip, but it wasn't enough. Bristow could hit, and he followed no set of rules, no pattern of fighting; he just came in close and chopped with his fists, and the blows were full of power, against which Holliday's stylized defense was useless.

After being flung back against the wall and feeling his legs wilt, Ben Holliday found that he couldn't get up. He wanted to and tried to, but the strength wasn't there. Holly Bristow turned to a side table and soaked a towel in the water pitched. He wiped his face, then threw it at Holliday.

"Do you want to try again, Mr. Holliday?" Then he laughed. "Clean yourself up; you look like hell!" He turned to his desk and sat down, his head pillowed in his hands.

Holliday put the towel to his face and felt better, then he looked at Bristow and wondered if the man had a headache; he hoped so. Ben Holliday wanted him to have something, anyway.

"I don't understand you," Bristow said, daubing at his cut lip. "You fight for this piddling railroad like it was all you had. So what the hell if you lose it? You'll go back to Chicago and your old man will give you a good job anyway. From the beginning I couldn't see why you wanted to hang on. Haven't you got sense enough to know that money's going to beat you? The stock's worthless, or practically worthless, and you don't have enough cash to buy a wagonload of ties."

Ben Holliday got up and leaned against the wall; he threw the towel in the corner and straightened his clothing. "Bristow, if the line's so worthless, why do Singer and the others want it?"

The attorney shrugged. "I don't know and don't care. As long as I get my commission, it stays that way. Holliday, I'm not against you personally. I just represent a client."

"Maybe I ought to get a lawyer," Holliday said, and went out.

His stomach muscles ached from the sting of Bristow's fists, and he took care not to take any sudden or deep breaths until the soreness left him. Harry Lovell was standing on the hotel porch when Holliday crossed over.

Lovell said, "I wanted to tell you, Ben, that you couldn't lick him, but I don't think you'd have listened."

"No, I wouldn't have," Holliday said. "Harry, you're out of it now. What's my chances?"

"Of besting the Singer bunch?" Lovell shook his head. "On guts, you're ahead, Ben, but this time the money's going to count. And Singer's got you there. He's going to buy you out, so why not take it now and be done with it? I realized this some time ago." He took Holliday by the arm. "Ben, I know why you've got to do a good job but believe me, your father isn't going to hold it against you if you fail. He's right: you've got to take one good licking in your life, and the earlier the better."

"It must be good," Holliday said, "to be able to see so clearly. I'm sorry, but I can't."

His intention had been to go to his room, but he changed his mind and walked down the street to the Western Union office. He still had his brother's check, which he cashed, then added two hundred dollars of his own money; the whole thing was deposited, then he composed a message.

Adam Holliday
Fischer Bldg.
Chicago, Illinois
Buy five hundred M-P stock in my name . . . urge you to beg, borrow, or steal to buy all you can . . . Lovell discharged this date . . . Need you here on important legal matters . . . Can you come?

Ben

As he walked back to the hotel, he considered this move. Midland-Pacific had not moved on the market for six months, and he was certain that any buying would cause a flurry of interest. He knew how closely investors watched the market, even the stocks that seemed dead, and this brief bit of buying would sharpen their attention. After all, they didn't know what was going on, and if Adam could come through with some money of his own, it might inspire others to invest. Then the stock would take a jump in price and some bull would hop in and hope to buy cheap and sell high. But Holliday didn't care about that. He just wanted to force the price up to where Singer's present offer would be laughable.

Maybe he will end up owning it, Holliday thought as he walked back to the Hotel. But he'll sure as hell pay more than thirty-five cents a share.

He felt good enough to smile about it, and when he stepped inside his room, Jim Bender looked up from the casino game he had going with Sergeant DuJoise.

"For a man who's been in a fight, you seem happy about it," Bender said dryly.

"I got licked," Holliday said. He wet a cloth and held it to the bruises on his face. "I was smiling about something else. Jim, are you much of a horse trader?"

"Tolerably good. Why?"

264

"Suppose you had a horse that was a little wind broke, and you wanted to get top price, or a little better. How would you go about it?"

"There's nothin' like biddin' to raise a price," Bender said. "Especially when a man thinks he's getting something for nothing."

"The stock market works the same way," Holliday said. "If I can get up a little buying of Midland-Pacific stock, I think I can raise the market price."

"What good's that goin' to do you?"

"The higher the stock goes, the more expensive it's going to be for Singer to buy me out." He pulled a chair around and sat down. "Look, I got a cattle train into Dodge, didn't I? The newspapers will pick that up, and my father will blow it around, and when the market opens tomorrow and a thousand shares are picked up, it'll make the investors wonder if something isn't about to break out here."

"Yeah, your back," Bender said. "For Christ's sake, can't you see that Singer and the others only shipped with you because they want the top price for their beef? Hell, once their range is clean, they'll throw that contract in your face and leave you sitting there, extended to the limit. Hell, you need them, Ben. If they don't ship on your line, you go broke."

"That's the core of the whole mess, isn't it? Well, Jim, I'm going to make them see that the shoe's on the other foot. They need me!"

"Cattle have always been driven to market," Bender said. "Sure it's expensive and it takes time, but that's an out you can't close off." He sighed and gave up the card game.

"Who do you know that will take a gamble?" Ben asked.

"How much of a gamble?"

"Long odds against winning, but if we get lucky, you'd make a small fortune." He painted a clear picture for Jim Bender. "I just wired my brother to buy five hundred dollars' worth of Midland stock. It'll open an eye or two, but not enough. I need a thousand more, or two thousand. With that much I could push the market value up."

"A man could lose his shirt puttin' his money in your railroad."

"Yes, and he could win the coat and pants and all the rest," Ben said. Then he slapped his side and turned away. "Do I sound like I'm grabbing at straws, Jim? Well I am. I've got a good roadbed and good rolling stock, if I could only get the blasted wheels to turn."

"Evidently Singer thinks *he* can," DuJoise said.

Holliday glanced at him, then laughed. "For what he wants to pay for the line, he could pull up the rails and ties, sell them along with the equipment, and make three hundred per cent profit. Then he could sell the right of way and alternate sections for more profit."

"All you need is money," Bender said. "Just money."

Someone knocked, and Holliday opened the door. A corporal stood there, then came to attention. "Which of you is Mr. Holliday?"

"I am."

"The colonel sends his compliments, sir, and asks you to call at Fort Dodge at your convenience."

"All right, corporal. Within the hour." He closed the door and fingered his puffed lip. "Am I in trouble with the army now? All I get is trouble. Not one damned piece of good news yet."

"Your luck is bound to change," Bender said wryly. "No man can always have it this bad—I don't think."

"You're real cheering," Holliday said, turning to the door. "I want to be out of this town by sundown. Tell the engineer, and go downstairs and tell Anna Neubauer and her father they can go back in the caboose."

Bender grinned. "It'll mean a refund on their ticket."

"Go to blazes," Holliday said. "Besides, Neubauer has a pass."

He went down and through the lobby and hired a rig at the livery for his drive to Fort Dodge. Then sentry stopped him and Holliday gave his name, then was passed on to the sergeant of the guard, who detailed a trooper to escort him to headquarters.

Colonel Ridgeway, like Dawson of Fort Elliot, was a string bean, with a lot of worry lines on his forehead, and prematurely gray hair. He saw that Holliday had a comfortable chair, and a good cigar, then said, "The first train north was quite an event. I've been waiting a long time to see it. Never thought I would, though."

"A train is just a train, Colonel, and they go where the tracks point. However, I've had a lot of trouble about that. Especially with Indians and Texans."

"There's going to be some dancing and painting over this one," Ridgeway said. "What does the railroad intend to do about it?"

"Dump it in Colonel Dawson's lap," Holliday said. "Every man to his job, sir. Ours is railroading."

"A dispatch by courier from Dawson informed me that your attitude was very frank on the subject. All right, Mr. Holliday. I can't really quibble the point. But if the army is going to fight Indians for you, we're also going to use your railroad. I have a hundred and thirty cavalry mounts I want taken to Fort Elliot. When can they be loaded?"

"They'd better be loaded by sundown," Holliday said. "The train leaves then, dragging a string of empties."

"Not all empties," Ridgeway said. "How large a detail do you want to accompany the horses? Fifty men?"

"One," Ben said. "He can ride to Elliot when we get to the closest point. The railroad will hold the horses in the cars until a detail from Fort Elliot arrives."

"I'll have the quartermaster officer prepare the freight waybills and bring them to the train," Ridgeway said. "Mr. Holliday, would you mind telling me how long you think you can hang on? I've heard rumors that you were broke, that you were selling, that you were coming along nicely. It's a little confusing."

"There is nothing wrong with Midland-Pacific that a hundred thousand dollars wouldn't cure," Holliday said.

"But my chances of finding it are about as good as an old maid finding a man under her bed."

"I appreciate the honest answer," Ridgeway said.

They shook hands in parting, and Holliday drove back to town. At the hotel he found Swinner waiting.

"Fifteen thousand, Mr. Holliday. That's the best I can do."

"When I said twenty thousand, I was doing you a favor," Ben said.

"I can't go over fifteen," Swinner said. "Man, it was hard pressing to get that."

"And I'm hard pressed to take twenty."

"The deal's going to be lost if you don't come down."

"I guess. But I can't take less. I've got the money spent, so to speak. What does Western Union want? A bleeding vein?"

Swinner sighed and shook his head, then brought a check out of his inner pocket. It was made out for twenty thousand, and he smiled. "Had to make that one last try, Mr. Holliday. Company man, you know."

"I wish I had a few," Holliday said, and pocketed the check. He wanted to look at it, just to read the zeros, but he didn't, and settled for the pleasure of thinking about how advantageously he could spend this. It meant a siding, a badly needed siding, and he modified his original plan to buy the rails. To hell with that now. Since Murray Singer was going to renege on his contract, Holliday would beat him to it and shorten end of track by a mile. Singer would howl and seek an injunction, but there wasn't anything he could do about it, and he'd find that out.

It was too bad, he thought, that this twenty thousand was railroad money; with just five of it he could skyrocket the price of Midland-acific stock, push it so high that Murray Singer would just have to forget about stealing the line. The temptation to juggle the books was strong, but he put it down; he had no desire to go to the penitentiary for embezzlement.

Instead of going to his room, he knocked on Anna Neubauer's door; her father opened it and motioned Holliday inside. Anna was stretched out on the bed, resting; she swung her feet to the floor and raised her hands to her hair, to see if it was all right.

"Mr. Bender came around," she said. "Thank you for inviting us. We didn't want to stay over another night."

"I'd like to take you to supper," Ben said. "I could have it brought to the room, if you like."

"That would be nice," Anna said. "Sit down, Ben. Papa, bring that chair over here." She studied the marks on his face. "Have you been fighting?"

"Men do," he said, then laughed. "It was a foolish thing to do, but that seems to be what I do best." He studied her a moment. "Anna, I think you're a smart girl, so let me ask you something. Should I hang on to the railroad?"

She shook her head. "I can't answer that."

"Answer anyway. I want an honest opinion."

She thought a moment, then said, "It's first important to know why you want to go on fighting. Is it for the railroad, or for yourself?"

"I want the railroad to succeed."

"Yes, I know. But is it the big reason? The all-important reason?"

He shook his head. "I've got to go back to my father with the smell of success on me," Ben said. "He admires it in a man, the ability to do. It's the way I was raised, Anna, not to fail, and because my father expects me to fail now, I feel more determined not to. Anna, if I have to, I'll take the whole blasted world down with me."

"That's wrong," she said.

"Wrong? I know it. But what can I do about it?"

Anna remained silent for a moment. "Ben, you have to do what you know you can live with afterward. I don't think you're the kind of a man who destroys anyone else to save yourself. If it came to that, I think you'd sell the railroad."

"I wish I felt that sure," Holliday said softly. "It's not easy to live when you're not sure what you are, or how far

269

you can go." He turned to the door. "I'll order supper."

He stepped out and collided solidly with Jim Bender. Bender said, "I've been looking all over for you, Ben. Your operator here got word from end of track that Indians have been gatherin' all afternoon. They're camped out on the prairie and it don't look good."

"They're not under attack?"

"No, not yet, but I wouldn't bet they won't be." He took Holliday by the arm. "We'd better not wait until sundown to pull out with that string of empties. You want me to tell the engineer?"

"Wait." Holliday gave it some thought. "The army is shipping some horses to Elliot. They won't be loaded yet."

"God damn the horses!" Bender said, then he saw Anna standing in the room, listening. "Pardon me. Ben, I don't think we should waste any time. Now that's the best advice I can give you."

"Is an hour going to make that much difference, Jim?"

"It could," he said. "Ben, do you want to take the chance?"

"If we pull out now," Holliday said, "we won't have much of a supporting force. But if I can wait, take the chance, we might be able to get some army help. Jim, get a horse and ride to Fort Dodge. Explain it to the colonel and ask for thirty men. Give him an hour. I'll go and telegraph ahead that re-enforcements are on the way."

"There's seven men out there, Ben. You're gambling with their lives."

"Hell, don't you think I know it?" He gave Bender a shove. "Get going. You don't have any time to waste." He watched Bender dash to the lobby, then he turned to Anna and her father. "I have to ask you to excuse me on the dinner."

She came up to him and took his arms in her strong hands. "Ben, go now. Right now."

"I can't."

"Can't or won't?"

"Either way, I guess it's the same."

270

"Is a report to your father more important than those seven men?" She studied him critically. "Ben, if they're dead when you get there, you'll think of it the rest of your life. I know you must gamble, but not this way. It's not right and you know it."

"Sorry," he said. "I'll see you at the train." Then he turned and ran out, pushing his way past people in the lobby.

Sergeant DuJoise was at the train, talking to the engineer, who already had steam up and an itch to push the throttle wide open. They turned when Holliday came up, and the engineer said, "Mr. Holliday, empty I can push her to fifty miles an hour."

"You'd blow her up," Holliday said. "Nobody ever goes that fast."

"I'd rather blow her up tryin' than set here and valve off steam," he said. On the other side of the tracks the army detail were holding the horses; loading wouldn't take long, but in view of this development the quartermaster officer had held up, pending word from a higher authority.

Holliday vaulted to the cab and jumped down on the other side. He saw the officer sitting on the corral fence, and waved to get his attention. "All right, get 'em loaded! We'll pull out as soon as you're through!"

The army was organized, and shouting sergeants got their details into motion and the loading proceeded rapidly. Holliday went back to the other side of the train.

Sergeant DuJoise said, "A problem for a man to wrestle, eh, m'sieu? Perhaps this will be the day of a new miracle, another Adobe Walls, where a handful of men hold off the Comanche nation."

"Aw, why don't you shut up," Holliday said. He walked up and down, feeling the cinders crunch under his boots. Damn it, what a spot for a man to be in. Just when he thought he was getting steam up, something had to puncture the boiler and let it out. Seven men against a trainload of paying freight and a chance to crawl out of the puddle of red ink. Not clear out, but up a little ways anyway.

And this whole thing could blow over without a shot being fired too; a man was a fool to be panicked by a threat. And that's what it was. Just a threat. Nobody was under attack.

He remembered the look on Anna Neubauer's face and wondered how she knew so much, how she'd learned what was right and wrong so that she did more of one than the other. And Bender was no angel himself; he didn't have any right to be righteous. Only one man ran a railroad, gave the orders, accepted the responsibility, and took the credit or blame.

DuJoise and the engineer were still standing there when Holliday turned around. "Hook the engine and tender to the caboose, and get the crew aboard, every railroad man in the yard who can shoot. Let's see if this damned thing will go fifty miles an hour."

He just stepped back out of the way so they could get the job done. He went over to the dispatcher's shack and found the Dodge telegrapher there.

"This just came in, Mr. Holliday. End of track under attack, but they're holding off."

"We're pulling out of a few minutes. Tomorrow, hook the cattle cars onto the passenger train. We'll pick it up in the Comanche yard."

"That's going to make a nice smell for the passengers," the dispatcher said.

"Do we have that many, that we have to worry about it? He turned to leave just as Swinner came in. He had a handful of contracts and a look of impatience on his face. Holliday said, "My signature on those is going to have to wait a week or so."

"We gave you our check," Swinner said. "As chairman of the board you can make policy without consulting your father or brothers. Western Union isn't going to cheat you."

"And I'm not going to go to South America with your check," Ben said. A train whistle hooted wildly and he pushed past Swinner. "I'll see you in a week when you come down on the work train."

"According to contract, we don't have to start building the telegraph until you sign."

Holliday took the check out of his pocket and thrust it at Swinner. "Do you want this back? The line goes up in two weeks, or you can forget it. I can't wait for an answer, so give it to me now."

Swinner's expression darkened a bit, then he said, "All right, Mr. Holliday. A work train in a week." He shook his head and grinned. "I could be fired for this. We don't do business on faith and a handshake any more."

"I don't have the time for a conference table," Holliday said.

The train whistle continued to blow; it was time to leave and he dashed out and ran across the switchyard. The brakie had his lantern in hand although it was not yet dark, and the engineer and fireman were in the cab.

DuJoise yelled, "Bender is not here!"

"We'll go without him," Ben said. "Likely he'll knock my head off for running off and leaving him. All right let's get out of here!" He swung into the engineer's cab as the throttle was cracked, and the driving wheels spun briefly before grip was made. They pulled clear of the yard and were heading for the last switch when Holliday looked around and saw Jim Bender flogging his horse, trying to catch up with the train. He watched as Bender came alongside the tender, made the jump, then came down into the cab.

"How the hell did you get to the post and back so quick?" Ben asked.

Jim Bender grinned. "I didn't go all the way there. I got to thinking and decided that you wouldn't wait. You just ain't the kind who'd do a thing like that, Ben. So I turned around and come back."

"We've got thirteen men aboard," Holliday said. "That's one hell of a force to repulse an Indian attack."

"Well, they can't shoot through the sides of the caboose

273

and push the engine off the track," Bender said. He took out his tobacco and rolled a smoke, bracing himself against the side of the cab.

The engineer passed through the last switch and eased the throttle open. The pound of the drivers increased in tempo and the train rocked along, swaying and jolting on the roadbed. "How fast will this thing go?"

"The engineer says fifty miles an hour."

Bender whistled. "That's too damned fast for any man to go." He studied the throttle and the engineer's hand there. "But if he took out that screw there, the one that's keeping the throttle from goin' too far, we might hit fifty-five."

CHAPTER NINE

As soon as the telegrapher left Murray Singer's house, the boss of Lazy T leaned back in his chair and smiled thinly. Carl Singer started to get up, and his father said, "Sit down, sit down. You've got no place to go." He bit off the end of a cigar and lit it. "There must be a hell of a lot of excitement at end of track, with seventy Comanches storming those tents. I've got twenty dollars that says they don't last two hours."

"I could take twenty men and get there in time," Carl said.

His father looked at him. "What would you want to do that for? The railroad is supposed to come to our rescue, not the other way around. Besides, Holliday's got considerable equipment there, and he can't afford to lose any of it."

"You'll have to square this with Holliday afterward," Carl said.

"Hell, do you think I worry about that? If he comes around here looking for trouble, we'll push him right off the face of Texas." He turned his head as Betty stopped in the doorway. "Carl and I are talking."

"I heard some of it," Betty Singer said. "Dad, are the Indians attacking the camp at end of track?"

"That's what the telegrapher says."

"Then why aren't you riding to help them?"

"It's railroad business."

"Ten years ago when the Comanches were raiding, it was everyone's business."

"Times have changed," Murray Singer said. "Betty, I wish you wouldn't bother with it now. I'm the one who has to decide."

"Because you want a railroad? Because there isn't any

more land for you to take, you want a railroad? Dad, I put my own desires aside once to take your side, yours and Carl's. Don't make me sorry for that now."

"You're talking like a fool woman," Murray said. "When you gave Bender up, that was your doing, not mine. Your choice, not mine. Don't make me the goat for it now."

"I see," Betty said. "You're not to blame, is that it?" She turned to the hall and stopped. "I've wasted my loyalty, haven't I?"

She didn't wait for an answer, just went down the and out the side door. The last light of day was casting long grayish shadows in the yard as she crossed to the barn.

The Mexican hostler came forward, hat in hand.

Betty said, "Saddle my horse, Luz."

Then she stood there while the light faded. From across the flats three horsemen came on at a dead run, and they swung off by the barn. Jerry Vale said, "I saw more Indians this morning than I care to think about. Your father in the house?"

"Yes."

Bert Hutchins said, "They've stopped work on the telegraph line, so I supposed they were hittin' the railroad." He looked around and saw no particular activity in the yard. "Ain't your dad goin' out?"

"I think he wants to finish his cigar first," Betty said.

Both Vale and Hutchins looked strangely at her, then the hostler brought up her horse and she was boosted into the sidesaddle. Vale said, "This is a poor time to go riding." Then he shrugged and stepped back. "None of my business. You Singers always did do what you wanted to do."

She left the yard at a run, then Bert Hutchins said, "Let's go to the house." He glanced at his foreman. "Stick around here, Rex. We likely won't be long."

As they approached the house, Carl Singer came to the door. "I thought I heard horses ride in. The old man's in the study. You hear about the Indians?"

"We guessed," Vale said. "That's why we came over, to do what we can."

"The place was quiet when we rode in," Hutchins said, "we thought you'd already gone." He stepped into the study, and Murray Singer waved his hand toward the liquor cabinet; they helped themselves.

"I heard that," Murray said. "Where's your brains? Let the Indians have the railroad. We only want the rails and equipment anyway."

"That's kind of hard to take," Vale admitted. "I've fought Indians, and I hate like hell to think we just stood by and——"

"If you're going to whine, go home," Murray said flatly. "Son, pour me a whisky. Well, we know what Holliday is going to do about the Indians. Fight 'em. He'll get licked. That crew of his is fine for setting railroad spikes, but no good fightin' Indians." He turned to his son, saying, "Go tell Betty to make us some coffee."

Bert Hutchins said, "She rode out just as we walked to the house."

Murray Singer's frown warned them that he wasn't in the mood for jokes. "What the hell do you mean, she rode out? Go take a look, Carl."

"It's a fact," Jerry Vale said. "She was heading toward end of track. What's the matter with you, Murray? You sick or something?"

"That stupid female!" Singer said. "Carl, catch up a horse and go after her before she gets killed."

"Hell, I couldn't catch her now."

Murray picked up a book and threw it at him, and Carl twisted so that it bounced off his shoulder. He got up and said, "It looks like Lazy T is going to fight Indians after all. I'll get the men together." Carl looked at his father. "I want to see you there too." He walked over to a cupboard and took out a holstered pistol with a cartridge belt wound around it. He tossed this in his father's lap. "Somehow it just bothers me, all of us getting killed off and leaving you sitting there, so smart and rich. I've taken your orders and guff for a long time. Now let's go."

For a moment Murray hesitated, then he pushed him-

277

self erect. As he put on the gun belt, he said, "If you don't watch yourself, Carl, you're going to show a shard of decency."

"Listen to who's talking." Carl Singer laughed. "I know what I am and it's all right with me." He glanced at Vale and Hutchins. "We're all alike; we'd steal the pennies off a dead man's eyes. So we're land hogs, money hogs, power hogs. Do we have to act like sons of bitches within our own families?"

He dashed out of the house and ran toward the bunkhouse, calling loudly to the men in the bunkhouse and barn.

Jerry Vale looked at Murray Singer, then said, "I never thought about this before, but you make me nervous as hell. One of these days I expect you to turn on me. I guess I'd have to kill you if you did that." Then he touched Bert Hutchins on the arm and they went out to wait by their horses.

Ben Holiday worked up a fine sweat, stoking the engine, keeping the fire roaring, keeping the pressure up as the train rocketed along the roadbed. Jim Bender spelled him at times, and they worked like mechanical men, backs bent, arms swinging as they sailed fuel into the open maw of the firebox. When the engineer began to lean on the whistle cord, both men raised up, and then the brakes were applied hard and the train lurched to a wheelsliding halt.

The work train from the wire-stringing crew blocked the last stretched of end of track, and they jumped down and ran alongside the cars. Bender sided Holliday and DuJoise brought up the rear, while the train crew followed a distance back.

Bender pointed to the flat prairie, but the gesture was wasted; Ben Holliday had already seen the Indians camped there. Kisdeen came to meet them.

"By God, I'm glad to see you," he said. "How many men you got?"

"Better than a dozen," Holliday said. He looked around the camp and saw that Kisdeen had already done a creditable job of fortifying the place. Railroad ties were banked around the telegrapher's tent and the cook tent, and the water supply was well guarded. Holliday asked, "Have they started shooting yet?"

"Well, not for keeps," Kisdeen said. "Some of the younger bucks have come in whoopin' and yellin' and showing off how brave they are. They've taken a few pot shots, but we're saving our ammunition."

"That's smart," Bender said. He squinted at the sky and judged the remaining daylight. "Might not be anything doing tonight. In the morning, you'll see twice as many out there. The word's out, and they'll gather like flies around an outhouse."

"Qui," DuJoise said. "And then, m'sieus, you will find your defenses inadequate." He pointed to the barricades. "With this type of a defense, the Indians can surround you easily, which is the way they like to fight. I would suggest you move your water and supplies to the trains. Tonight, of course, when it is dark and movement will be unobserved. Spread your men out along the length of the train and make them attack in a line. If they do that, you have the advantage. And if they choose to ride along the length of the train, the odds are with you even more."

"Suppose they hit the train in a wedge and break through?" Kisdeen asked.

"They can't jump across the train," Holliday said. "A line of men, yes, but not the train. I think DuJoise has the best plan. Good military procedure."

"We will wait until dark to move supplies and water," DuJoise said.

"They won't attack tonight," Bender said. "We can post guards and get some sleep. But at dawn we'll have our work cut out for us."

Bender and DuJoise began to supervise the activity around the camp, while Ben Holliday and Kisdeen talked. "It hate to think of morning," Kisdeen said. "We've got to

279

make peace with the Indians, not fight 'em. How much chance do you think we'll have after tomorrow?"

"We may not be around to worry about it," Holliday said, and drew a frown from the maintenance super. "Emil, do you want to please everyone? Let's work for the railroad and step on the toes of anyone who gets in the way. I made a deal with Western Union; they're taking over our existing telegraph lines and stringing new wire to Fort Elliot. Seeing that we don't have the funds to develop the lines, I thought it best to make the deal."

"That'll throw a lot of our men out of work."

"They can get other jobs, or stay on with Midland in other capacities. What the hell, am I supposed to hold up progress for someone's job?" He shook his head. "I left a string of cars on the siding at Dodge; there's a shipment of army horses for Fort Elliot. So tell the brakie, engineer, and fireman to get out of here with the engine and caboose we came down on.'

"Send them back to Dodge?"

"Why not?" He tapped Kisdeen on the chest. "We'll fight the Indians. And by the time they get back, we'll have licked them or they'll have licked us. Either way, it doesn't make much difference to the railroad; cars will still be rolling."

"You're the boss," Kisdeen said. Then he grinned. "And you're turning into a pretty good one. You won't last, but likely you'll kick up one hell of a dust cloud while you're around."

He walked back along the line of cars, and Ben Holliday went over to the cook tent where supper was in the making. DuJoise was eating a cold potato, and he spoke when Holliday came up. "Can I offer some advice, m'sieu le boss?"

"Advise away."

"There are more pick handles in this camp than bullets. I've looked around, and I'd say there was no more than twenty rounds per man."

"That's not surprising news," Holliday said. "They'll

just have to shoot straighter and less often. What's the advice, John-Jack?"

"Pick out the best shots and put them near the engine. The Indians will attack there first; they think it is alive, or a thing of evil. Do you agree?"

"All right," Holliday said. "Pick whoever you want."

"You, and Bender, and myself. Perhaps three others. I'll find them before morning." Then he laughed softly. "It will be a noisy dawn, m'sieu."

"Who wants to die quietly?" Holliday asked.

When darkness came, they quietly transferred the water and food to the train, but took care to keep up an appearance of activity around the cookshack and telegrapher's tent. Holliday sent the telegrapher away, for he could see no sense in keeping him there; any message sent would only be wasted effort, for help couldn't arrive in time to do them any good.

He joined Bender at the engine and they waited there. DuJoise finally came around with three men, sometime meat hunters who claimed they could hit what they aimed at. Bender's cigarette glowed and died as he puffed on it, his attention turned to the Indian camp out on the prairie.

They could hear the dancing and singing and see the fires dotting the flats. Bender said. "That's poor music for a man who likes to sleep.

"This is some country," Holliday said. "Back in Illinois, you build a railroad, then sit back and make money. Out here you build it, then fight like hell to keep the rolling stock on the move."

"You'd get fat in Chicago," Bender said dryly. "Admit it, Ben, win or lose, you've had a time of it. A lot of men go through life with nothing happening to 'em."

"This I could skip," Holliday said. "To tell you the truth, I've met a German girl I'd like to know a lot better. It irritates me to have to end something before it got started."

"You can always fire up the engine and get the hell out of here," Bender said.

Holliday shook his head. "The Indians would turn on the ranchers then. No, we'll hold our ground. Run now, and it will be hell for the next man."

"Shhhhh!" Bender said, holding up his hands. "DuJoise, you hear anything?"

"I heard something I don't believe."

Then the sound came to Ben Holliday, a curb chain rattling. Some man on guard duty fired his gun, and someone else shouted at him to "put that goddamned thing away!"

They left the engine and ran over to the end of track camp as Colonel Dawson and fourteen-man detail dismounted. Lieutenant Gary was there, handling the second section, and he waved at Holliday, then attended to his duties. Dawson was peeling off his gloves and saying, "We rode right to hell through 'em, and they let us. That bothers me." He offered Holliday his hand, then turned as Gary came up with Betty Singer. "We found her on the prairie."

"When it got dark, I lost my sense of direction," she said. Jim Bender stepped out of the shadows and she straightened a slight bit. "Hello, Jim."

"Come on," Bender said softly, taking her arm. "I'll get you some coffee." His glance touched Dawson briefly. "The reason you rode on through is because they wanted you here in the morning. I guess they must expect some friends tonight."

"That's a grizzly thought," Dawson said. "From the fires, "I'd say there were a hundred now." He looked around to find Ben Holliday, but he was already moving off to catch up with Bender and Betty Singer.

"I don't want to intrude on your two," Holliday said, taking Betty's free arm. "But what are you doing out on the prairie with an Indian scare in full swing?"

"Coming here," she said softly. "I've changed my mind, Jim." She looked around at him when she spoke. "Is it too late?"

"Never too late," he said. "We'll talk about it over

coffee." He went inside the cook tent; it was vacant, but a fire in the sheet-iron stove kept the coffeepot warm. He poured for the three of them, then stood with his back resting lightly against the tent pole. "Did you make a clean break, Betty?"

"As clean as one can make with my father." She looked at Ben Holliday and could see that he wanted an explanation. "Did you know that Jim and I once planned to get married?"

"I heard about that, yes."

"We should have," Betty Singer said. "Only we didn't. Family loyalty got in the way. Father and Carl were grabbing land then. Carl lost his head and killed a man. I was there and saw it all. When Jim demanded the truth, what could I say? He was my own brother."

"I forced the issue," Jim Bender said. "I demanded that she consider the truth of the thing and to hell with her family. I had no right to ask that of you, Betty. It took me a year to get it through my head that I was asking her to put a rope around Carl's neck. It's better that he got away with it, Ben. Do you see that?"

"Yes, I see it," Holliday said. "People say a lot of things that are hard to take back." He fell silent for a moment. "But you'd better understand something, Miss Singer. I'll either have to get your brother, or someone else will. He killed Ollie Skinner."

Jim Bender said, "Don't pump her, Ben. If she knows anything, she keeps it to her self. It'll be bad enough, living after Carl gets what's coming to him, without having to know she tipped the scales against him."

"All right," Holliday said. "I've got enough anyway. Nothing I could take to court, but I'm learning that out here you do with what you have." He finished his coffee and got up. "Jim, you watch out for her. Tomorrow, put her in the caboose and lock the doors."

"Don't spend any time worrying about her," Bender said softly.

After hesitating a moment, Holliday went out, thinking

that this was a hell of a time for two people to get together. But then he supposed any time was good when you were in love. Colonel Dawson was by the locomotive, talking over the situation with Sergeant DuJoise; he turned to Holliday as he came up.

"DuJoise estimates that the total force may swell to a hundred and fifty. Which makes a knotty problem of it, Holliday." He fingered his mustache. "I've put Gary and a squad at the rear of the train. A little enfilade fire might turn an attack. At least the first wave."

Jacques DuJoise made a wry face. "With a force such as that, they could lose thirty men in the first attack and never miss them."

"We can't stand to lose five," Ben Holliday said. "Did you take a nose count?"

"*Qui*. Forty-six, counting the cook, and the colonel's detail." He gave his waxed mustache a twirl. "Well, m'sieus, it might be more glorious to die outnumbered than the other way around."

"I'm too old to die," Cameron Dawson said, smiling. "Just getting to the point where life is fun." He slapped his lean stomach. "We'll be smart to get some sleep. Breakfast ought to be an hour or so before dawn, Holliday. We'll all fight better on a full stomach."

Holliday and DuJoise settled down in the cab of the engine, stretching out on the steel floor with only a blanket to soften it.

"It is sad to think of," DuJoise said, "but before this day, your plan for making peace held some hope; there was only the railroad for them to forget. But now, there's going to be dead brothers to forget. I'm afraid there won't be any peace, m'sieu."

"A man can't have everything, Ben Holliday said.

"Bender seems to have," DuJoise said. He turned his head and peered at Holliday. "He's a wandering man these last few years. I know him well enough to say that. He loves the Singer woman. Maybe she loves him too, or she wouldn't have come here."

"She didn't know he was here," Holliday said.

"So? He was here." He lay back, hands behind his head, then he suddenly reared erect, as did Holliday; they bumped their heads and cursed. Out on the flats, from the Indian camp, came the rattle of small-arms fire and the whooping surprise of many men.

One of the railroaders, startled from his sleep, panicked and yelled, *"Attack!"*

Instantly Jim Gary's shrill voice shouted, "Quiet that man! Knock him out if you have to!"

The soldiers maintained order and Colonel Dawson came up; they stood there together and studied the fight taking place out there. It was too far to distinguish even the shadows of mounted men, but they could see the lances of bright muzzle flares as the fight grew hot, then dropped off to spasmodic shooting.

"What the hell caused that?" Dawson asked absently. "If I didn't have better sense, I'd say a force rode through the Indian camp."

"Riders coming!" A guard shouted this, then the sound of mounted men approaching grew louder. Holliday grabbed up his rifle and ordered a bright fire built up. The guards let them through, eleven Texans; a few horses with empty saddles tagged along.

Murray Singer flung off and his face was gray in the firelight; he shook his head like a man struck numb. "We lost twelve at least. Carl, for Christ's sake, find out how many. Vale? Where's Vale?" He looked around for the man and saw that he was gone. "Dead? Jesus, I didn't think there was more than forty-fifty. A hundred anyway." His attention focused on Ben Holliday and a smear of anger came into Murray's eyes. "Your goddamned doing with the railroad."

Holliday knew that Murray was going to jump him; it was simply a feeling he had, and when Singer swung toward him, Holliday brought the butt of the rifle up in an arc, laid it alongside Singer's jaw hinge, and dropped him instantly. Carl, hanging back, growled something,

285

and John-Jack DuJoise pulled his pistol and cocked it.

"Dying is an easy thing, my friend."

"What the hell's the matter with you people?" Dawson snapped. "Don't you have better sense than to ride through an Indian camp?"

Bert Hutchins shifted his feet awkwardly and said, "We used to hit 'em like that in the old days, Colonel. It worked then."

"Sure, with a hundred Texans against thirty Comanches." He waved his hand in disgust. "Well, get settled for the night. They'll get even in the morning for this, and I hope you haven't lost all your fight."

"Now just a damned minute——" Carl flared.

Dawson spun toward him, his manner threatening. "Shut your mouth! I've just seen some Texas stupidity. Now don't tell me how tough you are; I already know how tough that is." He pivoted on his heel and went back to his blankets. When Holliday turned, he saw Jim Gary there.

They walked back to the locomotive together. "The old man's got his back up," Gary said. He glanced at Holliday. "I hope that if I get shot tomorrow, It'll be from the front. A man never really knows how he will do, does he?"

"You'll do all right," Holliday said. "Don't worry about it."

"Well," Gary said, "It's nice that someone has confidence." He walked back to his own place, and Holliday got into the locomotive. One of the railroad men DuJoise had picked stirred and said something about damn-fool Texas cowboys, and Holliday let it go, not wanting to talk about it.

He couldn't figure why Singer had showed up at all, but he soon got his answer when Carl Singer came up with Sergeant DuJoise.

"Where's my sister?" Carl asked flatly.

"With Bender," Holliday said. "Leave them alone."

"She's going back with us," Carl said.

"Why, because she knows too much?"

Singer laughed. "Look Holliday, I don't want to argue about it. You just tell me where she is and we'll leave."

"What, and miss the fun in the morning?"

"I'm not going to fight the damned Indians for the railroad," Carl said. "Pa already got too many men killed ridin' through that camp. I thought he had better sense."

Holliday came to the ladder and stood there a moment. "Carl, I don't think you're going to leave here. You want to know why? I'd already made up my mind to come after you for killing Skinner. You saved me the trouble by coming to me."

For a moment Singer said nothing, then he laughed. "What the hell are you talking about?"

"You killed Skinner."

"Prove it."

"I'm not going to try," Ben Holliday said. "I'm going to hang you on my own say-so. From what I've heard, it's long overdue."

Singer laughed again, but it wasn't a laugh of pleasure. Hearing it, Ben pulled his weight up by his arms, arched his body, then came flying down, his knees striking Carl Singer squarely in the chest. The blow stunned him, and Holliday's weight carried the man to the ground. And when Holliday rolled away, Singer lay there, gagging for breath.

"Put a guard on him," Holliday said, and DuJoise disarmed the man. "I want him to survive, John-Jack. His neck will just fit a good rope."

"M'sieu, let me turn him over to the colonel."

"I'll take care of it myself," Holliday said.

"You're making a mistake. Let the law do it. Not railroad law, but everyone's law."

Holliday shook his head. "There's no jury of Texans who'd convict him and you know it, and if you try a man once for the crime he can't be tried again."

"A chance we all take. Bender waited, didn't he?"

"I'm not Bender. Now put a railroad man to guard him, and keep the Texans away from him." He turned and mounted the cab again, knowing that DuJoise would do as he was told, whether he liked it or not.

Lying there, trying to get to sleep, Holliday understood fully that he was wrong, yet he felt helpless to change anything. He just had to hit out at the Singers and hurt them now; he felt that the death of the son would break the father, and he kept telling himself that it was for the railroad, but he knew it wasn't.

He just wanted to draw some blood of his own, right or wrong.

Jim Bender woke him and the air was very chilly; Holliday suspected that dawn was not far away.

"What's the matter, Jim?" He sat up and pawed sleep from his eyes.

"Got somethin' to tell you," Bender said. "You won't like it."

"So tell me."

"I turned Carl Singer loose."

Holliday fisted a handful of the man's coat and tried to shake him. "You what?"

"Told you you wouldn't like it," Bender said. "Ben, I wanted Carl once myself, and I still do. So go get him with a rifle or a six gun or a hand ax. But get him fair, Ben. You'll sleep better."

CHAPTER TEN

With dawn so near, Ben Holliday forgot about sleep and left the locomotive cab; he walked over to where the cook was building a fire, and stood by it for a time to drive the chill from him. The soldiers were up and moving quietly about, and while Holliday stood by the fire, Lieutenant Gary walked over, his young face grave.

"Those Texans—ah—I took their guns away from them, Mr. Holliday. The old man is in a fit; I think he'd kill you on sight."

"Let's go talk to him," Ben Holliday said. "Where are they?"

"Locked in the supply car," Gary said. "Hell, I didn't know what to do with them."

He led the way, walking along the dark roadbed beside the train. The railroad men were stirring and walking around aimlessly with rifles and shotguns. Two soldiers from Gary's section guarded the supply car, and he motioned for them to open the door. Bert Hutchins stuck his head out and Murray Singer rudely pulled him back in. When he saw Ben Holliday he swore softly.

"I'm going to kill you. Carl!" He turned and gave his sleeping son a kick in the ribs. "Get up, goddamit!"

"It's almost dawn," Holliday said. "If you want to leave now, I'll give you the chance." He stepped close to Murray Singer and took a handful of lapel. "I don't need you here, and I don't want you here. You can get out if you travel west. When this is over, look for me. I'm going to clean house good."

"You ride on me, Holliday, and you'll get yourself killed." He jumped clumsily to the ground, then spoke to his friends. "Come on, let's get the hell out of here. I never wanted to fight Indians for the railroad in the first place."

Bert Hutchins got down and said, "Since I'm here, I'll stay. You go to hell, Murray. I should have told you that years ago."

"Don't get your back humped," Singer said. "A few years back when you were grabbing all the land you could get, I helped you, made you what you are today."

"Sure, and I've kissed your ass ever since. What am I today, Murray? I don't have any friends except you and Vale, and he's dead. What am I going to tell his wife, Murray? His kids? That he died doing what Murray Singer wanted? I think they're getting a little tired of hearing that. My family is."

"If you turn on me now, Bert, you've turned for good. No one gets a second chance."

Bert Hutchins laughed softly. "Hell, who wants a second chance to go on with you, Murray?"

Carl nudged his father. "It looks like it's going to be light pretty soon. If we're goin' then let's go. I want to be a few miles away before the sky turns pink."

"All right," Murray said. "Where're our horses?"

"Get their horses," Holliday said to Lieutenant Gary.

"Colonel Dawson isn't going to like this," Gary said, then shrugged. "Come on then. It's no skin off my nose."

Four of Murray Singer's men remained still while the rest started to move away. Singer said, "Well, what the hell's the matter with you?"

"This looks like a good time to quit," one man said. "We'll stay. Can't see any sense of going on with this." He glanced at the others for approval, and found it.

Singer was angry and it made his voice raspy. "All right, you yellow bastards. Any man who'd desert his brand is a yellow bastard."

"It's getting light, Pa," Carl said. "You want to stand here and cuss 'em out, you go ahead. I'm leaving." He swung his head around to face Ben Holliday. "Where's Betty? She's coming back with us." His voice was full of stubbornness, and Ben Holliday almost laughed at him for being so stupidly single-minded. But he didn't laugh. Instead he thought that here was a Singer weakness, an inability to give from a predetermined course, to change their minds once they'd made them up.

Holliday said, "Get the hell out of here while the getting is good. This is your last chance."

Carl was all for staying, arguing this out, but his father roughly shoved him into motion, and they followed Gary to where their horses were being held. A few minutes later they were mounted and leaving the camp, turning west where the prairie was void of Indians. It would mean a few extra, miles skirting them, but well worth the trouble.

Around the cook tent, men clustered for their coffee and bacon, and Ben Holliday got a cup and filled it, then went back to the engine where DuJoise and Jim Bender sat.

"Sky is getting lighter," Bender.

The ink shadows were gradually rinsing away, and Holliday turned his attention to the Indian camp; considerable activity indicated that their painting and singing was done with. He said, "John-Jack, how's this going to be? Will they come straight at us?"

"They are simple, and it's the only way they know of doing a thing." He reached for his rifle, checked the action, then laid out a belt of cartridges. "Watch the sky. At the first tinge of pink, they'll come."

Colonel Dawson approached the locomotive cab and climbed partially up the ladder. "I'm going to run my detail on the 'horn,' Holliday," he said. "The sound of a bugle has some effect on Indians. Mr. Gary has his section in place and will pay particular attention to guarding the caboose." He blew out a long breath. "I believe everything is ready. The waiting is hell though."

He stepped to the ground and went back to his duties, and the end of track camp grew silent and watchful. As the dawn bloomed, visibility reached out onto the prairie, then the sky turned a pale rose and a deeper hush fell.

Holliday kept wondering what the first sensation would be when the Indians attacked, and when it came the drumming thunder of running ponies, he was relieved to find it not frightening at all. They came on in a clumsy drawn knot, blackening the prairie, shouting, waving their weapons, lashing their ponies to a frenzy of speed.

It was inevitable that some of the railroad men would start shooting too soon, when the range was too great, wasting precious ammunition, but it couldn't be helped, and Holliday didn't worry about it. He and Bender and DuJoise and the three others waited until the range was less than a hundred yards, then they fired on Colonel Dawson's bugle call, holding steady, squeezing off, and reloading.

The steel butt plate gave him a solid thump in the shoulder, and it felt good, almost pleasurable when he saw an Indian spin off his horse. The Indians hit the train in a milling jumble, wheeling and shooting, unable to change direction or organize themselves into a solid attacking force. The besieged fired down on them, scattered them, and sent them away to form again.

Fallen braves dotted the prairie, and Holliday thought that their numbers were miserably small. It was a strange thought for a man to have, he decided—regret that more of the enemy had not been killed. But this was war, in a small sense, and the winner would be determined by the number he could slay.

"Here we go!" Bender shouted as the Indians formed a line abreast and rode directly at the entire length of the train. They came on without pause, as though they intended to run right over them all, and they met a withering, determined fire before breaking into two lines, riding along the train until they came to the ends, there circling to attack the other side.

It was a heartbreaking maneuver, destined to fail because the train was too long, and as the Indians rode along, they came under the full fire of every man. A few railroad men died that time, but the Indians suffered a staggering loss.

When they pulled away, powder smoke hung heavily over the line of flatcars and John-Jack DuJoise roughly counted the dead. "They can't stand much of this, m'sieu. Another wave, and if we hold, they are beaten."

"It's almost too easy," Holliday said without thinking, and both men looked at him.

Jim Bender grinned. "You're getting some prairie sense, Ben. I was thinking that myself."

The Indians retreated out of rifle range and drew together for a lengthy discussion. And after fifteen minutes of this, Ben Holliday decided that there wasn't going to be another attack. Not just yet.

"They're cooking up something," Bender said. "I don't like it."

Colonel Dawson came trotting up; he pulled himself into the cab. "Something's going on out there that I don't figure. They know now they can't push the train off the tracks, and we're well enough barricaded so they can't hope to kill us off in another attack. Mr. Holliday, it might be prudent if we backed this train out of here and left the field. I think there'll be enough death-song singing to convince them they didn't lick us."

"Hey! Hey!" Bender said sharply, and pointed.

The Indians were spreading out into a huge circular line that threatened to surround the train. They took care to stay out of rifle range.

"I've never seen that maneuver before," Dawson said. frowning.

Bender and John-Jack watched the Indians carefully, then the Frenchman swore. "They're going to fire the prairie! Look at the grass, like tinder And there's no wind to speak of."

"With all the creosote around here," Holliday said, "this train will burn like a candle."

"There goes the first one," Bender said, pointing. Even as he spoke, the Indians were lighting their fires and fanning the small blazes to life with blankets. "Backfire!" he said, and jumped down.

They seemed to accept Bender's authority without question, and Dawson and Holliday took charge of a section as a pall of smoke began to rise from the Indian fires.

They worked along both sides of the train, spading loose soil away from the train, then lighting their own fires. Blankets and slickers kept it away from the train and moving into an ever-widening circle, and the smoke choked them and made their eyes burn, and sparks burned holes in their clothes.

Holliday lost track of time, but finally the train rested in a blackened, smoking, patch of land, and they were safe, albeit exhausted and indescribably dirty. The fire was burning itself out, leaving a dirty patch of smoke to soil the blue morning sky, and the Indians rode around the circle, angry at being outdone but unable to do anything about it.

The fight was over and the railroad was still there. for all purposes undamaged, and the Indians knew it. With a final wail of disappointment, they turned and rode away; Ben Holliday then started to assess the damage.

At the final tally, six men were dead and three more wounded, but not too seriously, and Holliday counted himself lucky. He supposed that as a gesture of defiance to the Indians, as a symbol of his victory over them, the camp should be restored as it was before, with a telegrapher and cook and work crew on duty. He gave Bender orders to see that this was done, then walked to the caboose and stepped inside.

Betty Singer was sitting on one of the hard benches. combing the dirt out of her hair. Smoke still remaining in the coach, and Holliday opened the other door to induce some air circulation.

"Your father and brother are gone," he said.

"I don't care now."

He shrugged. "All right. What are you going to do now?"

"Go where Jim Bender goes," she said. "I've waited too long, Mr. Holliday."

"It makes sense. I'm not going to ask you anything about your father or Carl. But I've got to tell you what I'm going to do."

"You don't have to tell me," she said softly. "I know."

He seemed relieved about it; he didn't relish the idea of telling her he was going to kill her brother. "I'm not going to take Jim Bender with me," Holliday said. "I don't want anything to stand between you. Not anything like this. The railroad will break your father, but Jim Bender doesn't have to be part of it."

"Thank you for that." She stood up and tried to brush the soot from her dress but only succeeded in smearing it. "What makes a man want to own everything, Mr. Holliday?"

"I don't know. Can't your answer that? Don't you know your own father?"

"No, and I'm sure he doesn't know himself. He has to have things for no other reason than just wanting them."

Holliday turned to the door. "It's Carl I'm after, Betty. He killed Skinner."

"Don't go after him alone," she warned, then pressed her lips tightly together; it was the only advice she was going to give him. He waited a moment longer, then stepped down from the caboose and walked rapidly toward Colonel Dawson's position. He was being a fool, he told himself, but he *was* going to do this alone, without Bender or Sergeant DuJoise.

It was railroad business, strictly.

Adam Holliday stepped down from the coach at Dodge City, then turned to help his father with the suitcases. Julius Holliday wore a frown and a wrinkled suit and an air of impatience. He said, "Check to see if there's a train south. It's too much to hope for, but check anyway. I'll sit in the shade."

Adam carried the suitcases over to one of the benches,

and Julius Holliday lowered his bulk with a sigh. He checked his watch against the depot agent's time while he waited, then Adam came back.

"A freight is leaving in about a half hour," he said. "There's a coach on the tail end of it."

"Damn it," Julius said. "Not even time for a man to get his supper."

"Father, you ought to make up your mind," Adam said. "First you fuss because there won't be a train, and now you're——"

"Don't tell me what I'm doing," Julius Holliday said. "I was a fool to come along in the first place."

"You insisted, Father."

"Who can argue with a lawyer," Julius said, then stood up. "Let's go to the coach. It may be cooler there." He hefted one of the suitcases. "Wouldn't you think that it would cool off at sundown?" They walked along the siding, cinders crunching beneath their feet, and Julius spoke in a grumbling voice. "Why the devil Ben couldn't meet us is beyond me."

"You didn't wire that you were coming," Adam said. "I wanted to, but you said no."

They found the train, loaded with army horses. The coach was next to the caboose, and when they drew near Anna Neubauer and her father stepped away from the door so they could step up. Julius hauled himself to the platform, then turned to take the bags from his son. Anna Neubauer looked at Adam Holliday, then stepped forward and touched him on the arm.

"Why, you're Ben's brother, aren't you?"

"Yes," Adam said, smiling. "And hello, hello. Any friend of Ben's is a friend of mine. But he never told me about you."

"He's been busy," Anna said.

Adam nodded and continued to smile. "And I don't blame him. Allow me to introduce my father, Mr. Julius Holliday, who either owns all the railroads, or is working on it. Miss, ah——"

"Anna Neubauer." She introduced her father, who shook hands self-consciously.

Then Julius said, "Can't we sit down?"

"I hope you're going south?" Adam said, taking Anna's arm to help her aboard.

"Oh, yes," she said. "We've been waiting for the train to get back."

Julius, who was finding his seat, said, "Where's it been?"

"To the end of the track," Anna told him. "Ben's there now. They're fighting the Indians."

Julius stared for a moment, then shrugged it off as foolish talk. But Adam took it more seriously. "Do you mean that? I can't believe it." He sat beside her with the assurance that he would be welcome. "Ben doesn't know anything about fighting Indians."

"I think he's learning quickly," she said, smiling at him. "Don't you have any confidence in Ben?"

"It's not a matter of confidence," Julius said flatly. "You can't fight Indians and run a railroad too."

Neubauer, who was lighting his pipe, looked around and said, "I tink he must fight first, or haf no railroad to run."

"This convsation is going to have some exciting possibilities," Adam said.

The conductor came into the coach and walked toward them; he had a fare book in hand and Julius Holliday seemed insulted by it. "I'm Julius Holliday, a board member of this line," he said. "Don't you have passes?"

"Can't pay the bills with passes," the conductor said dryly. "Mr. Holliday, ah, Ben, that is, did away with those the first week. That'll be four eight-five apiece."

"Remind me to talk to Ben about this," Julius said, and paid up. "What a way to run a railroad! Conductor, do you know anything about the trouble at end of track?"

"Well, there were considerable Indians about," he said. "But I don't think they'll tear up the rails." He touched a finger to the hard brim of his cap and moved on to the rear platform. A half dozen passengers wandered aboard, and the conductor took their money like a streetcar change maker.

Julius Holliday settled back in his seat and stripped the wrapper from a cigar. After he lit it, he said, "I don't suppose you could tell me, miss, just what my son hopes to gain by fighting the Indians?"

"They believe the railroad is a bad thing," Anna said. "It frightens the buffalo."

"Somewhere," Julius said, "there must be a connection, but I fail to see it. Well, we'll get it all straightened out at the board meeting. Even if we have to elect a new chairman. Now, what's pleasant to talk about? I understand it's a long ride."

Ben Holliday did not discuss his plans with Jim Bender or Sergeant DuJoise. Instead, he sent Bender along with the work train, and the Frenchman was left in charge of the end of track camp. The train pulled out for the main yard shortly after sundown, and the army left to make a wide four-day sweep to keep the Indians under constant eye. Holliday sat in the cook tent and waited for the camp to settle down for the night before leaving.

DuJoise would want to come with him, and Ben Holliday thought it best if he did not. There would be a stink over this, and there was no need to mix the army into it. Any man as big as Murray Singer had political friends who'd see that some sweating was done, and Ben wanted it to be a railroad affair.

There was no definite plan in his mind when he quietly saddled a horse and eased out of camp. He took a pistol with him and some spare shells, and a determination to finish a nasty job; anything else was just excess baggage. He'd been in the Singer house enough to know his way around it, and he wasn't too worried about the hands in the bunkhouse. They'd be thinking about the dead friends they'd left on the prairie after that ride through the Indian camp, and Holliday didn't think any of them would take a side in this personal fight. There was no way of knowing how they felt about Satchel's killing, but four men had quit the brand, and he suspected that the whole thing sat poorly with them.

He had a long ride ahead of him, and he was tired and dirty and a long way from his Chicago-bred ideals. The thought that he could ride after a man to possibly kill him didn't alarm him as much as it amazed him; there was nothing in his background that offered a foundation for violence. He'd had a few fights in his life, but not over anything serious.

But he really couldn't see any alternative. There was no law to turn to, and if there was, what could he really say? That Carl Singer killed in cold blood? True or not, there was a matter of proof.

Well, he thought, there was one thing about Texas that had its good point. A man could settle his own trouble here, any way he saw fit, and if justice seemed to be served by it, people were willing to let it go at that.

If he settled this tonight, he'd have to go on, finish what he started, which was making the railroad pay. One way or another, piece would have to be made with the Indians; a man couldn't have them shooting up the coaches or setting fire to the prairie. And Murray Singer wouldn't be the only man who'd come along and try to saw the props out from under a tottering enterprise. You could spike the guns of one, but another always wheeled machinery into battery. Probably Holly Bristow would represent them too; he was a man who liked a fat commission.

Holliday thought a bit about the report he'd be writing to his father; that would make some reading. Be some howling over it too. But that was somewhere tomorrow and this was tonight, and the two bits of business were a long way apart.

The Singer place was dark when he arrived. He dismounted some distance from the house and hunkered down to look things over. He couldn't quite make up his mind as to whether the dark house was a natural state, or whether it was dark for other reasons. As he recalled, there was always a light on somewhere, but he couldn't be sure.

Carefully he approached the bunkhouse and circled it twice before stopping at the door. A heavy wrought-iron hasp hung on its hinge, and he moved on to the tool shed and there found a spike. With this securely wedged into the loop passing through the hasp, he felt sure that they weren't going to boil out of there shooting. Of course they could break out the windows, but he'd hear that and be warned by it.

Holliday returned to the house and stayed close to the walls, moving quietly and slowly all the way around it. The back door was locked and so were the windows, and he tried them all, finding only the one on the side porch open.

He didn't go inside immediately, but thought about this a bit. It struck him as strange that all the doors would be locked except one. And all the windows too. He could understand the doors, but not the windows for the night was warm and windows were opened to cool a house.

The suspicion that he was being invited to use one door only firmed up in his mind, and he became cautious. Quite likely either Carl or his father had taken him very seriously and had something waiting for him in the nature of a fatal surprise. Now what would it be? Was Carl sitting in that darkened room waiting for the door to be opened?

Holliday didn't think so. Carl might have to sit up too many nights, and it just wasn't his way of doing a thing. The man had a sneaky mind, so Ben suspected that Carl had rigged up something else, something to do the job while he slept.

It would have to be simple, something in the line of a snare; Carl wasn't very original in his thinking, so Holliday mulled this over for a few minutes. A gun was probably set to go off as soon as the door opened; Holliday assumed it was a gun because Carl was familiar with them, more so than with other weapons.

A shotgun quite possibly, for a single bullet from a pistol or rifle might miss. A double charge of buckshot would do nicely, Ben thought, and went on that assumption.

He considered the possibility that Carl had wired the door knob, but discarded that for two reasons: the setup would be overly complicated, and the charge would have to pass through the door to get the man.

No, it would go off after the door opened. Probably a string or a stick trigger that would release when the door opened enough to admit a man.

Leaving the porch, Holliday rummaged around the corral until he found a stick at least eight feet long. He took this back with him and, crouching down to one side, reached up and turned the knob. The stick eased the door open, way open, until it bumped gently against the back wall, and there was no blast, no string attached.

Unwilling to abandon his theory. Holliday turned this over in his mind and decided that there was a string stretched across the room, something for a man to tangle his feet in, and he laid down, belly flat, and poked into the room with the long stick. He couldn't hope to set off the snare by contacting the wire with the butt end, so he raised the stick up gently until he contacted something. Then he gave it a tug, and a double-barreled shotgun roared and sprayed shot a few feet over his head.

Yelling like a man cut in half. Holliday jumped up and ducked into the darkened room. From another part of the house, he heard a pair of boots hit the floor; Carl had obviously been waiting in bed. From somewhere else, a door slammed, and Murray Singer yelled, "You got him, boy!"

Holliday plucked the pistol from his belt and cocked it and stood there, holding it in his hand. It was an odd feeling to hear Singer yell like that, use those words, for if he were really dead, that was all Singer would think of it. He'd be elated and not a damned bit sorry.

A smear of lamplight started down the far hall and Holliday watched it grow in brightness, then Carl burst into the room, playing the light on the floor where he expected the body to be. He looked expectant—and surprised and disappointed when he saw nothing.

Then Ben spoke. "Over here, Carl."

Singer threw the lamp and whipped up his pistol just as Ben Holliday shot. He heard Carl grunt as the bullet found a home, then there was a slithering as he fell to the floor.

The burst lamp spread coal oil over the rug, and the flames caught instantly, leaping to great brightness. Holliday could see Carl Singer, a well of blood in the middle of his chest, and eyes already growing dead.

He didn't stay. Ducking out, he was already dashing around the house when he heard Murray Singer's anguished shout. Holliday ran for his horse, then stopped and ran back to the bunkhouse. The hands were driving their shoulders against the door, trying to get out, and with the barrel of his pistol he broke away the spike, freeing them.

They seemed to explode from the door, some falling down in their hurry. They saw him, but ignored him, and ran toward the house, which was now hopelessly afire.

No one noticed Ben Holliday leave.

CHAPTER ELEVEN

Sergeant Jacques DuJoise was up and about when the cook lit his breakfast fire, and he took the first cup of coffee from the pot. He stood outside the tent and watched the dark sky give way to the dawn flush. His sleep had been troubled since he had discovered that Ben Holliday had gone without him, and DuJoise's first impulse had been to catch up a horse and follow him. Then he thought about it and stayed in camp, for a man's business was his own; Holliday obviously had wanted it that way for he had gone to a lot of trouble to see that Jim Bender had gone back to Comanche and that DuJoise had remained in camp.

Still this logic didn't keep the Frenchman from worrying. He liked Ben Holliday, like the man's straight-out approach to his problems, liked the way he thought things out, without a lot of mental muss and clutter and no deep regrets afterward. I would be a pity, DuJoise thought, if some wild Texan like Carl Singer did him in; the future held something for men like Holliday.

He finished his coffee and let the cup dangle from the hook of his finger, unable to give up his vigil. The sky turned rose, then a sliver of molten sun shot brightness across the flats, and he saw the lone horseman approaching, far out, coming slowly, in no particular hurry. DuJoise stared a moment, identified Ben Holliday, then laughed with relief and went inside for another cup of coffee and his breakfast.

Dujoise was finishing his meal when Holliday stopped outside and dismounted. He came in, his step weary, and went directly to the coffeepot. Lack of sleep cast harsh lines into his face and made his shoulders round. DuJoise said, "I know it's done or you wouldn't be back."

"It's done," Holliday said, sitting down. "More than I figured. Carl threw the lamp just before I shot him. The place was going up in smoke when I left." He folded his hands around the coffee cup. "So it's either over with Murray Singer, or just beginning. He's got enough influence to bring legal action."

"Doesn't the railroad have any lawyers?"

"Lawyers cost money, especially railroad lawyers." He sighed and sagged forward, his forearms flat on the table. "But that's something I'm not going to worry about now, John-Jack. I don't want this Indian business hanging where it is, with blood spilled. We've got to try again for peace."

"*Qui,* it's a good thing. But how can you bring about a meeting?"

Holliday shrugged. "Lieutenant Gary's pretty original. Why don't you ride to Elliot and talk it over with Colonel Dawson? If you come up with an idea, let me know. I'm going back to Comanche."

"We can try," DuJoise said. "I'll leave for the post right away. When are you going north?"

"When I wake up," Holliday said. "I may sleep for a week."

He went out and walked a few yards away to one of the maintenance supply tents and made a bed for himself on some sugar sacks. The camp was turning noisy now as the railroad men went into the cook tent for breakfast, but this didn't bother him; he fell asleep and didn't wake up until late that night.

Without waking the cook, Holliday put some cold meat and a half loaf of bread in a sack, filled his canteen, then put the handcar onto the tracks and began to pump himself north. He was in no particular hurry, but kept steadily at it until dawn, then wrestled the car off the tracks and slept in the shade of it. At dusk he woke, ate cold meat and bread, then began to pump away the last miles of his journey.

When he reached the yard, he put the car away and walked to the headquarters building. It was dark except for a lamp in the bottom hall. Making his way up the stairs, he opened the door to his room and crossed immediately to the bed. The moment he sat on it, he knew someone was in it, and when the man pawed out for him, Holliday balled his fist and hit where the jaw ought to be. He connected solidly and the man shouted, half in anger and half in pain. Then he scrambled out of bed and lit the lamp, swearing all the while.

"This is a goddamned intrusion!" Adam Holliday said, then looked around to see who he was talking to. "Ben! Well, for gosh sakes, Ben!"

"What the hell are you doing in my bed?" Ben asked.

"Sleeping, until you hit me in the face." He rubbed the welt on his cheekbone. "You're getting violent as hell. Father's here. In the hotel in town. And I met your blonde. Some dish." He got up and pulled on his pants. "You don't seem too happy to see me, Ben."

"I'm glad to see you and you know it," Ben said. "But I didn't expect Father. Truthfully, I'd be a lot happier if he was in Chicago." He went over the night stand, filled the washbowl, and scrubbed. "I suppose he's ranting as usual ?"

"Well, it's Father's only way of speaking," Adam said. "You get used to it. He's very impatient to see you."

"Well, it's Father's only way of speaking," Adam said. you buy that stock like I asked you to?"

"Yes. And what a row that caused. If you want a reason for Father being here, blame it on that. You see, I'd just received a check from the Cartwright estate—a very handsome one, so I loaned you eight thousand. And I borrowed another six thousand from our dear, conservative brother. He thought I was buying some lake-shore frontage with it." Adam rolled his eyes toward the ceiling. "So when Father read the market report and saw the flurry, he hit the ceiling. Well, the upshot is that Father considers me a fool and you a madman for not accepting that offer."

"It wasn't legitimate," Ben Holliday said. "Besides, there is no more offer."

"Oh? It's been withdrawn?"

"Definitely. I shot him the night before last." Ben knew that Adam would be shocked, and it pleased him; he wanted Adam to know that he'd changed. Maybe Adam would communicate that to Julius Holliday, prepare him in a way for the rough sailing ahead.

"You mean, it was an accident," Adam said.

"No, I mean that I took a gun and went after him, and when I found him I shot him before he shot me." He dried himself and took off his shirt, then threw it in the corner. "When it comes right down to it, a lawsuit can't hold a candle to a bullet for getting the job done."

"Good grief! Is the law after you?"

"No," Ben said. He shaved, using cold water and much stropping of the razor. "Did you happen to meet Jim Bender? I want to find him."

Adam Holliday frowned pleasantly. "A tall, thin man? I think I saw him at the hotel. He had a woman with him." He reached out and took Ben's arm. "Don't you think you ought to sleep, or wait until morning?"

"Dirty jobs," Ben said, "I like to do now."

"No, he's a railroad man. I only shoot the ones who aren't." He reached out and pushed Adam flat in bed and threw the covers over his head, then went down the back stairs. The town was quiet when he walked toward it, well past the general closing hour, even for the saloon. The clerk was sleeping when Holliday entered the lobby, and rather than wake the man, Ben had his look at the register, saw which room Bender had, and went on up.

He knocked twice and got no response, then the door opened a crack and Bender thrust the muzzle of his pistol against Holliday's stomach.

"You're a cautious man," Holliday said, and stepped inside.

Bender lit the lamp and put the gun away. "I ought to have shot anyway. What the hell's the idea of leaving me behind? Did you think I'd draw the line because of Betty?"

"You've got enough troubles," Ben said. "I've got to tell Betty how it is now."

"Just how is it now?" Bender asked.

"Carl's dead. He wired a shotgun trap for me, but I smelled it first. The place is burned to the ground."

Bender whistled softly. "Man, you really went Injun, didn't you?"

"The fire was an accident," Ben said. "Carl threw the lamp at me before the shooting started. The place caught afire. I'm going to have to tell Betty."

"Just say that it's over," Bender said. "She knows already how bad it is." Holliday frowned briefly and Bender explained. "Ben, she knows what Carl deserves. Let it go at that."

"All right," Holliday said "I sent DuJoise to the post to see if Dawson couldn't get the Indians together for a talk.

Bender shrugged. "Slim chance, but worth a try. What can you lose?"

"That's what I figured. I'm still determined to use the original plan, with the hot wires." He toed a chair around and sat down. "For the first time, I really think I can save this railroad, build it into something. For a fact, I worried more about Singer's attempt to buy it up than I did the Indians. Singer's kind of business is hard to fight. I'm glad it's off my back."

"Someone else will come along, just as greedy as Singer."

"Sure, but maybe I'll be in a better financial position to fight them." He slapped his knees and stood up. "I think I'll go root the old man out of bed; he hasn't seen the sun come up in thirty years."

Bender stared at him for a minute, then laughed. "Kind of like the mouse that got into the whisky bottle?"

"How's that?"

"He went out looking for cats to kick."

"Well, something like that," Ben Holliday said. "Look, I know my father. He didn't come here for some grouse hunting." Holliday put the chair back against the wall and turned to the door. "Of course I've got an advantage with my father that I never had with Singer: I know my father and what he'll say."

"Knowing that much about some men has caused me to pack up and leave for healthier country," Bender said. "But go ahead. I admire a free-swingin' man."

Returning to the lower floor, Holliday decided that if this whole thing went up in smoke, he wouldn't go back to Chicago at all, but team up with Jim Bender; he really liked the man, liked the way he thought about things; they could find some business venture, and not railroading.

Ben knew that his father would be in the best room available, so he walked along the hall to the back suite and knocked on the door. He had to ball his fist and pound several times before he got an answer, and that was a grumble.

"What do you want? And who are you?"

"It's Ben. Open the door."

This did not erase Julius Holliday's irritation. He flung the door open and motioned the young man in. "You damn fool, it isn't even daylight outside." He fumbled around for the lamp, lit it, then sat heavily on the edge of the bed and pawed the sleep from his eyes. "What possible reason could you have for this outrageous intrusion? Ooooo, what an unearthly hour for a man to rise." He held his head in his hands for a moment, then looked at his son. "I think you've lost your mind."

"Adam thought so too," Ben said. He went over to the windows and raised the curtains, letting them flap on the rollers. "What did you come out here for, Dad?"

"Well, I wasn't getting proper action from you, Ben."

Ben turned and looked at him. "What did you want?"

"I wanted you to listen to me!" Julius snapped. "That's what I wanted!" He calmed himself. "Lovell wired me that you'd fired him. I made up my mind to come then."

"I'd rather have you do your own snooping than hire it done," Ben said. "If you didn't fully trust me, then why give me the job?" He knew he wouldn't get an answer to that, and didn't wait for one. "You sent me here to make the line pay, then recommended that I take Singer's offer. Why? So it would look good? So it wouldn't be put down as a failure for Julius Holliday?" Ben laughed softly. "Well, if you want to sell it now, you'll have to rustle up another buyer. The three men that made the offer aren't interested now. Jerry Vale is dead. Bert Hutchins has backed out, and Murray Singer's been burned out, clean to the ground. And the price has gone up. Or don't you watch the markets?"

"I saw that flurry," Julius snapped. "Ben, that was the cheapest bit of conniving I ever saw. I suppose you wanted the stock up a half or so, then you'll dump yours and pocket the profit."

The impulse to his him was strong; he had never known it so strong before. But he resisted it. "I want working capital. Not one share of my stock is for sale."

Julius Holliday was surprised. "What's that?"

Ben walked over and stood near his father, looking down at him, and it was an odd sensation; he had never know it before. "I don't want to sell the line at any price, Dad. I want to stay with it, rise with it if it succeeds, and fall if it fails. All my life I've wanted to go it on my own. That's the way it's going to be this time."

"I've only tried to help you," Julius said.

"Sure, but I don't want any more help, Dad." He pulled a chair around and sat down, facing his father. A gray light was seeping into the room; it would be dawn in another ten minutes. "I don't want any advice, or money, or anything. This is going to be straightened out my way, or balled up hopelessly through my efforts. Either way, I'm going to learn my own lessons. Getting money is always going to be a problem, I'm afraid, so I might as well get used to the idea of it. The Indians—well, I hope that the railroad can make peace with them. At least that's one of my top priority projects for the near future. Maybe I'll succeed and maybe I'll fail. But I'll try, you see."

309

"You're turning into a man, Ben," Julius said. "I like you better. And I'm sorry if I held you back."

"Don't be sorry. It's a lesson I've learned in Texas: never be sorry. Good or bad, do what has to be done and don't cry about it." He sighed and got up and walked back to the window and watched the sky turn rose. "I don't know as you understand me, Dad. I don't really understand you. But why don't you go on back to Chicago and let me be? Not because I want to get rid of you. But because I want to be on my own. Will you do that for me?"

"It won't be easy. I'm full of advice. You know that."

"Yes, but I'll get along without it."

Julius Holliday chuckled. "I met the German girl. Serious with you?"

"It might be in time," Ben said. "You'll like her; she isn't afraid of you at all."

"I sure found that out," Julius said. "Ben, I'd like nothing better than to see you make it. Would you take my word that I won't interfere and let me stay a week or so? Just as a favor?

"Sure," Ben said, turning, a smile on his face. "Why not?" He walked over to the chair that held his father's clothes, and tossed them to him. "Come on, I'll buy you a Texas breakfast."

It was a good feeling, Ben decided later, to get the railroad on a schedule. It was good for business, too, for the freight manifests grew steadily fatter, and the revenue came in slowly but in steadily increasing amounts. In one week Midland-Pacific fulfilled an army contract and shipped Bert Hutchins' cattle. Vale's widow and half-grown son came to see Holliday; he was sorry the man was dead but didn't show any false grief, since the man had picked his side and lost.

She was selling out, and he gave her a good freight rate, then sent the train north with the largest single shipment so far. It created a stir in Dodge and in the Chicago market. Midland-Pacific stock took a substantial gain, and even shrewd investors began to consider it with something else besides disdain.

Yet Ben knew that the line was a long time away from being on firm financial footing, and he hoped he could keep the boat from rocking. Western Union cleaned out the telegraph equipment and sent in their own operators, and the line to Fort Elliot was finally finished. Some hailed this as a major communications advance, but Julius Holliday thought it was a bit of financial foolishness; the day would come when the railroad would regret parting with communication control.

On Thursday afternoon, Jim Bender brought Holliday the news that Murray Singer had ridden into town with six men, and that Singer wanted to see him at the hotel. Holliday took his .44 pistol from the drawer, made sure it was loaded, and thrust it into his waistband.

Then he walked uptown to find out what Singer had to say.

CHAPTER TWELVE

As Ben Holliday walked down the street, he wondered if the men with Murray were all he had left, and if they were, it was a pitiful number, considering the number Singer had once employed. Holliday could see that nearly everyone in town was gathered; if there was trouble, they wanted a front-row seat.

Approaching the hotel, Holliday didn't think about the odds; he knew how strong was Murray Singer's pride; this would be between the two of them, either talk or a fight. Singer and his men were arrayed across the front of the porch, and as Holliday stopped in the street, Jim Bender came out of the hotel and stood just behind the Singer faction.

Bender said, "No need to turn around, gents. But just keep it in mind that I'm behind you. You go right ahead, Murray. Mr. Holliday's waitin'."

Julius Holliday and Adam wheeled down the street in a buggy and pulled in by the feed store; neither man got down, but Julius said, "Ben, this damned thing has gone far enough." He started to dismount, but Murray Singer pointed a finger at him.

"If you're not carrying a gun, don't get down!" He turned his head slightly to speak to Jim Bender. "My men will stay out of this. You don't have to interfere."

"If they stay out," Bender said, "I won't interfere."

Ben Holliday said. "What do you want to talk about, Murray?"

"Us," Singer said softly, "You killed my son and burned me to the ground. Did you think for a minute I'd let you get away with it?"

"I had hoped you had sense enough to," Holliday said. "Murray, ask yourself who's to blame. Who killed Skinner? Who set himself up against the railroad?"

"That part don't matter," Murray said. "I'm going to kill you just because I'll take pleasure in it."

"Are you going to start shooting, Murray?"

"Hell, yes," Murray said, and flipped his hand beneath his coat for his gun. He was slow by some standards, but compared to Holliday's inexperience he was very fast.

Holliday jerked at his pistol in his hurry to get it into action, and the hammer snagged on his shirt, ripping it slowing him so much that Murray Singer had his first shot off before Ben was even ready to cock his gun. The bullet spun Ben around completely, and caused Murray to miss his second shot. Ben fell down but did not drop the .44. He brought it up, sighted, and shot Murray Singer high in the breastbone. Murray staggered back a step, hooked his heel against a crack in the porch planks, and went down hard. He kicked his legs and tried to rise, but the strength was leaving him and he died amid a fit of bloody coughing.

Julius and Adam left the buggy in a rush, and Singer's men just stood there as though they couldn't believe it had turned out this way. Jim Bender stayed behind them while a crowd gathered around Ben Holliday.

Julius was shouting, "Someone get the doctor!"

Some wag standing by said, "Hell, mister, he was on his way the minute he heard the first shot. Like a damned bird dog."

"Ben, are you badly hurt?" This was Adam's concern; he raised Ben to a sitting position and looked at the blood on his coat, his manner horrified.

The doctor arrived, brusquely pushing people aside. He made a brief examination of the wound and said, "I'll have to dig that out." He stood up and motioned for Ben to be lifted. "Cart him over to my office."

"Gently there!" Julius snapped as two men grabbed Ben's feet. "By God, I've never seen such people!"

The man lifting Ben's shoulders took offense at Julius' tone. "You his mother or somethin'? Get the hell out of the way."

Julius Holliday was infuriated because the doctor

wouldn't allow him to be present when the bullet was removed, and it was an hour later before he and Adam were permitted to pull up chairs at Ben's bedside.

The young man's face was gray and he was in pain, but it didn't seem to bother him much. He looked at his father and said, "Don't fuss around so much, Dad. You look like you've been sick."

"I'm thinking of the lawsuit you're going to have."

Ben shook his head. "No, it's settled now. For good." Someone knocked and Adam got up to open the door.

Jim Bender came in and grinned. "You were slow as hell, Ben, but you got the job done. Which is what counts." He sighed and sat down. "Got to give Murray credit though; he went all the way." His glance touched Julius Holliday. "I don't expect you understand that."

"Frankly, I don't."

"Well," Bender said, "Murray wanted your railroad. And he went after it the only way he knew how. If he'd been like you, Mr. Holliday, he'd have tried some clever stock swindle or maneuver. But he wasn't a complicated man. He was just a hog who wanted it all and he grabbed and hung on and kicked until the other fella let go. Only Ben wouldn't let go, so Murray had to start shootin'."

"You make it surprisingly clear," Julius Holliday said softly. "I was going to stay here a week or so until a few of these matters pending were settled. I think now that I'll go back to Chicago. Adam, you ought to stay and help Ben until he gets on his feet. And I don't think you ought to stay here, Ben. Perhaps if I spoke to that German girl—It seems to me that she'd gladly——"

"Dad," Ben said, "will you stop running things for me?"

Julius Holliday laughed and seemed embarrassed; he got up and turned to the door. "You're right, Ben. It's time I got out and let you handle your own business."

He stepped out and closed the door softly. Jim Bender rolled a smoke and said, "He's all right. Well, Betty's going to be needing me. In a couple days we ought to do something about the Indians, huh, Ben? A man's troubles never end but what something else comes up. I wonder what it'll be after the Indians?"

"I won't worry about it," Ben Holliday said. He shifted, searching for a comfortable spot. "This is the worst bed I've ever slept in."

Jim and Adam went out and he was relieved to be alone. His wound pained him like blazes, but he could tolerate that. In his mind still was the memory of that moment when Murray Singer drew his gun; the thought had been strong then that he stood a good chance of dying, and the amazing part of it was that he had entertained no regrets at all; within him there was no apology for what he was or what he had done.

I'm going to be all right, Ben thought, then fell into a deep resting sleep.

Will Cook is the author of numerous outstanding Western novels as well as historical frontier fiction. He was born in Richmond, Indiana, but was raised by an aunt and uncle in Cambridge, Illinois. He joined the U.S. Cavalry at the age of sixteen but was disillusioned because horses were being eliminated through mechanization. He transferred to the U.S. Army Air Force in which he served in the South Pacific during the Second World War. Cook turned to writing in 1951 and contributed a number of outstanding short stories to *Dime Western* and other pulp magazines as well as fiction for major smooth-paper magazines such as *The Saturday Evening Post.* It was in the *Post* that his best-known novel, *Comanche Captives*, was serialized. It was later filmed as *Two Rode Together* (Columbia, 1961), directed by John Ford and starring James Stewart and Richard Widmark. Sometimes in his short stories Cook would introduce characters who would later be featured in novels, such as Charlie Boomhauer who first appeared in ''Lawmen Die Sudden'' in *Big-Book Western* in 1953 and is later to be found in *Badman's Holiday* (1958) and *The Wind River Kid* (1958). Along with his steady productivity, Cook maintained an enviable quality. His novels range widely in time and place, from the Illinois frontier of 1811 to southwest Texas in 1905, but each is peopled with credible and interestering characters whose interactions form the backbone of the narrative. Most of his novels deal with more or less traditional Western themes—range wars, reformed outlaws, cattle rustling, Indian fighting—but there are also romantic novels such as *Sabrina Kane* (1956) and exercises in historical realism such as *Elizabeth, By Name* (1958). Indeed, his fiction is known for its strong heroines. Another common feature is Cook's compassion for his characters, who must be able to survive in a wild and violent land. His protagonists make mistakes, hurt people they care for, and sometimes succumb to ignoble impulses, but this all provides an added dimension to the artistry of his work.

AL CODY

Two Action-Packed Westerns For One Low Price!

Rimrock Vengeance. Curt and Keogh ride into Montana, determined to give a passel of rustlers a six-gun send-off to the territorial hoosegow—or see them rot in hell.
And in the same rip-roarin' volume...
The Sheriff of Singing River. When luckless cowhand Boone Sarsfield is elected sheriff of a frontier town, he is more than ready to pin a tin star to his chest and begin teaching his enemies some hard lessons.

_3489-1 RIMROCK VENGEANCE/THE SHERIFF OF SINGING RIVER (two books in one) only \$4.50

Deadman's Gold. Somebody has to protect a cargo of gold from fast-drawing bandits, and Johnny Styverson seems like the man who can do it—if he doesn't catch a fatal dose of lead first.
And in the same action-packed volume...
Powdersmoke Payoff. When Rebel soldier Jeb Honeycutt returns home, he finds his old sweetheart married to a ruthless land-grabber. Even if it takes a war, Honeycutt will win his woman back.

_3526-X DEADMAN'S GOLD/POWDERSMOKE PAYOFF (two books in one) only \$4.99